For King, Country, and Love

A World War One Love Story

By

Mark Barie

Barringer Publishing, Naples, Florida
www.barringerpublishing.com
Cover, graphics, layout design by Linda S. Duider

ISBN: 978-1-954396-70-8

Library of Congress Cataloging-in-Publication Data
For King, Country, and Love/Mark Barie
Printed in U.S.A.

DEDICATION

For Christine Racine, my best friend, my closest confidant, and the woman I love.

OTHER BOOKS ON LOVE AND WAR, AUTHORED BY MARK BARIE

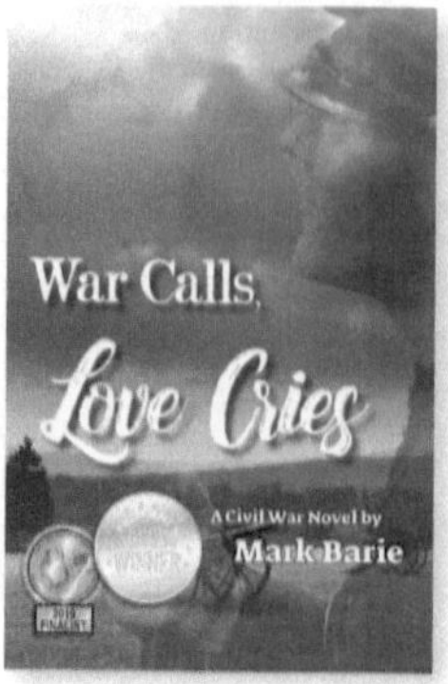

War Calls, Love Cries
(CIVIL WAR)

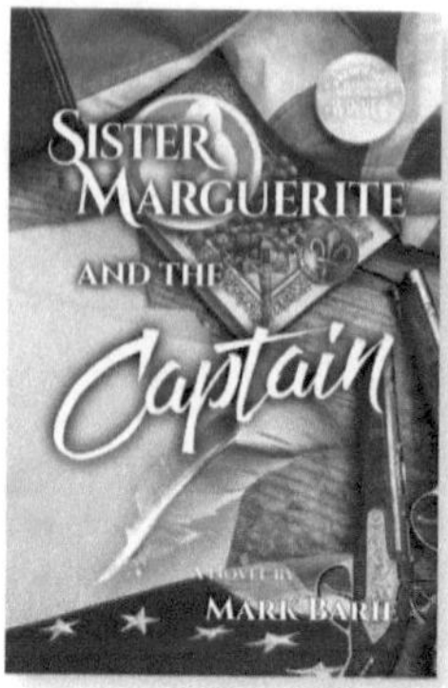

Sister Marguerite and the Captain
(REVOLUTIONARY WAR)

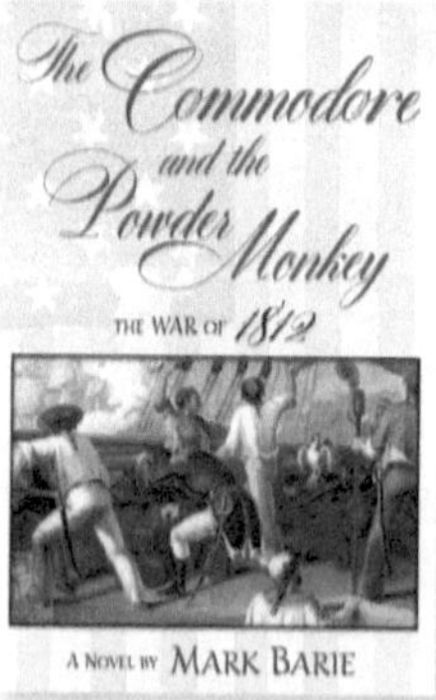

The Commodore and the Powder Monkey
(WAR OF 1812)

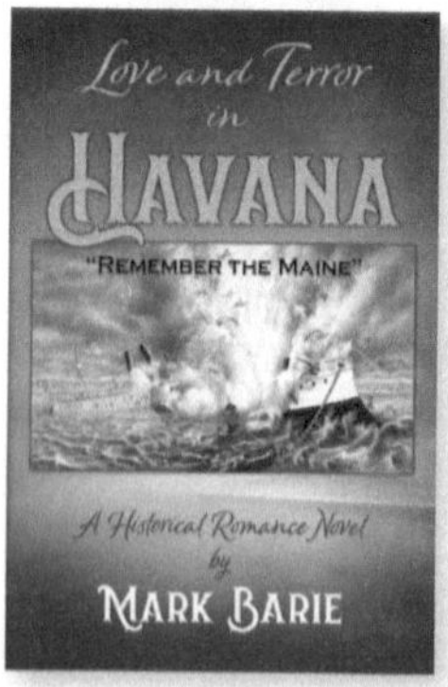

Love and Terror in Havana
(SPANISH AMERICAN WAR)

If you enjoyed any of these books,
PLEASE CONSIDER LEAVING A REVIEW!

Note: Mark Barie's books are available at:

★ amazon.com
★ barnesandnoble.com, and
★ markbarie.com (for signed copies at no extra charge)

Contact the author at: authormarkbarie@gmail.com

ABOUT THE AUTHOR

Mark Barie's historical romance novels have attracted state, national, and international recognition.

The Florida Authors and Publishers Association, the nationally recognized Eric Hoffer Book Awards, and the internationally respected Independent Publishers Group, have all acknowledged the author's historically accurate and riveting stories of life and love during times of war.

Mark's most recent novel, ***For King, Country, and Love***, details the life of Elizabeth Parsons, an 18-year-old girl who volunteers as a nurse in the Great War. Join Elizabeth as she travels from the friendly neighborhood of Saint John's, Newfoundland, to the desert sands of Gallipoli and onto the war-torn towns and cities of England and France.

If you enjoy novels that leave you spellbound and desperate for the next page, this story of life, love, and war will not disappoint.

Order your copy now at: **amazon.com, barnesandnoble.com** or, for a signed copy: **markbarie.com**

TABLE OF CONTENTS

ABOUT THE COVER

The original artwork on the cover of this novel was accomplished by Luke Leadbeater, a native of England.

Although he worked as a glazier, cutting and installing glass, he was also a tremendously talented artist. Luke attended Dewsbury School of Art where his award-winning artwork was on display for all to see.

On Valentine's Day, February 14, 1917, the 18-year-old young man enlisted in the British Army. As a parting gift to his fiancée, Jessie Wood, he presented her with several of his favorite pieces, including the depiction of a beautiful woman poised for battle.

On October 11, his training complete, Luke was ordered to the Western Front. On November 22, he was killed in action at Ypres in Belgium. The decorated war hero was buried at the Aeroplane Cemetery just outside Ypres.

Although Jessie would marry much later, she never forgot her first love, regaling her only child with stories of Luke's bravery in battle and his amazing talent as an artist. When she died, at the age of 101, Jessie's lifelong wish was realized. The man, whose generosity made this cover possible, sprinkled his grandmother's ashes on the grave of the man she once loved.

We thank you, Paul Tyler, for this beautiful story and for the unmistakable proof that in love and war, love will always triumph.

ACKNOWLEDGMENTS

A 100,000-word novel is not created in a vacuum.

Friends, family, professional colleagues, and readers all contribute to the effort, leaving the author in a quandary as to who gets thanked, first and most. In no special order, I would like to acknowledge the following people.

I must thank Paul Tyler for the contribution of Luke Leadbeater's artwork which was used for the cover of this book. The details of the artist's life and death can be found on page viii.

I would also like to thank and acknowledge the very kind folks at J.E. Hangar, of Pittsburgh, Pennsylvania. They have been making artificial legs for decades. And if they treat their customers half as well as they treat little known authors doing research for their next novel, J.E. Hangar must be the best artificial leg company in the world.

It is also necessary to thank Victor Piuk, my tour guide in France. Victor spent a few days with me, touring the Somme battlefields and surrounding area. His knowledge, his stories, and his books are amazing. He is England's finest export to France!

I take great pleasure in thanking the two best Beta readers in the world: Lurana H. and Susan L. If there any errors, inconsistencies, or nonsensical passages in this book, it is not their fault. Thank you, ladies. Your assistance is priceless.

And finally, a word about my publisher, Barringer Publishing of Naples, Florida. I consistently read about authors who have been poorly served, even mistreated, by their publishers. Jeff Schlesinger, the owner of this very fine hybrid publishing company, is the best there is. We work as a team and I would not be writing, much less selling my novels, were it not for Barringer Publishing.

HISTORICAL NOTES

Chapter One

- The 1914 Newfoundland seal hunt disaster claimed 77 lives. Although easily preventable, no criminal charges resulted from the negligent actions of the boat captains.

Chapter Five

- Reginald Windsor is a fictional character and, as such, will not be found on the roster of those loyal Newfoundlanders who served on the Newfoundland Patriotic Association executive committee.

Chapter Six

- Tom Kelly was indeed a fire man on the *Lusitania* and went down with the ship.
- The Supreme Commander of the British Expeditionary Forces visited the 1st Newfoundland Regiment on two separate occasions.
- The Queen Mary's Hostel for Nurses existed as described and served as temporary quarters for hundreds of VAD nurses.

Chapter Seven

- The use of a helmet held aloft by a bayonet to locate an enemy sniper became a commonplace tactic in World War 1.

- Self-inflicted gunshot wounds and injuries were not uncommon in World War 1. Approximately 3,900 members of the British expeditionary Forces were convicted of this offense during World War 1.
- The *Maheno* hospital ship used its derricks to hoist patients on board. The ship also featured an unusual side door which, weather permitting, allowed for easier and speedier on-loading of patients.

Chapter Eight

- Star shells acted as a flare and would light up an entire battle field. Because of the initial glare, however, the enemy could see movement only, hence the British strategy of remaining perfectly still during a star shell attack.
- The fog of war, archaic identification tags, unmarked graves, and human error caused many World War 1 families to be notified, in error, of their loved ones' injuries, death, or even, survival.

Chapter Nine

- "Drip" or "pop-off" rifles were invented by Australian soldier, William Scurry.
- A severe shortage of officers in the beginning of the war, made an enlisted man's rise through the ranks up to and including an officer's rank, a distinct possibility.
- There are documented cases of army soldiers from Newfoundland who received a medical discharge for their wounds and then re-enlisted in the Royal Flying Corps, as pilots.

Chapter Ten

- The acronym OC stands for officer in charge. In the United States, however, CO (Commanding Officer), is more common. The author used CO to avoid confusion by the reader.
- The reputation and career of Lt. Col. Arthur "Fighting" Hadow is well documented.

Chapter Eleven

- The average soldier in the BEF, during World War 1, carried "baggage" into battle which was often more than 70 pounds.
- It is well documented that British command's decision to use a metal triangle cut from a biscuit tin, to identify British forces from the air, also made the men easy targets for enemy sniper and regular rifle fire. The metal triangles reflected both sunlight and moonlight.
- The initial name given the battle of the Somme was "The Big Push."
- A New Zealand Surgeon organized what is believed to be the world's first hospital for reconstructive surgery at the Cambridge Military Hospital in Aldershot, England.
- The metal frames of World War 1 flying machines were wrapped in canvas which was treated as described. As a result, the aircraft's wings would burst into flame on contact with enemy fire.

Chapter Twelve

- The author has credited the 252nd Tunnelling Company with the construction of a number of tunnels. In fact, there were several Tunnelling Companies involved in these projects.

Chapter Sixteen

- The J. E. Hanger Company, known world-wide for its prosthetic devices, has its corporate offices in Austin, Texas. See **Acknowledgements** for the details about this very fine company.
- The German's Officers Prison in Freiburg was established in May, 1916. Captain Billy Windsor arrived several months earlier. The discrepancy is acknowledged but deemed insignificant.

General Notes

- Characters and places of historical note are, as much as possible, accurately depicted. The same is true of activities which took place in Newfoundland. This list includes: the trolley cars of Newfoundland, the St. John's Armory building, the Bell Island mines, Bishop's Library, the practice of midwifery, gas powered automobiles, the regimental training grounds at Quidi Vidi Lake, blue putees, and the training regimen for VAD volunteers.
- Historic events abroad are also accurately depicted. This list includes: the Hawthorne mine, the first appearance of tanks in war, the lack of parachutes on aircraft, the locations and training regimens for the 1st Newfoundland Regiment, transport ships to and from St. John's, conditions in the trenches of Gallipoli and France, Britain's aircraft and pilot training, the use of VAD nurses in the OR, medical treatment for battlefield wounds, plus the battles at Gallipoli and the Somme, in France.

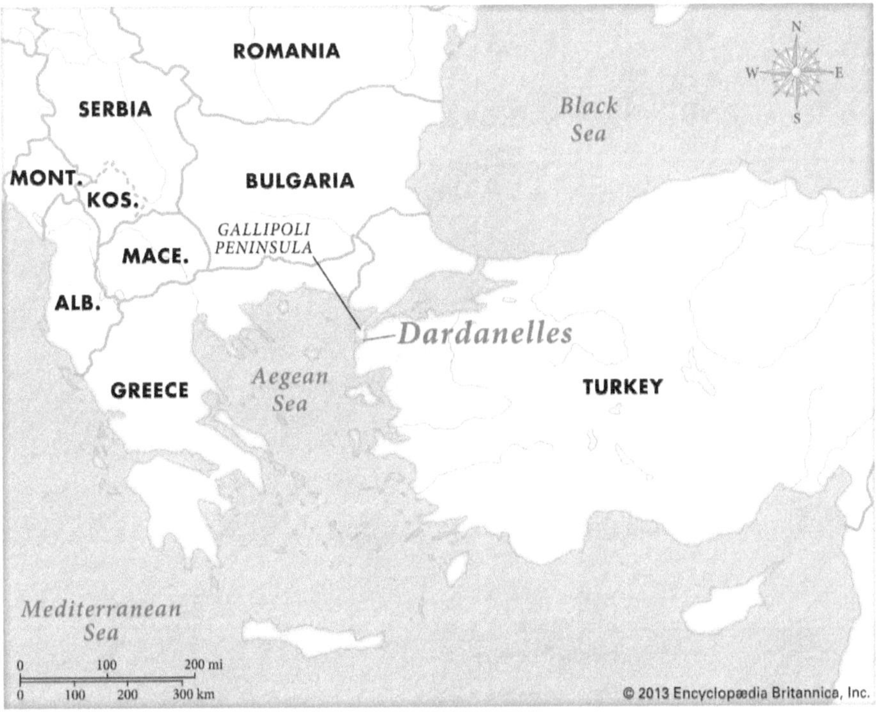

THE GALLIPOLI REGION OF TURKEY

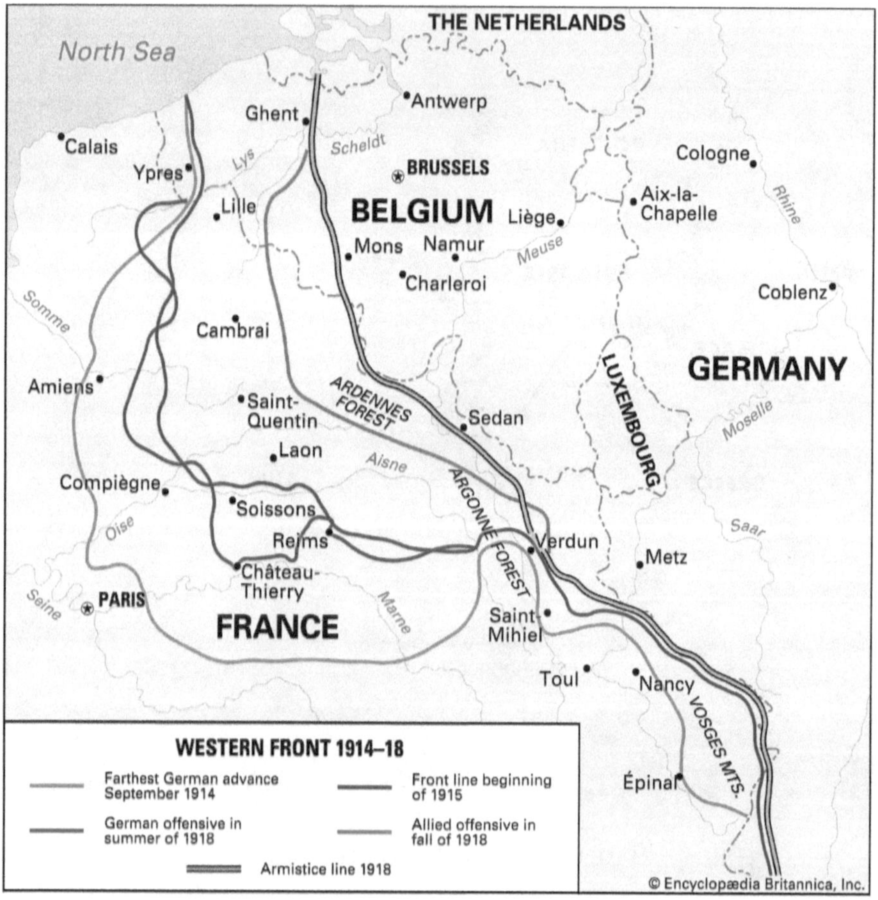

THE SOMME REGION OF FRANCE

Chapter One

THE HUNTER AND THE HUNTED

"On the hunt and in the fat."

For the young men of Newfoundland, this oft-repeated phrase referred to the three-week season for hunting baby seals and the prospect of windfall profits to follow.

After two brutal seasons on the ice floes of the North Atlantic, Luke Hobbs, a St. John's, Newfoundland native, knew better. Long days, a starvation diet, frostbite, injuries and even death, were a more likely conclusion to the annual slaughter. And much of the profits, if any, went to boat owners and large corporations, all of whom controlled the market for pelts and oil.

"I got a berth on the *Newfoundland*. The skipper is Wes Kean," said Luke.

"How did you manage that?" asked the boy's father. "Everyone in St. John's wants a berth."

The old man had worked the seal hunts for eight years. He knew the business. A berth entitled the chosen sailors to a percentage of the profits. His son explained further.

"I ran into Wes Kean at the Gear and Company Store on Water Street. He needed hardware for one of his pumps. I helped him find the right part. He was grateful."

Lucas Hobbs nodded approvingly. "You could make some good money, son. Some very good money. You got lucky."

Mary Hobbs, the boy's gray-haired mother, cast a sorrowful look at Luke, her eyes glassy with concern. She placed the tureen filled with fish and brewis on the table and removed the lid. The trembling in Mary's soft voice betrayed her fear.

"You told me last year there would be no more seal hunts. It was too dangerous. You promised me, Luke."

Her husband sneered at the woman as he helped himself to the traditional mixture of salt cod and hard bread. The old man's disposition rarely changed. He never smiled, possessed no patience, and preferred to be alone.

"Mary, this is none of your concern. Now hush."

The callous comment made Luke wince. He understood his mother's concern. Seal hunting was the most dangerous job in Newfoundland. As the sole wage earner in the family, Luke did not have a choice. He accepted employment wherever he could find it. The old woman persisted.

"But . . ."

Her husband hollered.

"I said quiet, woman! And where in bloody hell are the scrunchions?"

Luke's mother marched into the kitchen and retrieved a small bowl filled with crisp-fried bits of fat, cut from a slab of salt pork. She slammed the bowl on the table and took her seat, arms folded in protest. Luke did his best to comfort the woman.

"I am truly sorry, Mother. But we need the money."

"No reason to apologize, boy," said Mr. Hobbs, in his surly voice—the closest he ever got to genuine tenderness.

"You will be twenty years old in a few months. I did it when I was your age."

Mrs. Hobbs jerked in her chair and scowled.

"Yes, Lucas. You survived the seal hunts. But did you forget? You're missing three fingers on your right hand and half of your left foot. Is that what you call luck? Is that what you want for our son?"

Lucas Hobbs slammed his fist on the table. Scrunchions scattered in every direction, landing on the white lace tablecloth. The old man's spoon flew to the floor. Mrs. Hobbs jumped to her feet. She crumpled her embroidered cloth napkin into a ball and threw it on the table.

"I've lost my appetite."

The woman retreated to her bedroom. The pained expression on Luke's face triggered a response from the old man.

"Just ignore her, son. She has yet to learn her place in this family."

Luke resisted the urge to defend his mother. *Arguing with his father would be* a *waste of time*, he thought. Luke changed the subject.

"Wes Kean is Abe Kean's son, isn't he?"

Luke's father nodded.

"Yes. And I have known the kid since he was little. He would follow Captain Abe everywhere."

"The *Newfoundland* is a wooden steamer. The rest of old man Kean's fleet have hulls of steel. They can break through the ice floes with no effort. I'm guessing the *Newfoundland* will be left behind."

"The *Newfoundland* will be allowed to leave the docks a day earlier than the rest," Lucas replied. "That should make up for the difference."

"Perhaps. But if we get frozen in between the ice floes, it could be two or three days before we are underway again."

"You will manage, son. You will manage just fine."

Mr. Hobbs left for the parlor, his pipe in hand. Luke walked to the barn, intent on feeding and grooming his old mare. An hour with Jewel transformed the six-foot two-inch man into a carefree adolescent. Luke's blue eyes shone with affection when the old girl nuzzled the boy's long locks of dirty blond hair. Jewel's favorite pastime, licking Luke's clean-shaven face, made him laugh and giggle like a young boy. Tonight, the boy-man's thoughts lay elsewhere.

So much of Luke's life left him angry and frustrated. From the time he was a young boy, his mother strongly encouraged him to read everything he could get his hands on. As a result, he happily spent most of his free time at Bishop's Library. He enjoyed his days at the library and retained most of what he learned. His memory was that good. In fact, Luke would often survey a room and, rather immodestly, conclude that he was the smartest person in the room.

Unfortunately, it became increasingly clear that the distance between father and son could be attributed to the difference in their education. The old man, barely able to read and write, could not compete with the boy's encyclopedic knowledge of literature, the sciences, economics, history, politics, religion, and philosophy.

His father came from a different world. A universe where the practical skills in life were more important than book learning or even women. Indeed, Lucas Hobbs would often say that men were the breadwinners. A woman's proper role should be limited to the kitchen and the bedroom. Perhaps a child's nursery. Women, he claimed, would never be wise in the ways of the world much less possess the common sense required to run a household, pay the bills, or discipline a growing child.

Luke also confessed to a deep resentment of the poverty that surrounded him as a child. The same poverty that cursed him as an adult. St. John's economy, failing miserably in the spring of 1914, offered few opportunities for an educated young man. Graduates from high school were offered the same low-paying jobs given to drop outs; backbreaking work in the mines, lumberjacking in the deep woods, or cod fishing. If a young man felt lucky, he could participate in the annual slaughter of baby seals. Some men got rich doing that kind of work. Most of them were lucky to break even. Too many men lost money, limbs, fingers, or toes.

Some men lost their lives.

Elizabeth Parsons double-checked the lock on the library's front door, stepping into a bitter cold swirl of wind-driven snow.

The twenty-minute walk to the modest home she shared with her father became routine for the 18-year-old woman. She walked everywhere. On rare occasions, the girl would hop on a Reid Newfoundland trolley car. The electric vehicles ran up and down Water Street and covered a portion of Military Road, where Elizabeth lived. A ride on the yellow cars cost five cents. A reasonable amount, but way too much for her frugal father, Clarence Parsons.

Although she walked alone, Elizabeth did not fear for her safety. She spent most of her young life alone. She possessed no memory of her mother. The woman died shortly after Elizabeth's birth. Nana, the girl's maternal grandmother, took the deceased woman's place. Nana was Elizabeth's only source of love and affection; the girl's father, constantly at work, was too busy to be bothered. Nana devoted her life to the girl, teaching her the practical aspects of life. Elizabeth mastered cooking, sewing, cleaning, gardening, the importance of hard work, and honesty. Nana also bequeathed to Elizabeth an unquenchable thirst for books. That her first job after high school graduation would be at the very library where she spent most of her teen years was a pleasant happenstance.

For years, Elizabeth learned from the woman's example. They delivered a pot of homemade soup for a poverty-stricken neighbor, a home-made remedy for a sickly acquaintance, a knitted item for a young mother, mended clothing for an overwhelmed parent, and a patient set of ears for each of them. Nana was the guardian angel of the neighborhood, taking care that everyone was taken care of. Elizabeth became her faithful assistant. When Nana took ill, it was Elizabeth who tended to her needs, utilizing the same home remedies, the identical hot soup, and the constant care and attention that Nana had shown to so many others. Nana died with Elizabeth at her side.

The girl, just 16 at the time of Nana's passing, found modest comfort and very little wisdom or guidance in her father's arms. Adulthood came early for Elizabeth. She often contemplated a declaration of independence from the man who never encouraged her independence. She looked forward to that day and hoped it would come soon. Her schooling now finished,

Elizabeth intended to save her money and continue her studies. She intended to become a nurse. Nothing would stop her.

The heavy snow accumulating on her coat made the walk more treacherous but her thinking remained positive. At Bishop's Library, surrounded by books and people who loved books, she could not be more pleased. During the quiet times, she studied and absorbed the contents of every medical book in the building. Her dream of a career in nursing was close at hand.

When her tiny home appeared at the end of the street, Elizabeth smiled. Alice, her all-black cat, would be waiting at the door. The feline, a gift from Nana when she turned 12, brought great joy to the young woman, whose social life could best be described as severely limited. She talked to Alice and she wrote in her journal. Every day. Thousands of words crammed into a series of notebooks detailed her thinking about Alice the cat, her father, her secret dream to become a nurse, her work as a part-time librarian, her favorite books, and her idea of the perfect man. (In her opinion, he did not exist.) The journals lay secreted underneath her bed. Tonight, she would write about the senselessness of war. The local paper, now filled with talk of a European war, made her depressed. She neither understood nor agreed with the reasons for war. If Elizabeth ran the world, all wars would be outlawed.

Her plans to become a benevolent dictator were rudely interrupted by the noisy growl of a gasoline-powered automobile. The smelly contraption approached the girl from behind. The unpopular vehicles first made their appearance in St. John's when she attended grade school. And while their number increased over the years, the malodorous vehicles remained a novelty in Newfoundland. Their wealthy owners, many of them arrogant snobs, became the subject of many complaints.

The repeated honk of a hand-squeezed horn grew louder. A nearby horse and carriage, its owner apoplectic, struggled to get out of the vehicle's path. The elderly man at the reins voiced his objections in a loud voice.

"Confounded contraptions. They are cursed by God and man and there should be a law against them."

The motorized vehicle stopped ahead of Elizabeth, near her home. The driver hopped out of the car and yelled over the vehicle's roof. His booming voice could be heard from a block away.

"Good evening, Beth."

Elizabeth walked on. The shortened version of her name irritated the woman. And she knew that voice: Reginald Windsor, a.k.a. Reggie. The man tormented her for most of the past year, demanding that she accompany him to dinner, the theater, public outings, and even church. Reggie's very wealthy father, Reginald Windsor, owner of the Windsor Land and Lumber company, artificially inflated the boy's popularity with women. But not with Elizabeth. She viewed him as an ignorant Neanderthal. She suspected that the young man's graduation from school would not have occurred but for his family's wealth and young Reggie's athletic prowess.

"Elizabeth, I'm talking to you."

Elizabeth continued walking.

"What do you want, Reggie?"

"A bit cold to be walking home, Beth. Wouldn't you like a warm ride in my brand-new automobile?"

Beth stopped, twisted in place, and glared at the man.

"It's not yours. It's your Daddy's automobile and no thank you."

Reggie snarled his anger, slammed the door shut, and sped off. Reggie Windsor, a six-foot, two-inch giant with a full head of unruly black hair and an oversized moustache, regularly and publicly displayed his temper. His unexpected appearance, after dark and on a lightly trafficked road, made Elizabeth nervous.

The sight of his fancy motor car crawling away at half the speed of a galloping horse made her snicker.

Alice the cat greeted her owner at the door.

Elizabeth abandoned her snow-covered wrap and hat, revealing a milky white complexion with long brown hair and eyes to match. The girl, always dressed conservatively, wore dresses that mostly hid her slender frame. Elizabeth held the purring feline close as she added a log to the wood stove.

"Did you miss me, Alice?" she asked, searching the kitchen cupboards for a dinner idea.

Her father would be home in two hours. She wanted to make him a nice meal. Father and daughter did not enjoy a close relationship but she enjoyed doing nice things for him. Clarence Parsons did not have the capacity to be unkind. At worse, he could be less than loving. Elizabeth did not try to change the man. Over the years, she learned to deal with it.

Perhaps a soup with some hot bread, she thought. An hour later, her hair and face spotted with white flour, Elizabeth heard the front door open.

"Father. You are home early. Dinner will not be ready for at least an hour. Perhaps a cup of hot tea to warm your insides, until the soup is ready," she said.

When he failed to respond, the girl went in search of him.

"You're awful quiet. You must be exhausted . . ."

The young woman's voice disappeared in a draft of warm air from the wood stove. Elizabeth used her hand to stifle a scream. Reggie Windsor's large frame blocked the door. He leered at the woman and removed his custom-made sealskin gloves. The giant hulk shed his great coat and offered an obviously phony response.

"Thank you for your concern, Elizabeth, but I am not exhausted."

He paused; his eyes glazed in lust.

"And I'm not here for the soup."

Elizabeth pointed to the front door and screamed.

"Leave this house right this instant, Reginald Windsor!"

"I think it's time we get to know each other, Beth. We have at least an hour before your father gets home."

She pulled a textbook off the coffee table, holding it aloft with one hand.

"I'm warning you, Reggie."

The intruder flashed a devilish grin. She threw the book, its pages flapping in the air like a helpless bird. He caught the volume with both hands and slammed it shut. Reggie sneered when he read the title. *A Treatise on Midwifery*.

"You wanna be a midwife, Beth? Well, I can show you how babies are made."

He licked his dry lips. Her eyes darted to the wood stove. A forged-iron poker lay on a small stack of firewood. Reggie followed the path of her gaze. Elizabeth sprang forward. He reached the woman before she reached the poker. With one smooth motion he slammed her to the floor and straddled her body with his oversized frame. Reggie's massive weight made it difficult to breathe. The girl gasped for air. She screamed and clawed at his face. He used an oversized hand to pin her arms to the floor. With his remaining hand he pawed at her blouse. She twisted and turned. He struck her face with the back of his hand. Blood oozed from her lacerated lip. She continued to resist. He backhanded her again and reached for her throat.

"No one can hear you, Beth. And if you don't lay still, you will never scream again."

His thumb pressed against her windpipe. Elizabeth wheezed noisily. He slowly released his grip. The monster's eyes dared her to move. She lay silent. When he fumbled with the buttons on her blouse she screamed again. He grew frustrated and yanked on the white material. Buttons flew into the air and rolled across the hardwood floor. The sight of her white undergarments sent the man into an erotic frenzy.

She freed one hand from his sweaty palm and pressed a thumb against his eye. He punched her in the face with a closed fist. She whimpered. Elizabeth's eyes rolled to the back of her head. Drifting in and out of consciousness, she resisted no more. He struggled with his trousers. She could feel the drops of sweat falling from his face. He yanked the woman's petticoat to her knees and pressed a hairy groin to her abdomen. The petticoat worked in her favor, making the separation of her limbs, difficult. She crossed her heels and locked them tight. When her eyes opened, she could see his flustered face. His breathing grew rapid. She could feel nothing save the weight of his massive frame. His exertions came to a sudden halt. For a moment he examined his groin. A look of embarrassed disappointment crossed his flaming red face. Her puzzled look triggered a growl.

"Forget it. You're nothing but a whore. And I can afford better whores than you."

He rose to his feet, hurriedly covering his exposed private parts. Elizabeth, one eye black and swollen, rolled onto her side and faced the wall. She heard the rustle of Reggie's coat and retreating footsteps. The door slammed.

Alice, the black cat, lay beside her and purred.

The *Newfoundland* got underway on March 28, 1914.

A single funnel puffed black smoke from the coal-powered steam engine which propelled the 568-ton brig through icy waters. The gloomy murmurings of a dozen old-timers forced Luke Hobbs to go topside less he too be frightened by their half-truths, gossip, and rumors.

The veteran sailors, a superstitious lot, chattered incessantly about the "winter of storms" which plagued the commonwealth of Newfoundland that year. The men recited terrifying details of stories about ships that were lost or missing, their entire crews presumed dead. They argued that exceptionally cold weather rendered the ice too tight for the ships to navigate through the large pans (sheets) of ice. Some of them predicted that the seal-hunting fleet might never leave the harbor. And then there was the matter of the stowaways. Two of them. Captain Wes allowed the teen-aged boys to remain on the boat, calculating that their minimal wages and hard work would pay off. The old timers insisted that stowaways were bad luck. The ship would be jinxed as a result.

Luke's younger shipmates remained optimistic. Each year, they hoped for and boldly predicted *their* ship would discover "the main patch." The big herd, as it was called, would generate record profits. In 1910, for example, Captain Abe's crew received $148 each. A small fortune for sealers who lived on a fraction of that amount each year. The men in search of such riches traveled to St. John's each season, by dogsled, horseback, and on foot. Many of them signed the ship's register with nothing more than an *X*. Once on board, each man would be assigned to one of four watches. Each watch would regularly leave the ship in search of baby seals. Luke's 'Master of the Watch,' his boss when on the ice, would be George Tuff. They tolerated each other. Tuff needed the services of an experienced sealer. Luke needed the money. They would never be friends.

On the evening of the first day, the crew sighted a good-sized patch of seals. They were hoods. That particularly large version of the species jealously guarded both their mates and their pups. The animals could easily attack and kill a seal hunter. The *Newfoundland* sailed on; its crew now excited. The presence of hoods often led to larger herds of baby seals. The men would soon be "in the fat."

In time, the steel-hulled ships, their departure delayed by 24 hours, overtook the *Newfoundland*. Thickening ice and massive ice floes slowed the wooden ship considerably. Luke overheard Captain Wes complaining about the lack of a wireless onboard the ship. The owner decided such communication devices did not pay and ordered the wireless removed. Now, Captain Wes could not communicate with the other ships, much less his father, on board the *Stefano*. Knowing his son lacked a wireless, the old man secretly promised a signal. When he discovered a large herd of seals, the senior captain would raise the *Stefano's* derrick. Wes watched helplessly as his father's steam ship disappeared over the icy horizon. The boy prayed that the derrick would be raised when he next saw the *Stefano*.

By nightfall of the next day, the *Newfoundland* came to a dead halt, wedged in between two large ice floes. Scattered herds of seals could be seen but darkness delayed the hunt until the next morning. At first light, all four watches were ordered off the ship. The hunt did not go well. During the night, many of the seals scattered in different directions. The crew returned to the ship with only a few pelts. The tiny amount of seal meat for their stew that evening would be a small consolation.

Luke learned later that the steel-hulled steam ships discovered "whelping ice" the very next day. Tens of thousands of mother seals, their white-coated babies swarming among them, would soon become victims of the big hunt. The men that exited those ships carried gaffs (sharp hooks at the end of long poles) plus sculping knives. They needed the gaffs to kill the seals and move the pelts. If a sealer fell off the ice flow and into the freezing water, the steel hooks could also be used to pull the victim back onto the ice pan. They used the sculping knives to remove the pelts and carve the seal meat. They also carried ropes, a lunch pail, and tall poles with flags. They used the poles and flags to mark the small mountains of sealskins and meat they would leave behind. They or their shipmates would retrieve the bounty on their way back to their home port.

The *Newfoundland,* still stuck in the ice, missed out on the profitable find. The men started to complain.

"We've been stuck in the ice for days on end. Did Captain Wes expect the whelps to find us?" grumbled one of the older sealers.

On some days, the *Newfoundland* traveled only two to three miles. Most of the men spent their days chipping at the ice, in a laborious attempt to free the ship from Mother Nature's steel grip. The captain, increasingly desperate, dispatched scouting parties to search for seals. The men returned to the ship with only a handful of pelts and no significant sightings. Captain Wes insisted the seals were nearby. He ordered the searches to continue.

"If only we could get moving," he said.

The ship's progress continued, albeit slowly, through heavy ice. After a week in Arctic waters, the *Newfoundland* carried no more than 400 pelts, considerably less than the thousands they needed to earn a profit. Several days later, the *Newfoundland* caught up with the main part of the sealing fleet. They chased after the *Stefano*. Its Captain, Abe Kean, enjoyed a years-long reputation for always being at the right place at the right time. Where he went, everyone followed.

A day later, the old man spotted a thick patch of seals. As agreed, he hoisted the derrick on the *Stefano*, as a signal to Wes that a large herd of seals had been sighted. Ironically, Wes predicted that seals would be found at that very location, more than a week earlier. Unfortunately, the *Newfoundland* lay stuck in the ice, too far away from the *Stephano* to join in the kill.

Captain Wes decided to take matters into his own hands. He announced to the crew that two of the four watches would disembark early the next morning. They would walk several miles of ice, to the *Stefano*. The crews would harvest as many seals as possible on that day, spend the night on board the *Stefano*, and return to the *Newfoundland* the next day. Wes felt certain his father would feed and board the men for one night.

Early that morning, two watches of sealers prepared to leave, Luke among them. Threatening skies and the prospect of a long, arduous return trip laden with pelts and seal meat, triggered a great deal of grumbling. Making matters worse, a rapidly falling barometer indicated that a major storm would soon make its appearance.

Meanwhile, Captain Abe moved on. The *Newfoundland* crews would never catch up to the *Stefano*. The two watches struggled on rough ice to reach Captain Abe's ship for more than four hours. Their constantly moving target grew further and further away. Rapidly falling snow reduced visibility by more than half. The skies showed no signs of relief. The men, already exhausted, could go no further. Luke's instincts kicked in.

"I'm going back to the *Newfoundland*."

"Shouldn't we ask Master Tuff?"

Luke scowled and shook his head.

"I don't need George Tuff to tell me what to do. The conditions are dangerous. The *Stefano* is not waiting for us. If we don't get back to our own ship before dark, we may never find it."

Despite protests from the Master and shouts of "cowards," Luke and 33 of his shipmates turned back in search of the *Newfoundland*. The remaining 132 crew members continued their search for the *Stefano*. Hours later, when Luke's entourage reached the *Newfoundland*, they received a less than cordial welcome. Captain Wes screamed his objections.

"Who gave you the authority to come back?"

"There's a bad storm coming and there are no seals," said Luke.

"There's no sign of a storm," Kean lied.

"The *Stefano* is steaming away from us, sir."

"If the men you left behind find any seals, none of you will be paid for the skins they bring in. You get nothing."

Kean stormed off to his cabin. Luke and the men boarded the *Newfoundland* in silence. Some of them, upset about the welcome they received, questioned the decision to return to the mother ship. Luke did not second-guess his instincts. He recalled that his father rarely questioned what he *should* have done or what *might* have been. And in every book Luke read, none of the great men of history second guessed themselves. They made their decisions and moved on.

Luke fell asleep, his dream a very real nightmare. He was yelling at his father but Mr. Hobbs walked away without saying a word. Luke stormed out of the house. The family home was floating out to sea on a large ice floe. His mother screamed for help from a second-floor bedroom window. He could not reach her. And then, he woke up.

That evening, when the balance of the crew failed to return, Captain Wes assumed that the *Stefano* took his men in for a second night. When the men failed to appear by nightfall the next day, the crew grumbled amongst themselves.

"Something is wrong," said one sealer.

"Where are they, that's what I would like to know," said another man.

"Is we gonna look for 'em or not?" asked another.

"It's getting bad out there. Looking more and more like a huge blizzard," said Luke.

Captain Wes ordered the *Newfoundland's* whistle blown every 30 minutes, as a signal to his missing crewmembers. Once again, he cursed the lack of a wireless onboard the ship. He had no way of knowing for sure that his men were safe on the *Stefano* or somewhere out there searching for the *Newfoundland*. The weather grew worse. The accumulation of snow could be measured in feet. The old timers, convinced that no one could survive two nights in the freezing cold blizzard, predicted disaster.

By noon of the third day, the sky began to clear and the high winds and freezing temperatures abated—somewhat. The break in the weather allowed the *Newfoundland* to dislodge itself and slowly steam ahead. By nightfall, the Newfoundland ground to a halt, once again. Captain Wes used his spyglass to confirm that less than two miles separated the *Newfoundland* from the *Stefano*. When he turned, still gazing absent mindedly through the spyglass, he noticed a few black dots on the horizon. A closer look revealed movement. Captain Wes concluded that the dots were his crew members searching for the *Newfoundland.*

The captain immediately dispatched a rescue detail. Luke and his ship mates left the ship with litters, ropes, food, and drink. The handful of frozen men, barely alive, reported that more than 100 members of the *Newfoundland's* crew, remained behind. They could be dead or alive. Captain Wes immediately flew the international maritime distress signal. Within minutes, the *Stefano* confirmed the signal and dispatched a rescue crew of its own.

The rescue parties searched the icy terrain and by four o'clock that afternoon, confirmed the tragic results. Thirty-seven sealers survived the ordeal on the ice, most of them, just barely. Sixty-four of their mates succumbed and several more were reported missing, presumably drowned.

Those steamships equipped with wireless notified the authorities at St. John's as soon as they learned of the tragedy. City residents, still digging out from under the 10 feet of snow which fell during the blizzard, began to gather at the docks. A temporary hospital and a makeshift morgue were organized. Doctors, nurses, and police officials stood by.

The fleet, its flags flying at half-mast, did not arrive until the next day. A canvas tarpaulin hid the frozen bodies from onlookers' view. The injured were immediately carried off the ship. In time, the tarp-turned-shroud was removed. One by one, the frozen remains of dead sealers were carried to shore. Arms and legs, frozen stiff, protruded from the blankets which shrouded their bodies. The crowd, visibly shaken by the horrible scene, gasped their shock and surprise.

Mary and Lucas Hobbs were among the thousands on hand to greet the survivors and mourn the victims. Mary thought she recognized her son, returning to the *Newfoundland* with an empty litter. She yelled.

"Luke. Luke. Is that you?"

The 20-year-old sealer stopped and stared into the sea of grief-stricken faces.

"Yes Mother. It's me."

Mrs. Hobbs made the sign of the cross, bowed her head, and sobbed.

Mr. Hobbs, stone-faced and dry-eyed, looked straight ahead.

A single chime of the old clock on the mantle stirred Elizabeth from her pain-filled stupor, on the parlor floor.

Father would be home in a half hour. *He must not learn of the attack,* she thought. Although an employee of the colonial government, Clarence regularly worked with the Windsor Land and Lumber Company. At times, it seemed like the other way around. Reginald Windsor, its owner, was not to be trifled with.

His vast influence and untold wealth made him one of the most respected and feared men in all of Newfoundland.

Elizabeth stared at her image in the mirror. Her upper lip no longer bled but the swelling was obvious. Beneath her right eye, a half-circle of black and blue, stained her otherwise unblemished milky white skin. A few strokes of a brush straightened her long brown hair. If she changed her ripped blouse, father would surely notice. She chose to don a sweater, buttoning it to the neckline. Tears filled her brown eyes. She ached from Reggie's blows. Nevertheless, Elizabeth required only a moment to compose herself. She returned to the kitchen and resumed her preparations for dinner.

At precisely 5:15 p.m., the front door opened. Her father's punctuality gave her some comfort. A sudden bolt of panic shocked her tiny frame. *The door was unlocked. Could Reggie have returned? What if he . . . ?*

"Elizabeth. I'm home."

The girl took a deep breath and exhaled loudly.

"Father. I am so happy to see you. I made soup and fresh bread and I hope you are hungry because . . ."

"Elizabeth. You have been injured. What happened?"

"I am fine, Father. Now sit down and I will tell you what happened to me while we have our soup."

Elizabeth, perhaps because she read voraciously, spun a very believable tale about the ice-covered steps that welcomed visitors to the library's grand entrance. She used the ornate, wrought-iron railing to explain the black eye. A large pile of snow and ice, near the walkway, took the blame for her swollen lip. The girl knew her father well. He could easily be distracted and she did not give him a chance to ask questions.

"Now tell me, Father, were you able to persuade the Director to your point of view? Will the Crown maintain its control over the interior, and protect the local sawmill operators?"

The issue, having to do with the local pulp, paper, and lumber industries, represented a complicated bureaucratic mess that occupied much of her father's time. Clarence Parsons, recently promoted to Assistant Director, discussed the matter *ad nauseam*, almost every evening for the past two weeks. Elizabeth could not be any less interested in the machinations of bureaucrats and business people. Her father quickly forgot about his daughter's injuries and droned on and on about government business. An off-handed reference to a businessman, triggered Elizabeth's sudden attention.

"Excuse me, Father. What did you say?"

"I said that Reginald Windsor has agreed to support the agency in the matter. The director said that I was instrumental in Windsor's decision to support the agency. In fact, he congratulated me for persuading Mr. Windsor to cooperate."

Elizabeth stared into space. She spoke as if in a trance.

"I know his son."

"Of course, you do. Didn't he ask you to attend Trophy night at the curling arena last month? You couldn't go because you were not feeling well at the time."

Elizabeth could feel the flush of hot pink covering her face. She recalled Reggie's invitation along with many others, all of which, she spurned. She reached down and gave Alice her empty bowl. Clarence continued his boring monologue.

"I met Mr. Windsor on several occasions. He is an extremely large man, chain smokes cigars, wears a large, dark mustache, and speaks so loudly as to cause damage to one's ears. Is the son anything like his father?"

Elizabeth blinked, repeatedly. The question startled her. Her evasive response did not come easily.

"I don't really know the boy. I am told he was a skilled athlete in school. And, I believe he works for his father's company."

"No doubt. Hundreds of people are employed by Mr. Windsor. He is extremely influential in government circles. I should like to meet his son, one day."

Elizabeth's stomach churned. Her head ached. If she harbored any doubts about keeping the incident secret, her father's words ended such thoughts. Clarence would be unable and, perhaps unwilling, to pursue the matter. Elizabeth blinked herself into the present.

"Would you like some more bread, Father?"

"No thank you, Elizabeth. There are a half-dozen reports I must review this evening."

Mr. Parsons left the dinner table, assuming that Elizabeth would clean up and wash the dishes. *Typical,* thought Elizabeth.

"I will clean up, Father but please forgive me. I am exhausted and wish to retire early."

Her father nodded, his head elsewhere.

Chapter Two

RETRIBUTION

"You are late for dinner, once again."

Reginald Windsor despised tardiness. Even when the culprit was his favorite son. The old man jumped to his feet. Young Reggie stopped and faced his father.

"Repeat after me," said the father. "I will not be late for my appointments."

Reggie dutifully repeated the words. His father raised a hand and slapped his son across the face. The boy staggered from the blow but remained standing.

"You may be seated," said the older man.

The penitent son, a red handprint covering most of his left cheek, sat opposite his father at the end of the overly long dining room table. A uniformed servant rushed to the boy's side and filled his bowl with a stew of beef and vegetables.

"What happened to your face, Reggie?" asked his father.

"Father. You just slapped me."

Reggie's younger brother, Billy, seated at the middle of the table, spoke up.

"I believe that father is referring to the long scratches on your face and the bruise on your cheek." Billy smirked. "Looks to me like someone beat the tar out of the great Reggie Windsor."

The senior Windsor glared at his younger son.

"Not another word, Billy. When I want to hear from you, I will let you know."

Billy, two years younger than Reggie, was a foot shorter and wore a mop of strawberry blond hair on his pencil thin frame. The clean-shaven 19-year-old worked for his father, regularly advising the old man on matters legal, financial, and political. Particularly when the business at hand had been reduced to writing. The senior Windsor suffered from "word blindness." Europeans now referred to it as dyslexia. Although Reginald Windsor could read with difficulty, too many letters and numbers confused him. Comprehension became difficult if not impossible. For that reason, Billy, unlike Reggie Junior, did not fear his father's wrath.

Reggie Junior made short work of the stew, noisily slurping the last drops from his bowl. The patriarch growled.

"I asked you a question, Reggie."

A thunderous belch announced the boy's full stomach.

"Sorry, Father, I was hungry."

"I am still waiting for an explanation."

"Mrs. Pendergast stopped me at the library. Seems her cat got up into a tree and would not come down. When I rescued him, the little bastard scratched me."

Reggie's father smiled knowingly.

"You are always trying to help someone in need, son. I am proud of you."

Reggie beamed. Billy looked askance. He could barely disguise his disbelief.

"You were at the library? I don't believe it."

"I do," said the old man. Your brother is sweet on that Parsons girl, aren't you, son?"

Reggie flashed a salacious smile.

Elizabeth sprang out of bed in a panic.

She overslept. Father would be waiting for his coffee and oatmeal. He always ate oatmeal for breakfast. She flew down the stairs and rushed into the kitchen. He was gone. A handwritten note triggered a sigh of relief.

Elizabeth,

You must have been tired. I made my own oatmeal.

Your father

On that day, Elizabeth would be working a full eight-hour shift at the library. The head librarian, away visiting her mother in Placentia, regularly relied on the girl to fill in. Elizabeth worked every shift she could. She also saved every penny she earned.

The very name of that place, Placentia, made Elizabeth smile. Although her lip started to bleed again, she could not stop smiling. The small Newfoundland town, described as a pleasant place to live, reminded her of the word 'placenta.' The organ grows in a pregnant woman's womb, giving nourishment to her unborn child. Elizabeth, having read as many books as she could about childbearing, grew very familiar with the word. And while her social and economic status made medical school extremely unlikely, she dreamed of starting her career in medicine as a midwife.

As she dabbed at the drop of blood on her lip, Elizabeth's thoughts turned to Reggie. *Would he attack her again? Should she complain to the police? Will he accuse her of leading him on? Would anyone take her word over his?* She wrestled with these thoughts as she walked to the library, with one ear cocked for the sound of an oncoming gas-powered automobile.

There were no waiting visitors when she unlocked the library door. Elizabeth retrieved her journal and started writing. She explained why no entry was made on the previous evening. She confessed her fears that Reggie might easily have killed her. She also observed that Reggie did not accomplish that which he clearly intended. She allowed herself a smirk, concluding that Reggie thought himself a stallion. In truth, he was a toothless dog that barked a lot.

Elizabeth knew everyone who visited library that morning, but one visitor, arriving just before noon, made her stomach churn. Billy Windsor, Reggie's younger brother, walked in the door. Billy, a frequent visitor at the library, conducted a great deal of research for his father's company.

"Good morning, Miss Parsons."

"Good morning, Mr. Windsor."

"Billy. Please call me, Billy. Oh, my. What happened to *you*?" he asked, pointing to Elizabeth's black eye and puffy lip.

Elizabeth dodged his question.

"Mr. Windsor, it is not polite to point."

"My apologies, Miss Parsons."

"Apology accepted. How may I be of help to you today? More research on forestry?"

Billy did not respond immediately. He focused his unblinking eyes squarely on Elizabeth. He did it for a half minute. Elizabeth squirmed in her squeaky wooden chair. Billy Windsor, an exceptionally smart young man, could not easily be fooled. He demonstrated an extraordinary attention to detail and knew the lumber and forestry industry like the alphabet. *Could he know about the attack*? she asked herself.

"I understand that my older brother paid you a visit yesterday."

Elizabeth's eyes filled with tears. She choked a sob, unable to speak or cry. Billy's head swiveled in every direction. He whispered, "My brother did not admit to attacking you. He simply said he was at the library last night, helping an old lady whose cat got stuck in a tree."

Elizabeth shook her head, slapped the desk with both hands, and shouted.

"No!"

Two elderly ladies inspecting an ornate, oversized bible displayed on a pedestal in the history section, frowned their disapproval. Billy tapped his ear and smiled at them.

"My apologies, ladies. I have lost the hearing in my right ear."

Elizabeth sniffled. Billy offered her a white, monogrammed handkerchief.

"Your brother entered my home without permission and attacked me."

"I know," said Billy. "My brother never goes to the library."

Elizabeth blew her nose and dabbed at her tears. "Thank you. I shall return it when you next visit the library."

"You are not his first victim, I am afraid. I will speak to my father."

Elizabeth, still unable to speak, simply nodded.

"How did you survive three days on the ice, unharmed?"

Lucas Hobbs' question, accompanied by a snarl, reeked of skepticism. Mary Hobbs sensed an argument and intervened on behalf of her son.

"The Good Lord was with him," she said.

Mr. Hobbs leaned forward in his chair.

"The boy does not need a lecture on the Deity from you, Mary Hobbs. Now leave us."

The large artery on the boy's neck pulsed a seething anger. Luke took a calming breath and spoke in a matter-of-fact tone.

"No, Father. Mother stays in the room."

Mr. Hobbs' head jerked up. His jaw dropped. Mrs. Hobbs gnawed on her upper lip. The old man raised his voice.

"I'm sorry, boy. What did you say?"

Luke Hobbs jumped out of his chair. Using both hands, he yanked the old man to his feet and pushed his father against the wall. The sound of Luke's screaming voice, filled the room. Mrs. Hobbs covered her ears. Spittle flew from the boy's mouth.

"I said she stays. Did you hear *that*, Father. She stays."

Luke, red-faced and panting, slowly released his father. Mr. Hobbs returned to his chair. Luke remained standing. Mrs. Hobbs reached for her cup of tea, the woman's shaking hands splashing the liquid on the tablecloth. She quickly returned the cup to its saucer. Luke stood at the kitchen sink and spoke to the window, his voice a near whisper.

"I turned back."

Luke could not see his father's deeply furrowed eyebrows. The boy's outburst did nothing to placate the old man's shame.

"What does that mean? You turned back."

"Captain Wes ordered us to the *Stefano*. It was steaming away from us. The blizzard had started. There were no seals. There was no chance we would catch up. It would be dark in a few hours. I told George Tuff I was going back to the *Newfoundland*."

"Were you the only one who turned back?" asked his father.

Luke faced his father.

"No sir. There were 34 of us that refused the watch master's orders."

"Tuff and the rest of the crew said we were cowards. A bunch of grandmothers."

The boy's father shrugged.

"I'm not surprised."

Luke challenged his old man.

"Is that what you think, Father? Do you think I'm a coward?"

Mrs. Hobbs did not wait for her husband to respond. She rose from her chair and reached for her son.

"You were *not* a coward, Luke. You were smart. You used your head and you saved the lives of 34 men."

Mr. Hobbs shoved his teacup to the center of the table. He used his napkin to brush bread crumbs to the floor.

"You disobeyed orders and abandoned most of your shipmates. All to save your own skin. You should be ashamed of yourself."

The old man turned his back to the boy.

Reginald Windsor examined his pocket watch for the third time.

"Are we done here yet? I promised to meet Will Ellis for drinks," said the senior Windsor.

"What does Mayor Ellis want with you?" asked Billy.

"Free drinks is my guess."

"We have one more item to discuss."

The senior businessman groaned.

"Let's have it."

"This is about my brother."

Billy's father, using both hands to free his large frame from the office chair, reached for his coat and hat.

"What the bloody hell are the two of you fighting about, now?"

"We are not fighting, Father. But Reggie was involved in a fight."

"Did he beat the man?"

"No sir. He beat a woman."

Reginald held the hat aloft, as if frozen in place.

"Oh Jesus. Who?"

"Elizabeth Parsons, the librarian at Bishops."

The old man jammed his hat on the coat tree and used another hook for his coat. He fell into the office chair, rubbing his face and smoothing his moustache with two fingers. The old man looked tired.

"What in blazes is the matter with that boy?"

Billy sat in silence.

"Well? Are you going to tell me what happened or are we gonna be here all night?"

"He was not at the library last night. I'm guessing he followed the girl home when she left the library. She looked awful, Father. A swollen lip and a black eye."

"What exactly did she tell you?"

"Nothing. She was too choked up. I kind of tricked her. I believe you know the girl's father. Clarence Parsons."

"Yeah, I know him. The Crown's Assistant Director. He certainly knows his stuff."

Reginald thought for a moment.

"Wait a minute. Why did you approach the girl in the first place?"

"Reggie said he went to the library. I didn't believe him."

The older man winced.

"No one likes a tattletale, Billy."

Billy ignored the insult and continued.

"Clarence Parsons works in Forestry. He is in a position to help us a great deal. He can also hurt us, if and when he discovers the attack."

"What makes you think she hasn't already told him?"

"She's a smart girl, Father. She knows it would be a Windsor's word against her own. I'm thinking she hasn't said anything to her father."

Billy paused.

"Not yet, anyway."

Windsor Sr. reached for his coat and hat, once again.

"Mayor Ellis is gonna have to buy his own drinks tonight. Cancel the mayor and tell Reggie I want to see him. Here. Tonight. Eight o'clock."

Reginald paused.

"Alone, Billy. I want to see him alone."

"Where are you going?"

"To the library. I've got research to do."

"Am I your only customer?"

"No, sir. It's usually quiet in here on Friday evening . . ."

Elizabeth swallowed the rest of her sentence. She recognized the large man with the booming voice, standing at her desk. He reeked of cigar smoke and wore a perfectly trimmed, thick, black mustache. He looked so much larger than the photos in the newspaper but her father's description was accurate. Her hands began to tremble, uncontrollably. He noticed.

"Miss Parsons, I wish you no harm. I would like to learn more about the incident with my son. A few moments of your time. Please."

Elizabeth feigned a cough. She needed time to compose herself. She spoke in a whisper.

"I have said nothing about this so-called incident to anyone."

"You spoke to my son, Billy."

Her voice grew stronger.

"He fooled me. Made it sound like he knew what happened."

"Is it true? Did my son Reggie attack you?"

Elizabeth's soft voice and shy demeanor disappeared. She jumped to her feet and leaned in to the man's face.

"Yes, sir."

The large man, stunned by her response, took a step back. He struck an apologetic tone.

"Were you? Did he? Are you . . .?"

The man's voice trailed off into an awkward silence. He tried again.

"Did he, I mean, were you . . .?"

Mr. Windsor's face grew red. Elizabeth snarled her response.

"He tried."

"I don't understand."

Elizabeth's eyes drilled into the man's face.

"You are a businessman, Mr. Windsor. I will therefore utilize the language of business."

She spoke in a harsh whisper.

"Your son was unable to close the deal."

Windsor swallowed hard and licked his dry lips. He blushed a slight pink.

"I think I understand what you are telling me, Miss Parsons."

"He attacked me, nevertheless."

"I will gladly pay your medical expenses."

"There are no medical expenses. And I have repaired the blouse he ripped."

"I should like to pay you for your troubles, then."

"I don't want your money."

"I will speak to my son. He will pay dearly for his mistake. This will not happen again. I promise you."

The man's promise did nothing to diminish her anger and shame.

"I am within my rights to file a complaint with the authorities. There would be a story in the newspaper. Your son might well go to prison. Will your money protect him from all of that?"

Windsor studied his highly polished shoes. He took a deep breath, clearly contemplating his next words.

"Miss Parsons. In my lifetime, I have been threatened by people of much greater consequence than you. If you wish to destroy my family, you leave me no choice but to defend my family. If necessary, I will destroy yours."

"I have no family. My mother is deceased and I have no siblings."

"Your father works for the Crown does he not?"

Elizabeth flinched. The man's eyebrows arched. He leaned forward and spoke softly.

"I was of some assistance to your father, just last week. He was most grateful. I wonder how long he would be employed by the Crown should I, shall we say, render *no* assistance. Perhaps even complain to my friends in government about your father's attitude, his work ethic, and his honesty."

Elizabeth's eyes filled with tears. Her voice shook with anger.

"None of that is true and you know it."

Windsor straightened and spoke firmly.

"You are correct, Miss Parsons. But I will do what I must to protect my family."

Elizabeth fell back into her chair. She gripped the pencil on her desk.

"Your son does not deserve your protection, Mr. Windsor."

"You have my word, Miss Parsons. My son will leave you alone. But I must have *your* word. This ends, here and now. Do you agree?"

Elizabeth hesitated. In her heart, she wanted to fight and never stop fighting. Neither the son nor the father frightened her. They could not hurt her. But they could hurt her father. A small voice in her head urged caution. Extreme caution. Clarence Parsons might very well pay the price for her anger. She could not do that to him. The loss of his job, the publicity, the accusations, the denials, the whole sordid affair. It would kill him. Elizabeth looked Reginald Windsor in the eye.

"Yes. I agree."

The business executive executed a slight bow.

"Good evening, Miss Parsons."

"Shut the door, Reggie. And lock it."

Reggie, a puzzled look on his face, did as he was told. The father removed his suit coat, loosened his tie, and rolled up his sleeves.

"Father. What are you doing?"

"Come here, son."

Reggie took a step forward. The old man pointed to a spot very near his feet and shouted.

"I said *here!*"

The boy did not quite reach the designated spot when his father delivered a crushing blow to the boy's jaw. Reggie fell back onto the hard wood floor with a loud thud. He lay unconscious for minutes. His father reached for a crystal pitcher of water on the office credenza. He poured its contents on Reggie's face. The kid came to, sputtering and violently shaking the water from his face. The old man pulled him to his feet.

"Are you going to make it, boy?"

Reggie, still a bit shaky, searched his father's face.

"Why did you hit me, Father?

Reginald smiled again as his closed fist plunged deep into the boy's solar plexus. Reggie fell to his knees, gasping for air. He made a wheezing noise that sounded like a braying donkey. Once again, his father pulled the boy to his feet. This time the kid stepped back and protected his face and head with both arms.

"Father. Please. Why are you beating me?"

Mr. Windsor returned to his chair, rolled down his sleeves, and straightened his tie. Windsor spoke softly to the boy, his voice dripping with affection.

"Reggie, you will leave that Parsons girl alone. If there is a next time, I will beat you again. If necessary, to within an inch of your life. Do you understand me?"

Reggie jerked his head up and down.

"Yes, Father. I promise."

"Now please leave me. I have work to do."

"Luke, you are just in time for dinner. I will fix you a plate."

The boy's mother scurried to the stove. The boy took a seat, opposite his father. Luke could smell the fish and noticed the milk gravy, and potatoes on his father's plate.

"Good evening, Father."

The man did not acknowledge his son. He focused on his cod, cutting it with his fork.

"I applied for a job at Bell Island Mines today. I start on Monday."

Mrs. Hobbs slid a plate with steaming food in front of her son. She placed a hand on his shoulder.

"Working in a mine is not the safest job in St. John's."

"No, Mother, but at least it's a job."

Mr. Hobbs stood and faced his wife.

"I'll have my tea in the parlor."

He flashed a dirty look in his son's direction.

"Alone."

Luke waited until his father was out of earshot.

"How long is he going to be like that Mother?"

"Your father seems to think you should have frozen to death on the ice, like so many of your shipmates."

Luke scraped his plate clean. Mrs. Hobbs donated the fish on her plate.

"Here. You can have mine. I'm not hungry."

"He's not talking to you either?"

"Only when he wants something."

"I don't understand that man," Luke said.

"I'm not sure your father is feeling well, Luke. I am worried about him. I think he hurt his arm. He keeps rubbing his shoulder."

"He may be my father but there are times when I wish he was not a part of my life."

Mrs. Hobbs grabbed the boy's hand and squeezed.

"Luke! That is a horrible thing to say. You must be patient. He will come around in his own good time."

Luke shook his head.

"I doubt it," he said, rising to his feet and reaching for his dirty plate. "I'll help you clean up."

"No, you won't, but thank you for offering. Why don't you take Jewel for a long walk. You've got a few more hours of daylight and it will do you both some good."

"Good idea, Mother. Thank you."

Luke gave his mother a quick peck on the cheek and left.

The short walk from his house to a large shed at the back of the property triggered a memory.

Luke purchased the old mare four years ago. She was a present on the occasion of his 16th birthday. After saving his money for two years and with his parents' permission, he brought the horse home. The light brown mare, seven years old at the time, quickly became Luke's best friend and closest confidant. Some would say the intimate relationship was inevitable, given the boy's aging parents and the lack of siblings. And tonight would be no different. He took his time, brushing her coat, cleaning her bridle, and picking Jewel's hooves for dirt, pebbles, and ice. He talked all the while, mostly about his father.

"I think he's ashamed of me, Jewel. He thinks I'm a coward. Mother says he'd rather I died out there on the ice with so many of my shipmates."

Jewel turned a single ear in Luke's direction. Luke continued.

"It doesn't matter. As soon as I can, I'm leaving St. John's."

Jewel turned her head, as if she understood Luke's announcement. Luke rode in silence to Water Street, the city's main thoroughfare. But for the trolleys and an occasional gas-powered vehicle, which spooked Jewel to no end, it was a pleasant ride. Luke relished the cool, crisp air and basked in a rare Newfoundland sun, as it began its descent in the western sky.

He tugged on the reins and pointed the horse down Prescott Street. They would return home by way of the Military Road, an avenue which roughly paralleled Water Street, carrying very little traffic. As they approached Bishop's Library and the monastery, a lone figure could be seen, walking in the same direction, but on the walkway.

The sound of Jewel's hooves, muffled by a thin dusting of snow, disappeared in the noise of an oncoming, gas-powered vehicle. The pedestrian, a female judging from her colorful knit hat, veered to her right, further away from the roadway. Luke gripped the reins, anticipating Jewel's reaction to the noisy engine. The engine's roar grew louder. The woman, the horse, and the vehicle converged. The driver, as a warning or because he did not know better, repeatedly squeezed the car's rubber ball horn. The strange sound startled Jewel even more. The old nag stepped away from the road and onto the walkway. Jewel's hindquarters pushed the pedestrian into a pile of dirty snow and ice. Luke jumped off his horse, tethered it to a lamppost, and ran to the girl.

"Are you injured, ma'am? I am terribly sorry. My horse spooked."

"I'm stuck. Help me, please."

Luke reached for the girl's hands and pulled her to a standing position. While she brushed herself off and recovered her hat, Luke apologized again.

"I am very sorry, ma'am. Please forgive me."

"I am no worse for the wear. I must be going now. The street lamps are few and far between and it will be dark, soon."

Luke extended a hand.

"My name is Luke Hobbs. Do you live nearby?"

"Elizabeth Parsons. I live at the corner of Military Road and Kings Road."

"May I walk you home?"

"Mr. Hobbs, I have known you for less than five minutes."

Luke smiled.

"A scoundrel abandons a woman in distress. A gentleman comes to her aid."

Elizabeth flashed a mischievous grin. Perhaps it was the long locks of dirty blond hair that escaped his gray toque that attracted her. The piercing blue eyes also impressed her. With some trepidation, she offered a somewhat presumptuous remark.

"But I am a victim of the gentleman's horse."

"With respect, Miss Parsons, you are a victim of a scoundrel's automobile."

Elizabeth, in need of a distraction and knowing that her father waited for her, relented.

"Very well, then. You may accompany me to my home."

"Do you ride?"

"Not since I was a child. But thank you anyway."

"You were coming from the library, I assume."

"I started my employment at the library just two months ago."

"I am a frequent visitor at Bishop's Library. I do not recall seeing you there."

"I work different shifts. And how do *you* earn a living, Mr. Hobbs?"

"I start at Bell Island Mines on Monday. I used to cut lumber and hunt seals."

Elizabeth stopped walking.

"Were you on the . . . ?"

The woman's voice disappeared in the cool breeze. Her face became a bright pink.

"Yes. I was on the *Newfoundland*."

"How did you manage to survive?"

Luke disclosed a portion of his narrow escape.

"Only half of the crew was dispatched at the time of the blizzard."

The couple resumed their walk in an awkward silence. Elizabeth changed the subject.

"What do you like to read, Mr. Hobbs?"

"I am partial to Shakespeare."

Elizabeth chuckled.

"Come now, Mr. Hobbs. There is no need to impress me much less prevaricate."

Luke stopped walking.

"Tell me something, Miss Parsons. Are you of the opinion that men who hunt seals and fell trees do not read Shakespeare? Or do you consider such men incapable of reading?"

Elizabeth, visibly shocked by her escort's biting response, stubbornly refused to apologize for her presumptuous remark.

"I shall call your bluff, Mr. Hobbs. Which one of the Great Bard's 154 sonnets do you favor?"

Luke hesitated but only for a moment.

"The first line of Sonnet 138 comes to mind," he said, a scornful smile decorating his chiseled features.

'When my love swears she is made of truth
I do believe her though I know she lies.
That she might think me some untutored youth
Unlearned in the world's false subtleties.'

Elizabeth stood motionless, her mouth agape.

"I believe this is your residence, Miss Parsons. Have a pleasant evening."

Luke bowed from the waist, mounted Jewel in a single leap, and disappeared into the darkness.

Billy, the first person in the office, jerked in his chair when the office door slammed shut.

Reggie Junior stood at the door growling his anger.

"I should give you the same beating I got from the old man."

"What are you talking about?"

"How did father find out about my little altercation with Miss Parsons?"

"I have no idea," Billy lied.

Reggie flew to his brother's desk. With one sweep of his arm, he cleared the surface of its contents. Pens, inkwells, papers, reports, and rolled up maps, flew to the floor. Billy screamed.

"You've gone insane, brother. Absolutely insane!"

Reggie marched around the desk, pulled Billy from his office chair, and slammed him against the wall. A large oil painting of their grandfather crashed to the floor. Billy scratched and kicked his assailant.

"Leave me alone, you overgrown ape."

After backhanding the boy, Reggie lifted his brother aloft by the neck. Billy thrashed and kicked, sputtering, and struggling to breathe. Reggie released his victim. Billy collapsed on the floor with his back to the wall. Reggie kicked the boy. Billy groaned and clutched his stomach. Reggie's closed fist rose in the air.

"That's enough."

The thundering voice of Reginald Windsor filled the room. Reggie, panting like a hungry lion, turned to face his father.

"You always said nobody likes a rat. Well, my little brother is a rat. And this is what we do to rats."

Reggie turned on one heel and for good measure, spit on the boy.

"I said, that's enough. Now leave," said the senior Windsor.

Reggie stormed out of the room. Billy struggled to his feet using a sleeve to wipe blood from his nose. His father shrugged.

"He's right, you know. Nobody likes a rat."

"I did what I had to do to protect the family," said Billy.

The old man snorted.

"So, did I. Now get yourself cleaned up. We've got a meeting with the Forestry Department in 30 minutes."

Chapter Three

NEW OCCUPATIONS

Elizabeth fumed as she sat at the head librarian's desk.

Her encounter with Luke Hobbs, the night before, began with great promise but quickly dissolved into an unmitigated disaster. She shook her head in frustration. How could a man look like a lumberjack but speak like a college professor? His appearance impressed the girl as did his command of the English language. She could not recall meeting anyone quite like Luke Hobbs.

And yet, she would not consider an apology. It was his horse, after all, that catapulted her into a dirty snowbank. On the other hand, he did apologize for the incident. A visitor broke her chain of frustrated thoughts.

"Excuse me, miss?"

A matronly looking woman stood in front of Elizabeth's desk.

"My name is Margaret Newcastle. I work as a midwife and I am in search of a basic text on childbirth."

Elizabeth's face lit up.

"We have several books on childbirth. And I have read each of them at least three times. Follow me. I know exactly where they are located."

"I require a very basic text. My young assistant has left the area and I'm afraid she took my book with her."

Elizabeth's face lit up.

"Are you in need of a new assistant? If so, I would be most interested."

Mrs. Newcastle smiled and politely shook her head.

"Thank you for your interest. I have a young lady who started working with me just this past week. If for some reason she does not work out, I will contact you. Is this a good place to find you? I'm afraid I don't know your name."

The two women exchanged names and addresses. For a moment, Elizabeth's disappointment with the previous night's encounter disappeared. A long-cherished dream might soon become a reality.

That evening, the events of the past 48 hours required six full pages in her journal.

Luke took a streetcar to the Portugal Cove ferry crossing.

For one dollar, the steamer would deliver him to Bell Island. The steamship *Mary*, owned by the Bell Island Steamship Company, could accommodate up to 80 passengers. But no horses. The young man was forced to leave Jewel behind in the care of his mother and father.

He quickly learned that working at Bell Island Mines would not be an easy task. For 13 cents an hour, 10 hours a day, and six days a week, Luke would use a shovel to load chunks of ore into a trolley car—backbreaking work. Horses would tow the cars to waiting locomotives. Two men were expected to load at least 20 cars per shift. Luke would spend his evenings in a "mess shack" where he would sleep and eat. He would sleep on a straw mattress. The dilapidated building had no indoor toilet facilities. The food, mediocre at best, was served by candlelight. In fact, the men lived and worked by candlelight. Sundays would be the only day of the week when they saw the sun. After less than two weeks in the mines, Luke's routine was interrupted.

"Hobbs, you're wanted in the office."

The foreman's orders drew stares and fearful looks from the other miners. The long trip to the surface could only mean one thing. You were about to lose your job. Luke considered everything that occurred since the first day of his arrival. Nothing happened that would trigger his termination. He made it a point to talk very little, less management discover that the "tall kid" was well-read and a potential threat to their authority.

The older woman that worked in the owner's office was kind and always smiling. And while no women were allowed in the mines, it was considered bad luck, the men spoke well of her. They described the lady as someone who genuinely cared for the men.

"Mr. Hobbs. Your mother called. You must go home immediately. Your father has been hospitalized. He is seriously ill."

Luke, unsure if he had enough money to get off the island, reached into his pockets, a panicked look on his face.

"I've taken the liberty of arranging for your first week's pay," said the woman, handing Luke a small envelope.

The trip back to Saint John's took too long. Luke recalled the last time he saw his father. Once again, the old man refused to speak to his son. The boy cleaned himself off as much as he could and headed straight to General Hospital. His mother greeted him in the hallway.

"Oh Luke. I'm so glad you're here."

"What's wrong with him?"

"The doctor says it was a heart attack. I found him unconscious in the parlor. He has yet to open his eyes."

"May I see him?"

"Yes, of course. I will wait here."

When Luke walked into the hospital room he encountered a nurse.

"You must be his son."

"Yes, ma'am."

"He's resting comfortably. The doctor administered morphine for the pain.

"Will he regain consciousness anytime soon?"

A blank stare covered the woman's face.

"I'm sorry, Mr. Hobbs. Your father may *never* regain consciousness."

Luke stood by the bed staring at the man who considered him a coward. He could feel the anger rising deep in his chest and a pink flush creeping over his face. Luke wanted to do something. Say something. But it was too late. The old man would die without so much as a goodbye. His father would go to the grave neither forgetting nor forgiving the boy's "cowardice" on board the *Newfoundland*.

A sudden smile crossed Luke's face. It occurred to him that his father, an extremely stubborn man, bequeathed a portion of that hardheaded attitude to his only son. Luke could also be pigheaded and often displayed a single-minded determination to do things his way or not at all. Ironically, it was that character flaw that kept Luke alive. Most of the crewmembers, unwilling or unable to challenge the authority of their supervisor, succumbed as a result. Not Luke.

The steady noise of his father's labored breathing came to a sudden end. The eerie silence was deafening. He reached for his father's hand. Nothing. The old man exhaled, a sound of air mixing with liquid, in his lungs. The death rattle brought Luke's mother to her husband's bedside.

"Is he . . . ?"

"He's gone, Mother. He's gone."

She bowed her head, made the sign of the cross, and wept silently.

Luke, dry-eyed and showing no signs of emotion, turned to the door.

"I'll be outside, Mother."

Mrs. Newcastle returned to the library, just days after her first encounter with Elizabeth.

"I am afraid my newest student is my student no longer. Are you still interested in midwifery?"

Elizabeth gushed her response.

"Oh, Mrs. Newcastle. You have made my dream come true!"

"I must warn you, young lady, midwifery can sometimes be a nightmare."

"I will do my very best. I promise."

After agreeing to her first week's schedule, Elizabeth splurged and rushed to her father's office on a trolley car.

"Is he with someone?" she asked the receptionist.

"No. But he does have an appointment in about 10 minutes."

Elizabeth waltzed into her father's office with a flourish.

"Father, I have some great news."

"Elizabeth, I have a very important meeting in just a few minutes. Please be quick."

Elizabeth's enthusiasm could not be dampened by her father's lack of interest. She explained the details of her good news. Clarence, his fingers tapping an impatient drum beat on the desk, grimaced.

"Will you be paid for your apprenticeship with Mrs. Newcastle?" he asked.

Elizabeth's smile, disappeared.

"No Father, not until Mrs. Newcastle formally appoints me as her assistant. She estimates my training will require at least three months."

Clarence sat pokerfaced. Elizabeth, frustrated with the man's intransigence, turned to the door.

"I would like your blessing, Father. But at my age, it is no longer required."

Clarence jumped to his feet.

"Elizabeth, I am not worried about money. I just . . ."

A receptionist knocked and entered.

"Mr. Parsons, your next appointment has arrived."

"Oh, please show Mr. Windsor in. I would like him to meet my daughter."

Elizabeth jerked to attention. Reginald Windsor strode into the office. The color drained from Elizabeth's face.

"Mr. Parsons, thank you for taking the time to see me. I am most . . ."

Reginald Windsor's voice weakened into a murmur and then ceased. Elizabeth spoke softly.

"Father, I do apologize for barging in. I will leave you now."

Clarence Parsons held up a hand.

"Nonsense. I want you to meet one of Saint John's most successful businessmen. Mr. Reginald Windsor, please say hello to my daughter, Elizabeth Parsons."

The senior Windsor stepped forward and bowed. He showed no signs of their previous meeting. Neither did Elizabeth.

"It is a pleasure, Miss Parsons."

"Pleased to meet you, Mr. Windsor."

She clutched at her wrap and nodded clumsily.

"Please excuse me, gentlemen. I must go now."

Mrs. Hobbs and her son scheduled a viewing for friends and neighbors on Saturday, several days after Mr. Hobbs' death.

Luke gave notice to Bell Island Mines that he hoped to return on Tuesday of the following week. His father's funeral would take place on Monday. Luke stood close to his mother during most of the proceedings. Under the circumstances, she seemed to be holding up just fine. While still in the receiving line, Mrs. Hobbs turned to Luke.

"I want you to meet Mrs. Newcastle. She is a midwife and assisted me when you were just a toddler," she said.

Luke and the midwife exchanged pleasantries.

"Your mother tells me you are now employed at Bell Island Mines."

"That is correct. I've only been employed at the mines for two weeks. I hope to return after the funeral."

"I know women whose husbands work at the mines. They work long hours and are away for weeks at a time. The mothers and the children see very little of their fathers. It is most unfortunate."

"Yes, Mrs. Newcastle. We work six days a week, live on the island, and get to come home one weekend per month."

"Oh my. That is a difficult work schedule, indeed."

"I am very fortunate, in that sense. I have my mother to worry about, of course, but she is a strong woman. After that, there is Jewel, my horse. I do miss my regular visits to the library, however. But I can manage."

"Yes, I recall your parents telling me that you grew up with your nose in a book."

Luke and the women laughed.

"It was nice to meet you, Mrs. Newcastle."

"And you too, Luke. Incidentally, I should warn you. There will be a new face at the library when you return."

"How do you mean?"

"Well, Miss Parsons has agreed to leave Bishop's and begin training with me as a midwife."

"Elizabeth Parsons?"

"Yes. I just assumed you knew her. Tuesday is her last day."

Luke hesitated for a moment but recovered quickly, with a half-truth.

"Yes. Of course. I remember her quite well."

"You have grown into a handsome and intelligent young man, Mr. Hobbs. My condolences on the loss of your father. Please take good care of your mother. She is a very fine lady."

"Thank you, Mrs. Newcastle."

Luke and his mother, exhausted at the end of the day, shared a pot of tea when the viewing came to an end.

Luke announced plans for the day of the funeral.

"When services have ended, Mother, I should like to go to Bishop's. I've not been to the library in weeks. Will you need me for any reason?"

"Not at all, son. Go and spend the day if you wish. The rest and relaxation will be good for you."

"Thank you, Mother."

Luke spied Elizabeth well before the girl noticed his presence.

She appeared to be reading yesterday's issue of the Evening Telegram.

"I just assumed you would be brushing up on your Shakespeare," he said."

Elizabeth blinked repeatedly but focused on the newspaper. She took great care to fold the paper on the established creases. A nervous smile crossed her face when she looked up.

"Mr. Hobbs. Are you in search of a good book or a sincere apology?"

"Good books are hard to fine. Sincere apologies are extremely rare."

"You are most fortunate indeed, Mr. Hobbs. I am in possession of both. Will you accept them in the spirit with which they are offered?"

"And what spirit is that?"

"Humility."

Luke flashed a triumphant smile.

"Apology accepted."

"Are you not curious about the book I would choose for you?"

"Oh. Yes, of course. Tell me, please."

"*Pride and Prejudice,* by Jane Austen."

Luke threw his head back and laughed. Elizabeth grinned from ear to ear.

"A marvelous choice, Miss Parsons. If I remember correctly, the name of the protagonist is Elizabeth and she makes a number of hasty judgments."

"Yes, she does. And *this* Elizabeth hopes to avoid similar mistakes in the future."

"I hope our paths cross again, Miss Parsons."

"As do I."

Luke worked 30 consecutive days at the Bell Island Mines.

Although the operation closed on Sundays, management needed someone for a bit of grunt work in the railyard. Luke volunteered. His work mates ate, drank, and slept on their day off. Luke needed the money. His late father did not earn a pension despite 40 years in the deep forests of Newfoundland. His mother, except for taking in some occasional mending, made no money at all. Luke continued to be the family's only source of income. Now, his burdens included unpaid funeral expenses, no one to accomplish simple chores around the house, plus the labor and expense of a horse.

On Sunday, his elusive day of rest, Luke rose at first light. The sound of men snoring, the pangs of an empty stomach, and a head filled with confusing and troubling thoughts, prevented a restful sleep.

"Hobbs."

The voice in the door belonged to the foreman.

"Forgot to give this to you."

Luke reached for the envelope.

"Thank you," said Luke, examining the envelope as he walked in the cool morning air.

The perfect penmanship suggested a feminine hand. The short missive, came from Elizabeth Parsons. She had invited Luke and Mrs. Hobbs to Sunday dinner. The note referenced 'this very difficult time' and expressed their sympathies on the occasion of Mr. Hobbs' passing. Luke recalled the exchange of pleasantries with Elizabeth at the library. Although excited about the prospect of some time with the woman, he also experienced a twinge of guilt.

The 'difficult time' which prompted the dinner invitation did not apply to Luke Hobbs. He did not mourn his father. Indeed, he rarely thought about the man. In the wake of his anger and frustration there came an emptiness. Luke, unable to rectify the broken bond between father and son, allowed his relationship with the man to die with the man. Luke would accept the invitation from Elizabeth Parsons.

Happily so and guilt-free.

Elizabeth's dinner with Luke, his mother, and her father, would occur in three days.

Her daily errands, home visits, long days, and hours of studying, gave the girl very little time to plan, much less enjoy, the prospect of Sunday dinner. In fact, she remained at a loss as to what she would prepare. She lay in bed waiting for sleep to come, jealous that Alice the cat slept soundly. Elizabeth also wondered about Luke's reaction when he received the invitation. She knew only that Luke accepted.

Elizabeth's thoughts raced from Mrs. Newcastle's no-nonsense training methods, to the preparations for Sunday dinner, and then to her mysterious dinner guest. Luke's menial job piqued her curiosity. It also triggered a red flag. *How could a man of such intelligence be employed as a simple laborer?* Elizabeth knew from her father that good-paying jobs were difficult to find in St. John's. But surely there must be a job somewhere that required a young man of Luke's intellectual ability. She wondered if Luke's lack of a university degree hampered his progress. She also considered the possibility that the man's strong personality, not unlike her own, could be a problem for many employers. Their conversation at dinner would prove very interesting, she concluded.

"Boiled dinner!"

Her voice, late at night and in the total darkness of her tiny bedroom, startled the girl. The cat too. Alice, now awake, appeared angry. Elizabeth's sudden idea for Sunday dinner would be easy to prepare and most likely be enjoyed by all. Salt beef, boiled with potatoes, carrots, cabbage, turnips, and perhaps some greens, would satiate anyone's appetite. And the leftovers would delight her father. The girl stared at her journal but did not reach for it. Perhaps tomorrow night. As her eyelids grew heavy, Elizabeth imagined Luke complimenting her cooking.

In her dreams, he spoke in Shakespearean sonnets.

Billy Windsor, delivering a series of approved permits to his father, found the executive's outer office void of secretarial help.

He discovered his father perched behind the oversized desk and alone.

"Father, may I leave this here?"

"Of course, Billy."

Billy placed the documents on a nearby worktable and paused. He held a newspaper in his hand.

"Have you seen this?"

He placed a folded newspaper on the desk and pointed to a small headline.

"Archduke Assassinated"

Windsor scanned the article but made no serious attempt to read it. He glared at Billy.

"Are you trying to give me a headache, Billy? You know if I read too much, I get a headache."

Billy looked penitent for having forgotten about his father's reading disorder. He immediately summarized the article as best he could.

"Why are you telling me this, Billy? Why should I care?"

Billy explained that a good portion of Western Europe had become a tinderbox of political tension. The possibility of war, at first between a handful of smaller nations, could easily spread among the major powers including England, Germany, Prussia, France, and Russia.

"If the fighting is in Europe, why should I care?"

Billy continued.

"Even a small war could collapse the exchange rates. The overseas market for fish, steel, lumber, and everything else would be impacted."

"It seems to me there's nothing we can do about it."

"Frankly, Father, war is usually good for business. But only for those businesses which have lots of cash on hand and can move quickly to take advantage of market disruptions."

"What in blazes are you talking about Billy?"

"We should tie up as much lumber as we can and use as little money as possible to do it. Lock it in now, before things get crazy," said Billy.

"What do you have in mind?"

"I am working on a full set of recommendations. I should have it done within a week or two."

"That's nice, Billy. Keep me informed. Oh, and I need some more cigars and whiskey."

Elizabeth paid little attention to the minister's sermon at Sunday services.

Her preparations for that afternoon's dinner took priority. Her father could not walk fast enough during their journey home. The girl needed to set the dining room table, put a bowl of raised bread dough into tins for cooking, and assemble a thin gravy from the cooking broth. She expected her guests at one in the afternoon and would serve dinner at two. Clarence Parsons noticed his daughter's anxiety.

"If Sunday dinner sends you into a tizzy, what will happen when you are required to assist a mother in childbirth?"

A knock on the door forced Elizabeth into the kitchen.

"The door, Father. Please get the door."

"Good afternoon, Mr. Parsons," said Mrs. Hobbs.

She introduced her son and both were seated in the parlor. After expressing his condolences and inquiring of Mrs. Hobbs' health, Clarence Parsons turned to Luke.

"Elizabeth tells me that you are employed at Bell Island Mines."

"Yes, sir. And it has been a genuine challenge."

"I am concerned that the events in Europe will seriously affect our tiny island," said Clarence.

"Mr. Parsons, I share your concern. So many of my friends and acquaintances are blissfully—"

"Father, are you boring our guests with political talk?"

Elizabeth waltzed into the parlor, smoothing her hair and checking her dress for unwanted evidence of chores in the kitchen. Luke jumped to his feet. Elizabeth went first to Mrs. Hobbs.

"I am so sorry about your husband."

"Thank you, Elizabeth. You, like so many others, have been especially kind and generous in our time of need."

Elizabeth turned to Luke. He wet his dry lips, cleared his throat, and stepped forward.

"Miss Parsons. My days at the mine were more bearable knowing that I would see you once again."

Clarence arched his eyebrows.

"Have the two of you met before? Elizabeth, have you been keeping secrets from me?"

Elizabeth smiled through a blush of hot pink. Luke, a twinkle in his eye, came to the girl's rescue.

"Mr. Parsons, your daughter and I ran into each other, quite by accident. Wouldn't you say, Miss Parsons?"

Elizabeth smiled gratefully.

"Yes, Mr. Hobbs. I can recall our first meeting with clarity. And Father, you will be pleased to know that Mr. Hobbs and I share an interest in Shakespeare."

Clarence did a poor job of hiding his lack of interest in the classics.

"Shall we proceed to the dining room?"

"Yes, of course," she replied.

Luke bowed slightly and waved his arm, allowing his mother and Clarence to go first. He and Elizabeth walked side-by-side. She caught his gaze.

"You must remind me to formally thank Jewel for her, shall we say, intervention."

"I have already thanked her. But I refuse to share my boiled dinner with a horse."

"I am flattered by your sentiments, Mr. Hobbs. Let us hope that you do not change your mind after we have eaten."

Both men reached for the ladies' chairs. When all were seated, Mr. Parsons bowed his head. A loud knock on the door interrupted his intended invocation.

"Excuse me, please," he said, as the visitor banged on the door, yet again. The threesome could hear voices, but not the conversation.

Mr. Parsons returned momentarily.

"Elizabeth. It's Mrs. Newcastle. She says it is rather urgent."

Elizabeth excused herself. The voices in the foyer took on a sense of urgency. Elizabeth appeared at the parlor's entryway, her eyes glassy and her face contorted as if trying not to cry.

"Mrs. Newcastle and I apologize for the interruption. There is an emergency delivery. She requires my assistance. I must leave. Please forgive me."

The men rose to their feet. Mrs. Hobbs tried to reassure the girl.

"We understand, Elizabeth. Please do as you must."

Elizabeth gathered her things and rushed out the door.

Mrs. Newcastle cracked her long whip over the horse's head. The animal responded immediately. The midwife and her young assistant flew down the street at a pace just short of a gallop. The older lady briefed her student *en route*.

"Gertrude Hynes is a first-time mother, age 19. She claims she fell down the stairs in her home. And now she is bleeding. Could be a miscarriage," said Mrs. Newcastle.

Elizabeth thought it odd that Mrs. Newcastle described the woman's accident as a claim. The young girl wanted to know more. Asking an impertinent question often got her into trouble. She hesitated. In the end, having abandoned a perfectly prepared boiled dinner, Elizabeth thought it only fair to abandon her reservations. She wanted an honest response.

"You don't believe her, do you, Mrs. Newcastle?"

The older woman scowled. She focused on the horse and cracked the rawhide once again. Elizabeth pressed the matter.

"I may be inexperienced, Mrs. Newcastle, but I am not ignorant. Why did you say that Mrs. Hynes *claimed* to have fallen down the stairs?"

The midwife chewed on the inside of her cheek and then shrugged her shoulders.

"Well, I suppose there are no secrets in this business. Truthfully, I suspect the woman's husband is beating her."

"Why is that?"

"A 'skeet,' if you ask me."

Elizabeth knew what the word meant. Skeets are aggressive, uneducated, unruly people, usually associated with petty crimes. Teacher and student rode in silence for the balance of their trip.

"Here we are," said Mrs. Newcastle, pulling hard on the reins.

The tiny ramshackle home, most of its white paint weathered away, stood on a small lot. Grass, more than a foot high, covered the front yard and made the gravel walkway nearly invisible.

An unshaven man, reeking of alcohol, answered the midwife's knock. He wore a stained pair of long underwear, no shirt, and a full head of dirty, unkempt hair. A cigarette dangled from his mouth. After inspecting Elizabeth from head to toe, an obvious leer appeared in his bloodshot eyes.

"Well, a very good evening to you, Madam midwife."

Mrs. Newcastle interrupted the man's fantasies.

"We are here to see Mrs. Hynes."

The husband jerked his head toward the flight of stairs, behind him.

"She's upstairs."

Elizabeth peered into the man's face.

"Your wife climbed the stairs after she fell *down* the stairs?"

The husband shrugged.

"Hey, I was asleep on the couch. Didn't see a thing."

Mrs. Newcastle pushed her way past the man.

"Elizabeth, please follow me."

The scene in the upstairs bedroom stopped Elizabeth at the door. The expectant mother, her baby bump obvious, lay in bed. Her face, hair, and nightgown appeared soaked in sweat.

She sat in a large patch of dark red blood. Bruises could be seen on her face, both arms, and shoulders.

"Elizabeth, my bag. What is your name, honey?"

The mother spoke in a weak whisper.

"Sarah Hynes."

"Is my baby all right?" the woman whimpered.

"We will do everything we can, Sarah. Now please lie still and let me do my work. Mrs. Newcastle listened to the woman's stomach. With a pair of scissors, she cut and then ripped a clean portion of the sheet.

"We will use this for the bleeding."

The woman groaned when Mrs. Hynes gently pushed the makeshift bandage between the patient's legs.

"Help me get her out of bed, Elizabeth. We're going to hospital."

Elizabeth took one side, Mrs. Newcastle, the other.

"Grab my bag, Elizabeth. Sarah, what is your husband's name?"

"Doyle."

Elizabeth yelled.

"Doyle, we need your help."

The man yelled from the bottom of the stairs.

"The sight of blood makes me wanna puke. Sorry, ladies. You're on your own."

The two women struggled down the stairs with their patient. The husband watched from the porch as they passed. He took a long drag on the cigarette.

"She gonna make it?" he asked.

Mrs. Newcastle ignored him and announced her plans to Elizabeth.

"The hospital is close by. We will take her in the carriage."

The husband barked his objection.

"I ain't paying for no hospital."

Elizabeth thought about hitting the man with Mrs. Newcastle's medical bag. She decided against it. She and Mrs. Newcastle squeezed the woman in between the two of them. The pregnant lady, still hemorrhaging, passed out. Mrs. Newcastle snapped her whip and glanced at Elizabeth.

"I was hoping you'd hit the bastard with my medical bag."

With no choice but to eat the meal, sans their hostess, Luke, Mrs. Hobbs, and Clarence Parsons enjoyed their dinner.

Mrs. Hobbs allowed and encouraged the men to dominate the conversation. After discussions on government, the economy, politics, religion, and science, an obviously impressed Mr. Parsons queried his young guest.

"Luke, I'm sorry, may I call you Luke?"

"Yes, of course."

"Luke, you are obviously a university graduate. Where did you take your degree?

Luke focused on the empty plate in front of him, toying with his fork. He spoke in a murmur.

"I've not been to university, Mr. Parsons."

"You may address me as Clarence. Please."

Luke looked relieved.

"Clarence it is."

"I cannot believe that a graduate of our local school could be so learned in the arts and sciences."

Mrs. Hobbs motioned with a hand.

"If I may."

She hesitated, glancing at her son, in search of his approval. Luke slowly blinked and nodded.

"Clarence. You should know that Luke's father was decidedly against higher education for our son. I disagreed but did not prevail."

Luke explained.

"Mother encouraged daily visits to the library. Much of what I learned can be credited to her and a decades-long love affair with a series of very kind librarians. Platonic of course, but life-changing."

Clarence, deep in thought, interrupted his guest.

"Luke. Are you familiar with the Windsor Land and Lumber Company?"

"Of course. They also own a rail line."

"The owner is Reginald Windsor. I work closely with him and his son, Billy, as part of my job with the Crown. They could use a smart man like you. I should like to put in a good word on your behalf. I require your permission, of course."

Mrs. Hobbs squeezed her son's arm.

"Luke, you could be rid of that awful place. Please say yes."

Luke sprang to his feet and reached for Parsons' hand.

"Yes, Mr. Parsons. I mean Clarence. My answer is an unequivocal yes."

Mr. Parsons refused an offer from the Hobbs to assist with the after-dinner clean up.

Luke and his mother enjoyed their leisurely stroll and were home before dark. Elizabeth did not return home until well after dark.

"Oh, Father, I left you in such a mess, and in more ways than one."

"Not to worry, Elizabeth. I enjoyed my visit with Mrs. Hobbs. Luke, especially. In truth, the entire affair was a pleasant distraction. And cleaning dishes is preferable to reading reports on the lumber industry."

"Thank you, Father. At least *your* day went well."

"I was about to make myself a cup of tea. Why don't you join me in the parlor?" he asked. Elizabeth slipped into a robe, shocked that her appetite for a plate of leftover boiled dinner no longer existed. She drank her tea and recounted the torturous hours spent with her first expectant mother.

"It would appear that your first encounter with midwifery did not go as planned."

"No, Father. We lost the baby and the mother remains seriously ill."

"May God have mercy on them both."

"And may He strike her husband dead, where he stands."

Clarence splashed hot tea onto his lap.

"Elizabeth Parsons. You cannot say such things."

"I can and I did, Father. I think this man beat his wife. I am convinced of it. He is an animal and deserves to die."

"Judge not lest ye be judged."

"I apologize, Father. I am feeling less than Christian this evening."

"Your job is to bring life into this world, Elizabeth. You must focus on that and that alone."

"I will try, Father. I will try."

Elizabeth padded to the kitchen and refilled her cup. When she returned, she took a deep breath.

"Now, you must tell me what you think of my friend, Luke."

"I am most impressed with the young man. But first you must tell me how it is that you know each other and for how long you have known him?"

Elizabeth explained the humorous and not so humorous details of their initial and subsequent meetings.

"Father, he is the most intelligent man I have ever met."

Elizabeth noticed her father's questioning look.

"Except for you, of course."

Clarence flashed an appreciative smile.

"He is quite knowledgeable in several areas. In fact, I have Luke's blessing to speak with Mr. Windsor about the possibility of employment at the Windsor Land and Lumber Company."

Elizabeth choked on a mouthful of tea. The liquid flew onto her robe, the overstuffed chair, and the hardwood floor.

"Elizabeth. What's wrong?"

The girl could not catch her breath. She rose to her feet, gasped for air, and coughed some more.

"Water. I will get you a glass of water," her father announced.

Mr. Parsons rushed from the room and returned. Elizabeth, looking pale and sickly, swallowed a mouthful of the cold liquid.

"Better?"

"Yes, Father. Thank you."

"Perhaps you should get some rest now. We can finish this conversation in the morning."

Elizabeth nodded, her eyes glassy and a fearful look on her face.

"Good night, Father."

Elizabeth wrote in her journal for more than an hour. She assumed that no one, including her father, would ever see the venomous prose.

Billy hopped off the trolley car; the stop was just two blocks from Bishop's library.

He took a deep breath hoping to calm his nerves. It didn't work. An unannounced visit with Elizabeth Parsons could easily backfire. He genuinely wanted to know how she was faring in the wake of Reggie's vicious attack. He also wanted to take some credit for the severe punishment visited on his older brother by the elder Reginald. Elizabeth did not have to worry about the monster, anymore. Billy wanted her to know. If a relationship developed as a result of their encounter, all the better.

"Yes, may I help you?"

The girl at the desk was not Elizabeth Parsons.

"No, thank you . . . well . . . I was looking for . . ."

His voice vanished in the library's thick blanket of silence. Billy's face blushed pink and beads of sweat formed on his forehead. He lied to the librarian.

"I was here several weeks ago. Miss Parsons and I were searching for a particular book on forestry."

The receptionist searched the shelves behind her and checked several of the desk drawers.

"I am very sorry, sir. I see nothing on forestry. Perhaps I can help you. Do you recall the title or the author of the book?"

"No, ma'am. I do not. I will come back tomorrow. Will Miss Parsons be available?"

"I'm afraid not. Miss Parsons is no longer employed by Bishop's Library."

Billy stood motionless.

"I'm very sorry to hear that."

"You were a friend of hers?"

One lie begets many more, Billy recalled.

"Yes, ma'am, we were good friends."

"Perhaps you can reach Elizabeth at her residence."

Billy's mind raced. He did not know the woman's home address. Asking the librarian would expose his lie.

"Yes, of course. Thank you. Thank you very much."

He trudged back to the office, a stiff breeze blowing in his face.

He told himself that the cold wind made his eyes water.

Sunday dinner at the Parsons' place destroyed Luke's usual clarity of thought and methodical approach to life in general.

The prospect of a job which made use of his intellectual gifts triggered a fit of ecstasy previously unknown to the boy. Simultaneously, he regretted the missed opportunity to spend an afternoon with Elizabeth. He continued to harbor some skepticism about her plans for a career in midwifery. He also thought it somewhat rude, that she would abandon her guests in such an abrupt manner. He remained curious about the woman—very curious.

His first instinct, to return to the mines without speaking to Elizabeth, fell victim to his curiosity. Instead, he sent word that he was ill. Luke wanted to learn more about the young woman, whose beauty distracted from her strong will, rapier wit, and well-developed intellect. His first impressions could be inaccurate of course. But he had to know for certain. As he and Jewel traveled the streets between his residence and hers, he justified the excursion because Jewel needed exercise. He prayed that the young woman would be home and grinned when Elizabeth responded to his knock on the door.

"Mr. Hobbs, I was not expecting you. It is, nevertheless, a pleasant surprise."

Elizabeth used both hands to fix her hair and smooth her dress.

"May I come in?" he asked.

"Well, I am alone in the house and it strikes me as inappropriate to be entertaining a gentleman, without a chaperone."

Luke noticed the hot pink flush that slowly covered the woman's face. He understood her reticence and remained on the porch. He pointed to Jewel.

"Perhaps my trusty steed would agree to be our chaperone if you would agree to walk with me. We would be in full view of the traveling public and your personal safety, assured.

Elizabeth thought for a moment. But not for long.

"Yes. That would be acceptable, Mr. Hobbs. I should like to retrieve my sun bonnet."

They walked in silence for a while. Luke thought it best to hide his disappointment with the events of Sunday afternoon.

"We missed you at dinner on Sunday but the meal was excellent."

"I am glad you enjoyed the boiled dinner. Father enjoyed the leftovers even more."

"Your father and I enjoyed our time together. In fact, he seems to think I could find employment at the Windsor Land and Lumber Company."

Elizabeth turned away in silence Luke interpreted her gesture as disapproval.

"You are opposed to the idea?"

"My father has worked with the Windsors for most of his 12 years at the Crown. Mr. Windsor, and especially his son, Reggie, can be very difficult at times."

"A position with the Windsors would be more suitable to my skills. Would you have me remain at the Bell Island Mines?"

"From the frying pan into the fire, as the saying goes."

Luke, irked by her harsh comment, decided to retaliate.

"And your own decision to become a midwife. Is this the most suitable occupation for your skills?" he asked.

"The medical field is a calling which I have secretly nurtured since childhood. Helping people who cannot help themselves, healing the sick, and comforting the dying is, in my opinion, a noble profession."

"Noble, perhaps, but hardly practical."

Elizabeth spun in the boy's direction.

"Explain yourself, Mr. Hobbs."

The exasperated young man blew a lock of hair from his brow.

"Miss Parsons, I do not wish to be argumentative. But surely, you are aware that, in Newfoundland anyway, most women work with their hands, primarily in the home and occasionally in the fields or on the docks. I am simply saying that you are unlikely to assume a position of significance in the medical field, anywhere on this island."

Elizabeth set her jaw and spoke in a whisper.

"You surprise me, Mr. Hobbs."

"How so?"

Elizabeth raised her voice.

"That a man of your intelligence would condescend to be seen in public with a woman of, shall we say, limited intellectual capacity."

"You are twisting my meaning. I am simply making an observation about the profession you are contemplating."

Elizabeth did not back down.

"And you have concluded that doctors of medicine are members of an impractical profession?"

"I have yet to meet a female doctor, Miss Parsons."

Elizabeth flashed a fake smile. Her voice dripped with sarcasm.

"Jewel is so very fortunate to have you as her owner, Mr. Hobbs."

"And why is that?"

"Because horses rarely feel threatened by a jackass."

Luke's shocked eyes grew wide with disbelief. Elizabeth stormed off in the opposite direction.

"I didn't expect you to be home for dinner."

Luke avoided eye contact with his mother.

"I'm not hungry, Mother."

"Did you enjoy your visit with Elizabeth?"

Luke pretended not to hear, bounded up the stairs instead, intent on packing for his trip to Bell Island mines. Mrs. Hobbs stood at the bottom of the stairs.

"It is unlikely that a man of your age would experience a hearing loss."

Luke jammed a few personal items into a rucksack and patiently waited for the sound of his mother's retreating footsteps. A loud creak suggested that she started up the stairs. He walked to the top of the staircase. The old woman stood on the bottom step, a firm grasp on the railing. He said nothing, biting his lip instead.

"I am unable to stand here for very long, son."

Luke blurted his frustration.

"Mother. The woman is impossible."

Mrs. Hobbs retreated one step.

"She's probably thinking the very same thing about you."

"Elizabeth cautioned me against working for the Windsors and yet, she has this silly idea of becoming a doctor. A woman, contemplating a career in medicine. A ridiculous notion, if you ask me."

Mrs. Hobbs picked a few loose threads from her apron and surveyed the checkered pattern of red and white squares. After several moments of silence, she looked up.

"You are your father's son, I am afraid. I love you dearly, Luke, but you are your father's son."

"What does that mean?"

"It means that your respect for women is lacking."

Luke shot his mother a dirty look, turned, and yelled over his shoulder.

"I'm late for the ferry to Bell Island."

Clarence waited for the meeting to end.

Reginald Windsor, accompanied by his sons and several lumber company executives, began to exit the room.

"Mr. Windsor, could I trouble you to remain behind for just a moment or two?"

"Certainly, Clarence."

Billy stayed close to the old man. Reggie remained seated and reached for a cigar.

"I met an extraordinary young man while at dinner this past Sunday. If you require additional help in the office, I would urge you to meet with him."

Mr. Windsor turned to Billy.

"Billy, that's your department."

"What is his name, Mr. Parsons?" Billy asked.

"Hobbs. Luke Hobbs. My daughter, Elizabeth, thought to invite Luke and his mother to Sunday dinner. Mrs. Hobbs lost her husband just a few weeks ago. Her son is their only provider. He is currently employed at Bell Island Mines"

"You want me to hire a miner to cut wood?" asked Reginald.

"No, sir. He's much more than that. Very intelligent. One of the smartest young minds I have ever met."

"I can arrange for an interview, Father," said Billy.

Clarence raised a finger.

"I must tell you. My daughter seems rather taken with the young man."

Billy bit his lip and studied his note book.

"Is she still working at the library?"

"No, she is not. She is now in training with Mrs. Newcastle for a career in midwifery."

The old man glanced at young Reggie. The older son puffed furiously on his cigar and squirmed in his chair. Billy smiled and winked at his older brother.

"Isn't that impressive, Father?" Reginald glared at Billy and turned to Clarence.

"Is there anything else, Mr. Parsons?"

"No, Mr. Windsor. And thank you for your time."

After dropping his father and Billy at the office, Reggie announced that he had errands to run.

He drove his father's gas-powered vehicle to the hospital. Reggie lingered in the entranceway, confirming that he neither knew nor had seen the hospital receptionist, in the past.

"Excuse me, ma'am."

"Yes, sir. How may I help you?"

"My sister-in-law is in a motherly way and in search of a good midwife. Are you able to recommend anyone?"

"Yes, of course. There are three in the St. John's area that we know of."

"Are you able to give me their names and addresses?"

"Certainly. Just give me a moment."

As Reggie walked to the vehicle, he scanned the list. The first name, he did not recognize. The second name, triggered a big grin. *Margaret Newcastle, midwife.* The street address, several blocks from the government buildings, would be easy to find. And if he remembered correctly, it was a street lined with trees.

Plenty of places to hide.

Elizabeth, alone at home, seethed with anger.

She sat at the vanity in her room, brushing her long locks of hair at a furious pace. When finished, she jumped to her feet and flung the brush across the room. She retrieved the brush and paced the room, brushing her hair, again. Finally, she sat on the edge of the bed, used both hands to cover her face, and cried.

She did not understand why she cried. Perhaps it was the rocky start to her new career as a midwife. The reality of midwifery clashed sharply with the dream. Perhaps the vanishing hope of a relationship with Luke made her cry. He impressed her as a strong, intelligent, independent, and honest man. When they were together, though, she saw another side. She saw arrogance, an unspoken disdain for women, and a simmering, deep-seated anger. Anger for what, she did not know. But Luke rarely exhibited true joy or happiness.

In truth, Elizabeth nursed a simmering anger of her own. The memories of Reggie's violent attack would not go away. The knowledge that she might easily have been raped by that animal festered like an unhealed wound. In her mind, the assault screamed for revenge and required a closure that only punishment and justice could deliver.

Her white-hot anger with Reggie, her first days on the job with Mrs. Newcastle, and her frustrations with Luke, combined into a Gordian knot of tangled emotions. She made a promise to herself. She would somehow slice through the knotted mess and discover true happiness.

With or without Luke.

Luke tugged on the stiff, white collar which chafed at his neck.

Getting dressed for his interview with Mr. Windsor and his sons triggered more anxiety than the interview itself. His only suit, worn two maybe three times, looked new. On the other hand, Luke felt confident that his knowledge of business, government, science, and things political, would hold him in good stead. The stakes were high.

Management at Bell Island Mines complained about his absences. First for his father's untimely death, then for his "sick day," and now for this "family emergency." Luke did not want to disclose the real reason for his absence. When the foreman threatened Luke with termination for excessive absenteeism, he questioned the foreman's wisdom. In Luke's opinion, the foreman's apparent willingness to lose a productive employee, at a time when good workers for backbreaking labor could not be found, seemed both foolhardy and shortsighted. And Luke told him so.

Luke was fired on the spot.

"Mr. Parsons has given you the highest recommendation," said Mr. Windsor.

Luke smiled.

"Clarence is a very kind and generous man."

Reggie looked bored and fiddled with a cigar. Billy, a serious look on his face, leaned forward in his chair.

"Why should we hire you, Mr. Parsons?"

Luke did not hesitate.

"I have an excellent memory. If I see or read something, I tend to remember it, in detail. As a result, I am a fast learner. I am also a fast reader and my writing skills are excellent. I have an extraordinary attention to detail and pride myself on the ability to anticipate the needs of those around me. I am equally comfortable with men of letters as I am with men who spend their days engaged in backbreaking labor. I, too, have worked hard for a living. I have worked in the forest, in the mines, and on a steamship, hunting for seals. Luke paused, pursing his lips and looking away. He looked almost penitent.

"I have not been to university, however. I am self-taught."

Billy looked at his father and then turned to Luke.

"My father and I were discussing the current situation in Europe. What are your thoughts in this regard?"

"I assume that you are not interested in my political views. I will limit my remarks to matters which could directly affect your company. The likelihood of war in Europe is high. Contagion, that is the spread of war amongst the larger nations, is also a distinct possibility. A great war would be good for the lumber business. But you must be prepared. Protect your cash, because exchange rates will fluctuate wildly. At the same time, you should leverage, with options I suspect, large tracts of standing lumber. If demand rises, you will be rewarded. If demand collapses, you will have lost very little."

The old man grinned.

"That sounds familiar, Billy."

Billy sat back in his chair.

"Impressive."

Reggie Junior sneered.

"I think he's smarter than you are, Billy."

Billy shot his brother a dirty look and then flashed an evil smile.

"Luke, your father says that you and Elizabeth Parsons are good friends."

Reggie bolted upright in the chair, angrily jamming his unlit cigar into the ashtray. Mr. Windsor, eyes darting in every direction, cleared his throat.

"I've heard enough. Welcome aboard, Mr. Hobbs. Billy will be your immediate supervisor. Billy, I would like him to learn our overseas pricing schedule as soon as possible. I would also like a detailed report from you, Mr. Hobbs, which describes precisely how, when, why, and where, we can expect the demand for lumber in North America and Europe to increase. And I want that as soon as possible."

Billy and Luke responded in unison.

"Yes, sir."

Chapter Four

ON THE JOB

After an uneventful meal, Reggie excused himself.

His father and Billy were in the throes of a mind-numbing conversation on lumber prices and the potential effects of war in Europe. In minutes, Reggie was cruising the government building section of St. John's. When he reached the street where Mrs. Newcastle lived, he drove past the residence, did a U-turn, parked several homes away, and lay in wait.

His plan triggered a sly smile. Mrs. Newcastle and her young assistant would soon suffer an accident. Reggie did not know or care about the older woman but he was obsessed and angry with Elizabeth. She embarrassed him. She spurned him. And now, she would pay the price.

As dusk approached, Reggie heard an on-coming horse and buggy. He could see Mrs. Newcastle guide the animal into the drive and disappear behind the residence. Reggie allowed her the time required to unhitch the animal, feed him, and then retire for the evening. He waited until just after dark, to find his way to the shed. He spoke in comforting tones to the horse, as he searched for the mare's bit, bridle, and attached reins. With a quick slice of his pocket knife, he cut the leather strap. But only partially. Several tugs on the bit would completely sever the reins.

Reggie, pleased with his sabotage, chuckled, and returned to his father's gas-powered vehicle.

Elizabeth fell onto her bed, exhausted.

Despite a full day with Mrs. Newcastle, Elizabeth was grateful. Since her angry conversation with Luke, Elizabeth deliberately immersed herself into the chaotic world of midwifery. She witnessed her first live birth, attended to no less than a half-dozen, near-term mothers, and administered to three sickly infants. For Mrs. Newcastle, the errands, the emergencies, and the endless house calls, were part of a daily routine. For Elizabeth, it was an exhausting ritual of 12-hour days, filled with tedious and time-consuming labor. The girl, proud of her performance thus far, basked in the afterglow of Mrs. Newcastle's comments, earlier that evening.

"Elizabeth, you have done your job well. Such instincts at so young an age, are unusual. You are destined to be an extraordinary midwife."

And then, after only 40 days of mentoring, Mrs. Newcastle handed Elizabeth a small envelope filled with currency and coins. It would be the girl's very first payday.

On that evening, Elizabeth wrote in her journal with great joy.

At breakfast the next morning, Elizabeth enjoyed a rare opportunity to speak with her father.

She shared Mrs. Newcastle's comments.

"You are a very special young woman, Elizabeth. Your mama would be very proud of you."

An awkward silence enveloped the room. Elizabeth argued with herself. Should she ask about Luke? Her father seemed to read her mind.

"You know, Mr. Windsor and Billy speak very highly of Luke. I saw him just yesterday. He looked very happy."

Elizabeth, angry and happy all at once, thought for a moment. Her anger stemmed from the fact that Luke paid no price for his arrogance. And yet, she rejoiced that his work in the mines had ended. Perhaps, Luke would change. With his own success assured, Luke might more readily recognize Elizabeth's potential and rejoice in her success. Perhaps. But not likely.

"Why don't you pay a call on Mrs. Hobbs?"

Elizabeth's wide-open eyes betrayed her shock.

"Father, that would be a bit forward, don't you think?"

Clarence shrugged.

"Why is that forward? She would be grateful for the company, don't you think?"

Elizabeth, struck by the genius of her father's suggestion, sat in stunned silence. Her pride demanded that Luke make the first contact. A social call on his mother might prompt him to call or visit. She would welcome such an entreaty. An apology from either of them would not be necessary. The visit with Mrs. Hobbs would be a face-saving strategy for both of them.

"Mrs. Newcastle says we will have a light day today. Perhaps I can see her this afternoon."

Mr. Parsons kissed her on the forehead as he left the table.

"I must go now. Good luck.

Elizabeth knocked on the door several times.

"Mrs. Hobbs, I hope I am not disturbing you."

"Not at all. I was upstairs where I should not have been, given my knees."

"I just came to check on you."

"God bless you, Elizabeth. You are a very kind soul. Do you have time for a spot of tea?"

"Yes, of course."

The older woman and her young visitor talked nonstop about the beautiful summer, midwifery, the prospect of war in Europe, Mrs. Hobbs' vegetable garden, and the shawl she was knitting.

"My Nana taught me how to knit. But lately I don't seem to have enough time in the day."

"Knitting is good for the soul, Elizabeth. You must find time somewhere in between the expectant mothers and the newborn babies"

The tick of a mantle clock filled the room for several minutes, Elizabeth did her best to avoid the woman's gaze. Mrs. Hobbs eyes twinkled.

"Luke has immersed himself in the job at Windsor Land and Lumber Company. But I am sure he would like to see you again."

Elizabeth could feel the sting of tears in her eyes. She blinked them away but struggled with her thoughts.

"He makes me so angry at times, Mrs. Hobbs. And there are other times when I could listen to him for hours on end. Is there something wrong with me?"

"There is nothing wrong with you, Elizabeth. It is not easy for a mother to admit that her son's view of women is seriously flawed. I blame his father. And I blame myself. We were a poor example of how a man and a woman should love and respect each other. Luke learned from his father's poor example and my lack of resolve. And now, you are both paying the price for his parents' mistakes."

As she walked the streets back to her home, Elizabeth considered the likelihood that Luke was a victim of his upbringing.

She thought of their last conversation. Her heated words triggered a pang of guilt. On the other hand, *he should know better,* she thought. He was not a stupid man. A son, once he has reached adulthood, should not let the sins of the father dictate his behavior. Perhaps Luke was aware of this deficiency. It would explain his moody approach to life and his anger.

Elizabeth knew the feeling. Frustration, even anger, with the fact that she grew up without a mother. Frustration, even anger, that her father would not openly disagree, much less argue, with anyone. Elizabeth was the man's opposite. She would argue with anyone, at any time, on almost any subject. She wore a chip on her shoulder. *Just like Luke.* Her words, whispered out loud, shook the girl to the core.

Elizabeth Parsons. No different and no better than Luke Hobbs.

Mrs. Newcastle arrived at Elizabeth's home just after sunrise.

The midwife and her student faced a long and difficult day. There were at least four expectant mothers who required examinations, each of them in various stages of pregnancy. Another woman, after experiencing sporadic contractions for most of the weekend, seemed likely to give birth in the next 24 hours. In addition to all of that, there were three newborn infants, all overdue for their one-month check-ups.

"Our first visit has to be Shirley Corrigan," said Mrs. Newcastle, as she urged the old mare into a trot. "She's been experiencing contractions all weekend."

Elizabeth nodded her approval as she checked the contents of their medical bag. As they climbed the hill, she offered to re-organize the list of visits.

"I could number them in approximate geographic order. That would mean less traveling and a more efficient use of our time.

"Excellent idea," said Mrs. Newcastle.

As they crested the hill, a fully loaded hay wagon tended by two farmers lay stopped in the middle of the lane. The midwife yanked hard on the reins and yelled.

"Whoa girl, whoa."

She pulled harder. The leather strap snapped. Mrs. Newcastle fell back against the seat cushion, the untethered reins still in her hands. The horse, with the bit now firmly in her grip, continued forward. When the severed reins fell to the ground, one on each side of the horse, they brushed against the mare's back legs. The horse panicked and surged forward.

The buggy's left wheel veered off the hard surface of the road into the muddy shoulder. The horse passed the hay wagon at breakneck speed. When the racing mare veered right, the two-wheel cart rolled left. Elizabeth was catapulted into the air. She landed in a field of uncut hay. Mrs. Newcastle hit the ground hard, immediately trapped by the overturned contraption. The horse continued to panic, dragging the wreckage over the woman's motionless body. The old mare continued to pull the overturned cart, exhausted herself, and came to a halt.

Elizabeth, bruised and shaken, struggled to her feet, brushing the hay and debris from her dress. She saw the two men from the hay wagon, running in her direction. When she noticed the crumpled heap on the side of the road, Elizabeth screamed and ran to the injured woman's side.

"Mrs. Newcastle!"

The woman moaned. Elizabeth, afraid to move her mentor, spoke calmly in the woman's ear.

"Lie perfectly still, Mrs. Newcastle. Help is on the way."

Luke stared, wide-eyed, at the Underwood Number five typewriter in front of him.

Mr. Windsor's secretary, out for the week with a suspected case of food poisoning, unknowingly surrendered both her desk and the typewriter to Windsor's newest employee. Luke studied his handwritten report which lay to one side. Despite the quick memorization of each letter's location on the keyboard, his progress would be slow. After a few pages, Luke's typing speed improved.

"I didn't know you was a secretary, too."

Luke looked up. The grammatically incorrect observation came from Reggie, whose large frame blocked the entrance.

"Trust me, Reggie, I am no secretary."

Reggie fell into the chair, resting his oversized shoes on the desk.

"What do you want, Reggie?"

Reggie's shoes came off the desk and hit the floor with a thud. He jerked to his feet and leaned over the desk, his sweaty palms resting on a newly typed page of Luke's report.

"I want you to stay away from Elizabeth Parsons."

Luke reached for a blank sheet of paper and fed it into the machine. He studied the paper for a moment. People like Reggie stirred the deep-seated anger that lay hidden just beneath the surface of Luke's otherwise stoic personality.

Money was never a problem for people like Reggie, he thought. *They were given what they wanted, when they wanted it, and with no strings attached. The Windsor money attracted the women and Reggie's sexist, domineering ways did the rest. Reggie was physically gifted. He could also afford the alcohol, the cigars, the food, and even the gas-powered automobiles required to attract an entourage of fickle friends. Luke did not have that advantage.*

Luke rose to his feet as if in a trance. His icy cold face looked down on Reggie. Reggie stood tall but not tall enough to match Luke's height. Luke's muscular right arm reached for Reggie's neck. Years of work in the woods, on the ice, and in the mines, gave Luke a vice-like grip. Reggie could feel the pressure on his Adam's apple. He reached for Luke's arm. Luke pressed harder. Reggie couldn't breathe. He started to wheeze. Luke pulled him closer.

"Your younger brother is my immediate supervisor, is he not?"

Reggie blinked repeatedly and nodded his head. Luke squeezed even harder. Reggie's eyes bulged. His beet-red face contorted in pain. His knees swayed like reeds in the wind. Luke squeezed harder and shoved Reggie to the floor. He lay there on his back, struggling to breathe. Luke circled the desk and offered a helping hand.

"Get up. You're going to be just fine."

Reggie, shock and terror in his eyes, reached for Luke's outstretched hand. With a single effortless pull, Luke brought the man to his feet. He pretended to smooth Reggie's shirt and fiddled with the man's tousled hair.

"Now listen to me, Reggie."

Reggie's eyes, glassy and dilated, fixed on his tormentor.

"Are you listening to me?"

Reggie jerked his head up and down and mouthed a silent yes. Luke spoke in a cold, slow whisper.

"You will never tell me what I can or cannot do. Ever. Again. Do you understand what I just told you?"

Reggie, still trying to catch his breath, spoke in a hoarse voice.

"Yes."

Luke leaned in.

"Do you understand me, Reggie?

"Yes, sir. I understand."

"Good"

Luke raised an arm to pat Reggie on the shoulder. Reggie flinched.

"You best leave now, Reggie. I have a report to type."

Clarence Parsons ran into the company's executive offices, out of breath and with no color in his face.

"Where is everybody?"

"Mr. Parsons. Is there something I can do for you?" asked Luke.

"I can't meet with Mr. Windsor this afternoon. Mrs. Newcastle and Elizabeth were in an accident this morning. Mrs. Newcastle is seriously hurt. Elizabeth claims she is uninjured. I'm heading for the hospital now. Please give the message to Mr. Windsor."

"I will."

Luke returned to his typewriter. Mr. Parson's visit distracted him. Should he go to the hospital? Elizabeth *did* visit his mother. She can't be too angry with him, he thought. Still, a visit to the hospital might be seen as a bit forward. The buggy will need repairs. Perhaps he should see to that, instead. Luke continued to work on the report. Billy Windsor interrupted him.

"Luke, what's wrong with Clarence Parsons? He just rushed right past me at the entrance to our office building. Didn't say a word."

"Mrs. Newcastle and Elizabeth were in an accident this morning. He said Elizabeth appears to be uninjured but Mrs. Newcastle is badly hurt."

"Elizabeth? In an accident?"

"I'm sure she will be just fine."

Billy shook his head.

"I must know for certain."

Billy ran out of the office. Luke worked for a bit longer.

Billy sighed loudly when he saw Elizabeth pacing in the hospital hallway.

"You appear not to be injured."

"I am fine. Mrs. Newcastle has a broken leg, a sprained shoulder, and multiple cuts and bruises. But she will recover."

"Thank the Lord."

"Billy, how did you know I was here?"

"Your father could not make his afternoon meeting with my father. He told us about the accident."

"It was nice of you to come."

Billy remained at her side. He and Elizabeth exchanged awkward glances.

"Why are you here, Billy? You don't even know Mrs. Newcastle."

Billy stuttered.

"I . . . I . . . guess I was worried. I was worried about you."

"I'm fine, Billy. And it is very sweet of you to be so concerned."

Elizabeth studied a wall hanging. Billy fidgeted.

"May I get you something to eat or drink?" he asked.

"No, thank you."

She glanced at Billy, forced a smile, and pretended to cough. She shifted from one foot to the other. Billy stood in silence. She assumed the boy suffered from a painful shyness.

"Thanks again for coming by, Billy. I am sure Mrs. Newcastle appreciates your concern."

Billy stared at the beautiful woman, but did not respond.

"Good night, Billy."

Billy turned to leave and then jerked to a halt.

"I came to see you, not Mrs. Newcastle."

Elizabeth stepped forward, her brows furrowed and a frown on her face.

"Billy, I don't . . . I am in the middle of . . . You are such a nice, young . . . oh, Billy, this is so awkward . . ."

"It doesn't have to be awkward, Elizabeth. I was hoping we could have lunch together. Or just tea, perhaps. Whatever you wish. I promise to be a gentleman."

Elizabeth slowly shook her head.

"I'm sorry, Billy."

Billy's eyes narrowed to slits. His lips curled into a snarl.

"I am not like my older brother."

"No, Billy. That's not it. That's not it at all."

"You're sweet on Luke Hobbs, aren't you?"

"Your question is inappropriate."

Billy hung his head and turned to leave.

"I apologize. You are correct. I am truly sorry and I will leave you alone."

When he finally disappeared, Elizabeth blew the hair off her face and collapsed in the chair at Mrs. Newcastle's bedside. She saw no change in the woman and yearned for a cup of hot tea. She muttered her frustration.

"Why are men so difficult?"

After finishing his report, Luke traveled to Mrs. Newcastle's place.

The damaged buggy lay in the back yard, the old mare in its stall. He fed the horse and assessed the damage. Luke replaced the reins and reattached the buggy shafts. He hand-stitched a tear in the overhead canopy and cleaned the entire carriage. He also checked the wheels. They were undamaged.

Luke did not dispose of the old reins, thinking they might be of some use in the future. His examination of the leather showed no dryness, cracks, or signs of age. Puzzled as to how leather in such good condition could rip apart, he repeated his inspection. Luke noticed, at the site of the tear, that both strips of leather had been cut. Sliced through with a knife to more than half of their width. He wondered if Mrs. Newcastle had made an enemy because of her work as a midwife. He thought about Elizabeth.

And then he thought about Reggie.

Mrs. Hobbs, asleep in her parlor chair, rose when Luke got home.

The mantle clock chimed twice. He excused his late arrival and related the details of the accident, leaving out any mention of sabotage. She offered to let him sleep in. He said no, and asked that she wake him at seven. She hugged him goodnight and he trudged up the stairs.

"I left yesterday's copy of *The Evening Telegram* on your nightstand."

"Thank you, Mother."

A front-page headline grabbed his attention.

Great Britain Declares War!

Luke read the article, hoping it would lull him to sleep. It didn't.

For him, his mother, the Windsors, and Elizabeth, a war would only complicate matters. Life would be considerably more difficult. As he folded the paper, an advertisement for tea, at the bottom of the page, caught his eye. **"Five pounds or more, 36 cents a pound."** T. D. Edens was located on Duckworth Street, just off the Military Road. Luke patronized the country store, quite often. The caption at the bottom of the ad was new, rewritten to reflect the immediate prospect of war. The caption applied to everything that Newfoundlanders held close in their heart. Not just tea.

"Tea will be much dearer."

Chapter Five

OFF TO WAR

The official notification to Newfoundland arrived at 9:14 on the evening on August 4, 1914.

Newfoundland, a self-governing colony of the British empire, was now at war. The 32,000 people of St. John's greeted the announcement with enthusiasm.

"This will be a short war," predicted Reginald Windsor, adding that "German and Prussian aggression must end and end soon."

His two sons plus Clarence, Luke, and a standing-room only crowd of employees gathered in the company's lobby area to hear their CEO expound on the previous day's declaration of war. Windsor continued: "I am certain that many of you would very much like to, shall we say, dispose of a few Huns. And I say, give 'em hell, boys!"

The room exploded in cheers and applause. Young Reggie, using his large hands as a public address system, encouraged his fellow employees to join the massive street demonstrations.

"Let's go, men! We've got a war to fight!"

Thousands of city residents paraded in the streets singing patriotic songs. They gathered on the sidewalks at the homes of the governor, the prime minister, and the office of the French counsel. The elder Windsor locked arms with his older son and marched from the office building and onto the streets. Luke Hobbs and Billy Windsor watched the demonstrations from the fourth-floor board room.

"Are you going to sign up, Luke?"

"I will speak with my mother, first. But yes, I will volunteer. And you?"

Billy nodded.

"Absolutely. I may be small, but I can ride and shoot with the best of them."

Luke flashed a weak smile. In a matter of months, death had become his unwanted friend. The frozen faces of his shipmates who died on the ice. His estranged father. The mutilated remains of a man who worked the trolleys at Bell Island Mines. Each man's death mask flashed before Luke's eyes. The loud revelry and jubilant celebration on the streets below, echoed through the windows and reverberated in the board room. *The suffering and death of your fellow man should never be a cause for celebration*, he thought. Billy stood at the boardroom window watching the revelers below.

"Maybe we should join the party," said Billy.

Luke shook his head.

"I'm going home."

Within days, an overflow crowd of mostly men and some women gathered at the Armory to hear Governor Walter Davidson.

He announced that, although the colony was "poor in money," it was "rich in men." He called for the establishment of a 500-man regiment as the colony's contribution to the war. He expressed his hope that the Newfoundland Regiment would grow to more than 5,000 men. With the prime minister's approval, Davidson authorized creation of the Newfoundland Patriotic Association. Its 12-member Executive Committee consisted of civic and business leaders from across the island. Reginald Windsor would serve on the committee.

On August 21, the governor's proclamation became official. Men between the ages of 19 and 35 were asked to report to the armory and enlist in overseas service. The term of enrollment would be for one year or when the war ended, whichever date arrived first. A few days later, the Women's Patriotic Association was formed. Elizabeth Parsons would serve as one of its 500 charter members. They would provide the men with clothing, various supplies, other comforts, and perform a variety of war-related work.

"Luke, you can't leave me. How would I support myself?" cried Mrs. Hobbs.

"There is already talk that we will be paid a dollar a day. I will send most of it home. Besides, Mother, it's only for a year. Maybe less. The war should be over by then."

Mrs. Hobbs reached for her son, holding him tight and sobbing quietly in his arms. Luke thought about his new job.

He thought about Elizabeth. He would abandon his job and he would abandon the girl. He would do that for a war, in some far-away land. For King, and Country.

And because he was not a coward.

"Don't be silly, Reggie said, a sneering grin on his face.

Reggie, Billy, and their father discussed the recent declaration of war as they finished dinner. Billy's announcement, that he too would enlist, prompted Mr. Windsor's intervention.

"Billy, you look like a kid. You're not tall enough and you don't have the physical strength. Besides, I need you here to run the company."

"But, Father . . ." Reginald's raised hand silenced the boy.

"That's enough, Billy. I don't want to hear it. Reggie snickered. Billy threw his napkin on the table and scowled at his father.

He took the stairs two at a time, as he ran to his room.

"I don't see how you can accomplish your duties as a midwife and be an active member in the WPA," said Mrs. Newcastle.

The old woman, still sidelined by her injuries, questioned Elizabeth's judgment.

"I am truly sorry, Mrs. Newcastle. It is something I must do."

"You are possessed of a character flaw, Miss Parsons."

Elizabeth's face turned to stone. She reached for the door.

"I have to leave, now, Mrs. Newcastle."

"Your character flaw is that you are a strong-willed, fiercely independent, and pig-headed woman."

Mrs. Newcastle smiled.

"Just like me."

Elizabeth's face lit up. She ran to the woman, hugging, smiling, and crying. The midwife squealed in pain.

"Elizabeth, my ribs!"

"Sorry, Mrs. Newcastle. We will talk tomorrow. I promise."

Elizabeth assumed that much of her day would be spent on arrangements for repair of the buggy.

She walked to Mrs. Newcastle's shed to assess the damage. The horse-drawn contraption blocked her path to the entrance. She stopped as she neared the buggy. The two-wheeled vehicle looked like new. Someone repaired and cleaned the carriage. The leathers lay on the seat. Mended and oiled too. Her mind raced, ticking off the possible "knights in shining armor" who would do such a thing.

The two farmers, tending to their broken-down hay wagon, delivered the buggy to Mrs. Newcastle's residence but did not linger for very long. She thought of Billy, her delusional suitor, but doubted he could be capable of such handiwork. That left Reggie and Luke. The very thought of personally thanking Reggie for his charitable deed triggered chills and goosebumps. She desperately wanted the anonymous benefactor to be Luke Hobbs. The two of them had not spoken since she called him a jackass. She called on his mother but thus far received no response from Luke.

"Are you pleased?"

Elizabeth spun around to confirm the man's voice.

"Mr. Hobbs. You scared me. And yes, I am most pleasantly surprised. Thank you."

"I came to say goodbye."

Elizabeth's eyes closed. Her head bowed.

"You signed up with the new regiment."

"I did. So did Reggie."

She searched Luke's blue eyes and solemn face. He showed no signs of knowing about the attack. But he was hiding something. She was convinced.

"When will you leave?"

"There's training. They say late September or early October. No one seems to know for sure."

"Luke. I'm sorry. Mr. Hobbs, I . . ."

"Luke is fine, so long as Elizabeth is acceptable."

"Yes, of course."

Luke waited patiently. Elizabeth tried again.

"Luke, I wish to apologize. You are not a jackass."

"Perhaps. But I *am* capable of it," he replied, a slight smirk on his face.

A large grin lit up her face.

"And you are similarly skilled," he added.

"Yes, you are correct. We are very much alike, aren't we?"

"Yes. I suppose we are."

Luke looked away for a moment. He bit his lower lip, clearly thinking about his next words.

"Are you pleased that Reggie too, is going off to war?"

He knew about the attack, she thought. *But how? Was it Billy? His father? Reggie?* Elizabeth started to tremble.

"Yes. I am glad to be rid of him."

"He's obsessed with you."

Elizabeth, now certain that Luke knew of the attack, turned her back. She did not want him to see her tear-filled eyes. She spoke in a soft voice.

"Yes. I know. And his brother seems to be of a similar disposition. Although Billy strikes me as harmless."

Luke approached the girl. The unexpected touch of his hand on her arm caught Elizabeth by surprise. She turned quickly. She stood just inches from his clean-shaven face. Elizabeth worried that he might hear the pounding in her chest. He leaned in. Their eyes closed. He kissed her. Softly. Briefly. On the lips. It was a slow, deliberate, and tender gesture. When he pulled away, she took a deep breath, as if frightened. It was her heart, leaping for joy. She focused on his blue eyes once again. Luke did not blink. He did not smile. He looked as if he could see right through the woman.

"Unlike Reggie, I am not *obsessed* with you, Elizabeth Parsons. But I'm getting there. Rather quickly."

Elizabeth blushed.

"Will you write?"

"Of course."

They stared into each other's eyes, comfortable with their last quiet moment together. He squeezed her hands, turned, and walked back to the road. Luke disappeared behind a stand of trees. She could hear the retreating sound of Jewel's hooves as they clapped against the hardscrabble road. The sudden realization that she might never see the man again, brought tears to her eyes. His was her first real kiss.

And perhaps, their last.

A cricket field near Quidi Vidi Lake, in the St. John's neighborhood of Pleasantville, would serve as the training camp for Newfoundland's First Regiment.

The training grounds, located in the east end of the city and directly north of downtown Saint John's, were easily accessed. Luke, surprised to see Reggie marching at his side as the new recruits drilled, concluded that Reggie harbored no hard feelings about their violent encounter of the previous week. Luke still suspected him of sabotaging Mrs. Newcastle's carriage.

"I used to play cricket there and jumped in the lake to cool off," Reggie said, pointing to the camp.

"Yours was a privileged childhood, Reggie."

"I guess."

The recruits would soon discover that preparations for their arrival at Pleasant Lake remained incomplete. A shortage of rifles allowed only 100 of the 500-man regiment to practice marching drills with real weapons. The musketry committee quickly purchased 500 Canadian-made Ross rifles at the cost of $28 each. The new rifles, although late in arriving, pleased the new recruits. Their new uniforms raised eyebrows.

"What in blazes are these?" asked Reggie.

Reggie, Luke, and most of the recruits, cautiously examined their new leggings. The puttees, as they were called, were supposed to be made of khaki-colored wool. The Newfoundland Patriotic Association decreed that the men's uniforms would be made entirely in Newfoundland. It would save money. Unfortunately for the men, khaki-colored wool could not be found anywhere in the colony.

"Blue puttees? Are they mad?" asked Reggie.

"We don't have a choice," Luke observed.

The new recruits trained for hours each day and well into the evening. Arms drills, foot drills, and marching became second nature to the men. When marksmanship training began, both Luke and Reggie excelled. Some locals resented the constant firing of weapons. Blueberry pickers, within range of the firing range, were denied access to their usual picking grounds. When "skirmishing" sessions began, however, the Pleasantville training camp became a tourist attraction. Hundreds of locals arrived, mostly on weekends, to witness the staged "battles."

When the cold nights of winter approached, the men could no longer be housed in their tents. Luke and Reggie, like most of the St. John's recruits, received permission to go home in the evenings. Out-of-town recruits made the necessary arrangements with host families. Luke, warmly welcomed by his aging mother, took the opportunity to call on Elizabeth. He made several attempts, all to no avail. The newly designated midwife, regularly working 12-hour days, spent most evenings at Mrs. Newcastle's residence. On one occasion Luke, in search of Elizabeth once again, sought the older woman's permission to house Jewel in her shed. He promised to send funds for Jewel's room and board.

"And tell Elizabeth, I said goodbye. Again."

By mid-September, the first 500 recruits from Newfoundland, finished their strict training regimen and received formal approval for their overseas embarkation. The cross-Atlantic journey would begin on October 3.

A huge crowd, the largest in Newfoundland's history, gathered at the docks to cheer the troops as they marched from the training ground to the ship that would take them abroad. Luke recognized the *Florizel* as one of the steam ships in the fleet of sealing boats, on that tragic day in April. Although refurbished to accommodate 500 men, he questioned whether the *Florizel*'s transatlantic journey would be at all pleasant.

Luke searched hundreds of faces in the crowd, many of them tear-stained and all of them waving goodbye with hats or handkerchiefs. He looked for one face, in particular. In vain. As he turned away from the ship's railing, he noticed a lone figure, far from the shore. He thought he recognized the woman's long locks of hair and the pink scarf she waved. It was the donkey at the woman's side that confirmed her identity. Luke could not remember the last time he laughed so much and for so long.

He climbed the railing and repeatedly swung his khaki-colored knit hat above his head in a wide arc. His 'woolen helmet,' as the men quickly nicknamed them, was nothing more than a knit toque made in Newfoundland. The woman with the jackass noticed the laughing man on the railing, waving frantically. She tied her pink scarf around the animal's neck and kissed the donkey on its nose. He blew her a kiss and Elizabeth Parsons pretended to catch it.

He vowed to remember her goodbye until the day he died.

Elizabeth recognized the address on her list.

The 'skeet' lived at that residence. Mrs. Hynes, the man's tormented wife, could not be pregnant. The woman lost her baby less than two months ago. Elizabeth knocked on the door, anyway. She waited minutes before the door opened. Even then, the young mother cautiously verified the identity of her visitor, staring through the narrow opening.

"I was expecting the midwife."

"She was hurt in an accident, Mrs. Hynes. I've come on her behalf. How may I help you?"

The door opened. Elizabeth's hand flew to her mouth, smothering a scream. The woman's left eye was swollen shut. Her lower lip was lacerated. Her face was bruised and discolored. A trail of dried blood, originating in the woman's ear, reached to her jaw. Her left arm lay in a crude sling made from rags. The woman spoke in a desperate whisper.

"Come in. And please shut the door."

"Mrs. Hynes. What happened to you?"

The woman began to cry. Elizabeth tried to calm her.

"Please, Mrs. Hynes. Sit down. I will make you a cup of tea."

"We are *out* of tea. That's why he got mad."

"Mrs. Hynes, tell me what happened."

"He'd been drinking. More than usual. He started to beat me. He chased me upstairs. He had a knife. I went into the bedroom and used the dresser to block the door. It worked. He said I would have to come out sooner or later and then he would kill me. Then, I heard a loud noise. It sounded like he fell down the stairs."

"Was he hurt?"

The injured woman's lips trembled. Her body shook violently.

"I will show you."

She brought Elizabeth into the living room. At the bottom of the stairs, a dingy colored sheet covered what appeared to be a body. Elizabeth pulled back the shroud. The man's bloodshot eyes stared at the ceiling. His hand still grasped the handle of a knife, its blade, deep in the man's stomach. Dark red blood covered his tee shirt and the top of his long underwear. Elizabeth, certain that the man's eyes followed her every move, touched the back of her fingers to his unshaven skin. Stone cold. She shuddered, covered the body, and turned to the injured woman.

"Grab some things. You will stay with Mrs. Newcastle tonight. But first, we will go to the police."

"Am I going to prison?"

"No, Mrs. Hynes. You will not go to prison. But you are going to escape from *this* prison, once and for all."

Clarence, home alone for dinner yet again, tossed two pieces of codfish into a frying pan with a bit of cooking oil, and returned to his easy chair in the parlor.

The white paper given him by Reginald Windsor and authored by Luke Hobbs detailed the expected demand for wood products once the European continent became engulfed in war. The report predicted that traditional methods of warfare would be a thing of the past. The author argued that this war would be fought mostly in the air, on the water, and in the trenches. The demand for construction materials to erect shelters, stabilize tunnels, construct airplane hangars, barracks, and so on would deplete most of the current inventory. The colony of Newfoundland, as well as countries such as Canada and the United States, would be the prime beneficiaries of this new type of warfare. Clarence searched Luke's report for the author's sources. He had trouble reading the print. The smoky haze in the parlor blurred his vision.

"Oh, my Lord," he yelled.

Clarence hurried to the kitchen. Flames and heavy smoke rose from the frying pan. He grabbed a pot holder holding the pan at arms-length. Clarence rushed to the door and tossed his dinner into a small snowbank. The flames and smoke quickly dissipated. Leaving the pan behind, he sprinted back into the house. *Everything will smell like burnt fish. Elizabeth is going to kill me*, he thought.

When all the downstairs windows were opened, he scurried up the stairs and repeated the process. His daughter's room was the last chamber to get aerated. Clarence collapsed onto the edge of her bed, out of breath from his exertions.

"I must be the dumbest man in all of St. John's," he muttered.

As he caught his breath, a composition tablet on the night stand sparked his interest. The notebook, the ubiquitous type with a black and white marble pattern on its covers, was labeled 'journal.' He reached for the diary and started flipping the pages. His curiosity had more to do with Elizabeth's penmanship than with the silly thoughts of a teenaged woman. He recalled that the girl's mother prided herself on perfect penmanship. Clarence smiled triumphantly as he scanned the neatly written and eloquent prose. He thumbed through a few more pages. The name Windsor caught his eye. After several pages he jumped to his feet and, for the first time in years, he cursed.

"That goddamned Neanderthal."

The words continued to leap from the page, like a snake biting its victim's flesh. Again, and again.

"With one of his giant hands, he pinned both of my hands above my head."

"I could feel his private parts against my bare skin."

"I found all of the buttons and repaired the blouse, the very next day."

"Father will be angry and disappointed. Angry with Reggie, but disappointed that I allowed such a thing to happen. I forgot to lock the door."

Clarence, rarely angry and never for very long, reflexively forced himself to calm down. His rage quickly melted into confusion and anxiety. *Should he confront the Windsors? Should he question his daughter? The fact that he read her journal would make the girl livid. Did she invite this attack? Perhaps she said something that precipitated the incident.* He returned the journal to its place, flustered and overwhelmed with the myriad troubled thoughts that filled his head.

Clarence predicted an ugly confrontation no matter what he did.

Luke, Reggie, and their fellow recruits, waited a full day before Captain William J. Martin ordered the *Florizel* out to sea.

They headed south to rendezvous with a Canadian contingent, also destined for Europe. The convoy of transport ships enjoyed a half-dozen battleships as an escort. They left on October 4, 1914, two months to the day, since Great Britain declared war.

Conditions on board the *Florizel* triggered widespread grumbling and constant complaints. The ship did not employ the manpower required to host five hundred soldiers. The newly minted recruits, pressed into service as crewmembers, found themselves working as cooks, waiters, stewards, garbage men, and errand boys. Crowded conditions and barely edible food made matters worse. The ever present threat of German U-boats, with a history of successful attacks on merchant ships, added to their worries and woes. Everyone on board kept a watchful eye on the swelling seas. They saw good things and bad.

"There's another one," Reggie shouted.

It was not a school of porpoises. Their daily appearance and acrobatic performances were no longer a novelty. Much to Luke's dismay, Reggie pointed to the floating remains of several dead horses. The Canadian convoy included 6,800 horses, many of them on board the *Montezuma*, a Canadian ship just ahead of the *Florizel*. Some of the horses did not survive the journey.

Another unexpected sight occurred just a few days later. The vision of the *Princess Royal*, a 26,000-ton battlecruiser named after a member of the royal family, impressed everyone. As it sped by, its cruising speed more than 22 knots, the crew on board the *Florizel* belted out a hearty chorus of 'God Save the Queen.'

The *Florizel* reached England on October 14. After a week at anchor in Davenport Harbor, the regiment boarded a train to Salisbury Plain, home of Stonehenge. The 135-mile ride ended with a 7-mile hike in the cold, wet rain to Pond Farm Camp.

It would be three in the morning before the 1st Newfoundland Regiment erected and occupied the tents that would become their new home for weeks to come.

"You had a visitor yesterday," said Mr. Parsons.

Elizabeth, during a rare weekend at home, noticed her father's nervous behavior.

"And who might that be?"

"Billy Windsor," said Clarence, peering intently over his spectacles.

Elizabeth rolled her eyes.

"What did he want?"

"He wanted to know if you recovered from the accident with Mrs. Newcastle's horse and buggy."

"But I wasn't injured."

Clarence whipped the spectacles off his face and leaned forward in his easy chair.

"That is precisely what I told him, Elizabeth. Is he stalking you?"

Elizabeth's eyebrows shot up.

"Father, why would you say such a thing?"

"Well, his brother impresses me as an overgrown ape with no manners. Perhaps it runs in the family."

Elizabeth could not hide her shock. She gnawed on the inside of her cheek. *Did he know about Reggie? How did he learn of the attack?*

"Father, I have never heard you speak like that. Is something wrong?"

Clarence took a calming breath and lowered his voice to a reasonable pitch.

"The Windsor boys are not to be trusted. You must be careful. You should never be alone with them. And I should not have to remind you that when I am gone, the door should be locked."

Elizabeth tried to reassure her father.

"Reggie is in England. And Billy is quite the gentleman. I think I am safe."

Her father, still on edge, jumped to his feet.

"No one is safe, these days. No one. Good night, Elizabeth."

Elizabeth woke to an empty house on Saturday morning.

A note from her father, left on her nightstand, explained he would be at the government building until lunchtime. Elizabeth lingered in bed, wrote in her journal, and then penned a letter to Luke. It would be her third missive since the young man left for England. Her letters went unanswered. Luke's mother claimed she received one letter, thus far. It included most of the new recruit's last paycheck but very few words. Elizabeth and Mrs. Hobbs blamed the British Army for the scarcity of Luke's letters.

The young midwife tore a page from her journal on which she would write the letter to Luke. When she finished the missive and while searching for an envelope, Elizabeth rediscovered her father's note. She initially found it on top of her journal. Her mind quickly connected the dots. She wrote in her journal about Reggie's attack. She stayed with Mrs. Newcastle for days on end. Her father enjoyed unfettered access to her room. She discovered her bedroom window opened, just the other day. She never slept with an open window in such cold weather. Her father was in her room. He read her journal. He read about Reggie's attack. In graphic detail.

Still wearing her robe and a pair of woolen socks, Elizabeth went downstairs in search of tea and toast. Her father's invasion of his daughter's privacy angered her. The fact that he now knew of the attempted rape made her anxious. Ironically, it was supposed to be a weekend of rest and relaxation. Mrs. Newcastle, almost completely recovered from their accident, offered Elizabeth some badly needed time off.

Before she could enjoy the first sip of tea, much less plan a response to her father's discovery, a loud knock on the door pulled the woman from her overstuffed chair in the parlor. She peaked through the curtained window. Billy Windsor, an expectant look on his face, waited at the door. A sudden chill triggered goosebumps on her arms and neck. Despite her father's admonition, she opened the door.

"Billy. I am still in my robe. I wasn't expecting company."

"I apologize, Elizabeth. I stopped by the other day but your father . . ."

"Yes. He told me. It was very nice of you to check on me, Billy, but I am quite all right. Really, I am."

"I don't wish to be a nuisance. I just . . ."

"Billy, I can't leave the door open. You might as well come in and say what you have to say."

Billy stood in the kitchen, shivering, his winter coat buttoned to his chin and its fur collar raised to cover the back of his neck. He wore an oversize bright-red toque, pulled low over his ears. He looked like a 14-year-old boy. Elizabeth, feeling safe and a tad flattered by the attention, saw no harm in being hospitable.

"Well, as long as you're here, you might as well have some tea."

"Thank you."

"Do me a favor, Billy, and throw another log on the fire while I pour your tea."

"Yes, ma'am."

Billy sat in her father's chair, fidgeting with his hat but still wearing the coat. Elizabeth returned with a steaming cup of tea on a saucer.

"Billy, you seem out of sorts. Is there something on your mind?"

"Well, yes, I guess there is."

Elizabeth tried to anticipate his concerns.

"If it's about Reggie, I don't want to talk about it."

"No, it's not about Reggie."

Billy wrung his hat as if it were soaking wet.

"It's about you."

"What about me?"

He sprung to his feet with his back to the girl warming his hands over the fire.

"It's about us."

Elizabeth exhaled, sharply.

"Billy, I've told you before. There *is* no us."

Billy spun in place, ignoring her protest.

"I have no experience in this sort of thing, Elizabeth."

"What sort of thing?"

"Courting a woman. Should I request your father's blessing?"

"My *father's* blessing? What about *my* blessing? Billy, I like you. I really do. And I feel safe when I am with you, unlike your older brother. But there will be no courting. Do you understand?"

Elizabeth heard the unlocked kitchen door open and then slam shut. Her father's face, red from the cold, peaked into the parlor.

"What in blazes is going on here? Mr. Windsor why are you in my home? And Elizabeth, have you no shame? Entertaining a gentleman in your bathrobe? You, sir, will leave the premises, this very instant."

"Father, what has come over you? Billy was not bothering me. Please restrain yourself."

Billy scurried to the door. Elizabeth confronted her father.

"You are acting like a deranged lunatic. And I will never forgive you for reading my journal. You are the worst father in the world."

Elizabeth fled to her room, sobbing. Clarence Parsons, his breathing suddenly labored, reached for his left arm, wincing in pain. Elizabeth slammed her bedroom door and locked it. He clutched at his chest and whispered her name. She did not hear his cry for help. He fell to the floor with a loud thud.

Elizabeth heard nothing, save the sound of her own sobs.

The Newfoundland Regiment, now under the command of a Canadian officer, rapidly assimilated itself into the British Expeditionary Forces.

On arrival, the regiment reorganized itself into two companies (A and B), of four platoons each. They received standard uniforms, including khaki-colored leggings, standard issue pointed caps, more Ross rifles, and a host of miscellaneous equipment. The battalion's Canadian commander, and the Canadians who shared the campsite, caused widespread confusion and a plethora of complaints.

"No. Newfoundland is *not* a part of Canada."

"We are a British colony."

"We are British, *not* Canadian."

These phrases became standard retorts in the barracks, at the firing range, during exercise drills, and at dinner. The 1st Newfoundland Regiment worked hard to preserve its identity.

Living in a tent and an almost daily deluge of rain, generated even more complaints. The construction of wooden huts could not occur quickly enough. It was not until the end of October that their new huts were all but completed and the men's morale improved. They enjoyed movies almost every evening in an oversized tent, funded by the YMCA. There were impromptu concerts, tables with stationery for letters to home, and a variety of entertainment.

Reggie Windsor, never one to obey the rules and always in possession of funds, managed to access a late model Daimler automobile, for his personal use. He invited a hut load of his friends to join him for a weekend in London. Luke tried to warn him.

"That is not one of your best ideas, Reggie. You will be caught."

They were. And each of the AWOL soldiers was given seven days of 'CB' (confined to barracks.) There would also be a significant delay should any one of them ever seek an officer's commission.

Dr. Macpherson, extremely busy as the newly appointed Chief Medical Officer of the Newfoundland Patriotic Association, responded immediately to Elizabeth's panicked phone call.

The doctor's examination of Clarence Parsons, now resting comfortably in hospital, left Elizabeth frightened and frustrated.

She listened carefully to Macpherson's diagnosis and his recommended course of action.

"Your father suffered a mild heart attack. The heart is likely damaged but not significantly. I recommend at least one month of bed rest and sedation if he is unable to sleep. If he begins to feel pain in his chest, contact me immediately."

"He will want to return to work immediately, Doctor. What should I do?"

Macpherson wagged his index finger at his patient.

"Clarence. You stay away from the office. That's an order."

Clarence glared at his daughter. Elizabeth reached for the doctor's arm.

"May I walk with you, Doctor?"

"Of course."

Dr. Macpherson and Elizabeth discussed her father's diet, his need for sleep, and the warning signs of trouble in the future.

"I will be checking on him as often as I can and I thank you for your prompt response," said Elizabeth."

"Not at all. He is in good hands, I am sure. Incidentally, I must compliment you on your work as a midwife. Mrs. Newcastle is most impressed. Indeed, she thinks you would be an excellent nurse."

"Thank you, Dr. Macpherson. She is an excellent teacher and I continue to learn from her, every day."

"If I may, Elizabeth, how old are you?"

"I'll be 19 in less than a month."

"Perfect. I want you to give serious consideration to the Voluntary Aid Detachment."

Macpherson explained that the VAD organization now had 7,000 volunteers throughout Newfoundland. More than 150 of them accepted assignments overseas.

"When the fighting begins in earnest, this war will create a tremendous demand for nurses and nurse assistants. There will be a short course to obtain your certificate, of course, but you would be able to work with qualified nurses. After enough training and an exam, you could then become a professional nurse. And, in my opinion, you would do a fantastic job."

"Thank you, Dr. Macpherson, you are most kind."

Elizabeth returned to her father's room. His closed eyes opened wide when she walked in.

"I wish to discuss something with you," he announced.

"You wish for another heart attack?"

Clarence ignored the remark.

"I do not like confrontation of any sort. I detest it. On the other hand, I think that Mr. Windsor should be confronted about his son's behavior."

"His son is off to war. What do you hope to accomplish by confronting Mr. Windsor?"

Clarence wore a confused look on his face.

"Well, I'm not quite sure."

Elizabeth frowned.

"Oh, I see. You have no objection to confrontation so long as someone else is doing the arguing."

"Elizabeth, I have a career to consider. I work with Reginald Windsor and his company, on a regular basis."

"Yes. And you would not want to jeopardize your position with the Crown."

"Precisely."

"I agree."

Clarence snapped to attention.

"You do?"

"Yes. Mr. Windsor told me as much."

"You have spoken to Mr. Windsor about the attack?"

"Yes. He is fully prepared to retaliate if I file a complaint with the authorities."

"What did you tell him?"

"We agreed to move on."

Clarence went limp after a loud sigh of relief.

"Well, I am pleased to hear that."

Elizabeth suddenly turned and slammed the door to her father's hospital room. She locked it and stood at the foot of his bed a hand on each hip.

"You read my journal."

"I can explain."

"I'm listening."

"I burned my dinner. I opened every window in the house to air out the place. I went to your room last. I sat on the bed to catch my breath and, honestly, I was admiring your penmanship. It was always perfect. But I spotted the Windsor name and, well, I kept reading."

Elizabeth growled.

"For almost 19 years now, you have treated me like a child. I will not forgive you for this, Father. You have betrayed my trust."

"Elizabeth. I am truly sorry. Please forgive me."

Elizabeth turned to the door.

"We will talk about this when I have calmed down and you have regained your strength."

"Elizabeth. Please don't go."

Elizabeth unlocked the door and stepped into the hallway.

"Elizabeth?"

"I need a cup of tea."

"Will you return?"

Clarence heard nothing but the sound of retreating footsteps.

Elizabeth walked home, thinking hard about all that happened in just the last few months. Reggie's attack, her new job as a midwife, Mrs. Newcastle's injuries, Mrs. Hynes' deadly encounter, Elizabeth's first real kiss, Luke's departure, and her father's heart attack. With Reggie off to war, her thirst for revenge became pointless. With Luke off to war, she had no reason to stay. In fact, she no longer wanted to be a part of the St. John's community. Dr. Macpherson's praise and encouragement rang in her ears. She reached a decision. Elizabeth would do more than just move on.

She would move away.

"What do you mean, Parsons is unavailable?"

Billy tried to hide his exasperation.

"Father, Mr. Parsons was released from hospital, just last week."

Reginald Windsor sprung out of his chair kicking an ornate mahogany wastebasket across the room. He rushed forward and cornered the boy.

"Track him down, Billy. The option I took on that 500-acre tract is good for only 48 hours. I need the Crown's permission to harvest the wood and I need it yesterday."

"Father, you're being unreasonable."

Reginald poked his son in the chest.

"You don't understand, Billy. We've got a lot of money riding on this. Now find Parsons. Go to his home if you must."

"Yes, sir."

Billy scampered from his father's office, less than anxious for a visit with Mr. Parsons but pleased that he possessed another excuse to call on Elizabeth.

His stomach did a flip-flop when he recalled their last visit. The old man had a heart attack. Billy, although sympathetic, had a job to do. And he refused to give up on Elizabeth.

"Billy, what in blazes are you doing here?"

Elizabeth shut the door behind her, shivering in the wind-driven snow.

"I'm sorry, Elizabeth. My father sent me. It's business. We need Mr. Parsons' approval on our permit request. There is a lot of money at stake."

Elizabeth blew a steaming jet of hot air into her cupped hands.

"Father is resting. I will not disturb him. I don't care how much money is at stake. Your father will have to wait."

"Have you had your lunch yet?" asked Billy.

"No, why do you ask?"

"Well, your father is resting. Wouldn't you like a respite? You've got to eat anyway."

Elizabeth, still angry with her father, rolled her eyes and grimaced.

"You are very persistent, Billy Windsor. But we are not courting. I am hungry. That's all."

"Understood," Billy replied.

"Let me get my coat."

After a brisk walk, Billy and Elizabeth ducked into a small family-owned diner. As they waited for their fish and chips to arrive, Billy reminded Elizabeth that they might both be in trouble.

"My father is going to be angry that I didn't get Mr. Parson's signature on the permit. And your father will be angry should he discover your choice of a luncheon partner."

"Billy. My father knows about Reggie's attack. He read my journal."

"You wrote about it?"

"I write everything in my journal."

"What did your father say?"

"My father will do anything to avoid confrontation. He would prefer that I move on. He just won't say it out loud. I reached that conclusion long before he did."

Billy took a sip of tea and scratched his head.

"What did you write about me in your journal?"

"That you were hoping to court me and that I had not heard that word in a long time."

"Anything else?"

"That you are so unlike your brother."

"Thank you. I take that as a compliment. Does that mean you would agree to have dinner with me?"

Elizabeth mouthed a silent no. The food arrived. Billy poked at his fish. Elizabeth attacked her plate.

"Perhaps I should enlist and go to England. You seem to prefer soldiers."

Elizabeth stopped eating. She took a sip of tea and dabbed her lips with the napkin. Her eyes drilled into Billy's head.

"I *do* hope you are referring to Luke Hobbs and not your older brother."

Billy crumpled his napkin into a ball and tossed it on his untouched food. He sat back in the chair, returning her stare.

"Yes, I am. And I apologize," he said.

"I don't want your apology. But I would like to tell you something, Billy Windsor."

"Is this going to hurt?"

"No. It's a compliment. I believe you are an honest, kind, and generous soul, caught in the dark shadow of a domineering father and a self-absorbed brother who is a better bully than he is a son or brother."

"My compliments, Elizabeth. You have portrayed my family with accuracy."

"I did not know your mother. I suspect you take most after her."

"She left when I was 12 years old. You could have been her twin. Beautiful, strong, independent, and intelligent. My father was afraid of her."

"I doubt very much that your father is afraid of anything."

"Trust me. He is afraid of what he does not understand."

"And you? What are you afraid of?"

Billy looked away, using the time to organize his thoughts.

"I am afraid of living my whole life and dying, without one person remembering who I was, what I did, or even that I once lived."

"I will remember you, Billy—always. And that is a promise."

"So, does that mean you will you get your father's signature on my permit?"

"There's a limit to my generosity, Billy."

They both laughed and finished their lunch.

At the beginning of December, the Newfoundland First Regiment received word they would be moving.

The recruits would spend their first Christmas away from home at a place called Fort George. It would be a pleasant stay, the men now occupying rooms, some small and some large, in a brick-and-mortar building. They enjoyed the luxury of iron cots with mattresses, a table on which to write letters home, and a fireplace, complete with a (rationed) supply of coal. Their diet also improved. They received milk in their tea, real butter on the bread, and roast beef, once a week.

The rigorous training continued, of course. Long hours on the firing range transformed some of the recruits into expert marksmen. Twenty-mile hikes in bone-chilling winds, with a full pack, left many of the men sore and tired. Mail call would ease the pain.

When Luke returned from a training session, he discovered four letters from home, lying on his cot.

A letter from his mother expressed her usual concerns about his safety. She thanked him for the funds he remitted each payday and reminded him to write more often. The remaining letters came from Elizabeth. The first and second messages described her interest in the VAD, the trials and tribulations of midwifery, and her considerable efforts to locate a donkey on the day of his departure. Her third letter required two readings before it truly registered. She described in graphic detail, the attack by Reggie.

The words burned into the soldier's eyes and screamed in his ears. Even worse, neither Elizabeth nor Mrs. Newcastle, suspected Reggie as the one who sabotaged their horse and buggy. Luke did. Now, he was all but certain. White-hot angry and vowing revenge, the soldier furiously paced the floor of his dormitory style room. He would require a plan of attack.

But attack, he would.

Reginald Windsor, the CEO, paced from his chair to the office door like a Bengali tiger in its cage.

Billy, standing in front of the old man's desk, waited for the explosion. His father faced the window.

"He refused to see you?"

"His daughter said he was resting and could not be disturbed. Doctor's orders."

The older Windsor spun in place and pointed to his son.

"We have all the original permits signed by Clarence Parsons, do we not?"

"Yes, father. Dozens of them."

"Bring me the most recent one, now."

Billy did as he was told, returning to his father's office in moments. His father reached for several blank pages of paper, handing them to Billy.

"It's best that you practice before signing the permit."

"Excuse me?"

"You heard what I said. Now, start practicing. And don't be so high and mighty. Nobody is going to look at the damn thing anyway."

"Father, Mr. Parsons is due back in his office, any week now. We could get in a lot of trouble, clearcutting forest land without a permit."

The old man slammed his fist on the desk.

"Just sign the damn thing. Now!"

Chapter Six

LEAVING TOWN

"Who could that be at this time of the morning?" asked Mrs. Newcastle.

Mrs. Hynes, still recovering from her injuries, went to the door.

Elizabeth, busy packing her bag for a day filled with appointments, continued with her task.

"Elizabeth. It's a young man asking for you. Says his name is Billy Windsor," said Hynes.

Elizabeth groaned and slammed a bundle of bandages into her bag.

"Not again. I will not subject myself to this man's begging and whining."

"Excuse me, I didn't hear you," said Mrs. Hynes.

"Nothing, I'll see the gentleman."

Elizabeth grabbed her wrap, flung the door open, and scolded Billy in a loud voice.

"Now listen to me, Billy Windsor. We've had this conversation at least twice, now. If you appear on my doorstep or Mrs. Newcastle's doorstep, unannounced just one more time, I will notify the authorities that you are stalking me and that I am afraid for my life."

Billy waved his arms and shook his head.

"No. No. No. I'm not here for that. We've got a problem. And it's serious."

"What are you talking about?"

"Your father and my father will soon be at war."

"What happened?"

Billy explained the forged signature on the forestry permit.

"We start logging in two days. When should I expect your father to be back on the job?"

"He starts half-days, next week."

"This could give your father another heart attack. And I won't be there to intervene."

"Are you traveling?" she asked.

"I suppose you could say that. I've signed up with the regiment. They are sending a third company to England in early February."

"I thought you didn't qualify."

"That's what I told everyone. The truth is my father prohibited it. In fact, I weigh 125 pounds and I am five feet, five inches tall. That's five pounds and one inch above the requirement. And I passed the physical exam this morning"

"You're not afraid of what your father will do or say?"

"No, I am not."

Elizabeth sat on the stoop, thinking.

"Maybe I won't be there, either."

"Where are you going?"

"Mrs. Newcastle and Dr. Macpherson suggested I join the Voluntary Aid Detachment. They are desperate for volunteers, now that the war has started, and I would have a chance to become a professional nurse."

"That won't get you out of Saint John's.

"It will if I offer to go overseas," she said.

Billy's eyebrows shot up and he giggled.

"What's so funny?"

"I'll be in a war zone and you will be close by. Perhaps we will see each other."

Elizabeth rolled her eyes but flashed a smile.

"I will still be too busy, Billy."

"Elizabeth Parsons, you will always be too busy for me."

She stepped forward, put her arms around the boy, and squeezed.

"Good luck, my friend. And please don't get yourself killed over there. I need someone to buy me fish and chips when I get back."

Billy reached for her hands and squeezed.

"It's a deal, Elizabeth. It's a deal."

Luke kept a low profile during the Christmas festivities at Fort George.

Reggie received more than a dozen packages from home. He shared his cigarettes, baked goods, chocolates, and even some extra pairs of socks. But not his cigars. Luke watched from a distance, wondering if Reggie's "friends" liked Reggie as much as they liked his reckless largesse.

On New Year's Day, Luke started his third attempt at a letter to Elizabeth. The words would not come. A precise description of his feelings for the woman continued to elude him. He admired her independence and her sense of humor. He wondered about her common sense, however, and questioned her impractical aspirations in the medical field. Most of all, he saw no reason to pursue what could only be a long-distance relationship.

"Hey Luke, want some cigarettes?"

Reggie sauntered over, his stride affected by alcohol. Luke saw an opportunity.

"No thanks, Reggie. But I wanted a moment alone with you. Are you up for a walk?"

"Sure, I'm not in trouble again, am I?"

"Not at all, Reggie."

They walked to the rear of the camp, very near the practice range. The lights from the fort shown bright enough to illuminate their way. Luke stopped. Reggie took a long pull on his expensive cigar.

"What's on your mind, Luke?"

Luke placed his hands on Reggie's shoulders and squeezed. Reggie smiled, welcoming the affectionate gesture. When Luke's knee suddenly crashed into Reggie's groin, the big man fell to his knees. Reggie moaned and writhed on the ground, clutching at his private parts. Luke retrieved the cigar that Reggie dropped and blew on its lit end. The red glow illuminated Luke's face. His evil smile triggered a reaction from Reggie.

"Please don't hurt me, Luke. Please. You're acting like a madman."

Luke's face took on a Satanic look, his eyes reflecting the cigar's red glow. He spoke in a slow monotone.

"Why do you think I'm mad, Reggie?"

He brought the glowing cigar to within an inch of Reggie's right eye.

"Please, Luke. I'm begging you. I'll do whatever you want."

Reggie squeezed his eyes shut. Luke could see tears.

"You cut the reins on Mrs. Newcastle's horse and buggy, did you not?"

Reggie, sobbing like a child, jerked his head up and down in agreement.

"And you attacked Elizabeth. But you didn't quite finish the job. Is that right?"

"No, I just roughed her up a bit. And then I left. That's the truth, honest."

"I received a letter from Elizabeth. She called you a monster. Are you a monster, Reggie?"

"I'm not a monster, any more, Luke. I've changed. Honest."

Luke blew on the burning end of Reggie's cigar, once again. Reggie watched in terror, as the cherry red tip moved to a spot on his forehead. Luke pulled the man's hair back and jammed the cigar into Reggie's exposed skin. Reggie screamed. Long and loud. The red glow soon disappeared. The smell of burnt flesh filled Luke's nostrils. Reggie moaned.

"Please don't kill me. Please."

Luke threw the cigar into the wind and yanked the crying man to his feet.

"I want you to promise me, Reggie, that you will leave the women alone, from now on. Can you promise me that, Reggie?"

"Yes, sir. I promise."

"*All* women, Reggie. You won't forget that, will you?"

"No sir. I won't forget."

"Are you sure you won't forget?"

"Yes, sir. I mean no, sir. I will not forget."

"I believe you, Reggie. I really do."

Reggie sniffed. His breathing slowly returned to normal.

Luke smiled. Reggie smiled.

Luke's hand suddenly closed around the man's neck. His squeezed and pressed hard with his thumb. Reggie sputtered, unable to talk. Luke spoke in a hoarse whisper.

"If you forget your promise, Reggie, I will kill you. I will kill you with one hand."

Luke released his grip and walked into the darkness.

"Father, we have to talk."

Clarence, relaxing in his chair with Alice on his lap, suddenly wore an anxious look on his face.

"I was hoping you would forget about the journal."

"What I have to say is more important than my journal."

Elizabeth reached over and scratched Alice on the back. The cat stood and arched into a half circle of black. Elizabeth took a seat in the chair opposite her father.

"When you return to your office next week, you will discover that Mr. Windsor has forged your name on a government permit. He started work on a large tract of forest, days ago. You will also discover that Billy is no longer working for his father. He enlisted and will be in England by the end of February."

"Well, we will see about all of that, won't we?"

"No Father, *we* will not see about any of that. *You* will see about that."

"I don't understand."

"I am leaving too. I have joined the Volunteer Aid Detachment. I have asked for and received an overseas assignment."

Clarence shook his head, his lower lip protruding like a pouting child.

"I don't want a confrontation, Elizabeth, but I will not permit you to do such a thing."

"I don't need your approval, Father. I turned 19 last week. With all the confusion and chaos, you forgot my birthday. But those things don't matter anymore."

Elizabeth got up to leave.

"Your little girl is all grown up."

"I forbid you. Is that clear? I forbid you."

Reginald Windsor, red faced and yelling, refused his second helping of codfish. He sprang from his chair and stood at Billy's side, looking down on the boy. Billy, showing no signs of anxiety, continued with his meal.

"Billy, I want your word as a gentleman that you will not go behind my back and enlist with the regiment."

Billy motioned to the family butler.

"More wine, please."

His father grabbed Billy's wine glass and threw it in the fireplace. The sound of breaking glass and hissing wine filled the room. Billy, still calm and collected, slowly dabbed at his lips with the cloth napkin. He pushed back his chair and stood within inches of his father. The boy stood almost a foot shorter than his father but tonight, Billy felt seven feet tall.

"You are too late, Father. I signed the papers, earlier this week."

"I serve on the executive committee. I will have the association declare your enlistment null and void."

"On what grounds?"

"You're too short and you're too small."

"Not true. I easily exceed the physical requirements and have been certified as physically fit by Dr. Macpherson, himself."

The old man searched his son's face. He slowly turned his back on the boy and faced the fireplace. He spoke to the flames, in a barely audible voice.

"Billy. I need you here. And you know why I need you here. I can't run this company without you."

Reginald turned and beseeched the boy with glassy eyes.

"I'm begging you, son. Please don't go."

Billy turned toward the stairs.

"Good night, Father."

After several months of training, Private William "Billy" Windsor departed Newfoundland for Scotland.

The *SS Dominion*, prevented from entering the harbor by large ice floes, required the assistance of a sealing steamer to break through the frozen waterway. The *Neptune* shuttled Billy and his colleagues to the *SS Dominion* and cleared a path for the regiment's transatlantic journey. Company C of the 1st Newfoundland Regiment would travel to Edinburgh. Billy learned that his counterparts in Companies A and B would leave Fort George and arrive two days after Billy's arrival. The boy laughed. Luke and Reggie would be stunned when Billy welcomed them to Edinburgh.

Reggie, Luke, and their comrades received a warm welcome from Company C of the 1st Newfoundland Regiment. Many of them, already known to Reggie and Luke, were friends, relatives, and neighbors from St. John's. They were shocked, however, when Private Billy Windsor emerged from the throng of 250 new recruits.

"Gentlemen, welcome to Edinburgh," said Billy. Luke greeted his former boss with a warm embrace. Reggie, a visible frown on his face, extended a hand.

"I'm surprised they let you sign up, Billy."

In an uncharacteristic display of bravado, Billy replied.

"They know a good man when they see one. And what in blazes happened to your forehead?"

Reggie instinctively reached for his black hair and pulled several locks over the wound.

"Oh. That's nothing. I fell asleep on my cigar."

Luke's unblinking stare made Reggie's face turn pink.

"Well, I must go. See you later," said Reggie.

Most of the men in the 1st Newfoundland Regiment, now more than 1,000 strong, slept very little that evening.

The new arrivals shared the news from back home. The first 500 recruits regaled the new soldiers with tales of woe, beginning with their miserable transatlantic journey and continuing on to their cold and soggy training at Salisbury Plain.

"You boys got the soft end of the plank," said Luke, a reference to the new recruits' relatively pleasant trip from Newfoundland to Edinburgh.

The regiment would spend 12 weeks at the Edinburgh castle. For the first time in history, the castle would be garrisoned by non-Scottish troops. The training regimen at Edinburgh would also be easier, given the warmer weather and lush grounds which surrounded the castle. Within a day, the soldiers settled into new quarters, their rooms accommodating anywhere from 6 to 30 men each. The chilly winds of March plus a single day's snowfall of more than one foot, made the Newfoundlanders feel right at home. What the local newspaper labeled as a 'howling blizzard,' the Newfoundland recruits referred to as "a mild snowstorm."

The men would continue their training for several months. The subsequent arrival of companies D, E, and F grew their numbers to 1,500. Twelve of the original 'blue puttees,' as they were called, received promotions to Second Lieutenant. Luke Hobbs was one of the twelve. The men, growing tired of the marching drills, the training, and the guard duty, grumbled loudly. They queried the new lieutenant.

"Will we ever get to kill us some Huns?"

"In good time, men. All in good time."

No one argued with Second Lieutenant Luke Hobbs. Especially Reggie Windsor.

The men, although quickly adopted by the locals, could not stay for long. In May of 1915, the regiment moved to Stobbs, some 50 miles southeast. The new location, although cloudy and very wet on the first day, quickly transformed into a training camp which featured plenty of sunshine, grassy fields in which to train, and something new in their daily regimen, bayonet fighting.

At Stobbs, most days started with reveille at 5:30 in the morning. There would be marches, drills, and skirmishing until

5 o'clock at night. When musketry practice was added to the normal schedule, usually for ten consecutive days, the men would labor for as much as 18 hours per day.

"Your mail, sir."

Luke, now enjoying the perks of a servant, welcomed the latest newspaper from London and received a letter from home. The letter from his mother recounted the sinking of the Lusitania, but with a local connection. Tom Kelly, a former neighbor and good friend to Luke, went down with the ship. He worked as a fireman in the engine room. Luke's boyhood friend, despite the four-year difference in their ages, served as Luke's big brother and at times, a substitute father. Luke mourned his friend's loss but worried about the geopolitical implications.

More than 120 Americans went down with the Lusitania. America's involvement in the war might come a lot sooner than everyone expected. At the very least, Americans' opinion of Germany, the country thought responsible for the disaster, would also sink to the bottom. Coincidentally, an uptick in the men's training regimen suggested to Luke that the 1st Newfoundland Regiment would soon be sent into battle.

Most likely the current front line. Gallipoli.

"Sir, you are needed in barracks. Now."

Luke, examining a letter he received that day, forced himself to leave it behind. The penmanship indicated it came from Elizabeth.

"What's the problem?" he asked the private as they quickstepped to the barracks.

"Windsor, sir."

Luke winced.

"Say no more."

When Luke arrived at the bunk room, one of the large ones, a circle of men surrounded several broken pieces of furniture. Reggie Windsor sat on the floor, in the middle of the group. The oversized bully, bleeding from the head and face, wore a panicked look on his face.

"Luke. You gotta help me."

"What happened here?"

"I was just . . ."

Luke cut him off.

"Shut up, Private Windsor."

Luke pointed to another soldier, his lip swollen and bleeding.

"You. Tell me what happened."

"He accused me of stealing his booze. I never touched it. He swung at me first. He would have killed me if the men hadn't stopped him."

"Private Windsor, alcohol in the barracks is strictly prohibited. You are aware of that fact, are you not?"

"Yeah, yeah, yeah."

"You will address me as lieutenant. Is that clear, Private Windsor? Perhaps a week in the guardhouse will improve your recollection of the rules and regulations in His Majesty's army."

Luke pointed to four of the men.

"Please escort Private Windsor to the guard house. Inform the men on duty that he is not to be released until I, personally, have authorized his release. Is that understood?"

"Yes, sir," said the men, in unison.

The rumored reassignment to Gallipoli was realized when the men received new uniforms.

"Hey, Lieutenant, you forgot to tell us about the fancy clothes."

Luke flashed a weak grin.

"Just make sure you get everything you need."

The men loved their new khaki colored, lightweight cotton shorts and matching shirts. They also received sun helmets, which would hold them in good stead when they arrived on the Gallipoli Peninsula. Temperatures in the late summer often exceeded 100°F in the shade.

"What in blazes is this?" asked one of the men.

He waved a several foot-long strip of khaki colored material above his head.

"It's called a puggaree. You wrap it around your sun helmet. It will keep you cooler," said Luke.

"One more thing," he yelled. "Today is your last chance to go home."

The room suddenly grew quiet. Some of the soldiers scratched their head. Luke explained. When the men first enlisted, it was for a period of one year or when the war ended, which ever came first.

"It will soon be your one-year anniversary as a member of this regiment. Is there anyone here who wishes to call it quits and go home?"

For a moment, the only sound in the building came from the buzz of too many flies. Luke spied Reggie in a back corner of the large room, fresh from a one week stay in the guard house. Reggie's head swiveled like a nervous owl. His right hand jerked up and then stopped suddenly. He pretended to be pulling locks of hair over the scar on his forehead. Their eyes met. Reggie blinked first. A loud voice in the back of the room broke the silence.

"Not till I kill me some Huns."

The soldiers cheered and hollered. The men of the 1st Newfoundland Regiment would stick together in life and, if necessary, in death. After a meal of roast beef, potatoes, tomatoes, peas, and plum pudding, the regiment received a warning. There would be an inspection in 30 minutes. Their Supreme Commander, Lord Kitchener, would be on hand to greet the troops.

Luke's dormitory, which he shared with several dozen others, buzzed with activity for the next half hour. The long rows of iron cots, filled with the paraphernalia of war, resembled a beehive in anticipation of the queen bee. Later that evening, the men in parade dress and standing at attention in perfectly straight lines, heard the words they anxiously anticipated for weeks.

"You are just the men I want for the Dardanelles."

The Dardanelles, a narrow strip of water approximately 38 miles long, separated Europe from Asia. Control of the Dardanelles would mean control of the Gallipoli Peninsula. It would have a significant impact on the outcome of the war.

Kitchener's message sent the men into a frenzy, prompting loud cheers which echoed in the night air.

In August of the same year, the regiment, now at full strength, would be transferred to Aldershot. The overnight journey to the 'cradle of the British army' triggered joy and excitement among the men. Aldershot, widely seen as the last stop for British troops before they transferred to Gallipoli, would be the regiment's home for just a few weeks. On August 12, Lord Kitchener visited the men once again. He made his earlier prediction official. The men would soon be shipped to the Dardanelles.

The weeks-long journey took the men to Malta, Alexandria, the harbor at Mudros, and to Sulva Bay, just a few thousand yards from the enemy's trenches.

"Please, Mr. Parsons. Have a seat."

"I believe you know why I asked to meet with you, Mr. Windsor."

"Yes, Mr. Parsons. My assistant said you questioned a permit which your office recently issued."

Clarence Parsons triumphantly tossed the permit on to Windsor's desk.

"That is not my signature."

"So, you say . . . but it does resemble your signature, Mr. Parsons, does it not?"

"It is a forgery."

Windsor leapt from his office chair. At six foot two, he towered over his visitor. He leaned over the desk and used an index finger to poke Clarence in the chest.

"Mr. Parsons, are you suggesting that I am guilty of forgery? Because if you are I will immediately petition the Crown to have you dismissed for the crime of slander and libel. And I will personally see to it that you are punished for such a reckless accusation."

Clarence, red-faced and trembling, retrieved the document from Windsor's hand.

"Mr. Windsor, I am not accusing you, personally, of forgery. I would never . . ."

Reginald Windsor did not allow Clarence to finish his thought.

"Then why in blazes are you here, good sir? Have you nothing better to do with your time than to harass the very people whose hard-earned money supports your livelihood?"

Clarence, his breathing labored and licking his dry lips, turned to leave.

"I apologize for the misunderstanding, Mr. Windsor."

Windsor stepped out from behind his desk. Clarence took a halting step backward. The giant businessman flashed an oversized smile.

"Please, Clarence. May I call you Clarence? We are all friends here, are we not? This entire matter is a simple misunderstanding. I would never question the validity of your signature. Perhaps someone in your office wanted to help, when you were at home recuperating. Oh, please forgive me, I should have inquired earlier. How are you feeling these days? Better, I hope."

Clarence stood motionless, a wide-eyed combination of relief and confusion, covering his face."

"Mr. Windsor, I . . ."

"Reginald, please call me Reginald. There is another matter I wish to discuss with you, Clarence. Walk with me and we can discuss it."

Clarence dutifully followed the huge man as he talked non-stop about the sudden rush of business caused by the war. Windsor expressed frustration with Billy's decision to volunteer with the Newfoundland Regiment and lamented the lack of quality employees. Clarence could only nod his head and occasionally mumble a few words like 'I understand' and 'yes, sir.' When Windsor, his hands firmly grasping the man's shoulders, spun Clarence around and pulled him close, Clarence could smell the stale cigar smoke on the businessman's breath.

"What I'm trying to tell you, Clarence, is that I want you to come to work for me. You would be my new Billy, if you know what I mean. I would double your current salary. Is that acceptable, Clarence?"

"Well, truthfully, Mister, er, I mean Reginald, I'm flattered."

"But does the proposition interest you or would you rather work for the government?"

"Oh, working for the government can be tedious at times. And the income is, shall we say, modest."

"So, you *will* accept my offer."

Windsor did not ask, he assumed.

"Mister, er . . . Reginald, may I have a day or two to consider your very generous offer?"

"Of course, of course. I will have my secretary draw up a contract and deliver it to your home, this afternoon. Thank you, Clarence, I am so happy you stopped by. Here, let me get the door for you."

As Clarence walked in the direction of the government office building, he retrieved the forged document from his suit jacket pocket. A second look at the strange signature triggered a frown. The frown disappeared and was replaced by a smile. In fact, Clarence giggled like a boy. He tore the paper in half and then in half again, carefully placing the pieces in his trouser pocket. Clarence whistled a happy tune all the way back to his desk.

Clarence rarely whistled.

"What's this?" asked Elizabeth, taking a wad of currency from her father's extended hand.

"Extra funds. You will have unexpected expenses, no doubt," he said.

"Is this a peace offering?"

"I suppose it is. I wish to apologize, again, for reading your journal."

"I will accept your apology but only if it is accompanied by your blessing."

"You've made your decision, Elizabeth. What difference will my blessing make?"

Elizabeth reached for his hand and slammed the money in his palm, a scowl on her face.

"Alright, alright. You have my blessing. I hesitated only because I will miss you."

The girl's face softened. Clarence smiled.

"Who's going to make my oatmeal?"

He returned the money, his eyes glassy with tears.

"Please be safe, Elizabeth. And promise me, you will write."

"I will. I promise."

He reached into a pocket and produced an envelope.

"This envelope contains a note. Please wait until you board the ship, before you read it."

"I will. And thank you, Father."

Elizabeth hugged her father, whose stiff embrace resembled a thick wooden plank more than it did a gesture of affection.

Elizabeth would board the *Portia* and head for New York City that afternoon.

The American city, although further in distance, would be the point of deployment for most VADs, assigned to Europe.

As she finished her last-minute packing, the young lady considered all that occurred during her five-weeks of preparation. The training and education required of VAD nurses, while boarding at the Seamens Institute Building, felt more like a passing blizzard. Her mind was a blinding snow storm of medical terminology, military protocols, and matron's admonitions. Matron Hamilton, a woman whose physical appearance and ear-piercing screams more closely resembled an aging banshee, supervised the VAD nurses' training.

"You will perform tasks ranging from basic domestic services to those of a night nurse in sole charge of an entire ward and all manner of work in between," said the matron.

That much responsibility made Elizabeth tremble with anticipation. Her strong desire to be a nurse was not diminished. She looked forward to her overseas assignment. A veteran VAD, home for a respite, tried to warn the new recruits.

"You will clean the wards, serve meals, change beds, and help to bathe and feed severely wounded men. You may even get the opportunity to help the nurses clean and dress wounds or assist in the operating theater," said the older sister. "And the men coming off the battlefield often suffer horrific and badly infected wounds. You will never get used to those sights and sounds."

Elizabeth would earn some money while overseas. Her annual pay would be 20 pounds. She recalled that a parlor maid in St. Johns earned 25 pounds per year. She would also receive a four-pound per year allowance for uniforms.

Her clothing would consist of a gray work dress, hemmed no more than eight inches from the floor. It featured a heavily starched white collar and cuffs to match. She would wear a white bibbed apron over the work dress, adorned with a VAD insignia. There would also be a dress uniform, several hats, and a great coat for outerwear. Most important to Elizabeth would be the widely recognized white kerchief or "veil" that sisters wore as a headpiece while on duty. Elizabeth grinned when she recalled the matron's compliment and the girl's new title.

"Excellent work, Sister Elizabeth."

All the nurses' aides would henceforth be called 'sister.' After weeks of lectures and practical exercises with bandages, splints, and slings, Elizabeth easily passed her exams in Basic First Aid and Home Nursing. When she boarded the trolley, Elizabeth mentally reviewed the lengthy checklist that certified her status as a VAD nurse. The required letters of recommendation from two responsible professionals had been received, from both Dr. Macpherson and Mrs. Newcastle, happy to oblige. The mandated inoculations and vaccines made her a bit queasy but they too had been accomplished. Pages of paper work, two photos, and a total fee of $4.00, earned the girl her first passport.

There would be a shopping trip, to purchase a new pair of boots, a light coat, and a variety of personal items. Elizabeth recalled an earlier conversation.

"Plain with no embroidery at all?" she asked the matron.

"Yes," said the woman, referring to the requirement for a sister's underwear. Elizabeth's night dresses would be similarly boring. She would use some of her father's cash but waited to open the mystery envelope when she reached the docks. The short, businesslike note explained that her father no longer worked for the Crown. He accepted a position with Reginald Windsor as Assistant to the President. Her father now earned a great deal of money. Elizabeth winced. Her anxiety about Mr. Windsor remained. And the frustration with her overly acquiescent father, continued.

Still, she rejoiced for her father. He would be happier working for Mr. Windsor rather than fighting with him.

The weeks-old letter from Elizabeth to Luke included good news and bad news.

Luke's horse, Jewel, sickly during the winter months, never fully recovered. The animal expired several weeks ago. She also complained once again that she had yet to receive a letter from him. She informed him that she was in route to England, her training for a position with the Voluntary Aid Detachment now complete. She would soon be assigned to a hospital in London. Elizabeth promised to send him a new address when it became available.

Perhaps it was Jewel's death or the loss of his childhood mentor on the *Lusitania.* Or maybe the fact that London was attacked by a German Zeppelin (airship), just last week. Either way, Luke suddenly knew what he wanted to tell Elizabeth. He put pen to paper and wrote from the heart.

Dear Elizabeth:

I apologize for not having written sooner. I also apologize for being skeptical about your desire and ability to enter the medical field. Clearly, I was mistaken.

I should like to tell you, that for the first time in my life, I feel as if my knowledge and experience have been recognized. That revelation came in the form of a promotion. In the British Army, anyway, money and status do not matter.

In addition, the death of my father has triggered an epiphany. For many years, I nurtured a tiny hope that he would one day respect me and love me, the way a father should, his son. And now I am forced to admit that it will never happen. He is gone and there is nothing I can do to remedy the situation. Additional angst would be a waste of emotional energy. It is time for me to move on.

I do not wish to be like my father. I want to love and be loved. Perhaps you and I can start over. You know . . . one jackass to another.

Affectionally,
2nd Lt. Luke Hobbs

Elizabeth and her colleagues, replete with new uniforms, boarded the *Saint Paul,* in route to England.

As the ship moved out of New York Harbor, two American destroyers constantly circled the steamer's bow and stern. Elizabeth compared the battleships to playful porpoises. In fact, they guarded against attacks from German submarines. She did not fully appreciate their purpose, however, suffering from seasickness for the entirety of her trip.

The nine-day journey included additional vaccines and high seas which made her nauseous for most of the trip. When the ship neared the British Isles, the American protective detail disappeared. Two British destroyers took their place. Elizabeth's last night at sea would be spent sitting on the deck, wearing a life belt and holding a small bag containing her valuables. Such was the captain's fear of attacks by German U-boats.

After docking at Liverpool, the VAD nurses boarded the train to London. They would stay at Queen Mary's Hostel for Nurses. The mistress of the palatial mansion introduced herself.

"My name is Mrs. Kerr Lawson. I will be your host until you are assigned to a hospital."

Elizabeth, mesmerized by every room, delighted in her surroundings. Her self-conducted tour included a writing room in the basement, complete with tables, Moroccan chairs, stationery, and electric lights. She also discovered a billiard room, oil paintings of Queen Victoria and King Edward, a library filled with medical books, a huge dining room, a sitting room, a parlor, and an oak staircase that led to countless bedrooms and bath chambers. Her glowing smile triggered a friendly warning from the mistress of the house.

"You will not be here for long, I'm afraid."

"That is most unfortunate," said Elizabeth.

In the next two days, Elizabeth toured the Lincoln Hospital, the Northern General Hospital, and the Wandsworth hospital, all located in London. Her assignment would be at the Third London General Hospital. A series of wooden huts, unconnected to the hospital but very nearby, would be her new home. She would share her hut with another VAD volunteer.

Quick notes to Luke and her father apprised them of her new address.

"You will be awakened at 5:30 each morning, have breakfast, and be in your respective wards, no later than 7 a.m. Is that clear?"

"Yes, matron," said the nurses, in unison.

"At 7 a.m., the sister in charge will knock on one of the tables, which is your signal to stand for morning prayers. We say the Lord's Prayer and there is a blessing afterwards. Understood?"

Elizabeth, quickly losing patience with the paramilitary nature of her new assignment, absentmindedly allowed her eyes to roll. The matron noticed.

"Sister Parsons. Am I boring you?"

Elizabeth stood erect, a transparent veil of hot pink covering her face.

"No, Matron. Not at all."

The Matron went on to delineate their daily obligations. They included the cleaning and dusting of furniture, fetching hot water, sweeping and scrubbing the floors, thirty minutes for a lunch break, laundry, changing bed clothes. A variety of other tasks that would be assigned by the matron or the VAD nurse supervisors.

"That is all. You may now return to your huts. Sister Parsons, come with me."

The Matron marched to a tiny office and stood behind the desk, a scowl on her face.

"You will be given no time for lunch tomorrow but will instead report to me in the Recovery Room. And you will not keep me waiting, is that understood?"

"Yes, Matron."

"Dismissed."

As she left the matron's office, a queasy feeling in her stomach, not unlike that which she experienced on the *St. Paul*, forced Elizabeth to skip the evening meal.

Chapter Seven

SERVING IN LONDON AND GALLIPOLI

Companies A, B, and C of the 1st Newfoundland Regiment landed on the shores of Sulva Bay at three o'clock on the morning of September 20, 1915.

When the morning sun made its appearance, so also did the Turkish Army. They gave the Newfoundland Regiment a very warm welcome. A barrage of artillery pummeled the men in a hailstorm of shells and shrapnel. On three sides of their landing zone, steep inclines of up to 900 feet stood between them and the rocky scrub-covered flats of Sulva Plain. Allied and Turkish trenches, located on the plain and in many instances just yards from each other, would house the combatants for months to come. Fortunately, the cliff-like structures provided some cover for the regiment, but only after a mad dash across the open beach. Although no soldier died in the landing operation, more than a dozen of the men would be wounded.

Billy Windsor, with Company C, disembarked and made it to the base of the cliff-like terrain, just before sunrise. Company A, which included Luke and Reggie, did not fare so well. Luke led the charge of his fifty-man patrol, stopping several times for wounded men and once for Reggie.

"Reggie! If you lie on the beach you will die on the beach."

Sweating profusely and trembling like a leaf in the wind, Reggie refused to move.

"I don't wanna die. Help me. Help me please."

Luke grabbed Reggie by the collar of his uniform, pulled him to his feet, and pushed hard. When they got to the steep incline, Luke barked.

"Now start digging."

Reggie did not have to be told twice. The sand flew everywhere. In moments the frightened man created a foxhole large enough to accommodate several men. After surveying his immediate environment and counting heads, Luke concluded that his entire platoon, except for two slightly wounded men, survived the landing. Luke reached for his canteen, hoping for a celebratory drink of water. When only a few drops fell onto his waiting tongue, Luke examined the empty cannister.

A bullet hole on each side of the metal container explained what happened to the water.

Within days, the 1076 men of the 1st Newfoundland Regiment took responsibility for a one-mile stretch of the British front line.

The regiment's portion of the lengthy trench formed a triangle without its bottom. The men who originally dug the six-foot-deep ditch made a foolish mistake. The triangular trench would expose the new arrivals to fire on two sides. The trench, less than a yard wide, included a fire step, which allowed the men to aim and fire their weapons above the parapet. The parapet, usually six to twelve inches in height and extending a foot or more above the trench wall, consisted of the dirt which resulted from digging the trench. Luke instructed his men to settle in as this would be their home for weeks to come. In the beginning, the soldiers would spend four days in the trenches followed by eight days of respite in the rest dugouts. That would change over time.

"Lieutenant Hobbs, when will we get some water?"

That question, asked by many of the men up and down the line, plagued Luke and every other officer in the regiment. Five large lighter ships, loaded with 80,000 gallons of freshwater and scheduled to arrive just behind the troops, arrived 24 hours late. Enemy attacks, and a collision among the ships, reduced the water-transport fleet to just two boats. The ship that arrived at Sulva Bay, ran aground on a nearby sandbar. Its hoses could not reach the shore line. The men of Company C, Billy Windsor among them, broke ranks, charged the beach, and entered the water. Some of the men, unwilling to wait their turn, stabbed the hoses and filled their canteens from the leakage. Most of the fresh water spilled into the sea. It required weeks of rationing and several rainfalls to make the shortage go away.

In October, when the rainy season began, there would be too much water.

"Keep your head down, Private. The Turk snipers are on duty, 24 hours a day."

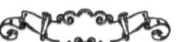

Luke regularly walked the length of his platoon's trench. The fifty soldiers in his care, custody, and control needed to hear his message and hear it often. Even a few seconds of exposure could cost a man his head. Literally.

"A sniper's bullet might be better than these bloody flies," said one of the men, waving furiously in the air.

"You can shoo the flies away, Private. It's not so easy with bullets," said Luke.

The flies came in swarms. The unburied bodies of both British and Turkish soldiers lay in no man's land, between the two combatants' trenches. Many of them, bloated beyond recognition by the sun's heat, remained above ground for weeks. Rats as large as cats could be seen feasting on the dead bodies. When the rodents tunneled into a dead man's chest cavity or bowels, the victim would appear to be alive, its body quivering and pulsating with movement. Any attempts at retrieval during the day would mean almost certain death for the stretcher bearers.

Removing the bodies at night required lights and posed a similar danger.

Several hundred yards down the line, at Company C's location, Billy Windsor offered a suggestion with respect to Turk snipers.

"Let's give the snipers what they want."

"What do you mean, Windsor?" asked the Lieutenant.

Billy explained how a helmet at the end of a bayonet would surely attract a sniper's attention. He proposed that one of their own marksmen use a periscope. The crude device, made of two small mirrors and wood, allowed a soldier to spy on the enemy, while remaining in the trench.

"We then expose the helmet a second time, a few yards from the first.

When the sniper lines up his second shot, I will line up the sniper."

"It just might work," said the officer.

In short order, the men arranged for a helmet to appear inches above the parapet. Seconds later, a shot rang out. The helmet flew across the trench.

"I see him," said Billy. "Do it again."

The men chose a spot three or four yards away from the location of the first "sniper victim."

"Tell us when you're ready, Billy."

"I'm ready."

The helmet bobbed a few times. The men then held it aloft, just inches above the earthen parapet. The sniper fired again. Billy did the same. He saw an explosion of red instead of the sniper's head.

"Got him!" he shouted.

The men cheered.

"Our first patient will be Private Thomas," said the matron.

"And what are the nature of his injuries?" asked Elizabeth.

"He's been shot in the thigh."

"I understand."

"I doubt that very much," said the matron.

Elizabeth followed the matron into the next ward, struggling as she walked. The novice nurse carried a heavy satchel filled with bandages, a bottle of solution, scissors, rubber tubing, and a variety of medical instruments.

"Private Thomas, this is Sister Parsons. She will be tending to your thigh this morning. She is still in training, but I will supervise. Your patience is appreciated."

"Yes, Sister, of course. And may I say that your assistant is a very beautiful young lady."

Elizabeth blushed.

"Why thank you, Private Thomas."

The matron scowled.

"Sister Parsons. We do not engage in such talk at London General."

"I apologize, Matron. It won't happen again."

Elizabeth looked to the matron with a bewildered look on her face.

"How shall I proceed?"

"First, we remove the bandages that are wrapped around the thigh. Then, we remove the bandages that have been packed into the wound."

Elizabeth unwrapped the bandages which circled the man's right thigh, six inches above his knee. When the wound came into view, Elizabeth swallowed hard.

"Oh my."

"Sister Parsons, such reactions are neither necessary nor professional. Please refrain from such comments in the future."

"Yes, Matron. I apologize."

"Use the forceps to remove the bandages that are inside the wound. And please be gentle."

Elizabeth probed deeper into the wound. The patient groaned in pain. She pulled more than two yards of bandage from the gaping hole, most of it stained red and green by blood and pus. The foul odor of putrefaction assaulted her nostrils. Elizabeth, in a hurry to finish her grisly task, yanked on the bandage. The patient hollered. Her stomach churned. She turned away.

"Sister Parsons. You *must* focus on the wound."

"I'm sorry, Mr. Thomas. I am truly sorry," she said.

"Please get on with it, Sister Parsons. Our time with each patient is limited."

When the bandage was entirely removed, Elizabeth stared at the gaping wound which ran five to six inches in length and very nearly penetrated the thickness of the man's thigh. She reached for a clean bandage.

"No, Sister Parsons. We must now debride the wound."

"I don't understand."

"You must cut away the dead tissue. Use the dissecting scissors. Begin with the exterior perimeter and work your way inside the wound."

Elizabeth held her breath. She cut dead skin from the edge of the wound and removed several pieces of obviously dead tissue from within the wound.

"You must now remove all debris from the wound. That includes loose pieces of dead tissue, dirt, thread, insects, and whatever else is foreign to human flesh. Please be thorough."

When finished, Elizabeth reached for the clean roll of bandages, once again.

"No, Sister Parsons. You must now irrigate the wound with Dakin's solution. Use the soiled bandages to collect the excess fluid."

"Yes, Matron."

"Please explain to our patient the main ingredient contained in Dakin's solution and for what purpose it is utilized."

Elizabeth, totally lost, turned to the older woman, her puzzled eyes opened wide.

"Very well, Sister Parsons. It is a solution of heavily diluted sodium hypochlorite. In layman's terms, it is a weak bleach."

"I understand, Matron."

"No. I don't think you do understand. What is the purpose and what are the benefits of Dakin's solution?"

Elizabeth smiled confidently.

"It cleans the wound."

"No, Sister Parsons, it sterilizes the wound. You do know the difference between sterile and clean, do you not?"

"No, Matron."

"The solution sterilizes the wound and acts as a solvent on the dead tissue and pus. Dakin's solution, however, does not damage any of the healthy tissue."

"I under . . ."

Elizabeth suddenly realized the extent of her ignorance.

"I think I have much to learn."

"Sister Parsons. Are we ready to close and stitch the wound or shall we bandage it once again?"

Elizabeth stuttered.

"I, I, I'm not certain."

"We will not close the wound until the bacterial matter has been eliminated and the wound is sterile. The presence of pus tells us that is not the case. Please pack the wound and then wrap the leg."

Packing the wound proved particularly painful for Private Thomas. He twitched repeatedly, drew several sharp breaths, and grunted. Elizabeth flinched throughout the procedure. When she finished, she looked at matron with a victorious smile on her face. Matron addressed the patient instead.

"Thank you for your patience, Private Thomas. Please come with me, Sister Parsons."

Elizabeth dutifully followed the matron to her office at the far end of the floor. The older woman stopped at the closed door, spun in place, and confronted Elizabeth, her eyes blazing.

"In the future, Sister Parsons, if you should find yourself bored, may I suggest you read the latest medical bulletins about the treatment of gunshot wounds. It is clear to me that, at present, you know only how to roll your eyes."

Elizabeth fought to keep her composure, blinking away the tears.

"Yes, Matron."

When Elizabeth completed the balance of her chores, she skipped the evening meal and fell into bed. She wrote a short note to Luke.

You were right. I will never be a nurse.

Elizabeth

"I've never been to a lumber camp. Are you sure you want me there?"

Clarence Parsons, overwhelmed with the number of tasks assigned to him by Reginald Windsor, tried his best to avoid the day-long trip to Trinity Bay.

"I want you with me, Clarence. I need your head."

"Why?"

"The numbers are not adding up and I own half of that place. It's time my partner and I had a little talk."

Clarence did not enjoy the ride to Trinity Bay. Unable to open the passenger side window because of freezing temperatures, Clarence struggled to breathe. The vehicle, filled with Reginald Windsor's cigar smoke, could not reach the lumber camp quickly enough. In between fits of coughing, Clarence pressed his boss for details.

"Tell me about the lumber camp."

"The Windsor Land and Lumber Company works with a dozen different contractors. Typically, the contractors own the lumber camps, pay the men working in the woods, and deliver the harvest to companies like us. I thought I could add to my profit margins by owning a portion of a lumber camp. A partnership with a contractor seemed like a good idea." Windsor paused. "At the time."

"So, what's the problem?"

"My partner, his name is Girard, says we can't get help and blames the war for the lack of workers. He wants to pay the men more but he knows we are not making any money as it is. And the haul-off starts in December."

"What's the haul-off?"

"It's when we deliver the lumber to the mills. First, the lumber must be cut into four-foot sections. Next, we employ loaders to pile the wood onto horse-drawn sleds. Then, we have teamsters to drive the sleds and tend to the horses. We also have roadmen to clear the roadway and finally, we have landers who unload the wood when it gets to the mill."

"I'll run the numbers when I get there. This fellow, Girard, do you trust him?"

"Yes. Until you tell me I can't."

After an overnight stay in the village, Windsor and Clarence spent all morning at the lumber camp.

"Mr. Windsor, may I speak with you please?"

Clarence looked at Girard. And then at Mr. Windsor.

"Alone, please?"

Girard scowled and stormed out of the cabin which served as the lumber camp's office.

"What did you find out?"

"Not much from the books. I learned a lot more from the guy that does the counting."

"The scaler?"

"Yes. He decides how much wood each man has cut during a work day. Is that correct?" asked Clarence.

"Yes."

"He says the men are getting the worst lots on the mountain. Calls them chances, I think."

"Yes. Each man gets a section of the forest, usually 100 meters by a thousand kilometers. We expect at least a cord and a half per day. Why does he say the chances are lousy? I walked this mountain myself. There is lots of good lumber out there."

"Most of your men are on the wrong side of the mountain. Steep terrain, wood that is difficult to harvest, wet conditions, and so on. My scaler friend also let it slip that he got here late because he was on the other side of the mountain."

"But I own both sides."

"In my opinion, there's another crew out there and they are not working for you."

Windsor jumped to his feet, breathing heavy and red in the face.

"I'll kill that bastard. I'll kill that bastard with my bare hands."

Clarence tried to intervene.

"Mr. Windsor, may I suggest you say nothing at this time. Send someone up here you can trust. Have him walk the entire property and talk to the men. We will give him written authorization from you. If he is chased off, you will know for certain. If he is allowed to do his investigation and makes a report, you will have all the evidence required for the authorities."

Reginald took a deep breath. He squinted one eye and pointed at Clarence.

"You're a smart fellow, Parsons."

The two men walked into the yard ready to leave.

"Well, I should at least say goodbye to the scoundrel," said Reginald.

Clarence nodded. Reginald shouted to one of the yard hands.

"Where is Girard?"

"I saw him walking toward the loading yard," said one of the hired hands.

Clarence and his employer walked amongst a half-dozen stacks of cut wood, all of them piled high. They did not find Girard. As the duo turned toward the automobile, Clarence noticed some movement.

"Watch out!"

He pushed hard, shoving Mr. Windsor from the path of falling logs. Clarence fell forward. Several logs struck Clarence in the leg. He was pinned to the ground. He screamed in agony. Several men came running. They pulled the logs off his leg. One of them helped Clarence to his feet. Reginald escaped injury.

"Can you move your legs?" asked one of the men.

Clarence, gritting his teeth and panting, mumbled a response.

"Yes, I think so."

They carried Clarence into the office.

"When you're ready, Clarence, try standing," said Reginald.

Clarence, able to put weight on both legs, smiled through his pain.

"It's not broken, anyway."

Reginald stepped forward, white with fear.

"I could have been killed, Clarence. You saved my life."

Clarence used a hand to wave off Windsor's comment.

"You would have done the same for me. It was nothing, really."

"Help him to my car, men. And tell Girard, we are leaving."

Reginald Windsor drove the luxury car back to St. John's without benefit of a single cigar.

Despite his pain, Clarence enjoyed the ride.

Elizabeth, unsatisfied with her performance in front of the matron and up half the night thinking about it, vowed to do better.

She vowed to never again be humiliated by ignorance, lack of skill, mediocre effort, or attitude. The matron's demands continued, unabated. Elizabeth welcomed the opportunity to prove herself. The girl worked ten times harder. She scrubbed floors, polished silver, dusted furniture, emptied bed pans, changed dirty bed linens, and gave sponge baths to dozens of bedridden patients. When an orderly, his boots covered with mud, walked across her spotlessly clean and freshly waxed hardwood floor, Elizabeth considered using the mop as a lethal weapon. Instead, she said nothing and cleaned up the mess.

When Elizabeth voluntarily assisted with chores assigned to other VAD nurses, the matron took notice. Elizabeth rarely took a break for lunch and often skipped the meal, entirely.

"Mail call, Sister Elizabeth."

Elizabeth received letters from her father, Mrs. Newcastle, Mrs. Hynes, and two more from Luke. They would have to wait until she returned to her hut. She continued with her assigned work and then volunteered for duty in the recovery room, the kitchen, the laundry, and elsewhere. She did this for weeks on end, with nary a comment, compliment, or even a thank-you from the matron. The patients and her fellow nurses fell in love with her. Elizabeth seemed to be everywhere at once, selflessly assisting staff and patients in any way she could.

"Sister Parsons."

Elizabeth's stomach did a flip-flop. The matron's loud voice, even when it invaded Elizabeth's dreams, made the VAD nurse tremble and sweat.

"Yes, Matron."

"I have been accosted by no less than a dozen patients in the recovery ward."

"Have they complained about my work, Matron. If so, I apologize and will do better."

"On the contrary, Sister Parsons. They speak highly of you and are truly grateful for your care and attention. If anything, they are concerned about your health and welfare. They are worried that you are working to the point of complete exhaustion."

"But I have said nothing, Matron. I did my work and then moved on."

"And so I have been told. Sister Parsons, in a few short weeks you have become an exemplary VAD nurse and have single-handedly made this hospital a better place. I am most pleased with your progress and quite impressed. I would like to thank you."

Elizabeth, almost afraid to breathe, stammered a response.

"It is I who thank *you,* Matron. I have done no more than follow your example."

"I should also like to tell you that every surgeon in the OR has commented on your work in the post-op portion of the recovery room. Clearly, you have impressed them."

"Thank you, Matron. It is a pleasure to work with each of them."

"This is good. Because you will report to the operating theater first thing Monday morning, at 7 a.m. sharp. Several of the surgeons have requested you by name."

Elizabeth blinked back the tears.

"But first, you will return to your hut and spend the entire weekend catching up on your sleep and eating healthy meals. And that's an order."

Elizabeth, in shock, watched as the matron turned and marched in the opposite direction. The woman stopped suddenly and pivoted.

"Elizabeth."

The young volunteer grew wide-eyed and smothered a gasp with both hands. The matron called her by first name.

"Yes, Matron?"

"I am very proud of you, young lady. Very, very proud of you."

For the first time ever, Elizabeth saw the matron smile.

Elizabeth returned to her hut and cried tears of joy.

She quickly read the letters from her father, Mrs. Newcastle, and Mrs. Hynes. They contained a great deal of good news. Clarence and Mr. Windsor were getting along fine. Mrs. Newcastle and Mrs. Hynes now worked as a team, each of them, grateful for the assistance. Elizabeth saved Luke's letters for last, crying a bit more when she read his words about wanting to love and be loved. Elizabeth laughed loudly when she read about his desire to start over, 'one jackass to another.'

The second letter from Luke reminded Elizabeth that the words in her last missive were no longer true. She could hear Luke's stern but eloquent voice.

> ***"I will assume that you experienced a particularly difficult day and wrote those words in a dejected and depressed state of mind. I will also assume that you have recovered from this temporary aberration and will soon return to your usual outrageously confident and opinionated self.***
>
> ***I am therefore rejoicing. I refuse to correspond with a woman who, for no reason other than an old and bitter matron, would give up her life's dream."***

The letter was signed, 'Affectionately, Second Lieutenant Luke Hobbs.'

Elizabeth laughed even as the tears rolled down her cheeks.

"What's a blighty? asked Reggie.

"It's when your wounds are serious enough to get you shipped back to London but not so serious as to be fatal."

The explanation, from a fellow enlisted man, got Reggie to thinking. He waited until nightfall and approached one of his drinking buddies, George Bower. Bower never had any money and constantly bummed cigarettes from his mates.

"Bower, come sit with me for a minute," said Reggie.

The man rushed to Reggie's side. Reggie offered Bower a cigarette. When Bower searched his pockets for a light, Reggie obliged the man with the red-hot tip of his cigar. Bower, who lost a tooth in a St. John's bar fight, grinned like a jack-o-lantern.

"Thank you, Reggie."

"How would you like to make five pounds, Bower?"

"I sure as blazes, would. What do I have to do?"

"I'll give you five pounds if you shoot me in the foot."

"Have you gone mad?"

"Not hardly. I need a blighty so I can get out of here."

"Five pounds?"

"Got it right here," said Reggie, waving the note in Bower's face.

Bower reached for his rifle. He pointed the weapon but stood in front of Reggie, motionless.

"Well, what are you waiting for?"

"It don't seem right, Reggie."

"I'll tell 'em it was an accident when you were cleaning your rifle."

Bower looked in every direction. He tightened his grip and placed his index finger on the trigger.

"Are you ready?"

"Gentlemen."

Both men stopped breathing. Bower jerked the rifle to his left side and saluted.

"Sir."

"Good evening," said Lieutenant Hobbs.

Reggie glared as he saluted. Bower started blabbering.

"Lieutenant, we was just kidding around. I mean Reggie and me, we're good friends, aren't we Reggie? I would never shoot him on purpose or anything like that. And Reggie sure as heck wouldn't pay me, would you Reggie?"

Reggie barked.

"Shut your trap, Bower."

Luke stepped closer to Reggie, brushing some invisible dust from the enlistee's shoulder. Reggie jerked away, his voice trembling with fear.

"Now Luke, you don't really want to lose your temper over such a little thing, do you? I mean we didn't mean no harm or nothing. You know what I mean?"

Luke dropped his head and grimaced, as if Reggie hurt his feelings.

"Reggie, you're supposed to address me as Lieutenant. Don't you remember?"

Reggie cleared his throat.

"I forgot. Lieutenant, sir."

Luke turned to Bower.

"Am I right, Bower? Isn't he supposed to address me as Lieutenant."

"Yes sir, Lieutenant. That's right."

As Bower spoke, Luke reached for the man's rifle. Bower did not resist. Luke aimed the weapon at Reggie's foot and placed his finger on the trigger. Reggie took a deep breath and held it.

"Reggie. Do you know the penalty for a soldier who willfully maims himself with the intent to render himself unfit for service?"

"No, sir."

"Well, there's a court martial of course. And then they throw you in prison. I figure twenty years of hard labor, at least. They might even execute you. Both of you."

Bower paled. Reggie flinched. Luke handed the weapon back to Bower. He glanced at both men.

"Do you understand what I have told you?"

"Yes sir," they said in unison."

When Luke turned to leave, his back to the men, he spoke to the night sky.

"And Reggie, the execution detail won't charge you a shilling. They will kill you for free."

Reggie snarled quietly and threw his cigar to the ground. Bower rushed to pick it up, dusting off the dirt, and grinning triumphantly.

"Thanks, Reggie."

"Go to hell, Bower."

Billy, despite the cold, fell into a fitful sleep using a high spot in the trenches as his bed.

A hand pulling on his shoulder woke him after what he thought was less than one hour's sleep. In fact, he slept till dawn. Billy jumped to his feet.

"What's the matter?"

"Nothing. It's time to stand at arms."

Billy quickly recalled a soldier's daily regimen. Every morning at daybreak and again at dusk, each man stood on the fire step with bayonets fixed. The precaution, taken at the most likely times of an enemy attack, insured the regiment's readiness. At the same time, a lieutenant stopping every three or four yards, distributed a periscope. Billy, passed over for the next guy in line, flashed a wide grin. The oblong tube of tin or wood, included angled mirrors at the top and bottom. This allowed a sentry to keep his head below the parapet and still observe the ground in front of him. Periscope duty, however, could be dangerous. A sniper's bullet might easily shatter the device, spraying shards of broken mirror into a soldier's eye.

With no suspicious activity being seen, the men spent the rest of their day accomplishing various 'fatigues.' (Work assignments.)

"Windsor, take four men with you and see what you can do to repair the trench, just west of here. It's that section right after the bend. Took a direct hit last night," said the lieutenant.

"Yes, sir," said Billy, motioning to the nearest soldiers.

"Bring your shovels, boys."

Billy led the way. Moments later he suddenly stopped.

"Halt."

An artillery shell from yesterday's attack had destroyed the parapet and caused the trench walls to cave in. Unless the men crouched low, their heads would be exposed to sniper fire.

"Well . . . I'm the shortest, so I'll go first," said Billy.

He used his entrenchment tool to clear the fire step and rebuild the dirt berm which served as a parapet. After 10 minutes of shoveling, the soldiers moved forward, working with Billy to finish the repairs. The sudden crack of rifle fire triggered a frenzy. They threw their tools to the ground. Billy lunged for his weapon. A man's wild screams filled the air.

"Allah. Allah. Allah."

Billy hopped onto the fire step and peaked over the parapet. A Turk soldier, covered in blood and running toward Billy, pointed his rifle. Billy fell back, pushing two of the recruits out of harm's way. He dropped to his knees, aiming his rifle at the spot where he thought the bearded man's head would appear. Billy and the Turk fired simultaneously. The fighter's face disappeared in an explosion of blood, bone, and brain matter. Billy flew backwards, his back slamming into the dirt wall. The crazed man without the face fell to his knees. For a few long seconds, he knelt in prayer clutching his rifle instead of a hymnal. The dead man plummeted headfirst into the trench, landing in six inches of mud. A brown muck, streaked with crimson red, mercifully hid the man's missing face. One of the soldiers yelled.

"Billy's been hit!"

Another man screamed for a stretcher.

"I'm all right. I'm all right," Billy mumbled, his eyelids fluttering to a close.

The stretcher bearers struggled to navigate the narrow trench. They took pains not to bump, much less dump, their critically wounded patient.

Billy's bib of dark red blood doubled in size during the time it took to deliver him to the regimental aid post. The medical facility, no more than a room-sized dugout some 300 yards behind the front line, housed the regimental medical officer plus two orderlies. When Billy's unconscious body arrived, the medical officer shook his head.

"He's not going to make it, boys."

"You gotta try, Doc," said one of the men.

"I'm no doctor, kid. I wish I was."

The officer sliced Billy's shirt, revealing a gaping hole on the right side of the boy's chest, very near the clavicle. He stuffed the bloody hole with a strip of white bandage. He then injected the wounded man with a serum for tetanus and then again, with morphine sulfate. The medical officer then used indelible ink to mark Billy's forehead with a cross.

"What's that for?" asked one of the men.

"That's to tell the men at the clearing station he's already had a shot of morphine. The casualty clearing station is not equipped to operate. There's nothing more there than a large tent, at the base of the cliffs. He will be moved to a hospital ship as soon as possible."

The converted passenger liners included operating theaters and a full medical staff.

"Get him on a shuttle to the *Maheno*. It's anchored in the open sea but it's safer and better than all the other hospital ships."

A fishing trawler, marked with a large red cross, brought Billy to Anzac Cove where the *Maheno* was docked. Once alongside the *Maheno*, the ship's derricks were used to winch Billy's stretcher onto the boat, through its unusual side doors.

Billy, still unconscious, underwent surgery, less than one hour after he was shot.

"Are you certain?" asked Luke.

"Yes sir. Billy Windsor. Probably the best liked guy in Company C," said the messenger.

"How bad is it?"

"He took one in the chest. The medical officer didn't think he was going to make it. Is it true, Lieutenant? Billy's older brother is in your platoon?"

"Yes. I'll tell him myself. Tell me exactly what happened?"

The man explained in detail how Billy pushed members of his work crew to one side and exchanged fire with the mad Turk.

"How did the Turk get across no man's land without being shot?" asked Luke.

"The guy was shot three times before he got to Billy. But Billy got him in the head."

"Sit down, Reggie."

"What did I do now?"

"Nothing. This is about Billy."

"What about him?"

"He's been shot."

Reggie blinked a few times and jumped to his feet. He shook a finger in Luke's face.

"The ole man is gonna be really mad. Are you sure?"

"I'm sure."

"Can I see him?"

"No. He's on a hospital ship in Anzac Cove. They will probably move him to London, if he makes it through surgery."

"Surgery?"

"Reggie. He took one in the chest."

Reggie shook his head in disgust.

"Stupid kid. I told him to stay home."

"That stupid kid pushed two of his men out of harm's way and killed the bastard that shot him. I'd say Billy deserves a medal for valor."

"Well, I ain't getting shot for no medal. Are we through here?"

"Yes, Reggie. We're through."

Reggie fumed as he navigated the muddy trench back to his work station. He just assumed that he would return to Newfoundland a hero. Not Billy. Billy barely qualified for military duty. He was all brains and no brawn. Reggie muttered.

"Billy gets all the luck."

Elizabeth arrived a half hour early on her first day in the operating theater.

The former orphanage-turned hospital now included electric lifts, an x-ray department, a room for insane patients, and a state-of-the-art operating room.

"May I help you? You look a bit lost," said the uniformed officer.

Elizabeth took a sharp breath. The man wore the uniform of a lieutenant-colonel in the British army.

"No, sir, I mean, I'm not lost. I guess I'm exploring. I'm not due in the operating theater until 7:30. I've only recently been assigned here and I wanted to get familiar with my new home."

"I understand. My name is Bruce Porter. I serve as London General's commanding officer."

The lieutenant-colonel extended his hand. Elizabeth responded with a firm handshake.

"Elizabeth Parsons, sir. An honor to meet you."

"I hope you are pleased with the facility, Sister Parsons. There is still much to be done, I'm afraid."

"Yes, sir. Quite impressive, in my opinion. And the bronze statue of Lord Kitchener at the entrance is spectacular."

"Thank you, Sister. Forgive me for asking, but a VAD nurse in the operating theater? A bit unusual is it not?"

"So I am told, sir. Matron tells me I was requested by the surgeons."

"A high compliment indeed. My congratulations."

"Thank you, sir."

"And from your manner of speaking, am I correct to assume that you are not a native?"

"Newfoundland, sir."

"The Commonwealth is most fortunate to have the loyalty of its colonials. Welcome to our humble island."

"You are most gracious, Lieutenant-Colonel."

"And you, Sister Parsons, are most impressive. Please let me know if I can be of any assistance to you. It would be my distinct pleasure."

"How very thoughtful of you, sir. Thank you, Lieutenant-Colonel Porter. Thank you very much."

"You must be the new VAD. I am the nurse supervisor, Alice McLean."

"Elizabeth Parsons, ma'am."

"Well, Sister Parsons, do exactly as you are told and you will be allowed to remain here."

"Yes, ma'am. I will do my best."

"You have been assigned to Dr. Browning. He is the senior surgeon here at in London General."

Nurse McLean's head suddenly swiveled in every direction. She leaned forward, her voice now a conspiratorial whisper.

"He is particularly fond of VAD nurses."

Elizabeth, her eyes wide, wondered if she should thank the woman. Somehow, it did not seem appropriate. She mumbled instead.

"I understand."

A short thin man, with jet black hair and a pencil thin mustache, approached the women.

"Nurse McLean. Is this our new VAD?"

"Yes, Dr. Browning. This is Sister Parsons."

The doctor reached for Elizabeth's hand. She returned the gesture but the man did not release his grip. He stroked the woman's arm with his remaining hand.

"I trust you are as skilled as you are beautiful, Sister Parsons."

Nurse McLean, standing behind the surgeon, allowed her head to drop. She used a hand to shade her eyes from the glaring nature of the man's suggestive response. A cold shiver with goosebumps crawled from the back of Elizabeth's neck down to the length of her arms. The doctor continued caressing her arm with his long, cold, bony fingers. Elizabeth jerked her hand away, reached for a handkerchief, and feigned a huge sneeze.

"Bless you, Elizabeth," he said.

The surgeon's use of her first name, confirmed Elizabeth's growing fears.

"Thank you, Dr. Browning."

"Scrub up. You will be assisting me with a leg wound this morning."

Elizabeth followed the doctor but turned her head to catch a last-minute glimpse of nurse McLean. The older woman's eyes rolled to the top of her head. She mouthed but did not speak her parting words.

"Good luck."

"Where am I?"

Billy's eyes darted in every direction, settling on the older man peering at his bandaged chest.

"You're on the *Maheno*, a hospital ship. You *should* be in a pine box. We are headed for London."

Billy struggled to keep his eyes open.

"What happened?"

"You don't remember?"

"No, sir."

"You took a bullet in the chest. Extreme right side. Went through and through. Didn't hit the ribs, the lung, or any major vessels. The bleeding stopped on its own. You're in good shape for a man who should be dead."

Billy closed his eyes. His body jerked and he winced.

"Are you in pain?"

"I remember now. The men. Were they hit? Are they all right?"

"One of them came with the stretcher guys. Said you saved his life and his buddy too. You were the only one that got shot."

"And that crazy mad Turk who ran across no man's land. What happened to him?"

"He stopped one of your bullets with his head. They buried him last night."

Billy took a long deep breath. His eyes fluttered shut. He slept for most of the journey to London.

The medical staff on board the *Maheno* called him their miracle boy.

Reginald Windsor marched into Clarence Parsons' office without knocking or announcing himself.

He tossed a telegram on to Parsons' desk, chomping on his unlit cigar and rolling it from one side of his mouth to the other. Parsons read the telegram.

SINCERELY REGRET INFORM YOU N861 PRIVATE WILLIAM WINDSOR, FIRST NEWFOUNDLAND REGIMENT, CO. C, WOUNDED IN ACTION.

ADJUTANT GENERAL

Clarence stared into Reginald Windsor's glassy eyes. They flashed with fear and frustration. The old man gnawed on an unlit cigar.

"How can I be of assistance, Mr. Windsor?"

"I want him back home. As soon as possible."

"I'll visit with all the Crown bureaucrats I can locate, but I suspect your political friends will be more helpful."

"You are most likely correct. Oh, I almost forgot. You were also correct about my partner, Girard."

"Did you send anybody out there to check on him?"

"Yes. The bastard admitted it. Said he'd pay me back as long as I didn't throw him in jail."

"What did you do?"

"I didn't need the money, so I threw him in jail."

"Yes, sir."

Luke Hobbs, although anxious, acknowledged the captain's orders, without comment. He would lead a six-man reconnaissance patrol into no-man's land. The night time exercise would be considered a success if they brought a prisoner back to the British lines. Field intelligence would be Luke's primary goal. The amount and location of barbed wire (used to protect the enemy's trenches), the location of freshly dug trenches, machine gun placements, and sniper nests, along with estimates of troop strength, would all be useful to the higher-ups.

Minutes later, Luke yelled.

"I need six volunteers for recon patrol, tonight."

A sprinkling of hands rose in the air. Reggie, uncharacteristically quiet, chomped on his cigar.

"I need one more," said Luke.

Reggie, thinking about Billy and a medal for valor, motioned with his hand.

"I'll go."

Luke's eyes opened wide.

"Thank you, Reggie. Keep that up and you might get a reputation for being a good soldier in his Majesty's army."

Luke cautioned each man to bring three empty sandbags and their entrenchment tool.

"Concealment is the name of the game," said Luke.

The digging tool, a miniature pickax with a hoe's blade on the opposite end, proved ideal when the need for temporary protection arose. In no-man's land, that moment could occur at any time. Digging a hole and filling a few sand bags could make all the difference.

"Bring only what you need. Your rifle, your small arms ammo, at least two pineapples (Mills bombs), your helmet, a water bottle, haversack, field dressings, and your identity disk. A waterproof sheet is a good idea, too. That should be a lot less than the 60-pound kit you are used to lugging around."

As the men prepared, Luke told them what he wanted.

"We want information first and foremost. Prisoners would be ideal. We go over the top at 01:00 hours. We spread out in a straight line and stay within a yard or two of each other. No noise and no talk. Got it?"

Six heads nodded.

Chapter Eight

TRENCH FIGHTING

"Let's go."

Luke took the lead, crawling over the parapet and walking slowly into the darkness of no-man's land. The enemy's trenches, just 200 yards from the Brits, were likely modified. SAPS, or communication trenches, dug in the middle of the night and in a perpendicular direction to the British trench, enhanced the likelihood of a surprise attack by the enemy.

A loud pop, followed by a ball of sparks shooting into the air, sent Reggie into a panic.

"Bomb! It's a bomb!"

The giant turned to run. Luke pounced, pushing Reggie deep into the mud.

"Don't move. It's a star shell. Stay exactly where you are. They can't see us," Luke growled.

In seconds, the men were bathed in the flare's bright light. But no one fired at them. The men on both sides of no-man's land, temporarily blinded by the bright light, could see movement only. Seconds later, when the light faded, Luke pulled Reggie to his feet.

"Move."

Luke could hear voices, just yards away. He held up a hand. The voices did not speak English. Some of the enemy soldiers could be heard laughing. The smell of hot food wafted in the air. Luke removed two of the pineapple-shaped hand grenades from his belt. He pointed to one of the men, who did the same. The Mills bombs would explode three seconds after contact. The Turkish soldiers used 'potato mashers,' so-called because the foot-long device resembled a kitchen tool. Turkish grenades exploded five seconds after contact. A handy bit of information, thought Luke, if a soldier was alert and quick enough to return the potato masher to its original owners.

Luke and a private walked very slowly in the direction of the voices. The SAP (a small tunnel dug perpendicular to the main trench) covered half the distance between the two lines. It had to be destroyed or taken. Luke signaled and both men threw their explosive devices into the enemy trench. Several men screamed. Luke chased his own grenades, rifle at the ready, bayonet fixed. The rifles would not be necessary. He counted six bodies, one of them writhing in the dirt. Luke turned and yelled.

"Get in here, all of you. Now."

The men came running, all of them leaping into the enemy trench. They landed on bodies, tipped over the small cooking stove, and loudly cursed the confusion. Two additional star shells flew into the air. Luke barked.

"Quiet and stay down."

The wounded soldier, bleeding from a shrapnel wound to his upper leg, groaned in pain. Luke searched the man and then retrieved a field bandage. As he finished tying the gauze, he noticed lights at the enemy end of the SAP trench.

"We've got company. We leave now. When we get over the top, run ten yards and toss the rest of your pineapples. I want nothing left of this trench, once we leave. Understood?"

Heads nodded.

Luke pointed to the wounded Turk.

"He comes with us."

The recon patrol, dragging the wounded Turk, scrambled over the top and ran. They stopped just as quickly, unloaded their grenades, and took off at a run, once again. Luke pushed the men forward, staying back a few steps to ensure that his men plus their prisoner made it to the British trenches.

Another fire star froze the men in place. Reggie, drowning in fear, continued to run. A machine gun sprayed the entire area. Luke, a sudden stabbing pain in his left arm, hugged the dirt. When the light faded, he did a head count. Two of his men, motionless and unresponsive would be left behind. Of the remaining three, one was hit but not seriously. Reggie and the Turk prisoner were missing.

"Let's move. Now."

Luke forgot about the bullet in his arm. He wanted to put one in Reggie's head.

Elizabeth, tending to a post-op patient, escorted the man's stretcher to the recovery room.

She checked the wound for bleeding, wrapped it in a series of loose bandages, and reorganized the bedding such that his leg would be slightly elevated.

"You did a fine job in there, Elizabeth."

Dr. Browning, approaching quietly from behind, startled the woman. Elizabeth could smell the alcohol and feel his hot breath on her neck. The bed prohibited her forward movement and the wall prevented her escape to the right. With no other choice she pushed left and brushed past the doctor.

"Excuse me, Dr. Browning, there are a number of patients I must check on."

"I have an amputation of the arm tomorrow. Would you like to assist?"

"Yes, Dr. Browning. I would like that very much."

"I should like to review the x-ray and his file with you beforehand. Are you able to come to my office after rounds this evening? Say, seven o'clock?"

Elizabeth could feel the hairs on her arm stand in protest. The goose bumps on the back of her neck made her shiver with fear. *I don't have a choice,* she thought.

"Yes, Doctor. I will be there."

Elizabeth knocked on the office door.

"Come in, Elizabeth."

She stepped into the tiny office, immediately noticing the bottle of spirits and two glasses on an otherwise spotless desk.

"Shut the door please and lock it. I don't wish to be disturbed."

Elizabeth shut the door and rattled the key, rather than turning it, leaving the door unlocked. She turned to face the doctor.

"Dr. Browning. You seem to have misplaced our patient's file and his x-rays."

Dr. Browning gulped the amber liquid in his glass and extended the second glass, filled to the brim, to Elizabeth. When she didn't move, he came out from behind the desk.

"Come now, Elizabeth. You are familiar with the old saying are you not? All work and no play . . ."

Elizabeth did not let him finish.

"I think I'm going to be sick, Dr. Browning. I really must go."

She spun around and opened the door.

"I told you to lock that door, young lady. Insubordination is grounds for dismissal, Sister Parsons. Do you understand what I am saying?"

"I understand what you are saying and I most certainly understand what you are trying to do. Good night, sir."

Elizabeth ran across the ward and all the way to her hut. Even after her breathing returned to normal, it would be several hours before she could sleep.

When a solution to her predicament came to mind, she fell into a deep sleep.

"Lieutenant-Colonel Porter? I just came to say good bye and thank you again for the kindness you showed me earlier this week."

"Sister Parsons, I don't understand. Are you leaving us?"

"Yes, sir. Dr. Browning requires a nurse with more, shall we say, flexibility."

Porter furrowed his eyebrows.

"Dr. Browning, you say?"

"Yes sir."

"Have you notified him of your decision to leave?"

"No, sir."

"I think it only proper, don't you?"

"Well sir, I . . ."

"And I shall accompany you," he said. "Follow me please."

"Dr. Browning, Sister Parsons tells me that you require a more flexible nurse. She has therefore decided to leave the hospital. She has come to say good bye."

"Well, sir, that is not necessary."

"Oh, but apparently it is. In the past six months, at least three of your nurses have also said goodbye. Is that not true?"

Dr. Browning glared at Elizabeth. Lieutenant-Colonel Porter circled the desk. A nearby bookcase caught his attention. A cork, still in its bottle, could be seen tucked behind the medical volumes. Porter removed one of the books and exposed the bottle of spirits. He opened the text and flipped a few of its pages, as if researching a medical question. The bottle of liquor stood in full view.

"Sister Parsons, what is the rule in this hospital with respect to the possession or consumption of alcoholic beverages?"

"They are not allowed, sir."

"And what is the penalty if someone were to be caught in violation of this prohibition?"

Elizabeth caught Dr. Browning's gaze.

"Dismissal, if you are a civilian. Court martial if you are an officer in the army."

"That is correct, Sister Parsons."

The lieutenant-colonel leaned forward. He stood within inches of Dr. Browning's face. He took a deep breath.

"Dr. Browning, if Sister Parsons is guilty of possessing or consuming alcohol while on the premises, you would report her, would you not?"

"Yes, Lieutenant-Colonel. I would."

"And Sister Parsons, were the roles reversed, you would do the same, is that correct?"

"Yes, sir. I would."

Porter replaced the medical text and strode to the door.

"Thank you, Doctor. And thank *you*, Sister Parsons. May I look forward to seeing the both of you, first thing tomorrow morning?

"Yes, sir," said Elizabeth.

After a slight pause, Dr. Browning also responded.

"Yes, sir."

Clarence Parsons contacted as many Crown officials as he knew, plus a few more he did not know.

Each of them claimed he could do nothing to help the well-known business executive. None of them knew if and how Billy could be brought back to Newfoundland. At the government house, just a few blocks away, Reginald Windsor waited impatiently to speak with the governor, Sir Walter Edward Davidson. After two hours and several cigars, an assistant escorted the businessman into the politician's office.

"Mr. Windsor, I have taken the liberty of inquiring as to your son's injuries and current location. The best information available at this time indicates he was transported to London on the hospital ship, *Mohena*. I know only that he underwent surgery for his wounds."

"Thank you, Governor. It was my hope that as commanding officer of the regiment, you could order my son's release."

"Mr. Windsor, whether your son is sent home is beyond my authority. It is strictly a medical decision. Even then, I know of several instances where our boys were told they could return to Newfoundland and chose to stay and fight with their regiment."

The governor and Reginald exchanged long glances, silently taking stock of each other. Reginald sat in the overstuffed chair, perilously close to tears.

"I told him to stay home. I needed him in the business. He didn't listen."

"How old is your boy?"

"19 going on 20."

"You should be proud of your son, Mr. Windsor. Independent, courageous, and willing to fight for king and country."

Reginald jumped to his feet.

"He's a good boy, Governor. I just want him back in one piece."

Luke went straight to the captain to make his report.

He winced in pain as the officer shook his hand and slapped him on the shoulder.

"Nice work, Lieutenant Hobbs. Very nice work. Oh my. You better have that looked at. We don't want gangrene to set in."

"It's nothing, really, Captain. I'll be submitting a written report, of course, but I thought you might want to hear the important details before then."

"Well, Hobbs, I've already spoken to your man, Windsor. The Turk POW he captured won't shut up. We're are learning all sorts of valuable intelligence."

Luke clenched his jaw. His fingernails dug into the palms of each hand. He swallowed hard and struggled to keep his emotions in check.

"Everything will be in my report, Captain. I suggest you withhold your judgment with respect to Private Windsor until after you have read the report."

"Nevertheless, Lieutenant Hobbs, a splendid job. Absolutely splendid."

Luke's wide eyes stared in disbelief.

"Captain, we lost two men. The bodies are still out there."

The captain stiffened. He blinked repeatedly.

"Windsor said nothing about casualties."

"Two killed, one wounded, two if you include me. And all of it could have been avoided, sir."

"What happened?"

"Private Windsor happened, sir. He didn't follow orders. Ran when the Turks fired off a star shell."

The captain's jaw dropped.

"Jesus Christ."

He took a deep breath and yelled at Luke.

"Get yourself back to the aid station and have that looked at, now!"

"Yes sir."

Luke saluted and turned to leave.

"And I want Windsor to hand-deliver your report to me, the minute it's finished. And make sure the damn thing is sealed."

"I want you to deliver this report to the captain. He is expecting it within the hour."

"I'm not your mailman."

"That's an order, Windsor."

A thought flashed in Luke's head.

"The captain requested you by name, Reggie. He's quite pleased with the Turk soldier you brought in."

Reggie smirked and studied his cigar.

"Does the captain like cigars? I think I'll bring him one."

"That's a good idea. He can't wait to talk to you."

Reggie turned and marched off, a definite swagger in his step.

When he disappeared around the corner, it was Luke's turn to smirk.

The medic spent more time completing the paperwork which documented Luke's minor injury than he did cleaning and bandaging the wound.

The bullet never entered Luke's arm. It simply plowed through a half-inch of flesh and muscle, leaving a four-inch-long trail in its wake. The triceps on Luke's left arm would be sore for a while. He would carry the scar for life.

"I must be going," said the medic. "We've got more wounded coming in. I'll finish your paperwork, later. Keep that wound clean."

Luke smiled his thanks and returned to the dugout he called home.

The lieutenant-colonel screamed at Reggie for ten minutes, straight.

"I could have you court martialed for disobeying a lawful command by your superior officer."

"Lieutenant Hobbs wanted us to stand still while the Turks were flooding the place with star shells."

"You idiot. That is precisely what you are supposed to do. You caused the death of two men, Private Windsor, because you did not listen."

Reggie, a sheen of sweat covering his face, glared at the lieutenant-colonel in silence. The large vein on the side of his neck bulged as he stuck his chin high into the air. Despite being a head shorter, the officer in charge poked Reggie in the chest.

"I'm told that you come from a very well-connected family in Newfoundland, Private Windsor. Well, that means nothing out here. You will be on fatigue duty for the next 30 days. Your rum rations are suspended until further notice and your pay will be suspended for the maximum of 28 days. Is that understood, Private Windsor?"

Reggie growled through his clenched teeth.

"Yes, sir."

"Now get out of my sight."

Reggie stood at the entrance to Luke's dugout, glaring at Luke with closed fists at his side.

"Private Windsor reporting for fatigue duty, as ordered. Sir."

Luke, cleaning his rifle at the time, rose to his feet and returned Reggie's salute.

"We are constructing a dugout for a new latrine. See Corporal Bailey for your precise assignment. Report back to me when the latrine is finished."

"Yes, sir."

"Dismissed."

Elizabeth's duties and responsibilities, while assigned to the Third London General Hospital, seemed both easier and more difficult, with each passing week.

Easier, because her work as a VAD nurse had progressed from cleaning windows, floors, dishes, and bed pans to assisting professional nurses, doctors, and surgeons as they made their daily rounds. More difficult, because her services, in constant demand, left little time for eating and sleeping.

"Nurse Parsons, you are needed in the Receiving Hall, immediately. More wounded," said the matron, shouting her orders as Elizabeth wheeled a post-operative patient past the matron's door. Elizabeth quickened her pace, knowing precisely what she could expect in the Receiving Hall. She had spent many hours there since her arrival two months ago.

The 'walking wounded' cases arrived first. They usually arrived in motorcars, able to walk without assistance and suffering from injuries or sicknesses that were not life threatening. Each man would be thoroughly quizzed by the

VAD as to their name, rank, ID number, previous diseases, wounds, their current condition, and even their religion. During this polite but painstakingly thorough interrogation, the VAD, with paper and pencil in hand, offered the patient a cup of hot cocoa. After months of tasteless tea, putrid water, and the extremely rare piece of chocolate, the soldier would gladly answer the nurse's questions.

The patient was then ordered to strip, escorted into the baths, and given a loose-fitting pair of navy-blue pajamas. By the time his clothes were inventoried and fumigated, the soldier was assigned to a specific ward and bed.

Even before the Receiving Room was emptied, a series of ambulances, some motorized, some horse-drawn, began to arrive. They carried seriously wounded patients, each of them with labels attached to their clothes. Based on the patient's label and the in-house medical officer's quickly rendered opinion, the soldier was given an engraved metal 'ticket.' The tag indicated the ward and precise bed number to which the soldier would be assigned.

Before proceeding, he too if able, would surrender his particulars to the pencil-wielding VAD nurse along with his clothes and his modesty. Most of the VAD nurses, charged with thoroughly bathing filthy and often lice-infested soldiers, were female. The cleansing procedure, very likely the soldier's first bath in months, could be time-consuming and awkward.

"It's a chest wound, Sister Parsons. He's still recovering from surgery," said the orderly.

"I'll take it from here," said Elizabeth.

"Are you awake, soldier?" asked Elizabeth, placing her stack of forms at the foot of the bed and reaching into a pocket for her pencil. The soldier looked dazed, dirty, and disoriented.

Elizabeth had not yet seen the man's face, focusing instead on the blank chart.

"I need your name, rank, and ID number, my friend."

"The patient responded in a weak voice.

"Windsor. William Reginald. Private. ID number 861."

Elizabeth's jaw dropped, her eyes blinking as fast as her racing heart. She took a few sharp breaths. The blank form fluttered in her trembling hands. She stepped closer to her patient.

"Billy?"

The soldier bit his lips. His face contorted in pain. He struggled to breathe.

"Billy Windsor. Is that you?"

Elizabeth's cheeks, streaked with tears, lost their color. She reached for the man's hand.

"Billy. It's Elizabeth Parsons."

Billy blinked and frowned until the woman's face came into focus. His words came slowly, deliberately.

"Please. Write to my father. Tell him I'm going to be all right."

"Sister Parsons. Is it your intention to spend the rest of your day with that man?"

Matron's shrill voice brought Elizabeth back to her senses. She apologized to Billy and completed her paperwork.

"Billy, I've got to get you cleaned up. Would you like some hot cocoa?"

"Yes."

Billy's lips formed a weak smile. Elizabeth grinned from ear to ear. She blushed when it came time to remove his clothes, taking care to cover his private parts as often as possible, as she administered a sponge bath.

"I'll help you with these," she said, holding his navy-blue pajamas.

"You'll also find a shirt, slippers, socks, a cravat, cigarettes, and assorted personal items in this bag," she said.

After putting one arm into a sleeve, Elizabeth reached for the small of his back and pulled the man into a half sitting position. She noticed a patch of dark blue and the glint of silver. When she finished dressing him, Elizabeth reached behind Billy's back. She retrieved a metal decoration in the form of a cross. Attached to the cross, was a tri-color ribbon. Two stripes of white with a stripe of navy blue in the middle. Elizabeth immediately recognized the award as Great Britain's Military Cross for Gallantry. She gasped.

"Billy. Did you see this?"

He stared at the medal and then at Elizabeth.

"I must have been sleeping."

"It's a Military Cross, Billy. A level three award for gallantry in battle."

Billy shrugged his shoulders and then winced from the pain it caused.

"I just want to get out of here and back to my company," he said.

"You're a war hero, Billy Windsor. I will return this evening and we will write that letter to your father."

Mrs. Hobbs held the telegram with trembling hands.

"What is it, Mary?" asked Mrs. Newcastle. The midwife and her assistant, Mrs. Hynes, visited Mrs. Hobbs each week, checking on the old woman and seeing to her needs. The old woman handed the unopened telegram to the midwife.

"I can't read it. I just can't."

Mrs. Newcastle ripped the cable open. Her lips quivered and both eyes slammed shut.

"I'm so sorry, Mary. I am so very sorry."

Mrs. Hynes snatched the telegram from the midwife.

"No. It can't be true. It must be some sort of mistake," she said reading the message one more time.

DEEPLY REGRET INFORM YOU SECOND
LIEUTENANT LUKE HOBBS NO 109 KILLED
IN ACTION ON SEPTEMBER 30, 1915.
ADJUTANT GENERAL

Mrs. Hobbs collapsed into the midwife's arms. Mrs. Newcastle and her assistant escorted the woman to a living room chair.

"I'll make some more tea," said Mrs. Hynes.

Mrs. Hobbs screamed in anguish.

"My son. My only son."

"How are you feeling, Private Windsor?"

Elizabeth stood at Billy's bedside, a tearful smile on her face. Billy looked rested and spoke clearly.

"I'm sore. But it's getting better."

"I have to replace those bandages, Billy. It may be uncomfortable," she said.

"It can't be any worse than getting shot. I promise not to scream."

As Elizabeth worked, she talked to her patient.

"Tell me how you earned the medal."

"I'm not sure. Maybe you get one just for getting shot."

"No, Billy. It's an award for gallantry. You did more than just take a bullet."

Billy closed his eyes, deep in thought. His breathing became quicker and deeper. Elizabeth noticed his trembling hands. She could feel the man's racing pulse in his wrist.

"Billy. I'm sorry. I didn't mean to upset you."

Billy talked as if in a trance, his voice barely above a whisper. He suddenly grabbed her hand and squeezed hard. She could see beads of sweat on his forehead. Slowly, he described that day in the trench. The Turk who fired the bullet that almost killed him. The man's exploding head, the mud, the blood, and the burning pain in his chest. He recalled every detail. Every horrible detail.

"Billy . . . let's take a rest now. I'll check on you later and we'll do the letter to your father. I promise."

Billy, his eyes filled with tears, mumbled.

"I'm sorry, Elizabeth. I'm sorry."

"No. I will not let you apologize for being the bravest person I know. Now get some sleep, Billy Windsor. Please."

Billy's head fell to one side, he closed his eyes, and drifted off to sleep.

"When? When did the damn telegram go out?"

"Yesterday, sir."

Luke grabbed the company clerk by his uniform and slammed the young man against the dugout's dirt wall.

"My mother thinks I'm dead. How about if I kill you and then your mother will get the same goddamn telegram. How would you like that, corporal?"

"I'm sorry sir. Your paperwork was delayed because we got slammed with more wounded. The private that finished the report was not the private who started the report. It was a mistake."

"A mistake? You call that a mistake?"

Luke paced the dirt floor and suddenly lunged for his writing materials.

"I want this telegram sent immediately. Do you understand? Immediately."

"Yes, sir."

The corporal read the telegram.

MOTHER MESSAGE OF NOVEMBER 2 SENT IN ERROR LETTER TO FOLLOW LOVE LUKE

"It will go out today," said the corporal.

"Any luck, sir?"

Reginald Windsor pulled up a chair in front of Clarence Parsons' desk.

"No. They can't help me. I spoke to the governor. He can't do a damn thing."

"We will get a letter very soon, Mr. Windsor. I am sure of it."

"How in blazes can you write a letter if you are seriously wounded?"

"The nurses write letters all the time. At least, that's what I've been told."

"I haven't heard a thing from my other son. Knowing Reggie, he's probably having a great time.

Clarence grinned.

"Yes, sir. I think you are probably correct."

"The latrine is finished, sir."

Luke Hobbs, still fuming about the errant telegram, rushed to Reggie's side and screamed into the man's ear.

"This is your fault, Private Windsor. All your fault. Two men are dead, one seriously wounded, and my mother thinks I'm dead. Are you pleased with your work, private? Are you proud of your accomplishments? You may be the son of a wealthy businessman but you are not a real man, Reggie Windsor. You are less than a man. You are an arrogant, selfish coward who preys on women and thinks only of himself. You are not fit to wear the British uniform and if it was up to me, you would be executed at noon tomorrow."

Reggie stood at perfect attention, sneering at the wall behind the lieutenant.

"Will that be all, Lieutenant?"

Luke wrapped his fingers around Reggie's neck and squeezed.

"Wipe that stupid look off your face, Windsor, or I'll kill you where you stand."

Reggie recalled their last physical confrontation. His arrogant sneer disappeared. Luke, his face a hot pink, spoke in a low guttural roar.

"Report to the corporal for your next work assignment."

"It's a letter from Billy."

Reginald Windsor jumped to his feet and yanked the envelope from Clarence's hand. He scanned the envelope and frowned.

"That's not my son's handwriting," he barked, ripping the envelope open.

Clarence smiled.

"No, sir. It's my daughter's handwriting."

Reginald read the missive, fell into his office chair, and read it again.

"Is he getting better?" asked Clarence.

Windsor explained that Billy was in London, transported to the very same hospital where Elizabeth worked.

"He wants to return to his regiment as soon as he's well enough," said Reginald.

"And your daughter added a message of her own. She says that Billy was awarded a medal for bravery on the battlefield. The Military Cross for Gallantry."

Clarence noticed the glassy look in Mr. Windsor's eyes.

"You must be very proud of your son, Mr. Windsor."

Windsor stared out the window, deep in thought. The room took on an eerie silence.

"I thought it would be Reggie who distinguished himself in battle. Hell, I didn't even want Billy to sign up."

"Our children have a knack for surprising us, don't they?"

"Yes, Clarence, they do. Billy is in the hospital with a chest wound and all he can talk about is rejoining his regiment. And I've heard nothing from Reggie."

"I'm sure you'll be hearing from him soon."

"This calls for a drink, Clarence."

Reggie reached into a desk drawer and retrieved a bottle of scotch. When he retrieved two glasses, Clarence politely declined.

"I understand, Clarence. But I need this. More than ever."

A letter from her "deceased" son, and the telegram announcing the Adjutant's error, arrived at Mrs. Hobbs' home, the very next day.

Mrs. Hobbs sat with pen and paper and wrote an especially long letter to Luke. She implored him to be safe and to write more often, like a good son should. She confessed, however, that even a rare letter from her only son was infinitely better than a telegram from regimental headquarters. After a walk to the post office, she arrived at Mrs. Newcastle's home for a previously arranged celebration with tea and freshly baked bread.

Her darling Luke was alive and well!

Luke struggled to keep his eyes open after a particularly arduous day but forced himself to write, yet again, to Elizabeth.

He recounted the incident with Reggie, his anger with the errant telegram leaping from the page. He ended the note with news about Billy, expressing his hope that the boy survived his wounds. He added an uncharacteristically personal post script.

> ***I don't know if Billy survived his wounds. But the men in his company love him. He's become the hero that Reggie Jr. could never be.***
>
> ***Luke***
>
> ***P.S. Please write back. I haven't received a letter from you in more than a month. I assume you are busy. I hope you are busy. Any other explanation would be very disappointing.***

"I received a letter from Luke, earlier this week. He asked about you," said Elizabeth.

Billy smiled, his strength slowly returning after several weeks in the hospital.

"Did you tell him I'll be back with the regiment in no time?"

"No. I have yet to write back to him."

Elizabeth checked Billy's bandages for the third time that day. Although the wound required no attention she fiddled with the bandage.

"Elizabeth. I feel like I'm wasting your time. I'm sure you have better things to do."

"Nonsense. I'm just looking after you. And it is not a waste of time."

"What is it then? You're not here for medical reasons. And if I remember correctly, today is your day off."

Elizabeth blushed and stuttered an explanation.

"I'm . . . Well, you're . . . It's my . . . We're like old friends, Billy. What do you want me to do? Ignore you?"

Billy searched her face.

"Have you changed your mind?"

"About what?"

"About men? About Luke?" Billy searched her eyes. "About me?"

Elizabeth turned her back, pretending to rearrange the items on the cart which she regularly wheeled around the recovery ward.

"I don't know anymore."

Billy thought back to her last request.

"I didn't forget my promise to buy you another lunch of fish and chips."

Elizabeth smiled through watery eyes.

"Look at me," said Billy.

Elizabeth refused to turn around. Billy spoke in a whisper.

"Elizabeth Parsons. Look at me. Please."

She turned to face him. He reached for her face and gently caressed the woman's cheek with the back of his fingers. She closed her eyes but made no move to push his hand away.

"Billy. You must not do that in hospital. It's against the . . ."

"I know. It's against the rules."

Elizabeth shoved her trembling hands into the pockets of her uniform and hurriedly walked away.

Reggie, assigned to reinforcing and expanding yet another latrine, groaned when it started to rain.

When the thunder grew louder and the lightning grew closer, he decided to quit.

"Where do you think you're going, private?"

Luke stood at the entranceway wearing a rubber sheet. His full head of hair, poking through a hole in the makeshift rain gear, appeared soaking wet. He carried a spare.

"Put this on and keep shoveling. I'll let you know when it's time to quit."

"Luke, I'm sorry about what happened. Now, please give me a break."

"I had to write a letter to their parents, you know. I told them that their sons were fearless and died in a hail of enemy bullets. But I wanted to tell them the truth, Reggie. I wanted to tell them that their boys were killed by a selfish, stupid, coward who doesn't deserve to wear the uniform of the King's army."

Reggie, unwilling and perhaps unable to argue with the lieutenant's logic, placed the rubber sheet over his head and resumed digging.

Luke continued his slog through the trench, now a rushing river of thick muddy water filled with the ruined debris of a soldier's day-to-day existence.

Sheets of rain reduced his visibility but Luke could clearly see the damage to that portion of the BEF's trench line which the Newfoundland Regiment occupied. Entire walls lay crumbled. The footpath through the trenches was no longer navigable. Where the walls remained, their parapets no longer existed. Soldiers labored unsuccessfully to drain the ditch. They soon found themselves wading through a waist-deep slurry of muddy garbage.

The downpour continued into the evening hours as the temperatures dropped. Luke anticipated that the flood would worsen even when the rain stopped, because the regiment's portion of the trench lay in the lowest portion of Sulva Plain on the Gallipoli Peninsula. Neither he nor his men got any sleep that evening. They watched helplessly as papers, books, personal possessions, clothing, foodstuffs, and supplies rushed past their posts in a fast-moving quagmire that very nearly drowned several of the men.

When morning came, all hands worked feverishly, with picks and shovels, to drain the deluge and repair the damage. As they worked, temperatures continued to drop. By day's end, a cold north wind converted the rain into sleet. Within an hour the sleet turned to snow. The frost continued for two more days; a phenomenon last seen on the Gallipoli peninsula 40 years earlier.

More than 150 men in the Newfoundland regiment suffered from severe cases of frostbite, a dozen of Luke's men included. After requesting winter kits (clothing and equipment) for his men, Luke learned that the kits were no longer available. A decision by the general staff to evacuate the Gallipoli Peninsula made the winter clothing no longer necessary. All of it now lay in a warehouse at Mudros. The men were forced to use whale oil and straw. The soldiers would rub their blistered feet with whale oil and insert them into sandbags filled with straw.

The men, their feet too swollen for regular footwear, looked like elephants as they trudged through the trenches.

Chapter Nine

LOVERS AND WARRIORS

A recent meeting of the high command made it official.

The evacuation of the Gallipoli Peninsula would take place in mid-December. The 1st Newfoundland Regiment would serve as the rearguard. Its job would be to defend the retreating troops against an attack by the Turks. The brass expected significant casualties.

"Hobbs. A moment please."

Lieutenant-Colonel Hadow, recently installed as the regiment's new commander, waved a paper in Luke's direction.

"Yes, sir."

"Your captain says you are a clever fellow, Hobbs. I want you to come up with some specific strategies that would convince those Turk bastards that we are still in the trenches, long after we've left. Do you understand?"

He handed Luke a folded sheet of paper.

"And this should help. You've been promoted to full Lieutenant."

Luke smiled politely, worried more about his assignment than pleased about his promotion.

"Get the regiment off this rock in one piece, Hobbs, and I'll make you a goddamn captain. Understood?"

"Yes, sir."

"All right then. Get to it. I expect a full set of recommendations by the end of this week."

Luke, accustomed to thinking about the fifty men in his platoon would now consider the evacuation of more than 80,000 soldiers. How could he protect the thousands of retreating troops and simultaneously extricate the Newfoundland Regiment, all the while keeping their movements hidden from the Turkish army?

"I assume there will be a barrage," said Luke.

The officers, including the lieutenant-colonel, all nodded.

"Yes. Of course."

Luke fidgeted with his notes.

"And the periscopes. Can we keep them in place?"

"Yes. We can do that."

"I have a proposal which I believe will convince the Turks that we continue to occupy our trenches, long after we've evacuated."

"Go on," said the lieutenant-colonel.

"We move the equipment and the men's kits the night before the Newfoundland Regiment's evacuation. We begin the embarkation the next night, after dark. The men's boots are muffled. Rifles and flare guns will be placed at various distances along the trenches, set to go off at different times."

"But those remaining men will never get out alive," complained one of the captains.

"The rifles and flare guns will fire on their own."

The lieutenant-colonel leaned forward.

"Explain yourself, Lieutenant."

Luke revealed that each rifle would be wired in place. A tin, partially filled with sand, would be suspended from the trigger, with a wire. Another can, filled with water and suspended above the first tin, would slowly leak the water into the can filled with sand. When the combined weight of the water and sand reached about seven pounds, the trigger would be pulled and the rifle would be discharged.

"I've got one set up. Would you like to see it?"

The officers quick-stepped a dozen yards down the trench. Luke filled the highest tin with water. It immediately began to leak into the sand-filled tin below, which was wired to the trigger.

"And now we wait," said Luke.

Luke's CO muttered under his breath.

"There's no way that thing can work."

The lieutenant-colonel, his lips pressed into a fine line, stepped in for a closer look. When the rifle suddenly discharged, he fell back, lost his balance, and landed in a mud puddle.

"I don't believe it. The bloody thing works."

Luke extended a hand and pulled the officer to his feet.

"Sorry, sir. Didn't mean to startle you."

"Best surprise I've had in a long time."

"We can do the same thing with our flare guns and I think we can rig something up with the grenades too, sir."

The lieutenant-colonel grinned.

"Brilliant, my boy. Absolutely brilliant."

Evacuation of Gallipoli began in earnest on December 19.

The Navy, ordered to launch a particularly heavy barrage of artillery, distracted the enemy for hours. Most of the British Expeditionary Forces were on board the waiting ships by midnight. Three hours later, amidst the sporadic fire of rifles, flares, and grenade launchers, the men of the Newfoundland Regiment joined their counterparts. The evacuation, requiring just hours, freed more than 83,000 men plus animals, equipment, and artillery.

"Where are we headed, Lieutenant?" asked one of the men. Luke, necessarily vague, responded with three words.

"Anywhere but here."

"Etaples, in France?"

The pained look and scrunched eyebrows on Elizabeth's face spoke the words she dared not speak to the matron.

"Yes, Sister Parsons. There is a large training camp there, two General Hospitals, and a half-dozen medical facilities of various sorts. They have the capacity for more than 7,000 patients. You will not suffer from a lack of things to do," said the matron.

"Why now?"

"There is talk of a big push by the British Expeditionary Forces. I believe they are anticipating a great number of casualties. That is my opinion of course. Not to be shared with anyone."

"And my assignment?"

"Officers Hospital No. 24. They expect and demand their nurses to be the best of the best. Do us proud, Sister Parsons."

The matron flashed a rare smile. Elizabeth stepped forward, grateful to the woman for all her help. She wanted to hug the woman but hesitated, stammering her gratitude, instead.

"I . . . You have been . . . Well, I just wanted to say . . ."

Elizabeth's voice trailed off into a cloud of awkward embarrassment. The matron reached out and pulled Elizabeth close.

"I will miss you, Elizabeth. I will miss you every single day."

Elizabeth struggled to hold back the tears.

She failed.

"The surgeon says I'm going home," said Billy, a confused look on his face. "I leave at the end of the week."

He blinked repeatedly, waiting for Elizabeth to react.

"Is that what you want?"

Billy ran the fingers of both hands through his hair and snapped at her.

"I don't know what I want. I'd like to rejoin my regiment, but they won't let me."

Elizabeth flinched. She quickly recovered from his unexpected outburst, slumped into a nearby chair, and exhaled loudly.

"I'm leaving too."

"Where are *you* going?"

"Tomorrow is my last day. I have two days to myself and then it's off to France. An officers' hospital in Etaples."

Billy looked away and talked to the wall.

"I've heard of that place. They have a large training camp there."

Elizabeth nodded, a blank look on her face.

"We should have a party or something."

Billy made a face.

"Not sure what there is to celebrate."

"I have an unopened bottle of French wine in my hut and a bit of cheese. A patient gave it to me. Said I saved his life."

"A man in your hut? Isn't that against the rules? I could report you."

"Nobody likes a tattletale."

"My father told me that once. Right after Reggie attacked me."

"Why did Reggie attack you?"

"I tattled on him."

"About what?"

"About you and Reggie."

Elizabeth scratched her head.

"I have neither forgotten nor forgiven what your brother did to me. I never told you a thing but you figured it out."

"Father talked to you and then he beat the living daylights out of Reggie."

"Did it do any good?"

"That jury is still out."

Elizabeth thought about the wine and cheese. *What would matron think. What would her father say?* They would never know. Her voice cracked with fear and anticipation.

"So, no going away party?"
"It would be front-page news."
"Why is that?"
Billy's eyebrows shot up and he grinned.
"Elizabeth Parsons breaks all the rules."
Elizabeth pointed a finger in his direction.
"Seven o'clock. Meet me at the gate."

The journey from Gallipoli to France required more than a week.

After a quick stop in Suez, where the canal enters the Red Sea, the regiment boarded the steamship *Alaunia*. They sailed into the harbor at Marseilles, France, boarded a train to Pont Remy, and crossed over the River Somme to Buigny l'Abbé. After a one-month billet in Buigny, they marched deeper into the French countryside, taking a reserve position in the small village of Englebelmer, two miles from the front line.

After its withdrawal from the Gallipoli Peninsula at the end of 1915, the 1st Newfoundland Regiment required reinforcements. Its ranks, depleted by sickness, injuries, and death, now numbered approximately 560 soldiers plus 23 officers. Fortunately, the recruitment effort back in Newfoundland continued throughout all of 1915. By April, 1916, the regiment would be at battalion strength once again: Thirty officers and 972 men of other ranks.

The regiment, now at full strength, would become a significant part of the "big push."

"Your job in His Majesty's army just got bigger."

"Sir?" asked Luke, puzzled by the knowing grin on Lieutenant-Colonel Hadow's face.

Luke's rare meeting with the regiment's commanding officer triggered a bad case of the jitters, unusual for a young man who rarely lost his composure.

"Company A is yours, Captain. Unless of course you would prefer to remain a Lieutenant."

Luke took several deep, calming breaths, struggling to maintain his composure.

"Captain? Did you say Captain, sir?"

"You heard correctly, Captain Hobbs. And you already have your first assignment. The general says we are going over the top in early July."

"That's a little more than a month from now. We have a lot of work to do before then, sir."

"And that's why you are now in charge of Company A."

"I heard the colonel's aide talking. And it's true. Lieutenant Hobbs is now a captain."

Reggie, lying on a cot in the men's billet, sprang to his feet and confronted his soldier friend.

"A captain? Luke Hobbs is a captain? I'm never going to get a break."

"Are you still on fatigue duty?"

"No," said Reggie. "And I'm getting paid again. But still no rum rations. Bastards. The lot of them. Bastards."

"Keep your voice down, Windsor, or your next stop is a court martial."

Reggie stormed off, chomping on his unlit cigar. The steady rain made it impossible to smoke. He walked through the village, deep in thought, contemplating how Luke's promotion might affect him. Reggie absentmindedly bumped into a young private. The soldier, also a member of the Newfoundland Regiment and just as tall and muscular as Reggie, threw his hands into the air.

"A damnable *omaloor.*" (A Newfoundland term for an ungainly fellow with big feet.)

Reggie stopped and spun around.

"Say it again and I'll drop you where you stand."

"That will take a better man than you, my friend."

The private swung hard at Reggie's jaw. The cigar flew in the air as Reggie slammed into the mud-soaked ground, clearly stunned by the man's blow. The assailant threw himself on Reggie. Reggie pushed him off into a nearby puddle. They rolled in the mud, throwing punches but landing none. A half dozen soldiers, hearing the ruckus, came running. There were no officers present. The fight continued. Reggie and the stranger connected with a series of crushing blows. Neither of them gained the upper hand. They rolled in the mud and, at one point, simultaneously rose to their knees. Reggie clambered to his feet first. A powerful uppercut with Reggie's huge fist smashed the man's nose deep into his skull. The soldier fell to the ground and didn't move. A lieutenant arrived on the scene. He pointed to a few of the spectators and then to the injured soldier.

"Take him to the medical tent."

The officer turned to Reggie.

"You just can't stay out of trouble, can you, Windsor?"

Reggie snarled.

"He threw the first punch. It was self-defense."

"Come with me, Windsor."

"I'm right here."

Elizabeth jerked to a standstill and spun in Billy's direction.

"Billy. You scared the daylights out of me."

Billy emerged from the shadows, looking in every direction.

"Sorry."

"I told you to wait at the gate."

"Too many questioning eyes."

"Quick. My hut's over here."

Billy inspected the tiny chamber. There were two cots, a small dresser, a nightstand next to each bed, and a shelf on the wall covered with boxes and folded clothes. A coal-fired heater stood in the corner, generating a modest heat.

"You have a roommate."

"She's gone for the week."

Elizabeth reached under the bed and retrieved an open bottle of wine.

"As promised."

Billy retrieved a metal flask from his jacket pocket.

"Save your wine for someone important. I brought rum."

"Did you steal that from the hospital?"

"War heroes are treated very well around here."

Billy sat on the edge of one bed, Elizabeth, the other.

She studied her guest.

"How are you feeling?"

"I'm not back to normal yet. I get winded rather easily but other than that everything is fine."

Billy offered the flask to Elizabeth.

"I don't think I've ever tasted the stuff."

"Me neither, till I got into the army."

She took a large gulp, coughing her surprise. Billy chuckled and took a large swig.

"It's an acquired taste."

She leaned forward, resting a hand on his knee.

"You've changed, Billy."

Billy took another gulp. She did the same. She made a face and waited for his response.

"Yes. I suppose I have. What have you noticed?"

"It appears to me that you no longer live in the shadow of either your father or your big brother. And that has made all the difference in the world."

"Is that why you invited me to your hut? You wanted to meet the new Billy Windsor?"

Elizabeth could feel a growing buzz in her head.

"I admit it. I'm curious. And I've never violated the rules for VADs and their patients. Perhaps I, too, have changed."

"I think you have changed."

"Is that why you accepted my invitation? You wanted to meet the new Elizabeth Parsons?"

"I liked the old Elizabeth Parsons. Remember?"

Elizabeth fidgeted, rearranging her dress, brushing fingers through her hair, and wetting her lips.

"Am I making you nervous?" he asked.

Elizabeth sprang to her feet, pacing the short distance to the door and back again. She whirled in place and faced her visitor.

"Why would you say that?"

Billy rose to his feet.

"I'll take that as a yes. Enjoy your trip to France, Elizabeth."

Billy rose to his feet. Elizabeth turned away.

"That's not why I'm nervous. I've never been . . . this is my first . . . I don't know what . . ."

Billy interrupted.

"That makes two of us."

Elizabeth went to the door. With her trembling hand on the handle and her back to Billy, she spoke in a shaky whisper.

"Would you like to stay?"

Billy approached from behind, both hands on her shoulders. He whispered in her ear.

"Yes. Very much."

Elizabeth locked the door.

Reggie paced the floor in the small room which served as his cell.

His nostrils flared. A pink rage covered his face. Two armed soldiers stood guard on the other side of the open door. He seriously considered the possibility of overpowering the men and making a run for it. The guards did not affect an imposing presence. He was the largest of the three and he was angry. Very angry. *Going AWOL might trigger a court martial*, he thought. *Perhaps even execution. But climbing back into the trenches could be equally fatal. If the artillery shells didn't get you, the snipers would. And then there were the rats, the lice, the awful food, and the mud. Lots of mud.* He was so sick of the mud.

"What happened, Private Windsor?"

Luke's voice startled Reggie. His head jerked up.

"Well, what do you know? It's Captain Hobbs to the rescue."

"I'm not here to rescue you, Reggie. I want to know what happened."

Reggie told Luke what caused the fight.

"He started it; I finished it," said Reggie. "He lasted longer than I thought he would. Has the loudmouthed bastard woken up yet?"

"He's dead, Reggie."

Reggie stopped pacing. His eyes bulged. He stuttered.

"Th-that's a cru-cruel joke, Luke. You shh-shh-shouldn't say such things."

"It's no joke, Reggie. I think he was dead when he hit the mud."

Reggie rushed the door. The two guards used the butts of their rifles to stop him, one blow to the prisoner's stomach and the other to Reggie's head. Reggie fell back onto the cot. The soldiers took aim. Luke never moved. Reggie slowly raised his hands in surrender.

"Luke. You must help me."

"It's out of my hands, Reggie. There's going to be a court martial."

Elizabeth woke to the sound of Billy's rhythmic breathing.

The early morning light, as it seeped through the flimsy curtains, caressed the boy's handsome profile. And yet, the naked man lying next to her did not resemble the Billy Windsor she knew before the war. She wondered if the restoration of a man's blood supply could trigger a new-found confidence. The nurse in her said otherwise. But the boy had changed. Significantly. The uncertainty in Billy's voice and mannerisms, much like his fallen comrades, lay buried somewhere in the blood-soaked trenches of Gallipoli. The wound that left a massive scar on his chest also left its mark on the boy's heart and mind. Billy, the younger son of Reginald Windsor, no longer existed. William Windsor, the decorated war hero, lay in his place.

The couple's spontaneous tryst left her frustrated and disappointed. Their initial attempt at lovemaking proved awkward and, at times, clumsy. Inexperience reduced their first carnal embrace to little more than a biology lesson, sans instructor, and in a dingy room. She expected her first time to be so much more exciting. Satisfying. Perhaps even romantic. It was none of the above. And the whole thing happened much too quickly.

She reached beneath the covers, her touch, soft and sensual. Billy stirred. Without a word, she tugged on the sheet and covered his body with the warmth of her silky soft skin. He reached for the nape of her neck, pulling her closer. She resisted. Now, in complete control, she ignored the impatient lust on his face. Elizabeth savored the growing pleasure in her writhing body. His breathing grew heavy. Her eyes squeezed shut. Billy moaned his pleasure. Elizabeth squealed in ecstasy, praying the moment would never end. She collapsed onto his heaving chest. They basked in the afterglow of their passion, the sound of his beating heart filling her ears. Billy whispered.

"Let's stay in bed until the war is over."

Elizabeth suddenly rolled to a sitting position and reached for her undergarments.

"Sorry, soldier. I have a boat to catch."

Elizabeth crossed the English Channel to Etaples, France, on board the *Asurias*.

The steamer, formerly a luxury passenger liner, evidenced remnants of its glory days. Mahogany trim, fine furniture, and elegant fixtures decorated the ship. On the open sea, however, a casual observer would reach an entirely different conclusion. Two wide stripes of bright green, painted on either side of the 12,000-ton vessel, were highlighted by large red crosses at the bow, the stern, and amidships. The *Asurias* served as a hospital ship now. It belonged to the Admiralty.

The floating medical facility included 900 beds, dozens of medical personnel, and all the attendant equipment and supplies. Despite her surroundings, Elizabeth looked forward to a rare respite from her usual labors as a nurse. She could now tolerate the nausea of seasickness but the steady sound of waves crashing against the ship's hull failed to silence the noisy voices in her head.

Uppermost in her mind: the guilt she felt for leaving Billy in such a rush. On her floating fortress of solitude, she could be honest. She left because she was too embarrassed to stay. What do first-time lovers say when their love-making has ended? *I love you?* That would not have been remotely true. For either of them. What they lacked in carnal knowledge, they made up for in curiosity. When the words would not come, they let the rum do all the talking. And the idealistic notion of commitment vanished in the face of their pending departures. They were not in love. They were in lust.

Over all of that, there lay a heavy, wet blanket of fear. She shuddered at the very thought of a domineering man in her life. A man that exercised control and demanded that *his* needs be satisfied first. Her father, the Windsor family and, to a lesser extent, Luke Hobbs, represented that male-dominated world. She wanted no part of it.

Despite the wondrous pleasures of her first physical relationship with a passionate lover, Elizabeth wanted none of the emotional baggage that came with it.

As the port city of Etaples came into view, Elizabeth recalled the descriptions given her by veteran nurses who were stationed there in the past.

The city, once a small fishing town, grew to an unrecognizable morass of buildings and uniformed bodies. Her new home housed thousands of soldiers in training and thousands of patients in hospital. Hundreds of officers, doctors, and nurses worked long hours to manage the chaos. The pastoral views of green meadows and plowed fields, which greeted Elizabeth upon her arrival, slowly morphed into narrow streets of cobblestone and colorful row houses. And then, with no more than a faded sign to warn her, a muddy conglomeration of tents and buildings buzzing with people and machinery ravaged the scenic vista. The camp hummed with the ant-like movement of more than 100,000 people. And somewhere in this city of ramshackle buildings, canvas tents, pond-sized puddles, and a maze of mud-filled roads, she would discover General Hospital number 24.

"May I help you?"

"My name is Elizabeth Parsons. I have been . . ."

"I am aware of your assignment, Sister Parsons. And if I may be brutally honest, a voluntary nurse with none of the formal training required of a professional nurse does not belong in a surgical hospital, much less General Hospital Number 24. Our reputation for excellence is beyond reproach and I hope and pray that you are capable of doing your job."

"Forgive me. I don't know your name."

"You will address me as Matron. I will be your immediate supervisor. At his request, you have been assigned to Dr. Hope's surgical team. And only the Lord himself knows why."

Elizabeth bowed her head, speaking softly.

"It is my understanding, Matron, that Doctor Hope . . ."

"What you understand, Sister Parsons, does not concern me in the least. You will do precisely whatever you are instructed to do. Is that understood?"

"Yes, Matron."

"You have been assigned to hut number 13. You are due in surgery by eight o'clock tomorrow morning. I will expect you to arrive no later than 7:30."

"Thank you, Matron, I promise you that I will do my very best."

"You are dismissed, Sister Parsons."

After negotiating a labyrinth of muddy roads, Elizabeth stumbled upon hut number 13, a weathered building of the flimsiest material.

Her roommate, enjoying a rare day off and sleeping in, did not disguise her irritation with Elizabeth's unexpected arrival. She pointed to a bed, void of bedding.

"Your bunk is over there. Keep your stuff in your half of the room."

Elizabeth, soured by her meeting with the matron, decided to forego the usual amenities. She nodded her acknowledgement and started to unpack. A few hooks on the wall would serve as her armoire. A small chest of drawers allowed for the minimal storage of personal effects.

"Is it true? You're a VAD nurse assigned to the surgical ward?"

"Yes. It's true."

"Who'd you sleep with to get that assignment?"

Elizabeth stood motionless.

"I'm sorry. I didn't get your name."

"I didn't give it to you."

Elizabeth flashed a sly smile recalling the dozens of incidents when she had to wrestle male patients into their beds or baths.

"I guess it doesn't really matter. The doctor will patch you up, regardless."

"What doctor?"

"The one you will require after I break your jaw."

The solemn threat that spilled out of Elizabeth's mouth, surprised her as much as it did the roommate. The woman sprang to her feet. Elizabeth did not wait for the girl to cross the floor. She leapt forward and shoved the woman back onto her bunk. The roommate fell backwards, hitting her head on a portion of the canvas-covered frame. The wooden upright made the girl grunt in pain. She rubbed her head and glared at her attacker. Elizabeth pointed a cautionary finger.

"Choose your words carefully, sweetheart. Or your next bed will be a gurney in the surgical ward."

The roommate pulled herself to a seated position.

"You're tougher than you look."

Elizabeth made several trips between the dresser and her luggage, talking to the canvas wall.

"War will do that to you."

"Where was your last assignment?"

Elizabeth hung a clean uniform on one of the hooks.

"Third London General."

"Why did they send you here?"

"I volunteered."

"Are you mad?"

Elizabeth's eyes closed for a moment.

"Yes. I suppose I am."

The girl hopped off the bed. Elizabeth flinched.

"Rosemary Redmond," said the girl, extending a hand. "I apologize."

Elizabeth crossed her arms. The girl persisted.

"Can we start over? Please?"

Elizabeth nodded and squeezed the girl's hand.

"Is everyone here as charming as the matron?" asked Elizabeth.

"Most of the VADs are nice. The professional nurses treat us like a case of trench foot."

"The patients come first. I don't really care if the nurses like me or not."

"The VADs will be jealous but in a nice way."

"Why? Working in the surgical ward and the recovery ward is the most exhausting assignment of all."

"But the glamour of it all."

"That doesn't last for very long. Trust me. You are a VAD too, aren't you?"

"Yes, ma'am."

"What do they have you doing?"

"Bed pans, dirty bandages, cleaning, and meals. Very little patient care."

"That's how I started."

"How did you get to surgery?"

"I worked twice as hard as everyone else, volunteered whenever I could, and rarely slept." Elizabeth paused. "It was easy."

Her impish grin made the roommate smile.

"Now tell me, Rosemary, where do I get something to eat in this place?"

Billy lay in Elizabeth's cot until midmorning.

The physical ecstasy of his first encounter with a woman left him excited and anxious for more. He doubted that Elizabeth would be interested in continuing their relationship. Her strength, her fierce independence, and her intellectual prowess, attracted him like no other woman. But the feelings did not appear to be mutual. He wondered if her heart lay elsewhere. Luke perhaps. In any event, their relationship would not continue. She ran off to France and he would soon be in St. John's, Newfoundland.

Billy made the decision to arrive home without advance notice. Two weeks on the Atlantic, much of it dodging German U-boats, gave the war hero all the time he needed to reflect on his future. His future with the army, his future with his father, and his future with Elizabeth. Days later, when the city of St. John's appeared on the shimmering horizon, Billy's mind was made up. As much as he yearned to be with his regiment, the army would not have him. And as much as his father wanted him to run the family business, Billy would not have him. Living in Reginald Windsor's shadow, much less under his thumb, would be worse than life in the trenches.

And then there was Elizabeth, an unrealistic dream he would not chase. Her physical charms, although mesmerizing, would not satisfy his urge to pursue an old passion. A passion that had yet to be satiated. An ardent love of long ago. And this daring dream could return him to the battlefields of France.

Billy's next tryst would be with a flying machine.

With those thoughts still reverberating in his mind, Billy took the stairs to his father's fourth-floor office. He preferred the exercise to an elevator crowded with familiar faces. Clarence saw him first, jumping to his feet and scurrying to the door.

"As God is my witness. Billy Windsor. You are a sight for sore eyes," said Clarence.

He pumped the soldier's hand and slapped him on the shoulder. Billy greeted his father's assistant warmly.

"How are you, Clarence? I heard you're working for my father. I hope he's not been too harsh on you."

"Not at all. I think we need each other," said Clarence.

Reginald Windsor's booming voice suddenly filled the room.

"But I need him more than he needs me."

Billy wore a nervous look on his face, uncertain if a handshake or a hug was appropriate. Reginald made the decision for his son, stepping forward with a grin that covered his face. The old man's bear hug lifted Billy off his feet. For a moment, he refused to release his son. When Reginald stepped back, he blinked tears away and swallowed hard, desperate to hide the emotion on his face. Reginald reached out and caressed the military cross which decorated the boy's uniform. His voice fell to a whisper.

"My son the war hero. And to think I wanted you to stay home. I am so proud of you, Billy."

"Thank you, Father. But all I did was forget to duck."

Clarence interrupted the reunion.

"Why don't the two of you get out of this office and find a place to eat and share a few drinks."

Reginald took a long puff on his cigar, giving his son a cloud-like halo. He pointed the stogie at Clarence.

"That's why I hired him, Billy. He's a genius. Come on, kid. I'll buy you a drink."

It took the father and son longer than usual to reach their destination.

Billy, continually approached by old friends and total strangers, politely acknowledged their kind words and hearty congratulations on the award for valor. A seat in the far corner of a restaurant afforded them a measure of privacy.

"What have you heard from your brother?"

"Nothing, Father. Nothing at all. He is in Company A and I served in Company C. We were often in different trenches and hundreds of yards apart. Communications are between officers not between enlisted men."

"He hasn't answered my letters."

"The last I heard, he was under Hobbs. Luke was promoted to captain, you know."

"I'm not surprised. Luke's a smart man. Good for him. Now let's talk about you. You're coming back to the company, I assume."

Billy flinched. The unblinking stare alerted his father.

"Did I say something wrong?"

"Father, I want to go back to France."

"You can't. You've been medically discharged, Billy. That's never going to happen. Now, I've given this a great deal of thought. I think you can run the entire company with a little help from Clarence.

"But Father . . ."

"It won't be easy at first but I'll be there to help when you need it."

"Father, I . . ."

"The hardest part is dealing with the vendors and the subcontractors. They can be a sneaky lot but . . ."

Billy slammed his open hand on the tablecloth. The glassware rattled. Customers stared.

"Father! Please!"

Reginald jerked in his chair, an incredulous look on his face. He spoke in a whisper.

"Billy. What's come over you?"

Billy closed his eyes, took a deep breath, and started again.

"I apologize for my outburst, Father. But I've been trying to tell you. I do not want to work for you or even run the company. I want to fly fighter planes. I want to get back in the war. The sooner the better."

"Billy, you are not fit for combat. They told you that."

"Combat, no. But flight operations, yes.

"No, Billy. That makes no sense at all. They won't let you. *I* won't let you."

Billy's lips stretched into a straight line. His eyes narrowed to slits.

"Are you going to do *that* again, Father?"

Reginald's eyes dropped to the white tablecloth. He looked up staring at Billy through glassy eyes.

"I didn't mean that, son. You are a grown man and I will not order you around like a servant. I am truly sorry."

"Father, the Royal Flying Corps is desperate for pilots. They will take me. I can prove it."

Billy related the story of Joseph Raymond, a St. John's, Newfoundland, native. After a serious wound in the jaw, Raymond was discharged because he was 'no longer fit for war service.' He later applied for and was approved for a position with the Royal Flying Corps. (Later called the Royal Air Force.)

"I might need you to make a few phone calls."

Reginald used a fork to fiddle with the food on his plate.

"I don't want you to go, son."

Billy looked away; his lips pursed and his jaw set like stone. Reginald noticed.

"But we both know what happened the last time I said that."

Billy saw the weak smile on his father's face.

"It is something I must do, Father."

Reginald leaned over his plate.

"Just promise me you won't get shot up again."

"I'll do my best, Father. I promise."

"You have been charged with committing the offense of murder."

Reggie Windsor stood alone. He faced three officers, each with a stack of papers in front of him. The officer with the highest rank, a colonel in the New Zealand regiment, spoke first.

"Do you wish to speak in your own defense?"

"I thought I was entitled to a barrister."

"We're at war, son. The usual protocols do not apply."

"I would like to speak on behalf of Private Windsor."

Reggie twisted in place, rattling the manacles and chains around his wrists and ankles. He usually greeted Luke Hobbs with a sneer. Instead, Reggie's face lit up and he stood a bit taller. He turned again to face his accusers.

"I would like Captain Hobbs to speak for me. Please."

The colonel motioned Luke forward.

"You may approach, Captain. Please identify yourself and tell the court how you came to know the accused."

"Thank you, Colonel. My name is Captain Luke Hobbs with Company A of the 1st Newfoundland Regiment. Private Windsor and I enlisted at the same time. Since that time, Private Windsor has served as a member of my platoon and now as a member of my company."

"Proceed with your statement, Captain Hobbs."

"I am unwilling and unable to speak about the private's honesty, trustworthiness, or dedication as a soldier in his Majesty's army. He has none of those qualities. In fact, he has thus far shown himself to be lazy, opportunistic, conniving, and, when the opportunity arises, a bully to those unable to defend themselves."

Reggie's nostrils flared. He snarled at Luke, his face red-hot with anger. Hobbs continued.

"On the other hand, I have known the defendant both personally and as his commanding officer for almost two years. And I can say with certainty that he has neither the will nor the courage to intentionally kill anyone, much less a fellow soldier. Although he was never in any real danger, Private Windsor struck the man who struck him first. And he killed the victim with a single blow. Private Windsor did not consider, much less anticipate, the consequences of his actions. I therefore request your utmost leniency."

Reggie looked away, desperate to hide his shame and embarrassment. The colonel spoke up.

"Captain Hobbs, the accused is guilty of murder, regardless of his intent. Are you suggesting that Private Windsor go unpunished for this crime?"

"No sir. But there are extenuating circumstances."

"Explain yourself, Captain.

"We are at war and in desperate need of additional manpower. I am told that our Tunnelling Companies are short of miners. And, as I am sure you know, we will soon require many tunnels."

"What would you have this court do?"

"Ten years of hard labor, sir. He can start with the tunnel company."

The colonel leaned to one side and then to the other, conferring with both of his colleagues. The conversations were brief.

"Very well then, Captain Hobbs, you have named your own poison. Private Windsor will be stripped of his rank and serve as a military trainee with the Tunnelling Division for a period of no more than ten years. He will serve under your care, custody, and control, until such time as he has earned his release or the war has ended, whichever comes first."

Luke's jaw dropped. The color drained from his face.

"But, Colonel, surely you don't expect me to . . ."

The colonel turned to Reggie.

"Mr. Windsor, were it not for the captain, you would be facing a firing squad at noon tomorrow. I suggest that from now on, you do precisely what you are told."

"Yes, sir," said Reggie.

"The defendant is released into the custody of Captain Hobbs. This court is adjourned."

Elizabeth arrived at the operating theater by seven, allowing herself a full hour to become familiar with her surroundings.

The surgeons at her previous hospital in London had the luxury of three nurses in the operating room. One "waited" on the operating table, one supplied the cleaned surgical instruments, and the remaining nurse removed the contaminated bandages and instruments. The surgical theater at Etaples, according to Elizabeth's roommate, operated differently. Each surgeon would work with a single nurse who would be responsible for everything the surgeon or his patient required.

In short order, Elizabeth memorized the location of everything she might require, from bandages and needles to tourniquets and tubing.

"And what exactly do you think you are doing, Sister Parsons?"

Elizabeth spun in place. The matron's angry inquiry made her stomach churn.

"I am familiarizing myself with the location of the supplies and equipment which Dr. Hope will require during the course of his surgeries."

"You will not enter the operating theater without my express permission, Sister Parsons. Is that clear?"

"Yes, Matron. Would you prefer that I arrive in the operating theater, totally ignorant as to where I might locate the supplies and equipment which Dr. Hope will surely require?"

The matron grew red in the face and shoved her face forward. Elizabeth did not blink.

"You will show me the respect I have earned, Sister Parsons. Is that clear?"

"And Sister Parsons will be shown the respect which she has earned."

Dr. Hope's gravelly voice spun the matron a full 180 degrees. The matron, her face now a sunburned red, wore a look of horror. She stuttered a nonsensical response.

"Doctor, I was just, you are correct of course, please, I didn't mean to . . ."

Her words melted into the heat of the moment.

"Matron, you will see to it that Sister Parsons is given everything her position requires. And that includes anticipating my every need and providing excellent postoperative care to my patients. Is that clear, Matron?"

"Yes, Doctor Hope."

The surgeon, in obvious good humor, grinned and winked at Elizabeth.

"Sister Parsons. How nice to see you again."

"You as well, Dr. Hope."

"I arrived early to show you around. I should have known you would have anticipated my visit."

Dr. Hope turned to the matron.

"Matron, please do not be angry with me or Sister Parsons. It is not my intention to violate the strict protocols required of your staff. You should know that Sister Parsons is an exception to the rule. She is the finest nurse I have ever had the privilege of working with. She may not have received the formal training of a professional nurse, such as yourself, but she has more experience, in and out of the operating room, than any nurse with whom I have worked. In fact, she has more experience than at least one of my fellow surgeons. That is why I requested her as my assistant. I trust you understand my wishes, in this regard."

Matron smoothed her dress with trembling hands.

"Yes, Doctor Hope. I understand."

"Great. Now be a good girl and fetch me a cup of tea, would you?"

Elizabeth assisted Dr. Hope with three amputations, two abdominal surgeries, and a compound fracture of the upper leg. Long after the surgeon disappeared, Elizabeth shuttled among patients in the recovery ward, examining their wounds for signs of bleeding, torn stitches, and unexpected inflammation.

"You have a good and loyal friend in Dr. Hope."

"I do not socialize with the surgeons, Matron. And I have very few friends," said Elizabeth.

"How did you acquire the skills to which he referred?"

"I was previously stationed at Third London General in England. They were very short-staffed. I had good teachers and very patient surgeons. I was most fortunate."

"Are you always this modest?"

"Some would say I have much to be modest about."

"You have more experience than most of my professional nurses."

"Sometimes, I wish I didn't."

"We have a dozen post-op patients that would benefit from your attention. Would you be willing . . . ?"

The matron's voice disappeared in flood of embarrassment.

"Yes, of course, Matron. Right away."

Elizabeth worked alongside the matron in the recovery room until midnight. The older woman approached Elizabeth as they prepared to leave.

"I wish to apologize for my behavior of this morning."

"An apology is neither expected nor required. In my humble opinion, there is a job considerably more difficult than surgical nurse."

"Pray tell, Sister Parsons. What job could possibly be more difficult?"

"Matron," said Elizabeth with a grin.

Matron smiled through teary eyes. Elizabeth scanned the room for other nurses. Seeing none, she stepped forward and hugged the woman.

The Matron whispered in Elizabeth's ear.

"Thank you, Sister Parsons."

"You will be assigned to the 252nd Tunnellers Division. It's the best I could do."

"I guess I owe you a big thank you."

"You guess? You prefer the Glasshouse Prison at Aldershot?"

(A federal prison that once featured a leaded glass, lantern-shaped, roof.)

"I didn't mean to kill that man, Luke. Honest."

Luke exhaled loudly.

"I know, Reggie. But this is your chance to turn things around."

"What do you mean?"

"Reggie, you will be one of the strongest men in those tunnels. Show them how it's done. Be the man I know you can be. Lay off the booze and treat everyone the way *you* want to be treated. We are not in St. John's anymore. Your name and your money mean nothing in the tunnels and trenches of France. Remember that."

"I will. And thank you."

"A lot of men die in those tunnels, Reggie. Don't thank me yet."

"Will you write to my father?"

"Yes. Of course."

Luke returned to his dugout and penned a letter to Reginald Windsor.

Dear Mr. Windsor

I have been asked to inform you that your son Reggie has been found guilty by Court Martial, of the

murder of a fellow soldier. Although he was provoked and did not throw the first punch, he has been stripped of his military rank and will serve as a military trainee with the 252nd Tunnelling division for no more than ten years. He is eligible for early release for good behavior or when the war has ended, whichever is earlier.

By order of the court, Reggie has been placed in my care, custody, and control. I know of no procedure by which you can challenge his conviction or the sentence he was given. Nevertheless, I am at your disposal if I can be of any assistance.

Sincerely yours,
Captain Luke Hobbs,
Company A,
1st Newfoundland Regiment

"Have you read the telegram from Luke?'

Reginald Windsor paced the floor in his office like a bull in his pen. Clarence, always with fresh and innovative ideas for his boss to consider, had none.

"I read it, Mr. Windsor. But I am at a loss as to what if anything we can do about it."

Reginald turned suddenly and slammed his fist on the desk, screaming.

"My son is not a murderer, Clarence. Do you understand? He is not a murderer!"

"Mr. Windsor, he is serving his sentence with the Tunnellers, a division of uniformed soldiers with great responsibilities. If Reggie performs as I expect he will, there is a good chance his sentence will be significantly reduced."

Reginald fell into his chair, crushing his newly lit cigar in a nearby ashtray. His heavy breathing slowed. His eyes turned glassy and the man's lips quivered.

"I gave that boy everything he ever wanted, Clarence. Everything.

Perhaps that was the problem, thought Clarence. But he dared not say the words aloud.

"I understand, Mr. Windsor. I understand."

"No. You don't understand Clarence. You have a daughter. Now please leave me alone."

Clarence reached the door and glanced at his boss. Reginald was pouring himself a glass of scotch.

Billy's effort to join the Royal Flying Corps (an extension of the British Army), began at the recruitment office in St. John's.

If necessary, he would argue that a pilot did not require the physical stamina of a soldier in the trenches. Although true, his desired job would be no less risky. Months earlier, the son of former Newfoundland Governor, Terrence O'Brien was killed in action while flying an observer airplane. In Billy's favor, the RFC recently launched an aggressive recruitment campaign. The initiative, spurred in part by significant losses in Gallipoli, became more urgent when plans for the 'big push' took shape. The need for new pilots became both critical and urgent.

The fact that Billy received a medical discharge from the army made his planned reentry problematic but not impossible. He could not request a transfer from one branch of the army to the other. He would be forced to start from scratch. Billy hoped that his father's political connections might help.

"I am inclined to reject your enlistment in the RFC on medical grounds, Billy."

Billy glared at Dr. Macpherson as he buttoned his shirt and finished dressing.

"Why? I'm feeling fine."

"Your breathing is shallow. And while you won't admit it, I believe you are experiencing shortness of breath on a regular basis."

"I am but there has been significant improvement."

"I also worry that your heart has suffered damage."

Billy stepped forward and poked the doctor's chest.

"But you have no evidence of that, do you, Dr. Macpherson?"

"No, Billy. I do not. But experience tells me that my assumption is correct."

Billy's steady gaze intimidated the old man.

"Why in blazes do you want to go back, Billy? You have done your duty and you have earned the rest."

"The Royal Flying Corps is in desperate need of pilots. The cockpit of an airplane is infinitely easier on the body than the trenches. And this war is a long way from over."

"I understand, Billy, but . . ."

Billy cut him off, wagging an accusing finger at the doctor and yelling.

"No, you don't understand, Dr. Macpherson! You don't understand what it's like to watch your friends get killed or horribly wounded while you sit at home and do nothing. You will never understand that. Never!"

The doctor fiddled with his stethoscope, a blush of hot pink covering his face. He spoke in a murmur.

"No. You are correct. And I guess I never will."

The doctor suddenly straightened, his eyes flashing.

"And if I wasn't so dammed old, Billy, I'd be fighting alongside them."

Billy's look softened. He rested a hand on the doctor's shoulder.

"Doc. I'm begging you. Please."

"And if I say no?"

Billy jerked his hand away. "I will go to Canada and enlist there. If *they* don't accept me, I will go to New Zealand or Australia. But I will not stop until I get the answer I want."

"So, I am simply delaying the inevitable."

"Yes, sir. That is precisely what you are doing."

Dr. Macpherson rolled down his shirt sleeves and reached for his suit jacket.

"The Billy Windsor I used to know was not nearly as combative as the one that showed up here this morning."

"If I have made you uncomfortable, I apologize, Dr. Macpherson. But I intend to serve my King and Country, with or without your help."

"I'm late for a luncheon with the Reserve Force Committee."

Billy lunged for the doctor's examination report lying on the desk. He shoved the papers into Macpherson's hands and pointed to the Medal for Gallantry pinned to his uniform.

"I would like to kill a few of the bastards who almost killed me."

Dr. Macpherson studied the form and slowly reached for his pen. He glanced one more time at Billy and scribbled on the paper.

"There are about one hundred reserve troops going to Etaples next week. Good luck."

Dr. Macpherson extended a hand. Billy's face lit up.

"Etaples?"

"Yes, Billy. They call it the 'Bull Room.' A very difficult and challenging training camp. Have you been there?"

Billy flashed a grin.

"No, sir. But I've always wanted to go."

Chapter Ten

THE FACE OF WAR

Reggie Windsor, assigned to the 252nd Tunneling Company as part of his prison sentence, enjoyed his new assignment.

His size, strength, and bear-like demeanor precluded harassment from his colleagues. His performance generated admiration from his superiors. And while he wore a khaki uniform, bereft of any military insignia, no one questioned how or why he joined the tunnellers. Yet.

Reggie learned the details of the tunnellers' current project from the other men. The first mine to blow, when the 'big push' occurred, would be under the Hawthorne redoubt. The shaft, 75 feet deep, would extend more than 1,000 feet toward and under the German lines. The explosion, when it occurred, would do significant damage.

Reggie took great delight from the shower of sparks that flew from his pickax as white chunks of chalk stone fell at his feet. The hard mineral permeated the region and made tunnelling very labor intensive.

"Windsor, you're shooting sparks like a Fourth of July firecracker," said the Sergeant.

Reggie took a breather, using a shirt sleeve to wipe the sweat from his forehead.

"Kinda pretty, isn't it?"

"Sparks are fine, for now, anyway."

"What do you mean, for now?" asked Reggie.

"When we get closer, the Bosch will hear every noise we make. We will soak the walls with water to soften the rock. There won't be any sparks. At that point, we'll use our bayonets and break the stuff up into small pieces."

Reggie scratched his head and furrowed his eyebrows.

"Those chunks will still hit the ground."

"You'll have a partner with a sack. He will catch the chunks of rock before they hit the ground."

"That's gonna take a lot of time."

"That's why we started early," said the sarge.

"It's also going to take a lot of explosives," said Reggie. "We're pretty deep."

The sergeant grinned.

"How's 40,000 pounds of explosive sound to you, Windsor?"

Reggie shook with laughter.

"There won't be enough pieces to find even one of those Bosch bastards."

"OK, boys, back to work."

Despite the hardness of the chalk and the need for silence, most of the tunnellers completed their work by the last week in June. As Reggie made his way back to the tunnel's entrance, a scrum of uniforms spied the newcomer and suddenly stopped talking. They stared at the new recruit in silence. Reggie stopped; stone faced. He placed a second hand on the pickax and brought it to chest level. He spread his feet and waited. The handful of soldiers approached. Reggie stiffened and tightened his grip on the digging tool.

"We wanna talk with you, Windsor."

"I ain't stopping you."

"Why aren't you wearing a uniform?"

Reggie's forehead wrinkled as he bit the inside of his cheek. *They didn't know he was serving a prison sentence*, he concluded. But he couldn't think of an explanation so he told them the truth.

"I got into a fight with another soldier. They decided that digging tunnels would be a good punishment."

"What did you do? Kill him?"

Some of the men snickered. Reggie looked away, pulling on the sweat-soaked collar of his shirt. He blinked repeatedly.

"I only punched him, once. It was an accident."

The soldiers whispered and murmured to each other, all the while staring at Reggie. Reggie's heart pounded in his chest. The soldiers grew silent. Their spokesman cocked his head.

"You're fooling with us, aren't you?"

Reggie saw an opportunity. He winked. His inquisitor grinned. Reggie smirked. One of the men snickered. Someone started laughing. Reggie joined them. The leader stepped forward.

"You're so full of shit, Windsor. But you can sure as hell handle a pickax. As far as I'm concerned, you can wear whatever you want. You're one of us now and we're glad to have you on board."

Someone slapped Reggie on the back. Someone else reached for Reggie's pickax.

"Lemme carry that for you, Windsor. You've done enough work for today."

Reggie hesitated but surrendered his weapon with a smile of appreciation. For the first time since grade school, he felt good about himself. And he did it by himself with no help from his father or his father's money. He worked hard and was recognized for it. Reggie liked the feeling. He decided right then and there to become the best tunneller in all of France.

As he walked with the men, he spotted Luke Hobbs in conversation with the tunnel unit's captain. They both looked up. Luke jerked his head in acknowledgment.

Reggie flashed a wide grin and kept walking.

After a hasty goodbye to his father and Clarence, Billy boarded the *Stephano* to Halifax.

From there, he would sail on a Canadian Pacific steamer, the *Missanbie*, to Liverpool. Billy joined a handful of reserve troops on board the 13,000-ton liner. He traveled almost 200 miles by train, from Liverpool to Oxford. His aeronautical training in Oxford would take place at the Number One School of Military Aeronautics. The instructors' college, formed in 1915, recently expanded into a full-fledged RFC training school. The RFC commandeered several of the buildings belonging to the University of Reading, and used the facilities to train both pilots and flight instructors.

Billy would learn the theoretical aspects of flying, including map reading, gunnery, and mechanics. After an introductory flight with an instructor, he would be given control of the aircraft. There would be additional instruction until he was deemed qualified to solo.

The school wasted no time in the training of new pilots because of the severe shortage. Just months earlier, the RFC ordered every reconnaissance flight to be accompanied by three fighter planes. In the same month, while defending England from a German attack, the RFC lost 10 of 16 planes plus three pilots. RFC pilots rarely survived a dog fight with the German Fokker. The fighter plane carried two machine guns synchronized to the plane's propeller, a technology which the RFC did not yet have.

Billy trained on a Maurice Farman 'Longhorn,' despite its near obsolescence. The French biplane, first built in 1910, was used by the RFC as a reconnaissance airplane. A 70 horsepower Renault engine powered the aircraft which included four wheels, duplicate controls for the instructor and his pupil, a stick for elevation, pedals for rudders, and yards of piano wire, to hold the contraption together. And while the operator felt more like a canary in its cage than a pilot, the plane was difficult to crash. A sleeker version of the Longhorn, dubbed the 'Shorthorn,' could only be accessed after a trainee received his wings. Even Billy, as anxious as he was to climb into a cockpit, marveled at the speed with which he "graduated" from flight school. After just 15 hours of solo flight, the Newfoundland native earned his wings and left for France.

As his transport crossed the channel and glided up the river from Le Havre to Rouen, Billy's recollection of the flying school became nothing more than a distant blur. His stomach fluttered with butterflies and his brain urged caution, but his heart pounded with excitement. Instead of a miserable existence in the muddy trenches below he would soon be soaring through the air, spying on the Germans and, from a safe distance, killing a few of them.

When the lorry (a military truck), arrived at Saint Omer, 85 miles from the Somme River Valley, Billy‘s eyes lit up. A row of BE2c's glistened in the sun.

"Take the one you want. It's yours."

Billy whirled in place and quickly saluted the commanding officer (CO).

"Sir?"

"I said take the one you want. It's yours."

Billy turned on one heel and jogged toward the flying machines. The CO yelled.

"There's no room in there for your kit."

Billy thought about leaving his bag on the hard scrabble apron but abandoned the idea. The CO, a tall, skinny fellow at least a foot taller than Billy and sporting a bushy black moustache, pointed to a large building.

"You will find your billet behind the mess building on the other side of the sheds. Don't worry, son. The plane will be there when you get back. I'll go up with you and give you a tour of the area."

The CO stepped closer and extended a hand.

"The name is Patrick. I don't bother with ranks."

"Billy. Billy Windsor. Why?"

"Why what?"

"Why don't you bother with ranks?"

The CO grew serious.

"Because most of my pilots don't hang around for very long."

Billy frowned.

"They just up and quit flying?"

"No son. They get killed."

Billy's face froze.

The CO slapped Billy on the shoulder.

"But I have a feeling you're going to be different."

"I hope so, sir. I sure as hell hope so."

Billy's first flight over the French countryside left a permanent grin on his face.

He fell in love with the BE2c flying machine, a World Aircraft Factory production, whose popularity with the pilots made it the most widely used aircraft for British reconnaissance missions. Billy's CO described the plane as safe to fly but advised against any dogfights with German fighter planes.

"You wouldn't stand a chance," said the CO.

Billy's two-seater plane came with a single Vickers machine gun and could reach elevations of 10,000 feet. The CO, riding in the front passenger seat, pointed to a series of landmarks with which Billy would find his way back to the aerodrome, the base station for his squadron's aircraft and pilots. Billy decided to impress his CO and quickly climbed to 5,000 feet. Without warning, he shut off the engine, and straightened out the controllers. As expected, the nose of the aircraft, containing the bulk of its weight, quickly pointed to the ground. Billy allowed the aircraft to plunge several thousand feet before restarting the engines and assuming a normal flight pattern.

"I'm impressed, Billy. But don't be trying tricks like that too near the ground. Only fools do that. It's a good way to get killed."

"Yes, sir."

"I'll teach you a more useful maneuver."

The CO explained how to recover from a tailspin by going full throttle, a counter-intuitive tactic when one is plummeting to the ground at breakneck speed. The strategy worked perfectly for Billy on his first attempt. When the aircraft stopped spinning, he was easily able to level off and recover control of the flying machine. Billy also attempted his first loop. After a steep dive with the engine at full power, Billy went vertical. When he passed the vertical, he began a downward plunge and eventually flattened out. The smooth, almost effortless exercise, triggered a compliment from the CO.

"You're a natural, Billy."

"The commander of the regiment is Lieutenant-Colonel Hadow," said Clarence.

Reginald Windsor leaned forward in his office chair.

"What do we know about him?"

"They used to call him 'Fighting Hadow,' a strict disciplinarian. He spent a few years in Egypt attached to their army. In charge of a very large district, answered to almost no one."

"Why would he care about Reggie's situation? Sounds like a dead end," said Reginald.

"He does communicate regularly with Governor Davidson."

"Davidson didn't do me any good the last time I called on him."

"You've got nothing to lose, Mr. Windsor," said Clarence.

"Set up an appointment with the governor. As soon as possible."

"Sister Parsons?"

Elizabeth turned toward the patient who called her name. The soldiers addressed every nurse, whether VAD or professional, as "sister." "Yes, Lieutenant. What can I do for you?"

"My leg is killing me. Can I have something for the pain?"

Elizabeth's body went rigid. She took a sharp breath.

"Lieutenant. You're still feeling the effects of the surgery. Why don't we give it some time?"

"It's swollen and infected. I just know it. Take a look."

When he yanked the bedsheet to one side, his face became a white mask of horror. He saw nothing but bed where his leg should have been. When he pulled the sheet down, the bloody bandage at the end of a foot long stump, came into view. The Lieutenant squeezed his eyes shut. Elizabeth could see the tears as they rolled down the man's cheeks. She rushed to the man's side, grabbing his hand.

"We call it phantom limb syndrome. The nerves in your upper leg transmit false impulses to the brain. I'm afraid it may continue for a few days."

The soldier opened his tear-filled eyes and focused on the stump.

"The doc *told* me they were going to take the leg. I forgot."

Elizabeth stepped away.

"I'll be back in a bit with a cup of tea."

"Yes, sister. I would like that very much. And I apologize for bothering you in the first place."

Elizabeth rushed off. She did not want the soldier to see her tears.

Billy continued his training.

"Think you can fly the plane and take pictures at the same time?"

Billy searched the CO's face. He didn't dare tell the man "No."

"Sure. But I don't know how to operate a camera."

"You're about to learn," said the CO.

As they approached the plane, Billy immediately noticed the rectangular mahogany box attached to the side of his BEc2. He learned from the CO that the handle on top of the box would be used to change the plates. Each plate, once exposed, would be a photograph. To expose the plate, he would pull on a ring attached to the end of a short cord. To aim the camera, he would lean over the side and look through a finder with crosshairs. The procedure would force Billy to fly the plane with his right hand only. After pulling the cord, Billy would pull on the handle and change the plate again.

On the ground it looked easy. The CO read Billy's mind.

"It's not as easy as it looks. That's why I will be going with you."

"What for?"

"I'll be on the gun in case we get company."

"Where are we going?"

"The Somme. Behind enemy lines. The brass wants pictures as soon as possible."

After examining the CO's map, the duo boarded the airplane.

Billy took the machine to 7,000 feet and dropped to 5,000 feet when his target came into view. With his hand resting on the handle, Billy leaned to the left. The 70 mile an hour wind got under his goggles and nearly blew them him off his face. With his fingers around the cord, Billy waited.

"Now," said the CO.

Billy sited the camera one more time and pulled hard.

"Now go to the next plate."

The CO grinned.

"Seventeen more to go."

"Where to next?"

"Keep going. Just follow the trench line."

Billy acclimated quickly to the wind, the cold temperatures, and the use of just one hand on the stick. He did not expect the puffs of smoke which suddenly appeared, 100 feet below and to the side of his aircraft. Before the smoke cleared, he heard two small reports.

He leaned forward and yelled in the CO's ear.

"What the hell was that?"

The CO smiled.

"Archie."

Billy knew what that meant. German anti-aircraft fire. This would be the first time he was Archie's target, however. Billy stayed focused on the camera, calculating that three plates remained. When he pulled on the handle and switched to a new plate, his fingers now numb from the cold, he heard a sharp tearing sound. A close crack of thunder jerked the plane upwards. A long tear in the fabric of the plane appeared and Billy could smell an acrid smoke in the air. The CC turned in his seat.

"That was an archie. They've ranged us."

Billy understood. The Germans could now estimate, to within a few feet, the plane's altitude. Billy took a sudden right turn and flew higher. The CO screamed.

"How many more?"

"Two."

"Get back down there but to a different altitude."

"Yes, sir."

Billy pulled on the cord, twice more, and notified his CO.

"We're done. I'm out of here," said Billy.

The CO pointed straight ahead and screamed.

"Fokker."

Billy could barely see the thin line of the German plane silhouetted in the bright blue sky. The CO trained his machine gun on the target and pulled the trigger. The weapon misfired.

"Jammed," he shouted, beating the ammo drum with his open hand.

The Fokker flew dead ahead. Billy pushed the aircraft into a deep dive. He heard a sharp crack and noticed a small hole in the glass windscreen. Billy's poor vision, now obscured by a spider's web of broken glass, made his job more difficult. The kill shot missed Billy's head by just inches. He put the plane into a wild tailspin, hoping to fool the German fighter pilot. The CO braced for a crash landing. The Fokker gave up the chase. Billy fought every instinct in his body and refused to pull back on the stick. He maintained full opposite rudder, instead. And he waited. Even as the ground below grew larger by the second, he waited. Finally, the flying contraption stopped spinning. He could now pull up on the stick and flatten his trajectory. The CO twisted around and screamed.

"Bring her home, Billy!"

When the aircraft rolled to a stop, Billy started to breathe again. He leaned forward and shouted in the CO's ear.

"Let's do that again sometime!"

"Reginald, we've been down this road before. I don't want you as an enemy but there is nothing I can do for your son."

Governor Davidson paced back-and-forth in his large private office. Reginald Windsor pouted in an overstuffed chair.

"You're the governor, for Christ sakes."

"And Hadow is the lieutenant-colonel in charge of the entire regiment. Not me."

Reginald sprang to his feet, stabbing the air with his cigar.

"My assistant tells me that sentences are often suspended. Why can't you ask Hadow to suspend Reggie's sentence?"

"He killed a man, Windsor. Think of that dead boy's parents. How would you feel if your son's murderer was never punished?"

Reginald jammed the cigar into a nearby ashtray and stormed out of the office.

Reggie's popularity with uniformed members of the Tunnelling Company grew as the tunnel to Hawthorne Ridge got longer.

He worked harder and dug further and faster than any of his counterparts. As they neared the German lines, the importance of silence became critical. Reggie and his colleagues worked quietly. So quietly they heard the Germans tunneling beneath the British tunnel. The men worried about being discovered and fully expected to be killed by a German mine. Each day the tunnel grew in size. And each day, the men grew more anxious and afraid.

The tunnellers now worked in their socks. No talking was allowed, only whispers. The men attached crude handles to their bayonets, the only digging tool allowed. One man would insert his bayonet into a crevice and twist the blade. A second soldier would catch the lump of rock-hard, white chalk, and place it on the ground. Dozens of other men would fill burlap sacks with the loose rocks and pass them down the line. The rocks would be used for tamping material when the explosives were installed.

With just days to go before the big push commenced, the CO approached Reggie.

"We're done here, Reggie. Time to pack the explosives."

"Can I help?"

"Afraid not. That's tricky work. We've got experts for that."

More than 40,000 pounds of explosives would be installed and wired to simultaneously detonate. Reggie, instructed to report back to Captain Hobbs, left the mine disappointed and crestfallen. For a painfully brief time, he served his country well and enjoyed the recognition for doing so. And while the crowded conditions and poor ventilation in the tunnels would make most men claustrophobic, Reggie despised the trenches, even more. The constant supervision, the filthy conditions, and the endless sniper fire made trench life a living hell. He dreaded his return

"Your CO said some nice things about you, Reggie," said Luke.

"Yes, sir. I liked the work. And I would like to keep doing it," he said, using fingers to comb through his unruly head of black hair.

"We've got about four miles of tunnels out there already. Once the big push is underway, I'm not sure the tunnellers will need extra help."

Reggie's lower lip protruded. He blinked repeatedly. Luke stepped closer.

"Reggie? Are you alright?"

Reggie's head drooped. He spoke in a whisper.

"They didn't know I was doing time for murder. I told them but they thought I was kidding. They were nice to me, Luke. Really nice."

"Why do you suppose that is?"

"Hell, if I know."

"Nobody likes a bully, Reggie. Maybe the bully stayed in the guard house this time. And when you're not being a bully, Reggie, you're a nice guy."

Reggie looked up and swallowed hard.

"Luke. What's going to happen to me?"

"Any word from your father?"

"He's seen the governor. He can't help us. I guess no one pushes the lieutenant-colonel around."

"Hadow is a crusty old fellow," said Luke.

"Yeah. So, I hear."

"Report back to the Tunnellers, Reggie. Tell your CO to sit tight until he hears from me."

"What are you going to do?"

"I will talk to Hadow. Everybody's thinking this war is going to be over after the big push. I disagree. Maybe Hadow has the same opinion. And if that's the case, we'll need all the tunnellers we can get."

"I'm not used to this."

"Used to what?"

"People being nice to me and caring about what happens to me."

"I'm looking out for you, Reggie. Don't screw it up."

"Yes, sir."

"Sister Parsons. Come with me."

Dr. Hope wore a glum look, walking briskly to the receiving ward which Elizabeth knew to be nearly empty. Each of the Etaples hospitals, busy preparing for the much rumored "big push," enjoyed a significant reduction in the number of admissions. Elizabeth, struggling to keep up with the man, questioned the surgeon with a quizzical look. He spoke in a quiet voice.

"Head wound. A bad one. Not sure we can do anything for him."

When Elizabeth and the doctor reached the patient's bedside, the man appeared uninjured and normal in every respect, save his head. From the neck to his scalp, the patient lay wrapped in bandages. Small holes appeared where his nose and mouth would have been.

"Help me with the bandages, Sister."

Their combined effort, time-consuming and tedious, led to a shocking discovery. Elizabeth heard the doctor gasp. She covered her mouth to stifle a scream. The soldier, the victim of a trench raid by German soldiers, did not have a face. Both eye sockets were empty. A gaping hole could be seen where the man's nose should have been. The lower half of the man's jaw and most of his upper lip no longer existed. Only a handful of his upper teeth remained. Elizabeth couldn't understand how the private suffered such horrific wounds and yet survived.

"Can you hear me?" asked the doctor, peering into the man's ears.

The patient nodded his head.

"The inner ears look undamaged," said Dr. Hope.

"Can you speak to me?"

The patient grunted, animal-like, and shook his head no.

"Are you able to breathe normally?"

Another nod.

"Please take a deep breath and hold it."

The private, Zachariah Sutherland according to his chart, filled his lungs with air. He did not appear to experience any problems. After listening to his chest, Dr. Hope nodded.

"That's good."

"I assume you cannot chew your food. Are you able to swallow?"

A portion of the man's face twisted. He repeatedly jerked his head backwards. After a series of grunts and deep guttural noises, the man stopped trying. He slowly moved his head from side to side.

"Elizabeth, we will have to fashion a method by which we can administer liquids to Private Sutherland. Can you do that?"

"Yes Doctor. We've done it in the past. You will be well fed, Private Sutherland."

"Are you in pain, private?" asked Dr. Hope.

Sutherland nodded vigorously, gripping the doctor's arm.

"Give him the maximum dosage of morphine. And clean bandages of course. See me when you are finished."

Elizabeth required almost 15 minutes to rewrap the man's head, using yards of clean gauze and pining it in place. After excusing herself for a few minutes, she returned with the morphine, a needle, a large bottle, a length of rubber tubing, and a pot of tea. After injecting the man's shoulder with 16 milligrams of the pain killer, she reached for the feeding paraphernalia.

"We will start with some warm tea, Private Sutherland. I'm sure it will make you feel better."

When she attempted to insert the tube into the man's esophagus, he gagged and started coughing. Elizabeth pulled on the tube.

"A gagging reflex is normal, Private Sutherland. Let's try that again, a bit slower this time."

Elizabeth didn't get the tubing entirely in the man's mouth, when he pushed her hands away, reached for the feeding device, and threw it to the floor.

"Private Sutherland, you will not survive without nourishment. Please let me help you."

Sutherland shook his head violently. He repeatedly pointed to the injection site on his shoulder.

"I understand, Private Sutherland. You are still in pain. I must speak with the doctor. I'll be right back."

"Give him whatever he wants, Sister Elizabeth. There is nothing more we can do. We might as well make him comfortable," said Dr. Hope.

Elizabeth winced but did not object. When she returned to Sutherland's bedside, she injected one-half of the previous dosage amount. The patient did not wait for the medication to take effect. He pointed to the injection site, tapping it with an index finger.

"Private Sutherland. You must give the morphine a chance to work. If I give you much more, you will go to sleep and you won't wake up."

He jerked his head up and down and reached for her hands. He pulled them to his chest and squeezed. The two large dark holes, where his eyes should have been, pierced the woman's soul. She quickly stepped away from the bed, shaking her head.

"No. I won't do it. Don't ask me to do that, Private Sutherland. I'm here to save lives, not take them."

Chapter Eleven

THE BIG PUSH

Luke slammed his field phone into its receiver.

The "big push," originally scheduled for June 29, would be postponed to July 1, at 7:30 in the morning. Four successive days of rain made it impossible for the Royal Flying Corps to accurately sight their bombs or pinpoint the precise location of enemy artillery positions. The five-day artillery barrage, designed to destroy the enemy's front line, would be extended for two more days. Unfortunately, it meant two more days of misery for his men.

Luke and his subordinates stood, ate, and slept in several feet of mud and water. Not surprisingly, morale was low. A date certain for the "big push" gave the men some desperately needed hope. They happily welcomed the opportunity to engage the enemy after months of delay. The experienced veterans of trench warfare at Gallipoli exhibited a more reserved demeanor.

"All commanders will use this whistle to signal or attack. We go together," said Luke, sounding his whistle and demonstrating its loud, high-pitched squeal.

"I am told we can expect minimal resistance from the German front line but their reserve trench could be just the opposite. So, let's be alert and let's be prepared."

The men's preparations included a fully loaded kit. In addition to their rifle and bayonet, each man would carry 170 rounds of ammo, two Mills grenades, a gas mask, their steel helmet, a water bottle, two field dressings for the treatment of wounds, and a waterproof sheet. The high command also required them to carry two empty sandbags. The bags would be used for repairs to the German trenches, which they hoped to occupy in the next 48 hours.

Soldiers were also reminded to wear their identity disc, a round piece of vulcanized asbestos fiber, approximately one and a third inches in diameter. The disc would hang from a cord around the neck with the man's identity stamped in indelible ink. In addition, almost half of the troops would be ordered to carry shovels or picks. There were also supplies to be brought forward, including flares, wooden pickets, sledgehammers, wirecutters, small cooking stoves, extra haversacks, and Bangalore torpedoes. The typical soldier would carry more than 70 pounds of "baggage" into battle.

One additional item triggered an objection from Luke. The divisional commander ordered that each man wear a triangular piece of metal cut from a biscuit tin. The triangle, seven inches on each side, would be sewn in between the shoulder blades, on the man's haversack. In theory, the shiny metal would assist pilots who, while observing the field of battle, would need to know which of the mud-covered soldiers belonged to the

German army and which of them belonged to the British Expeditionary Forces.

"It might also be a big shiny target on their backs," muttered Luke.

But no one was listening.

The tunnel to Hawthorne Ridge, on which Reggie Windsor worked so long and hard, would be detonated at 7:20 a.m., on July first.

The precise timing would allow British Expeditionary Forces to occupy the large crater immediately after the explosion occurred and before the Germans could reach the site. The explosion would also signal the beginning of the "big push"

At 7:20 a.m., the earth trembled and tons of dirt, debris, rock, and rubble flew thousands of feet into the air. The explosion killed and then buried hundreds of German soldiers. The Newfoundlanders, a thousand yards away, rushed over the top of their trenches, anticipating that the Hawthorne Ridge explosion, and the preceding seven-day artillery barrage, already accomplished most of their work. Luke, scanning the horizon to his left and right, could see thousands of men in wave after wave, walking slowly toward enemy lines, their bayonets glistening in the sun.

The calm determination which characterized the British attack disappeared when an ear-shattering cacophony of machine gun fire, artillery fire, and rifle shots filled the air. The German army, thought to be all but eliminated by the artillery barrage, were alive and in fighting form. In fact, they beat the British Army to the Hawthorn Ridge crater and used the crater,

130 feet wide and 60 feet deep, as a superior position from which to attack British forces. The volume and accuracy of the German onslaught triggered chaos and confusion amongst the men of the 1st Newfoundland Regiment. Everyone fell to the ground. A few of the men searched desperately for cover. Most of the soldiers fell because they were killed or wounded. As the Germans sprayed death in every direction, Luke could not believe the massacre unfolding before his eyes.

"Down! Everybody down!" he shouted.

For many of the men, the warning came too late. Luke rolled into a small crater, landing on the motionless bodies of men he knew by name. He could hear the anguished cries and sickly groans of men screaming for help or begging for death. He rolled to his knees to survey the battlefield, panicked as to what he should do next. As the bullets screamed past his head, a sudden force slammed him back into the crater. His body, pulsing with adrenaline, did not immediately register the bullet which entered the left side of his chest. Minutes later, when breathing became painful, Luke could feel the sticky red liquid which oozed from his torso and soaked his uniform. He slipped in and out of consciousness. He cried out.

"Mother! Where are you?"

His eyes grew heavy. Finally, he surrendered to the darkness.

One of Luke's men saw the captain when he fell back into the crater.

When Hobbs failed to return that evening, the man led the stretcher bearers right to his CO. Under the cover of darkness, they brought Hobbs, barely alive, to the casualty clearing station.

They could do little more than apply clean bandages and administer morphine. The absence of an exit wound indicated that the projectile ricocheted wildly after entering Luke's body. Major surgery would be necessary. They placed Captain Hobbs on the Ambulance Train, convinced that he would not survive the trip to Etaples.

After almost 12 hours in the air, Billy, his CO, and the other pilots, lay exhausted in their billets.

"The "big push" did not go as planned," said the CO.

"I heard most of the Newfoundland Regiment was wiped out," said Billy.

"The reports I saw estimated a fifty percent casualty rate," said the CO. He continued. "I could see the Germans pouring out of their dugouts. Our troops didn't have a chance against the Bosch machine guns or their artillery. Most of the Brits were mowed down."

Billy objected.

"It was supposed to be a walk-over."

"The Bosch were dug in. Deep I expect. The barrage didn't take 'em out. And I'm not sure it destroyed their barbed wire, either. The Germans installed it two and three rows deep. Only a handful of our men got that close anyway."

"I've got quite a few friends in the Newfoundland Regiment," Billy grumbled.

"You can hope for the best, Billy. But if I were you, I'd plan for the worse."

Billy closed his eyes, intending to say a prayer for his older brother.

He fell asleep instead.

A rising sun and the CO's voice forced Billy's eyes open on the morning after the big push.

"We got orders from HQ."

"What did they say?" asked one of the pilots.

"Bomb everything."

Billy's eyebrows shot up.

"How am I supposed to carry a couple of 100-pound bombs? I can barely afford the weight of a spotter."

"The spotters sit this one out."

Billy tilted his head.

"Are you sure?"

"Don't be giving me any crap, Windsor. You haven't been here long enough.

"Sorry, sir. It's a death sentence if you ask me."

The CO stormed toward the exit and yelled over his shoulder.

"It's an order, Windsor."

The RFC enjoyed air superiority going into the "big push." In the weeks that followed, the balance of power threatened to shift. In addition to the 'Fokker scourge,' the Germans now utilized a new aircraft manufactured in Germany, called the Halberstadt D.II. The biplane, much more maneuverable, performed well as a low-level attack plane and posed a significant threat to RFC pilots.

Despite their weakened position in the skies over France, Billy and his colleagues prepared to go on the attack. There would be one day of bombing practice at the aerodrome. The pilots would dive to 1,000 feet, dropping their explosives on a target located in an abandoned farm field. Billy received the highest marks for accuracy but his skepticism remained.

"Tomorrow, we do it for real," announced the CO.

Billy's orders sent him to a large building behind German lines, thought to be a supply depot.

A busy rail station lay nearby. He would drop bombs on both structures. He flew to the rail station first. Just as he practiced, Billy put the BEc2 into a deep dive, screaming over the rail station at 1,000 feet. After dropping one of his bombs, he banked sharply to the right, looking over his shoulder to confirm the hit. Dancing flames and large clouds of billowing smoke triggered a big grin. The train station was demolished.

He circled, searching the horizon for his second target. Loud popping noises alerted him to incoming ground fire. At least one bullet penetrated the tightly stretched fabric on his machine. When the stick began to jerk wildly in his hands, Billy knew that his rudder had been hit. He put the plane into a steep climb, desperate to get out of the range of enemy machine guns and rifle fire. Even at 5,000 feet, he would still be in the range of the enemy's 'flaming onions.' The Brits called the special Gatlin-type gun that fired these projectiles a 'light splitter.' The gun could be loaded with 37 mm shells or pyrotechnical shells (flares). Either way, they would destroy the highly flammable wings on Billy's plane on contact.

When he reached 10,000 feet, a loud banging noise could be heard from the engine. Believing it to have been damaged, Billy cut the engine. Still in German territory, he dropped the remaining bomb, calculating that a forced landing would trigger the explosive and kill him, instantly. Now, despite a flapping rudder and a dead stick, he headed for home. The deathly quiet trip to lower and lower elevations, seemed to require hours. In fact, he spotted several familiar landmarks within thirty minutes. He circled repeatedly, to lower his altitude and speed. His landing, although rough, occurred without incident.

The condition of his machine, visible to the other pilots already back from their mission, prompted the men to run in Billy's direction. When Billy climbed out, he could hear a series of cheers.

"We thought you were a goner," said one of the men.

"Sorry to disappoint you," said Billy, an oversized grin on his face.

He scanned the scrum looking for the CO.

"Where's the CO? Don't tell me he's pissed at me again."

The pilots stared. Nobody moved. After a minute, one of them spoke up.

"I saw him go down. Looked like a flaming onion got him. He didn't have a chance."

Elizabeth heard a woman's loud scream and ran to the recovery ward.

She immediately suspected Private Sutherland as the culprit. An inexperienced, newly arrived VAD, could be seen running from the ward, crying hysterically. Elizabeth ignored the nurse, and marched straight to Sutherland's bed. She winced when her patient came into view. The horribly disfigured soldier, sitting in bed with his arms folded, had removed every bandage from his head. Elizabeth spoke firmly.

"Private Sutherland. Why did you remove your dressings? You do want your wounds to heal, do you not?"

Sutherland shook his head violently from side to side. Again, he pointed to the injection site in his left shoulder, repeatedly slapping at it.

"You have received the maximum dosage of morphine, Private. I am not allowed to give you any more."

Again, the private shook his head from side to side and used a finger to poke, first at his shoulder and then in Elizabeth's direction.

"I will speak to Dr. Hope. But first we must replace your bandages," she said, noticing the bloody gauze strewn on the highly polished wooden floor.

When she returned with a tray for supplies and reached for the man's head, he swung wildly hitting her in the chest with his forearm. Elizabeth fell backwards crashing through one of the fabric walls and landing on the floor. She scrambled to her feet and rushed to the man's side.

"Hit me again, Private, and I will hit you twice as hard, in your privates."

For a moment, Sutherland sat perfectly still. Slowly, his head drooped forward. He hit the top of his head with both fists. He did it repeatedly until Elizabeth intervened, this time, in a whisper.

"Zachariah. Listen to me. Please."

She squeezed both of his hands, bringing them to her cheeks.

"You mustn't give up, Zachariah. I'm told there is a hospital in Aldershot which specializes in reconstructive surgery."

Sutherland angrily jerked his hands away.

"Will you at least let me replace the bandages?" she asked.

When the soldier didn't move, Elizabeth assumed consent. She instructed him to lean forward and wrapped several lengths of gauze around the man's head. Totally engrossed in her task and with her view of the tray blocked, Elizabeth could not see her patient's wandering hands. He gingerly used his fingers to search the tray. Although Elizabeth returned from the supply room with additional morphine, she carried it in her pocket. Sutherland retrieved a pair of scissors. In one smooth motion, he brought the shears to his head and used both hands to point the sharp end in to one of the empty sockets. The gauze she held, fluttered in Elizabeth's trembling hands.

"Zachariah. Please no. Not that way."

The scissors did not move.

Elizabeth reached into her pocket.

"I brought the morphine."

The suicide scissors remained in place. Elizabeth filled her syringe. She pinched a slab of loose flesh on the man's shoulder and inserted the needle. She estimated the amount to be twice the fatal dosage. When finished, she tossed the empty syringe on to the tray and reached for the scissors.

"You won't be needing these," she whispered.

Sutherland lowered the scissors. Elizabeth placed them on the tray and reached for the man's hands.

"Would you like me to stay with you?"

The man nodded. She fluffed the pillows and suggested he lay back. Elizabeth could feel his slowing pulse. She smothered a sob and sniffed. His hand reached for her face. She tried to blink the tears away but failed. He searched her face with a gentle caress and discovered the tears. Zachariah pulled the nurse to his chest. He dried the tears with his bandages and hugged the woman he could neither see nor speak with.

"Thank you," she choked.

He shook his head, pointed to her, and then placed both hands over his heart. Minutes later, the man lay motionless. Elizabeth rested a stethoscope on his chest.

She heard a woman sobbing. Nothing more.

Elizabeth mourned the death of her faceless friend by keeping busy.

Casualties from the "big push" arrived by the train load. She wondered how Captain Luke fared, worried that a full two weeks after the battle of the Somme, she received no letters from him. She could set her watch, or at least a calendar, by the regularity of his missives. It always amazed her to receive his letters, given that she rarely responded in kind.

"I saw what you did to that man with no face."

The woman's voice caught Elizabeth by surprise. The inexperienced VAD nurse, hysterical after seeing the man's unbandaged face, now confronted Elizabeth with arms folded and a scowl on her face. Elizabeth played dumb.

"I'm not sure what you mean, Sister Fletcher."

Elizabeth calculated that the woman did not leave the ward that morning, and most likely hid behind a door or bedside curtain. The young nurse shook a finger in Elizabeth's face.

"You gave that man an entire vial of morphine," she said, stepping forward.

"That man, Sister Fletcher, has a name. Private Zachariah Sutherland. And I suggest you show some respect for the men who died in the service of King and Country. Please refer to them by name."

"It is my intention to pursue the matter," said the young nurse.

Elizabeth flashed a fake smile.

"I hope you have a good day, Sister Fletcher."

The VAD nurse marched off. Elizabeth continued to inventory the medicine cabinet.

The glass bottles and vials clinked loudly in her shaking hands.

"Windsor."

"Yes, sir."

Reggie scrambled to his feet when his lieutenant appeared at the doorway.

"Orders from Lieutenant-Colonel Hadow. You are to continue your work with the 252nd."

Reggie allowed a slight smile.

"Thank you, sir."

"But the lieutenant-colonel says if he gets one more communication from the Newfoundland governor or your father, he will lock you up himself."

"Yes, sir. I'll take care of that, right away, sir."

The lieutenant turned to leave. Reggie called out.

"Sir?"

"Yes."

"I would like to thank Captain Luke."

"You mean Hobbs?"

"Yes, sir."

"Didn't you get the news? He took one in the chest when we went over the top. Not sure he made it."

Reggie's eyes bulged.

"How do I find out for sure?"

"His next of kin, I suppose."

Reggie made a beeline to the cable office. He slipped the dispatcher a pack of cigarettes with a handwritten note.

"Can you read it?" asked Reggie.

Luke seriously wounded. Condition unknown. Contact his mother. Still digging tunnels. Happy. Do NOT interfere.

Reggie

Reginald Windsor threw the cable into the air.

Clarence, forced to wait until the paper fluttered to the floor, read it twice.

"I'm sure she's received a telegram by now," said Clarence.

"What about Reggie?" asked Reginald.

Clarence could smell alcohol on the old man's breath.

"Perhaps, Mr. Windsor, we should leave well enough alone."

"What do you mean by that?"

"If he's happy and there's nothing we can do, why interfere?"

Reginald jumped to his feet; eyes blazing. He threw his lit cigar at Clarence, hitting the man's suit jacket. Clarence flailing at the sparks and ashes with both hands, raised his voice.

"Mr. Windsor. My suit!"

"Do nothing? Is that your advice, Mr. Parsons? I am paying you a small fortune as my assistant and that is what I get for my money? Do nothing?"

Clarence pleaded.

"I am simply suggesting that we do nothing for the moment. We do not want to jeopardize Reggie's situation. He is happy doing what he's doing. Isn't that the most important consideration?"

"Of course. Of course. Above all, let's keep my son happy. And when he comes home in 10 years, we can have a big parade for my son the convicted murderer."

Reginald reached in to a desk drawer for the bottle of scotch he regularly secreted.

"I need a drink."

He waved an empty glass at his assistant.

"No, thank you, Mr. Windsor."

Windsor swallowed the contents in two gulps and poured another one.

"I want you to check on Luke's mother. Do it now."

Mrs. Hobbs received a telegram about her wounded son, but refused to believe its contents.

Clarence summoned Mrs. Hynes, the midwife's assistant, to keep the old woman company.

"Perhaps Mr. Windsor will make some inquiries and tell me if my Luke is coming home," said Mrs. Hobbs, her weak voice cracking with emotion.

Clarence nodded.

"I'm sure he will, Mrs. Hobbs. I'm sure he will."

As trainloads of wounded arrived at Etaples, Elizabeth recalled that Officers Hospital Number 24 would accept officers only.

That proviso, sometimes ignored for the critically wounded, disappeared in the face of the overwhelming number of casualties. Patients could now be found in beds and litters, on floors, in hallways, in lobbies and recreation rooms and in dining rooms.

"The receiving ward has a serious chest wound that only Dr. Hope will be able to handle. Can he stop in for a quick visit?" asked the matron.

Elizabeth, now scheduling surgeries for Dr. Hope and exhausted, shook her head. She spoke in a hoarse whisper.

"I am terribly sorry, Matron. It just can't be done. He has a double amputation in just a few minutes."

"I will leave the patient here, for now. Honestly, I don't think he'll live much longer, in any event. A very bad chest wound. And he's a captain too. Let me know if Dr. Hope has a last-minute opening."

Elizabeth nodded and resumed her tasks. She calculated that she slept less than eight hours in the last three days. The woman's ghostly white complexion and dark circles under both eyes, betrayed a lack of sleep and a poor diet.

"You need some rest, Elizabeth. Now," said Dr. Hope.

"Thank you, Doctor, but we have one more surgery before you go. A double amputation I believe."

"No, we don't. I just checked on him. We are too late. So, we both get some rest."

Elizabeth fell into a bedside chair blowing the hair from her face and closing her eyes.

"I can't remember what it was like to get a good night's sleep," she said.

"Come on, I'll walk you to your billet."

As they traversed the long hallway, Elizabeth saw the receiving ward room entrance and came to a sudden halt.

"Oh no, I forgot."

"Forgot what?"

"We've got a captain in the receiving ward. A very bad chest wound. Matron wanted you to look at him. She didn't think he was going to make it through the night."

Dr. Hope closed his eyes and shook his head.

"You're impossible, Elizabeth. Absolutely impossible."

As they marched across the oversized lobby, Dr. Hope pointed to a young VAD nurse.

"Do you know her?"

Elizabeth recognized the young woman who accused her of killing Private Sutherland.

"Yes, Dr. Hope. We've met before."

"She has filed a complaint with the colonel, you know."

Elizabeth, uncertain as to what the doctor knew, feigned ignorance.

"About what?"

"About our faceless friend."

"Private Zachariah Sutherland. You instructed me to give him whatever he required. And I did."

Doctor Hope furrowed his eyebrows.

"Yes. I did say that, didn't I?"

"I stayed with him until the end. He was in such pain. I'm not sure the morphine even made a difference."

"Perhaps not. But I suspect *you* made a difference."

"I hope so, Dr. Hope. I really do."

"Don't worry about the complaint. I'll take care of it."

When they reached the receiving ward, Elizabeth surveyed the sea of beds, carts, and stretchers.

"I have no idea where this fellow is located," she said, motioning for a VAD nurse.

"You have a captain with a very serious chest wound. Matron wants Dr. Hope to have a look."

"Yes, Sister Parsons. That would be Captain Hobbs. I'm surprised he's still alive. Follow me, please."

Elizabeth reached for the doctor's arm. Her knees went wobbly. Her vice-like grip made the man wince.

"Elizabeth. What is it?"

"It's my friend. It's my friend, Luke," she murmured.

The commander of the Royal Flying Corps, Hugh "Boom" Trenchard, used a telegram to announce Billy's promotion to captain and his new assignment: Temporary Squadron Commander.

Billy would move sixty miles north to Candas, a number 2 depot. The second-class landing field featured a single hangar and billets for four flights of four pilots each. Flights were led by captains. Squadrons were led by a major. Billy was now a captain, doing a major's work.

Trenchard planned to visit the depot at Candas. He commanded the RFC from its headquarters at Saint Omer. Billy and the lieutenant-colonel had yet to meet, making the promotion especially surprising.

"Now why did he go and do a stupid thing like that?" asked Billy.

The clerk arched his eyebrows.

"You're pulling my leg, aren't you?"

"No, I'm not pulling your leg. The guy doesn't even know me."

"It might have something to do with that medal on your chest."

"That and the fact that our CO went and got himself killed," said Billy.

Billy took a deep breath and tossed the cable on the CO's desk.

"Assemble the men at Candas for a meeting in their mess tent for 1800 hours."

"Yes sir."

"The Major has designated me as your acting CO."

The pilots, all of them older than Billy, wore surprised looks on their faces. A few of them frowned.

"Yes, I know. I was as shocked as the rest of you."

The men laughed. A loud voice in the back of the room got everyone's attention.

"That's all right, Captain. We've heard about you. The way you fly, you won't be our CO for very long."

The men laughed and applauded. Billy blushed pink and grinned. He paused and then donned a somber look.

"All right. Listen up. Our commander, Lieutenant-Colonel Trenchard is coming for a visit, day after tomorrow, 08:00 hours. He will conduct an inspection and would like to meet both you and members of the ground crew."

"What are our orders?"

"More reconnaissance. Plus bombing raids, balloons, and trench work. Each flight will take their turn. Two missions per day. After you have done all three sorties you will start over. Questions?"

The men nodded and Billy assigned each flight (four pilots per flight) their first assignment. Until the morning of Trenchard's visit, the men would practice. They took photographs, dropped bombs on a nearby farm field, and target practiced with their machine guns. When the day came, Billy greeted the commander with a salute and a handshake.

"Welcome to Candas, sir."

The men liked "Boom" Trenchard, from the start. He credited them for recent successes.

"But you get only half of the credit," he added.

The commander awarded the second half to the ground crews. To a man, the pilots agreed with Trenchard. Everyone knew just how important the ground crew was to their survival. Trenchard also urged the men to be as aggressive as possible.

"We must grind the Huns down. That means we photograph everything, we shoot everything, and we bomb everything. Is that understood?"

The men clapped and cheered.

Billy's flight, four BEc2's took the first LOP assignment.

Line Offensive Patrols required the pilot to cruise up and down enemy trench lines as a means of distracting the Germans while the RFC's observation planes took photographs. Billy and his colleagues could do little more than strafe the German trenches and pray that the usual casualty rate would not apply. One third of pilots who engaged in such high-risk flying were captured or killed. On the morning of the attacks Billy made another surprise announcement.

"We have a dozen steel plates. Any takers?"

All of the plates disappeared. The 450-pound steel slabs would worsen the performance of the already sluggish BE2c's. They would also afford an extra measure of protection from the close-range ground fire that such sorties triggered. Billy did not reserve a plate for himself. He did not think it appropriate for the squadron commander to pull rank in such matters.

In any event, there was no protection against fire. Billy, one of the few pilots to have studied the manufacturing process, knew that the tightly stretched fabric which covered the machine's air frame was highly flammable. To waterproof and strengthen the material, a colorless liquid of cellulose mixed with acetone, benzene, and tetrachloroethane, was applied in the manufacturing process. Six coats of it. Long after the solution dried, it remained extremely flammable. A red-hot projectile, such as a bullet, could start a fatal conflagration. When a plane caught fire, the pilot had three choices. He could jump to his death (parachutes were not issued), he could burn to death, or he could use the pistol strapped to his hip and finish the job himself.

Billy led the observation flights deep into enemy territory. He banked and then flew low over the German trenches, his engine screaming just 100 feet above the German positions. He constantly varied both his speed and elevation to make the enemy's job more difficult. After several passes he searched the sky for the RFC observation planes. The photographers had finished their work.

Billy put his machine into a deep climb and leaned forward in search of landmarks, which would guide him back to Candas. When he did so, the goggles which protected his eyes and face, flew off and out of the cockpit. Seeing clearly in a 70 plus mile-per-hour wind suddenly became difficult. When he checked the stick, he could see daylight through a coin-sized hole in the floor of the airplane. A small trickle of blood extending from his hairline to an eyebrow, gave him the answer. A bullet had penetrated the cockpit from the bottom of the aircraft, hit the goggles, and creased his forehead.

The newly minted promoted squadron commander survived his first mission because of inches.

As Elizabeth and Dr. Hope examined the captain, she recalled her often nonchalant and tardy responses to Luke's weekly letters.

A pang of guilt washed over the woman as she and the doctor removed the bloody bandages from Luke's chest. They searched for an exit wound and concluded that the bullet remained somewhere in Luke's chest cavity or, worse, his abdomen.

"We've got to get the bullet out but I have no idea where to cut," said the doctor. Elizabeth agreed.

"He's still bleeding. The bullet may have nicked one of the main arteries after ricocheting off a rib."

"The x-ray people will argue the futility of it all. He's not going to make it, Elizabeth. Is he a close friend?"

Elizabeth nodded and suddenly shook her head no, repeatedly blinking.

"No . . . I mean yes . . . well . . . not really. We were . . . I was . . . well . . . let's just say the relationship never went anywhere."

"The x-ray people are backed up as it is," said Hope. I cannot justify an x-ray on this man. I can't help him. I am truly sorry, Elizabeth."

Elizabeth rubbed the tears from her eyes and cleared her throat.

"I understand, Dr. Hope. And I agree with you. If your schedule permits, I would like to stay with him."

"By all means, Sister. Stay as long as necessary."

Although Elizabeth's eyelids fluttered from exhaustion, she remained at Luke's side. The man now wore the sickly gray color of death with which Elizabeth was so familiar. Elizabeth recalled the last time they saw each other. She had just discovered the repaired buggy. Luke appeared and confessed to the good deed. They shared her first kiss. When they said goodbye that morning, she thought his eyes glistened more than usual. Later, that same day, as she made her midwifery rounds, Elizabeth wondered if their tumultuous relationship would change. Whether the man's anger would melt in the face of her genuine affection. Whether her joyous optimism would overcome his natural cynicism. Whether two jackasses could ever get along.

And then, the world went to war and each of them went their own way.

She examined Luke, once again. His appearance did not change. His labored breathing, continued. She rose to her feet, thinking that a few laps around the man's bed would ease the stiffness in her joints and keep her awake for a while longer. She absentmindedly reached into the pocket of her apron and rediscovered the envelope that arrived two weeks ago. Elizabeth ripped it open and sat at Luke's bedside, reading the man's last words. She read it twice.

My dear Elizabeth

Given the tardiness of your responses, I must now assume that my weekly missives are boring you or being used as kindling.

Regardless, I bring you greetings from where the "big push" will soon commence. We are being told that it will be nothing more than a "walk over," the Bosch supposedly "destroyed" by our days-long artillery barrage. It should not surprise you that my natural skepticism has rendered a celebration of our anticipated victory as premature, if not entirely misplaced.

Interestingly, we have distributed writing materials to the men, for letters to their loved ones, should they fail to return home. (Perhaps HQ shares my cynicism!) If nothing else, I must set a good example for my men, hence this letter to you. Please forward it to mother, should I remain in the French countryside. Literally.

All of which brings me to the real purpose of this note. Like so many others, I too have been changed by this miserable war. First and most, I have discovered humility. The admission itself is humbling. For my entire adult life, I just assumed that I was the smartest person in the room (sound familiar?) and should be accorded the respect and blind fealty that such intelligence deserves.

I was mistaken. There are ways of earning respect that require considerably more than book learning. In the midst of the mud, the blood, the death, and the destruction of this awful war, I have witnessed bravery in the face of unspeakable horror. I have seen heart-rending occasions of kindness in a sea of cruelty and I have watched ordinary men displaying an extraordinary courage in the face of certain failure.

I have often read of such things but never believed it. I never took it to heart. I never learned from it. My men, many of them with little or no schooling, have taught me by their example, more than any professor at the best university could have imparted to me in a thousand lectures. Becoming a captain has taught me how to be a good private. Leading soldiers has taught me how to be a good soldier. And watching a man in his final minutes on this earth, talk of nothing except the family he loves, has made me realize the absence of love in my own life.

I like to think that, absent this horrible war, I might have discovered such truths on my own. Perhaps not. After all, I failed to notice your courage, your intelligence, and your independence. And all of it was

on display each time we met. I truly was, as you once said, a jackass.

Please forgive my stubborn ignorance, Elizabeth, and be assured that if I survive this war, I will mend my ways. I will also do what any man in his right mind would have done on the first day he met you. I will ask for your hand in marriage.

With love,
Luke

Elizabeth sobbed into her brilliant white apron. Her fatigue and Luke's heartbreaking words brought her own life into a painfully sharp focus. She regularly disguised her own arrogance as ambition but it was there, never the less. And she thought it only natural that the librarian in the room would be the smartest person in the room. And love? In truth, the only person she really loved was herself. Everyone else was someone who could satisfy her needs. In the end, she was not much different from Luke. Her life too, was filled with regrets. And she too lived, unloved and alone.

Luke's unblinking eyes, now open, stared in her direction. She noticed the dilated pupils and the ashen color of his skin. His chest no longer rose with each labored breath. Instinctively, she reached for his wrist and searched for a pulse. Tear-filled eyes burned Luke's face into her memory. With a soft caress of her fingers, she closed his eyes and whispered in his ear.

"Yes, Luke. I would have said yes."

Chapter Twelve

CASUALTIES

A handful of the men who served under Captain Luke Hobbs, all of them recovering from their own wounds, stood at attention as the late captain's remains slowly descended into the French countryside.

The popular leader, eulogized by one of his fellow captains in the 1st Newfoundland Regiment, received the usual military honors. After a few days, Luke Hobbs became just another name, in a list of thousands who gave their lives for King and Country.

Mrs. Hobbs, when she received the telegram, fervently prayed that the British Army had, once again, erred. A letter from Elizabeth and Luke Hobbs' last words before he went into battle, made it painfully clear. The old woman's prayers would not be answered.

Reggie Windsor, one of hundreds who listened to the Regimental Commander's solemn announcement, no longer feared a physical confrontation with Luke Hobbs. He feared the dead man's absence. *Who would watch over him? Who would keep him in line? Who would be his wise counsel and confidant?*

Reggie scattered with the other troops when the commander dismissed the regiment. He snarled and avoided eye contact with his colleagues, giving everyone the impression that the captain's death left Reggie angry and frustrated. He was. He was angry and frustrated with himself. Luke Hobbs saved his life. On and off the battlefield.

And now, Reggie would never be able to repay the debt.

In the immediate aftermath of the big push, the tunnellers found themselves repairing and constructing roadways.

That would soon change. The Battle of the Somme produced no significant gains on either side of 'no man's land.' As a result, British troops, unable to get through or even around enemy strongholds, had no choice but to go under them. Reggie and the 252nd Tunnelling Company returned to the front lines within a month.

Reggie, taking advantage of his newfound popularity with both his colleagues and the CO, quizzed the lieutenant.

"How deep? How long?"

"Our goal is 400 feet from the shaft. That should put us behind enemy lines. We estimate sinking a sloped entrance to about 25 feet and then the tunnel itself."

"Count me in," said Reggie, triggering a gale of laughter from the crew.

In truth, the diggers had no choice. The assignment, to be completed by the end of August, would culminate in an explosion of 3,000 pounds of ammonal. The explosive, made up of ammonium nitrate and aluminum powder, would be a substitute for TNT. Reggie watched with glee as the mine exploded on September 3, 1916. It enabled the Black Watch (Scottish troops) to immediately occupy the large crater which resulted from the blast. Unfortunately, the Huns counter-attacked with bombs and crossfire from a string of machine guns. The Scots, forced to evacuate, retreated to their original lines.

Reggie and his team then dug a second tunnel. It too was loaded with 3,000 pounds of explosive. The second explosion, arranged to coincide with an attack by BEF infantry, inflicted heavy losses on the enemy. The crater gave the Brits a commanding position. This time they managed to hang onto the newly conquered piece of real estate.

It would play a large role in future victories.

"Trenches and dugouts? Are you serious?"

Reggie openly challenged the lieutenant's latest announcement. The constant rains, so characteristic of France in the fall, transformed trenches and dugouts into rivers of mud. The dirt walls, even when reinforced, collapsed. Parapets, the elevated portion of the trench which faced the enemy, crumbled to the ground, leaving the men exposed to enemy sniper fire. Several members of various regiments drowned in the soupy mess which often reached to waist-level and beyond. The men, forced to live, eat, and fight in the muck, suffered from trench foot and were unable to keep their weapons in firing order. Sleep was extremely difficult, and moving about in the trenches became impossible. The soldiers in the trenches needed help.

Desperately. Reggie's assignment, to drain and repair the trenches, was a matter of life and death.

While busy in one of the trenches, Reggie spied a parade of strange vehicles.

"What in blazes is that?" he asked.

He pointed to a caravan of four monster vehicles heading south. The lieutenant spoke up.

"Them are tanks, boys, on their way to Flers-Courcelette. And they're gonna scare the pants off them Huns."

The huge machines, a secret weapon until that day, would be used for the first time. The diggers, mesmerized by the sound and sight of the BEF's latest weapon, stood in silence. Reggie's eyes fixed on the massive metal machines as they lumbered across the battlefield. Although pockmarked with craters and strewn with barbed wire, the war-torn obstacle course did not hinder the tanks. When the machines disappeared over the horizon, Reggie's CO barked.

"All right, men. Show's over. Back to work!"

Days later, the men unexpectedly stopped their digging, once again.

They heard a muffled explosion, deep in the ground. It came from a long-ago abandoned tunnel.

"We haven't worked that tunnel in two months," said the lieutenant.

"I'll check it out," said Reggie.

The lieutenant barked his objection.

"No, Windsor, you won't. Keep digging. Leroy, you go. And be quick about it."

Reggie's lower lip protruded. The CO ignored him. Leroy and Reggie were friends. Always together but exact opposites. Short, skinny, and painfully shy, Leroy rarely spoke. He treated Reggie like a big brother and dutifully laughed at Reggie's jokes, even when they weren't funny. In return, Reggie supplied Larry with a steady stream of cigarettes, chocolate, and alcohol.

Neither Leroy nor the CO gave any thought to a breathing apparatus. The chest-mounted canvas breathing bag with its oxygen cylinders, rubber tubing, and mouthpiece, protected the men from carbon monoxide poisoning. The odorless gas appeared when large amounts of explosives detonated deep underground. Unlike diggers and stretcher bearers, who entered a tunnel immediately after an explosion, Leroy did not intend to linger. His exposure to carbon monoxide would be minimal, if any. Or so they thought.

The CO would regret the decision.

After Elizabeth forwarded Luke's letter to Mrs. Hobbs, along with a note of her own, she decided to go home.

It would be a short stay. She needed to get her mental bearings and rest a little. The matron would surely grant her request, Elizabeth never having requested leave in the past.

"I spoke to Dr. Hope about your request for leave," said matron.

"And?"

Matron folded and refolded the clean bandages in her hands.

"Elizabeth. You renewed your overseas volunteer status just a few weeks ago. You have more than five months remaining in your contract."

Elizabeth's eyes glazed over.

"I guess I forgot. But I have never requested leave. I should have weeks of unused leave, remaining."

"The agreement stipulates that you will receive one day per month, personal leave time."

"Yes, Matron. I am aware of that."

"But if you do not use the leave during the term of the contract, you lose it. As of now, you have earned a half day of leave."

Elizabeth's eyes grew wide and glassy.

"But I want to go home. I am *so* tired."

"I am truly sorry. Your request for leave is denied."

Elizabeth blew her nose and wiped her eyes.

"I understand, Matron. Thank you for your consideration."

"Dr. Hope tells me that your friend, the captain, has passed on. Please take the balance of the day. A rest will do you some good."

"Thank you, Matron. But I would prefer to work. It will keep me distracted."

"As you wish, Elizabeth."

Clarence arrived at Reginald Windsor's office, unannounced. Although well before noon, he saw Windsor at his desk, pouring himself a full glass of scotch. Again. Windsor eyed Clarence and tossed the empty bottle in to the wastebasket. The old man raised his glass.

"Clarence. So nice to see you. Have a drink."

Windsor took a large gulp and slammed the glass on the table. He splashed a portion of the alcohol onto his shirt sleeve.

The same shirt he wore yesterday. Clarence concluded that the man was inebriated.

"Mr. Windsor. Did you go home last night?"

"Home? Why would I go home, Clarence? It's empty."

"You need your rest, sir."

"What's that in your hand, Clarence?"

"Another telegram, sir. I'm afraid it's bad news."

Windsor jumped to his feet.

"It's Billy, isn't it? Something has happened to Billy."

"No, sir. It's from my daughter, Elizabeth. Luke Hobbs was killed at the Battle of the Somme."

Reginald fell back into his chair. He slumped over his drink studying the amber colored liquid, in silence. He suddenly scowled, reached for the glass, and drank the remaining alcohol in one large gulp. Once again, he slammed the glass on his desk.

"This god-awful war. I know it's been good for business, Clarence, but it just isn't worth it."

Clarence stood motionless, his mind racing for the right words. The old man reached for the empty glass and tipped it into his open mouth. A single drop fell on to his waiting tongue. His head fell forward. He whispered softly.

"Check on Mrs. Hobbs, Clarence. Make sure she has whatever she needs."

"Mrs. Hynes, the midwife's assistant, is staying with her for the time being," said Clarence.

Reginald's head snapped up.

"Wait a minute."

"Sir?"

"Didn't you tell me your daughter was sweet on that fellow?"

"Yes, sir."

"How is she holding up?"

"She doesn't write very often."

"Where is she now?"

"Still at a hospital in Etaples, France. That's the last I heard."

"Well, at least she's safe there."

"The Germans are using zeppelins to bomb London. It's only a matter of time before they go after the hospitals in France."

"She's a volunteer, for God's sake. Tell her to come home."

"She just signed up for another six months, Mr. Windsor."

Windsor reached for his cigar box. He fumbled with a box full of matches. After several attempts, the room filled with smoke. Clarence began to cough.

"I'll be going now, Mr. Windsor."

"Get me another case of scotch, Clarence."

"I'm in the mood to roast sausages."

Billy's announcement to his new squadron at Candas raised a few eyebrows. One of the pilots smiled, knowingly.

"He means zeppelins. He's going after the Hun zeppelins."

Billy pointed to the man and grinned.

"That's right. The remaining flights can choose between camera work, bombing runs, or strafing trenches. I'm going to do zeppelins. We will each take our turns."

Billy turned to the three members of his own flight.

"And you fellows can follow me but I get the first one."

German zeppelins, although used primarily for reconnaissance, could also be used in bombing raids. An attack on London, in September of 1915 by a single zeppelin, killed 22 people and wounded 87 more. By May of 1916, the German airships, known as super zeppelins, were 650 feet long, had six engines, and carried 10 machine guns plus tons of bombs.

Billy searched the skies over the German positions for most of that day, without success. It wasn't until just before dusk, when he spied his first airship. The zeppelin was flying at 5,000 feet and slowly descending, most likely headed to its base of operations. Billy banked hard and plunged into a deep dive. His machine gun blazed as he approached the balloon from the rear. His bullets had no apparent effect. The airship began a rapid descent, hoping to get within protective range of the Germans' land-based machine guns. Billy turned his flying machine around and approached the airship from the bottom, firing at the zeppelin's fuselage. Nothing. He estimated there would be just enough time to take another stab at the balloon before hitting the 3,000-foot deck, where machine-gun fire could reach him.

This time, he raked the length of its side, emptying his ammo drum. The zeppelin initially appeared unscathed. A second look revealed a growing red glow in the middle of the airship. In less than a minute, the entire balloon glowed red hot like an enormous Chinese lantern. When he climbed to a higher elevation for a better view, Billy saw the enormous conflagration plunge quickly to the ground.

The fatal fireball allowed the crew, at least a dozen men, no chance for survival.

Fifteen minutes passed and Leroy had yet to return.

Reggie stopped digging and glared at the lieutenant.

"It's taking him a while, sir. Should I check on him?"

The lieutenant glared at the tunnel entrance.

"Yes. And be quick about it."

Reggie scrambled down the shaft, using a torch to navigate. The shaft's slight incline allowed him to walk briskly but his height required him to crouch down for most of the walk. He discovered his friend, Leroy, in a small enclave, where the CO2 from even a single explosive would be fatal. The crater-like hole in the ground told Reggie that the noise he heard was indeed an explosion. A Hun booby trap, a dud, or one of their own, Reggie could not say. Regardless, he had no time to spare.

He reached for Leroy's crumpled body. The man's breathing was shallow. Reggie could feel a slight pulse. Leroy needed fresh air as soon as possible. Reggie struggled with the lifeless form, forced to crouch low as he carried Leroy back to the surface. He could hear the Lieutenant yelling as he approached the entrance.

"Windsor. What's going on down there?"

Reggie dumped his human cargo in the dirt and dropped to his knees, out of breath. The lieutenant screamed for a stretcher bearer. They arrived in minutes. The medic, examining Leroy, shook his head.

"Sorry, sir. He's gone."

Reggie fell forward and rolled to one side. Overcome with nausea, he began to vomit. Violently. He felt dizzy and gasped for air with each breath. A half dozen tunnellers surrounded the fallen giant.

"Windsor. Are you all right? Can you hear me?"

Reggie did not respond. He heard the lieutenant and could see the man's face, blurred against the gray sky. Reggie's eyelids fluttered. His head pounded. He could hear every painful heartbeat in his chest.

"He passed out," said one of the men.

Elizabeth took her cup of tea into Dr. Hope's office.

At two in the morning, an interruption would be unlikely. She needed a long moment of solitude. The pace of her work, Luke's death, and the desperate need to share her frustrations with someone, anyone, consumed the nurse.

She reached for paper and pencil, intent on writing to Billy. The decision surprised her. Billy's letters, unlike Luke's correspondence, arrived sporadically. They spoke mostly of his exploits as a pilot. The boy seemed obsessed with flying and killing Huns. Elizabeth did not share his interest in the hunt for Huns or the death and destruction which resulted. The fact that he wrote to Elizabeth at all made her curious. Did Billy view her as more than a casual acquaintance? She considered their unplanned tryst as having resulted from the lust of two curious young people. Nothing more. Perhaps he viewed their assignation differently. Since arriving in Europe, Elizabeth focused almost exclusively on her work as a nurse. Nothing took priority over her patients. Luke's unexpected death changed all of that. She did not want to die alone and unloved.

Her mind raced with thoughts of what might have been. She struggled with guilt for having all but ignored Luke's entreaties. And she yearned for someone, other than a doctor or nurse, with whom she could share her innermost feelings. But who? Her father, distant at best and consumed with his work, would neither listen nor understand. She despised Reggie Windsor and tolerated his father, but nothing more. There was no one else. No one in which to confide. No one who would care. No one who would understand. Billy Windsor would be her choice. By default.

She began her pages-long epistle by describing Luke's last moments. She also related the substance of Luke's last letter, apologizing to Billy for burdening him with matters of the heart. She confessed to drowning in her sorrow and wondering if she too, would die miserable and alone. There were more apologies for her less than affectionate actions of the past. She also promised a more regular correspondence, Elizabeth's way of compensating for her unfeeling actions of the past.

She signed the letter, "Fondly, Elizabeth."

Reggie regained consciousness after several hours in the casualty clearing station.

A medic approached Reggie's stretcher.

"How are you feeling, Windsor?"

"I have an awful headache."

"You're lucky to be alive."

"Leroy. What about Leroy?"

The medic's eyes darted to a litter at the far end of the tent. A pair of muddy boots could be seen protruding from the plastic sheet-turned shroud.

"He didn't make it, my friend. I'm sorry."

Reggie flew into an adrenalin-fueled rage. He sprang from the litter, shoving the medic to one side. He quickstepped to the body and yanked on the sheet. Leroy's deathly, gray face and fixed stare returned Reggie's angry scowl. Reggie shook the body and slapped his dead friend's cheek.

"Wake up, Leroy. What's wrong with you? Come on, Leroy. We've got a tunnel to finish."

Reggie's eyes brimmed with tears. He spoke gently, his voice cracking.

"Leroy? Please, Leroy. Wake up."

Reggie reached for his friend's face, softly caressing the dead man's cold cheek. His head fell forward and rested on the man's chest. Reggie, for the first time in years, cried. The sound of his sobbing filled the bunkered room. The medic stood beside Reggie, his hand resting on the big man's shoulder.

"Windsor. Let's get you back in the litter. I'll give you a shot of rum. Maybe you can get some sleep."

Reggie didn't move. His crying continued.

He spent the entire evening standing vigil over his friend's body.

Clarence, sitting uncomfortably at Reginald Windsor's oversized desk, stared at the candlestick-shaped phone.

The earpiece and the mouthpiece, as if refusing to acknowledge the strange man behind the desk, stared back in silence. A full week passed without a call, much less a visit, from the boss. For all intents and purposes, Clarence Parsons now ran the Windsor Land and Lumber Company. He knew what to do in Windsor's absence but his stomach churned. Reginald Windsor, a difficult man to please, would be decidedly unhappy if something were to go wrong while he was away.

It did not seem to matter. The old man remained at home. He drank to excess, slept it off, and repeated the process. Clarence, wrestling with potential solutions to Reginald's drinking, welcomed an interruption.

"Telegram, Mr. Parsons."

Clarence read and reread the telegram.

REGRET TO INFORM YOU THAT REGINALD WINDSOR WAS INJURED WHILE INSPECTING A TUNNEL. HE IS EXPECTED TO SURVIVE.

LT. THOMAS 252ND TUNNELLING COMPANY.

Clarence debated whether he should visit the Windsor home. On the one hand, the old man would want to know that his son was injured. On the other hand, the news might send his boss over the edge. In the end, Clarence compromised. The bad news would wait until tomorrow morning. If the old man did not show up, Clarence would visit the Windsor home.

When word of Billy's encounter with a German zeppelin reached Lieutenant-Colonel Hadow, at headquarters in Saint Omer, the commander responded immediately. The cable was brief.

YOUR CURRENT ASSIGNMENT AS TEMPORARY SQUADRON COMMANDER IS HEREWITH MADE PERMANENT.

LIEUTENANT-COLONEL H. TRENCHARD, COMMANDER RFC

Billy stole a page from his deceased predecessor.

He announced his permanent assignment by reminding the men that titles and last names were unnecessary when the "brass" was not present. The 15 pilots in the squadron, especially the three that served in Billy's flight, responded with approving nods and broad smiles. Like most pilots, they readily acknowledged superior officers. Their respect and loyalty, however, had to be earned. Billy earned it with his natural skills in the cockpit and his genuine concern for the men.

"I'm canceling the afternoon runs, gentleman. Your new orders are to empty these jugs."

With a flourish, Billy yanked on a piece of rubber sheet which covered a nearby table. Four containers of rum triggered a loud round of cheers and applause. Billy could be heard over the outburst.

"Get the maintenance crews in here. They've earned it, too."

Billy waited until the surprise party grew noisy and then quietly slipped away. His new quarters, both quiet and private, afforded him the opportunity to reread the letter from Elizabeth. He read it several times, surprised that a serious relationship with the woman might become a reality. Her note suggested it, anyway. A pang of guilt made his stomach turn. The untimely death of Luke Hobbs would make his romantic mission much easier to accomplish. He whispered a quick prayer for Hobbs and started writing.

Dear Elizabeth

Yours of the 15th arrived last week, and I must say, brought great joy to this war-torn heart.

Billy repeated his words of condolence, first expressed to Elizabeth in a previous letter. He then went on to inquire about her job as a VAD nurse and congratulate the woman on her skills in the operating theater. He complimented her on the widespread respect she now enjoyed from surgeons, doctors, and professional nurses. He also disclosed his new role as squadron commander and made a modest reference to his recent promotion to captain.

Clearly the RFC is desperate for help, no matter how young and inexperienced the candidate may be.

He ended the note on a hopeful note.

When this miserable war comes to an end, and it will, I hope and pray that you and I will be together: sharing our memories, mourning our losses, and celebrating our survival. I feel privileged to have you as my friend.

As ever,
Billy

Clarence rang the doorbell at the Windsor home, a stately mansion situated in St. John's nicest neighborhood.

The housekeeper immediately recognized Clarence and showed him in.

"Mr. Parsons, I am so pleased that you have come to visit. I need your help."

Clarence handed his raincoat to the lady.

"I understand, Harriet. Is Mr. Windsor in his office?"

The housekeeper spoke in a whisper.

"Yes. He fell asleep on the couch. Again. He has been there for days. The man isn't eating. He refuses to bathe and he's drinking heavily. I don't know what to do."

"I'll speak to him."

Clarence walked into the office and hesitated. The air reeked of sweat, booze, and stale cigar smoke. When he first saw Mr. Windsor, passed out on the red leather sofa, Clarence squeezed his eyes shut and turned away. The snoring man wore no jacket, tie, or vest. His badly wrinkled, white shirt, scarred with food stains and burn marks from cigar ashes, gave Windsor the appearance of a hobo.

The colorful Persian rug, which covered most of the hard wood floor, featured empty bottles of whiskey, cigar butts, and scraps of food. His pillow, a beige rolled-up bath towel, appeared to contain traces of vomit. A plate of partially eaten food lay on the coffee table, now an object of interest to a half dozen flies.

"Mr. Windsor?"

The snoring continued.

"Mr. Windsor. It's Clarence Parsons."

The body snorted and stirred.

"Mr. Windsor, please. We have to talk."

Windsor opened his eyes and quickly squeezed them shut.

"The light. Why in blazes do you have all the lights on? And close those damn curtains."

His aide's eyebrows shot up. The lights were off and all but one of the shades were closed. Clarence opened the door a crack and instructed the housekeeper to put on some coffee.

"As strong as you can make it, Harriet."

Parsons returned to the couch and pulled Windsor to a sitting position. The old man groaned, blinked repeatedly, and yawned.

"I've got some coffee coming, Mr. Windsor."

Windsor used fingers on both hands to rub the sides of his aching head.

"I need a drink."

"A bit early for that, Mr. Windsor."

"What time is it, Parsons?"

"It's ten in the morning, sir."

"What day is it?"

"Friday, September 29th."

"How long have I been here?"

"Almost a week, sir."

Windsor closed his eyes and slowly shook his head.

Both men watched in silence as Harriet brought in a sterling silver tray, two cups, and a steaming pot of freshly brewed coffee.

"Are you still taking your coffee black, Mr. Parsons?" she asked.

"Yes, ma'am. Just like Mr. Windsor."

Reggie reached for a cup with hands that trembled. The hot liquid splashed onto the carpet. Windsor blew on his beverage. He thought to acknowledge the housekeeper.

"Thank you, Harriet."

"You're welcome, sir."

After Harriet left the room and closed the door behind her, Clarence sat in the overstuffed chair, opposite the couch.

"I received another telegram, Mr. Windsor."

Windsor's head jerked.

"Read it to me. Now."

Clarence commented on the positive update of Reggie's status.

"It sounds like Reggie is going to be fine, sir."

Reginald shrugged and took another sip of coffee.

"Any word from Billy?"

"No sir. But I heard from my daughter. Billy has been promoted to captain. He has his own squadron now."

Reginald reached for a partially-smoked cigar lying on the carpet.

"Mr. Windsor, should I get you a fresh cigar?"

"Nothing wrong with this one, Clarence. Get me a match."

In seconds, the room filled with smoke. Clarence reacted instantly, coughing, and wiping the tears from his eyes. He choked his next question.

"Mr. Windsor. We have a company to run. Your presence is required. If you do not intend to return your office, what would you have me do?"

Reginald rose to his feet and searched the deep drawers on either side of the huge desk. He retrieved a single bottle. Empty. He tossed it aside and ransacked the credenza behind him. Books and papers flew everywhere. He yelled over his shoulder.

"I need more scotch, Harriet."

Clarence opened the office door.

"Did you hear him, Harriet?"

"Yes sir. Shall I fetch some?"

"Yes. Please."

When the housekeeper returned, she placed a sealed bottle on the desk. Windsor wasted no time opening it. Clarence scratched his head as Mr. Windsor poured his drink into a dirty glass.

"Will there be anything else, Mr. Windsor?"

Reginald drank half the glass, belched, and poured some more.

"For now, you are in charge of the company, Parsons. Now get out of here. I wanna be alone."

Chapter Thirteen

THE CHALLENGE OF HEALING

After much coaxing, Reggie returned to the litter and reclined there, quietly.

The medical attendant consulted with his colleagues and learned that victims of carbon dioxide poisoning respond in a variety of ways. Reggie could experience breathing problems, sporadic dizziness, convulsions, or impaired judgment. The consensus was that Reggie should be placed on a hospital train where presumably more experienced medical personnel would know what to do.

The attendant completed Reggie's Medical Case Sheet, but left portions of the form blank. He did not know Reggie's rank, ID number, or even the number of the Tunnelling Company. When asked, Reggie responded with a blank stare. No one in the room, save the patient, knew that Reggie was serving time for manslaughter.

Despite complaints of a headache, breathing problems, and dizziness, Reggie did not want to spend another moment at the Casualty Clearing Station.

"I'm going back to my company. Let me out of here."

"You're working on a blighty, Windsor. We're putting you on a hospital train. My guess is you're going to St. Omer."

Reggie cursed the attendant and rose to a seated position. The rapid movement made his head spin. He fell back on to the litter and passed out.

"Let's get him out of here. Now," said the medic. "He's getting on that hospital train whether he likes it or not."

Harriet, hearing no sounds from Reginald Windsor's home office, grew anxious by the moment.

The boss usually demanded his breakfast by 11 in the morning. When the grandfather clock in the parlor chimed one o'clock, she tiptoed to the office door. Harriet tapped softly. Nothing. She knocked louder. Still no sounds of life.

She opened the door slowly. Seeing no one on the couch, she checked the office bathroom. Reginald Windsor had disappeared. In a panic, she searched the entire mansion. No sign of Mr. Windsor. As she stood at the top of the staircase wondering what to do next, she absentmindedly gazed through the windows which framed the mansion's large entrance. A dark mound appeared in the front yard, partially covered with falling leaves.

Harriet scrambled down the stairs and ran to the motionless figure. He was still breathing. Snoring, in fact. Her first instinct, to call the St. John's Ambulance service, gave way to her better judgment. She called Clarence.

"I'll be there in minutes," he said, breathlessly.

Clarence raced to the residence. His mind raced even faster. St. John's was the epicenter of the temperance movement. While the city now counted almost 35,000 people as residents, the news that one of its most prominent citizens was found passed out in his yard in a drunken stupor would spread like wildfire. There would be weeks and weeks of gossip. A recent and well-attended public demonstration by the Women's Christian Temperance Union led to a Dominion-wide plebiscite on prohibition. The referendum passed by a large margin and would take effect January 1, 1917. If Reginald Windsor's drinking problem become public, it would ruin the man and the company he founded.

"Help me get him inside, said Clarence.

Clarence and Harriet struggled to get Reginald to his feet. He would take a few steps and then drop to his knees.

"I'm tired. I wanna sleep," he muttered.

When he finally collapsed onto the office couch, both Clarence and Harriet struggled to catch their breath.

"What are we going to do, Mr. Parsons?"

Clarence ran the fingers of one hand through his thinning hair. He took a long deep breath.

"I'm going to call Dr. Macpherson. He'll come to the house and he will keep his mouth shut."

"Should we clean him up first?" she asked.

"Yes, of course. And please accept my apologies for placing you in this rather awkward set of circumstances."

"My late husband was a drunk, Mr. Parsons. No need to apologize. I'll clean him up and get him into a robe."

The hospital train transported Reggie to Number 10 Stationary Hospital in St. Omer, France.

The former boarding school, constructed in 1729, included a large recovery room which used to be a chapel. The modified chamber featured several walls of majestic stained glass windows. Number 10 was just one building in a sprawling complex of more than a dozen hospitals located throughout Saint Omer. Reggie's hospital included an operating theater, x-ray facilities, a dental department, and beds for more than 1,000 patients.

"Where am I?"

The nurse, a tiny woman with wisps of flaming red hair escaping from both sides of her white headdress, smiled.

"Welcome to Number 10 Stationary Hospital, Mr. Windsor. You are in Saint Omer."

"I thought Saint Omer was an airfield."

"Oh, we have one of those too," she said.

Reggie managed a slight grin.

"I'd rather be back in the tunnels."

"Is that what you did, Mr. Windsor?"

"Yes. I was a digger or clay kicker. Call me anything you want. I dug tunnels."

"I'm sorry, Mr. Windsor. Your case file does not indicate your rank. Are you an officer?"

Reggie snorted in derision.

"No. I worked as a private."

Reggie's half-truth satisfied the nurse.

"Well, Private Windsor, tell me how you're feeling. Carbon monoxide poisoning is still a bit of a mystery to all of us."

"I have a splitting headache, it's difficult to breathe at times, and it seems like I'm always tired. Sometimes I just fall asleep. I can't help it."

The nurse scribbled furiously on her chart.

"I understand," she said. "Are you hungry?"

"Yes, but I haven't been hanging onto my food for very long."

"We will start you with some hot tea, bread and jam."

"Thank you."

Reggie started thinking.

"Billy was stationed here. I'm sure of it. But is he still here?"

Reggie's eyelids fluttered shut, once again.

"I don't know who will replace him," said the matron, biting her lip and shaking her head.

Elizabeth's deeply furrowed eyebrows reflected her shock.

"I don't understand. Why is Dr. Hope leaving us?"

"He has had a persistent cough for more than two weeks. And you already know the number of surgeries he rescheduled or reassigned. I will let you draw your own conclusions, Sister Elizabeth."

"I would like to have said goodbye to him, to thank him and express my appreciation," said Elizabeth.

"I have his home address. You can write to him."

"Thank you, Matron."

"Well, *there* you are. I was beginning to think this hospital did not employ a matron. Why aren't you in your office, where you belong?"

The strange man stood with his legs apart and arms crossed. His arched eyebrows and tilting head triggered the matron's famous scowl. She moved slowly and deliberately toward the man.

"I have been the matron at this hospital for three years. And who, may I ask, are you?"

"Maxwell Kane. Dr. Maxwell Kane. I am Dr. Hope's replacement."

Matron blushed. Elizabeth tried to defuse the awkward encounter. She extended a hand.

"Sister Elizabeth Parsons. Doctor Hope's surgical assistant."

Maxwell ignored Elizabeth's outstretched hand and sneered.

"You're dressed like a VAD nurse."

"Well, Dr. Maxwell, as a matter of fact . . ."

"Precisely where did you receive your surgical training?"

"At Third London General Hospital and here, with Dr. Hope."

"Where did you receive your formal education?"

"I was trained as a VAD nurse in Newfoundland. The balance of my education has been on the job."

Maxwell's eyes burned into Matron's face.

"Please tell me that Doctor Hope was aware of the fact that his so-called surgical assistant was an uneducated volunteer with no formal training."

"Sister Parsons was requested by Dr. Hope because of her knowledge and experience. I am of the opinion . . ."

"I am not interested in your opinion, Matron. You will find me a properly trained and formally educated professional nurse. And you will do it today. I have a full day of surgeries beginning at seven tomorrow morning."

Elizabeth cleared her throat.

"Dr. Maxwell. Please permit me . . ."

"And you, Sister whatever-your-name-is, are dismissed. I am quite certain you will find plenty of chamber pots to empty and patients to delouse."

Maxwell pivoted to the matron.

"I would like a tour of the operating theater. Now."

Matron followed Dr. Maxwell like a frightened puppy on a leash. Elizabeth, feeling abandoned, went where she would be needed most. The Receiving Ward.

"Convoy coming."

The loud announcement by an orderly brought more orderlies and a flock of nurses streaming into the large room. Stretcher bearers filled the chamber with wounded men, soon to be lying in beds, litters, and on the floor. Elizabeth tackled a plethora of tasks. Paperwork, injury assessments, ward assignments, delousing, baths for the men, plus the demands of patients who, too often could do no more than groan, preoccupied the woman until three in the afternoon. Her tea grew cold as she leaned against a pillar, her eyes closed.

"I'm sorry, Elizabeth."

Matron's voice startled Elizabeth. She stiffened to attention.

"No need to apologize, Matron. There is plenty do around here."

"Would you be willing to supervise the Receiving Ward, Elizabeth? Sister Randall is off on leave for two weeks."

"I spent my day here. I figured you needed me here the most."

Matron smiled; her eyes filled with appreciation.

"Dr Maxwell is making a huge mistake, letting you go."

"You have been most kind, Matron. Thank you."

Billy examined the envelope and smiled when the word 'Etaples' leapt off the page.

It would be his third letter from Elizabeth in ten days. Clearly, the long-distance relationship had blossomed. He winced when he read that she no longer served in the operating theater. And he grinned when she disclosed a third request for a week of leave in London. She wanted to meet him there. Elizabeth signed the letter differently this time. "Thinking of you, always, Elizabeth.

A hastily scratched note below her signature made Billy jump to his feet.

> ***Billy, a cable from my father reported that Reggie was hurt in a tunnel accident. He is at Number 10 Stationary Hospital in St. Omer. Can you check on him?***

Billy's aerodrome at Bailleul, lay just 45 km west of Saint Omer. If he took a flying machine, he could be there in minutes. But then what would he do? What could he do? Reggie served in Luke's regiment. Billy served with the Royal Flying Corps. He notified the clerk and ran to his plane, anyway.

"Good morning, Reggie."

Reggie bolted upright in his bed. His jaw dropped when Billy strode into the room.

"Billy! How did . . . Who . . . Where did you . . . ?"

Reggie gave up and took a deep breath.

"Thank you, Billy. It's really good to see you."

"I haven't done anything, Reggie."

"You came to visit me."

"How are you feeling?"

"Headaches, dizzy at times, I'm always tired, and I feel like throwing up, whether I eat or not."

"Any talk of sending you back to the Tunnel Company?"

"I've been after them to let me go back. But so far, no one has been honest with me."

"I'll see what I can do."

"Father managed to anger Lieutenant-Colonel Hadow. He is not your best bet."

"I'll ask my boss to intervene. Lieutenant-Colonel Trenchard. He likes me. He may be willing to help."

"Hey! You're a captain now. Congratulations!

"You take a bullet and they give you a promotion plus a medal. Happens a lot in this crazy war."

Reggie studied Billy through glassy eyes.

"My little brother ain't so little anymore."

"You've changed too, Reggie. Can't put my finger on it yet. But you have changed."

Reggie teared up. He turned his head away, worried that Billy might notice.

"I killed a man, Billy. I didn't mean to. But I killed a man."

"I heard. Elizabeth mentioned it in a letter. Father is driving Clarence crazy, trying to get you sprung."

"I told the ole man to leave it alone. I like the tunnelling work. It's better than the trenches, you know."

"I think you made a good decision. You can't change what happened, Billy, so put it behind you. Focus on the things that you *can* change. Show the brass that you've changed. That you're a new man. That you're a good man. They will notice and you will be out of here before this war ends."

"That's good advice, little brother. Thank you. And thank you for the visit."

"We are at war, Billy. And we're family. We need to stay together."

Reggie bit his lip.

"True. But we lost our friend, Luke."

Billy's eyes grew wide.

"*Our* friend? I thought you hated his guts."

"He helped me a lot, Billy. I owe him my life."

Reggie hesitated, a look of uncertainty covering his face.

"How is Elizabeth doing? I know she hates me with a passion. But is she all right?"

"She's doing fine. We are trying to meet in London. I'll tell her you were asking about her."

"Be prepared to duck."

Billy laughed. Reggie didn't want his brother to leave.

"How's father?"

"The ole man hardly writes anymore. Clarence has been very quiet. Talks business only. Something is going on, but I don't know what. And frankly, I have my hands full here."

Reggie frowned.

"Father will outlive us all."

"I gotta get moving, Reggie."

"Thanks again, Billy."

Reggie suddenly held a finger in the air.

"Just a minute."

With some effort, Reggie sat upright. He stiffened and snapped a perfect salute.

"I almost forgot. Thank you, Captain Windsor. Thank you very much."

Billy laughed out loud, returned the salute, and left the room.

Reggie could hear him, laughing still, as he walked down the corridor.

Dr. Macpherson, despite loud objections from his patient, lectured Reginald Windsor in full view of his administrative assistant and housekeeper.

"If you continue in this manner, Mr. Windsor, you will not live much past Christmas."

Harriet put a hand over her mouth, smothering a cry. Clarence pursed his lips and shook his head. Reginald wiped beads of sweat from his forehead using the sleeve on his bathrobe. The man's hands shook constantly. Three pairs of eyes watched. Reginald knew what they were thinking.

"I'm gonna cut back. And I know what you did with the booze. Did you have to destroy all of it?"

"Clarence and Harriet were following my instructions," said Macpherson.

"Doc, I haven't had a drink in a day and a half. You've got to help me. I'm dying."

"I am prescribing a limited amount of Brown's Bronchial Elixir."

"I'm not having any trouble breathing. What in blazes is that stuff gonna do?"

"It's a cough medicine, actually, but with a small amount of alcohol in it. This bottle must last you for a week. If you consume all of it before then, you will go without any alcohol whatsoever. Is that understood?"

Reggie reached for the bottle in Macpherson's hand. The doctor stepped away and held the bottle aloft.

"One swallow, Reginald. That's all."

"Oh, for god's sake. He grabbed at the bottle and took a large gulp. When he struggled to find the pocket on his robe, the doctor wagged an index finger.

"No, Mr. Windsor. Harriet will store the medicine."

Macpherson turned to the housekeeper.

"Please hide the bottle where Mr. Windsor will not find it. Is that understood?"

Harriet nodded. Windsor scowled again. Macpherson continued.

"You will also exercise, Reginald. Mr. Parsons has agreed to accompany you on long walks, at least twice, daily. He tells me that the two of you can talk business. It will be a healthy thing for you *and* your company."

Windsor focused on Clarence with flashing eyes.

"Yes, I can hardly wait for his progress reports."

Macpherson spoke softly.

"Reginald. I want your word as a gentleman that you will comply with my recommendations. They are for your own good."

Reginald took a deep breath and exhaled loudly.

"Yes, Dr. Macpherson. I will comply. Now, if you will excuse me, I have to dress. Clarence and I will be taking our first walk."

"That's the Reginald Windsor, I know," said the doctor.

Clarence bit his tongue. In his head, he screamed his objections.

"This is not going to work, Dr. Macpherson. You are kidding yourself."

Reggie underestimated Billy's influence within the ranks of the British Expeditionary Forces.

The war hero wasted no time. An orderly delivered the good news, just days after Billy's visit. Reggie read the telegram, several times, to convince himself that it was real.

> YOU WILL REPORT TO THE 252ND
> TUNNELLING UNIT, UPON YOUR RELEASE
> FROM HOSPITAL.
>
> ADJUTANT GENERAL

A larger-than-life grin slowly covered Reggie's face, as he faced the orderly.

"I'm out of here, my friend."

"As soon as the doctor signs off, you're free to go."

Reggie scrambled out of bed.

"I'll start dressing."

The orderly, his back to Reggie, did not see his patient stagger and grip the bed for balance.

Reggie slept through most of the train ride and the transport vehicle trip, which delivered him to the 252nd officers' dugout. Careful not to disclose the remaining symptoms of his near-fatal bout with carbon monoxide poisoning, Reggie calculated he could still do a credible job in the tunnels.

"What are you doing here, Windsor?"

The sergeant, his eyes squinting in disbelief, studied Reggie from head to toe.

"The doctor said I could go back to work."

The sarge stepped closer, forced to look up as he studied Reggie's bloodshot eyes.

"Are you sure, Windsor? You look a bit hungover. We can't afford any mistakes in the galleries (mineshafts)."

"Yes sir, Sergeant. Positive."

"Very well, then. God knows we need all the help we can get. We have orders to construct four new saps (tunnels), just north of the Ancre River. I think HQ is planning a little surprise for the Huns."

"Where do I start?"

Reggie worked the sandbags first, filling each of them with chunks of rock-hard chalkstone. He would not mount the "cross" until he felt stronger. The cross, a wooden seat used by the diggers, consisted of two strong boards, assembled at right angles to each other. It was positioned in the underground passage at a 45° angle to the working face of the tunnel. The digger, also known as the "kicker," would stab the wall with his grafting tool and then drive the tool with his legs. After prying the pieces from the wall, he would hand them off to the men behind him. They, in turn, would place the chunks into bags and remove them from the tunnel.

Later in the day, Reggie took his turn on the cross. After less than an hour of stabbing and stomping at the rock wall, he looked and sounded exhausted. One of the men noticed.

"Reggie, how about if I spell you for a while?"

Reggie, unable to catch his breath, fell off the cross and collapsed to a sitting position on the ground, his back to the tunnel wall.

"Thanks, buddy. I'm still feeling the after-effects of that gas, I guess."

"Get some rest, Reggie. I'll cover for you."

Reggie did not acknowledge the offer. He was sleeping.

Billy read the cable from Trenchard's office, several times.

He took time to memorize the cable, word for word. His clerk, twisting in his chair, strained to read the message. Billy threw it into the wood stove and waited until it caught fire.

"London, eh? Tell me more, Captain Billy."

"I am leaving for London. Tomorrow. That's all I can say."

In fact, Billy did not have to be in London until days later. An early arrival would allow him to meet Elizabeth, assuming she got leave. When the corporal left on an errand, Billy called the hospital in Etaples and left a message. The response was almost immediate. They would meet at Queen Mary's Hostel for Nurses, very near Buckingham Palace. Elizabeth chose the location, having stayed there when she first arrived in London.

She requested and received permission for one week of leave.

The cable from Trenchard contained very few details.

Billy would meet his mystery passenger at the North Centre gates of the palace. The man would tip his black hat and request a lift to Shoreham. (Billy intended to use the Shoreham aerodrome, when he first landed in England.) He would respond to the man's request by saying, 'I have a boat.' The passenger would not disclose their destination until they were in the air.

Billy assumed the mysterious passenger, most likely a spy, would be deposited somewhere behind enemy lines. The late squadron commander had described a similar mission.

"A bit nerve-wracking, flying that deep into enemy territory."

Reginald Windsor didn't last a full week under the strict regimen ordered by Dr. Macpherson.

After a brisk walk to the office, ostensibly to review some financial statements, the CEO excused himself.

"Sorry for the interruption, Clarence. I drank too much coffee this morning.

Ten minutes later, Clarence went in search of the businessman. Reginald Windsor vanished into the streets of St. John's, where the purchase of spirits required no more than a modest effort. Clarence huddled with Harriet at lunch.

"I have no idea where to search for, much less, find him."

Harriet stared at Clarence with unblinking eyes.

"I fear for his life, Mr. Parsons. He is not a healthy man."

Clarence remained at the mansion through the dinner hour and well into the evening.

"Should he return this evening or even tomorrow, Harriet, please call me immediately."

"Yes, Mr. Parsons. And I will pray for his safety."

The newly dug mines in which Reggie worked were fired on November 13.

The explosion did considerable damage to German positions in the Hawthorne Crater and well beyond. When the 252nd Tunnelling Company returned to the scene of the huge explosion, all of them, including Reggie, donned their gas masks. They also made a shocking discovery. Dozens of German soldiers, including three officers, greeted them, arms held high and weapons abandoned. The 252nd escorted the enemy soldiers into the regimental camp amidst loud cheers, slaps on the back, and congratulatory remarks from their colleagues.

After the explosion, the 252nd company cleared and repaired the German dugouts for occupation by the Brits. The company also assisted with the construction of road and railroad beds. Reggie, given considerable leeway by the sergeant, was not as productive as in the past, but he managed to accomplish his share of the labor.

"Reggie, if you're feeling up to it, you can clean up that German sap, straight ahead and on your left. Our artillery barrage did too good of a job on their trenches. Now we get to fix them. See what you can do."

Reggie enjoyed the assignment. He worked hard, meticulously removing the loose dirt and mud on the trench floor, using the excess material to heighten and strengthen the parapet. He also replaced and rearranged the duck boards which lined the floor of the trench. The wooden planks, an absolute necessity given the steady rains which fell in the fall season, protected the troops against the rivers of mud and water that would otherwise occur.

As he scraped the loose dirt and slowly increased the height of the new parapet, the blade of his shovel unexpectedly scraped metal. With his hands, he uncovered most of the metal object. Reggie stood perfectly still. An unexploded artillery shell lay buried in the mud. Such "duds" were not uncommon. The malfunction could be due to a manufacturer's defect. The fact that the shell landed softly in several feet of mud might also explain the lack of an explosion.

Reggie called out for help. The shell might explode if moved or even slightly jarred. When no one responded to his yells, he marked the spot with his trenching tool and tiptoed around the projectile. Reggie returned with the sergeant and a munitions man.

"Whereabouts?" asked the sergeant.

"I marked it with my shovel," said Reggie. "There," he said, pointing.

The sarge glared at the munitions man who looked like a 15-year-old boy.

"Well, what in blazes do we do with it?"

"Sorry, Sarge, I just load 'em and deliver 'em," said the so-called munitions expert.

The sergeant shot a dirty look in the man's direction.

"I'll get the captain. A helluva lot of good you are," said the sarge.

Reggie reached for his shovel.

"I'll get it," said the munitions boy. The kid tripped in the mud. He fell forward and knocked the shovel onto the artillery shell. In the split second that followed, Reggie tackled the sergeant, covering the officer's small frame, with his own.

A deafening explosion sent dirt, flames, debris, and dust in every direction. Reggie, still on top of his CO, could hear the sergeant's heart pounding in the man's chest. His right eye burned as if covered with a red-hot lump of coal. His left leg, throbbing and numb at the same time, would not move. Reggie assumed it was stuck in the mud. With his remaining eye, Reggie could see the bloody pile of flesh and bones that used to be the munitions boy.

"I can't breathe, Reggie," said the sarge.

Reggie could feel the sergeant pushing him to one side, impressed that such a small man would be that strong. The light in Reggie's working eye started to fade.

"Oh God," said the sergeant, gagging when he saw the bloody pile that covered the spot near Reggie's shovel. Reggie, now on his back and in six inches of mud, stared at the sergeant with one eye. The other eye, a circular patch of crimson red blood, appeared to be missing.

"Help me get up, Sarge. My leg is stuck."

"Stay where you are, Reggie. I'll get a stretcher."

Reggie's good eye fluttered shut. He passed out, before the stretcher bearers arrived.

"His leg is a mess, Sarge."

"I know that. Just do what you can. He's the best man I got."

Elizabeth's second stay at Queen Mary's Hostel for Nurses left her drowning in luxurious comfort.

The popular establishment held as much appeal for Elizabeth as did her planned rendezvous with Billy. As the hour of their meeting approached, her anxiety grew. What if he expected to spend the night with her? She could not "entertain" him at the hostel. Male visitors were strictly prohibited, although she knew of nurses who regularly violated the regulation.

She considered the fact that her relationship with Billy had changed—considerably. The tone, volume, and substance of their most recent correspondence stood in sharp contrast to earlier times. Their reckless tryst and her sudden departure would normally end most friendships. But that didn't happen. The gale storm of death, destruction, and heartbreak, which characterized wartime relationships, changed all of that.

As Elizabeth strolled to their planned meeting place, she wondered if they could enjoy an honest and sincere relationship? Would it be based on the things that now mattered most to her? Respect. Affection. Understanding. And most of all, love. A familiar voice interrupted her silent prayer.

"Looking for someone?"

Captain William Windsor looked dashing in his crisp, clean uniform. A splash of blue from the Military Cross on his chest added to his rakish appearance. Elizabeth mouthed but could not speak his name, rushing into Billy's waiting arms. She clung to him for several long moments, bathing in the warmth of his affection. His arms held her tight. Her head lay perfectly on his shoulder. And the aroma of a spotlessly clean uniform worn by a man who was neither wounded nor covered with mud and blood, brought tears to her eyes. She did not want the moment to end. She stepped back, nevertheless.

"Let me look at you, Captain Windsor. Oh my. You look absolutely smashing," she said.

"I had the best nurse in all of Europe," he replied. "And you, my dear Elizabeth, are still the most beautiful woman I have ever seen."

"Let's walk," she said.

Billy reached for her bag and quickly turned her in the opposite direction.

"This way, please."

"Where are we going?"

"It's a surprise."

While they walked, they talked. And talked. Nonstop. The dark and angry clouds of war finally burst and set into motion a torrent of pent-up emotion, immersing the one-time lovers in a welcome shower of laughter, relief, joy, and affection.

"We're here."

They stood in front of the St. James.

The luxurious hotel traced its history back to a series of alms houses, built by a friend of Queen Elizabeth. The homes were to be utilized as safe havens for the underprivileged children of London. Years later, when the site was acquired by a retired military man, the structures became eight luxurious red-brick town houses. They would eventually be transformed into one of London's finest hotels.

Elizabeth hesitated, her mind flashing back to their first and only encounter. She regretted it and wondered if he felt the same way. He must have noticed the apprehension in her eyes.

"We're having dinner here tonight. And I have arranged a room for each of us. Despite months in the trenches and in the cockpits of flying machines, I have not forgotten how to treat a lady."

She rushed into his arms once again.

"Oh, Billy, how could I have known you for so long and yet, not know you at all?"

Clarence, on the verge of calling the St. John's Constabulary, could not imagine where Reginald Windsor could be hiding.

Clearly, the businessman did not want to be found. Other than a withdrawal of cash at his bank, Mr. Windsor's activities remained a mystery. The CEO's absence, almost a week now, raised eyebrows at a variety of business meetings, public events, and social gatherings. Once again, Clarence spent most of his day perched behind Mr. Windsor's oversized desk. As he contemplated his next step in the search for his boss, a female assistant knocked on the open door.

"Mr. Parsons, I am so sorry to interrupt you but I've just received a rather strange phone call and I think you should know about it."

"Yes, of course. Who was it?"

"Well, that's the problem. He would not give me his name."

"What did he say?"

"I wrote it down. He said, *the armory has lots of hiding places*."

"Did his voice sound familiar?"

"No, sir. Not at all."

Clarence dismissed the woman and was prepared to dismiss the call when an image of the armory flashed in his mind. The Christian Lads Brigade (CLB) established their headquarters at the facility in 1882. The popular youth group worked to provide area young people with a structured and positive environment.

The Armory became a popular location for social gatherings and community events of every kind.

When the war began, many of the CLB's members were the first to volunteer for service in the 1st Newfoundland Regiment. The Newfoundland Patriotic Society, responsible for the Newfoundland war effort, organized itself at the Armory. Recruits went there to sign up and to swear in. The facility quickly became the regiment's central recruiting station.

More importantly, Mr. Windsor served on the commission that headed up the recruitment effort. Both of Reginald's sons volunteered and then took their oath of service at the Armory. For several months, after the declaration of war, the Armory became Reginald Windsor's home away from home.

Clarence tore out of the office on a dead run. The secretary dropped her pencil and jumped to her feet.

"Mr. Parsons? Is everything all right? Do you require my assistance?"

"I've got to go. Talk to you later."

Although familiar with its location, Clarence rarely visited the Armory.

He entered the building at its main entrance. The large set of double doors, mahogany in color, were framed by large, rectangular pillars of white stone, their width tapering in size as they rose skyward. The balance of the two-story building, entirely in red, was also made of stone. Inside, a lone volunteer, charged with the responsibility of the CBL's stores, which included clothing, food stuffs, and uniforms, greeted Clarence in a soft voice.

"May I help you?" he asked.

"My name is Clarence Parsons. I work for Reginald Windsor at the . . ."

The young man quickly brought an index finger to his lips and silenced Clarence.

"He gave me a five-pound note to keep quiet. He's upstairs in the room we use for medical exams. He's in a bad way, Mr. Parsons. Here's the money."

Clarence refused the currency and thanked the boy. He climbed the wooden staircase as quietly as he could. He could hear the old man snoring before he reached the door. Clarence entered the room, and sat in a nearby chair. For a few moments, he studied the snoring man wondering what he should do or say. Clarence struggled. Perhaps it was the old man's loud snoring. Or the fact that Reginald's drunken oblivion had become a heavy burden for Clarence. Clarence could feel the frustration and anger bubbling in his stomach. Windsor would most likely ignore the advice he truly required. The business executive would soon lose everything he worked so hard to build. Windsor stood on the edge of ruin. Clarence could think of nothing that would convince the executive to end the death spiral of self-destructive behavior. Hundreds of lives would lay in ruins. The company would collapse. The life of Reginald Windsor would be ruined. And the life of Clarence Parsons, also.

Clarence jumped to his feet. For the first time in his life, the innately timid man surrendered to the white hot anger coursing through his veins. Mr. Windsor's behavior could only be described as selfish and reckless. He deserved to be told. To be punished. As Clarence stood over his unconscious employer, he also recalled the ugly incident with Elizabeth and young Reggie. How the old man protected his son's predatory behavior, utilizing seductive deceit to manipulate Clarence and Elizabeth. It was Reginald Windsor's way of life. Bullying his subordinates, badgering bureaucrats, and manipulating weak-kneed people and politicians. Clarence decided that the abuse would end then and there. His body trembled with anger. His lips twisted into a snarl, the fingers on both hands curled into fists.

"Now. The time is now."

Clarence, surprised by the loud sound of his angry voice, watched as the old man stirred. He marched to the sink, filled a pitcher with water, ice cold at that time of the year, and approached his employer. Windsor's eyes remained closed. Clarence emptied the near freezing water onto Windsor's face and head. The old man woke, confused and angry, sputtering a string of curse words. He rose to a sitting position, choking on a mouthful of water and swallowing a portion of it. He struggled to breathe but managed to yell.

"Clarence, you sniveling, self-righteous, old lady. What the hell did you do that for? Never mind. I don't wanna hear it. You're fired."

Clarence quick stepped to the sink, refilled the pitcher, and stood over the drunk, once again.

"I'm fired, you say?"

Before Windsor could respond, Clarence doused the man again. Reginald knocked the pitcher from Parsons' hand, struggling to his feet with threats and curse words.

"I'll kill you with my bare hands, you snake. After all I've done for you."

Clarence noticed the big man swaying wildly as he tried to stay on his feet. Using both hands, Clarence pushed on the big man's chest as hard as he could. Windsor fell onto the cot, seated but hitting the back of his head on the cement wall.

Reginald screamed in agony. Clarence, drowning in adrenaline, slapped Windsor in the face, leaving a pink handprint on the man's cheek. Windsor yelled.

"How dare you hit me?"

"It was quite simple. I can demonstrate the procedure once again, if you wish."

"Don't you dare."

Clarence struck the man, once again and with greater force. Reginald now bled from the lip. He wiped the blood with the sleeve of his dirty white shirt and glared at his attacker. Clarence spoke up.

"Now you listen to me, Reginald Windsor, and listen carefully. I have worked too hard and for too long to make your company a success, just to watch you throw it all away because one of your sons is a killer and the other one secretly despises you. Fire me, if you wish, but your company will not last six months after I am gone. And you will not find the answers to your problems at the bottom of a bottle. And one more thing. You can't fire me because I just quit."

Clarence spun around and marched to the door. When he reached for the door knob, Reginald called out in a soft voice.

"Clarence?"

Clarence stopped but did not turn around.

"Clarence. Please. Don't go. I need help. And I can't do it without you."

Clarence wanted to keep walking. *The drunk didn't deserve any mercy*, he thought. *Mercy was for the merciful*. Clarence remembered his bible. Matthew Chapter 5, Verse 7.

"Blessed are the merciful for they shall receive mercy."

The Good Book hit Clarence in the face. Those words applied to everyone. Elizabeth, Reggie, Clarence himself, and even Mr. Windsor. With a scowl on his face and a snarl in his voice, Clarence pivoted.

"Get yourself cleaned up and meet me at the office. If you are not there by noon, you are on your own."

The stretcher bearers carrying Reggie marveled that he survived the explosion.

After placing a tourniquet on Windsor's upper thigh, they hurried to the field hospital. The dead soldier's grisly remains required two more orderlies, three burlap bags, and a rubber sheet, for transport to the regiment's temporary morgue. Reggie, screaming from the intense pain of his wounds, slipped in and out of consciousness. They administered the maximum dose of morphine. He would be transported by horse and carriage to the Casualty Clearing Station (CCS). The CCS, situated several miles behind the front line, featured a minimum of 50 beds, a half dozen medical officers, and a full complement of nurses and orderlies. Reggie, unconscious once again, did not hear the discussion which ensued upon his arrival.

"We can remove the surface shrapnel, right now. A lot of it is embedded too deeply however. Those wounds will require surgery. The left eye is destroyed and that leg has got to go," said a doctor.

A team of three, working furiously, did their best to remove a portion of the shrapnel and stop the bleeding. They cleaned and bandaged wounds on his face, neck, torso, and right arm.

"Let's get him to the ambulance train. It should arrive within the hour."

Additional morphine was administered, insuring that Reggie would feel no pain and remain unconscious during the bumpy train ride. Hours later, the groggy patient regained consciousness.

"Where am I?"

"You're on a hospital barge, Windsor. You're going to London and then you're going home."

"My sergeant, did he make it?"

"Yes. He was not injured, thanks to you. His report says you saved his life."

Reggie's world went dark before the medical officer could relay the rest of his report. The sergeant asked for and received permission to suspend the balance of Reggie's prison sentence. He also recommended a medal for valor on the battlefield. The request landed on Lieutenant-Colonel Hadow's desk. The commander's response surprised no one.

"He took a man's life and he saved a man's life. We're even. But I'm not going to decorate a soldier convicted of murder."

The barge to London, painted gray with a large red cross on either side of the hull, included 30 beds, a kitchen, and a full staff of medical personnel including doctors, nurses, and orderlies. The boat carried coal in its previous life. Although towed by a steam tug, it was now used to transport seriously injured soldiers to London area hospitals.

Reggie's barge would dock at Portsmouth. From there a lorry would deliver him to Queen Alexandra's Military Hospital, also located in Portsmouth. They specialized in the treatment of wounds from munitions along with trench fever and gas attack victims. The surgeons at Queen Alexandra's spent several hours with Reggie, tending to dozens of shrapnel wounds. The removal of his left leg required 15 minutes. An enucleation (removal), of the left eye also occurred. A glass eye would be inserted later.

"How are you feeling?"

Reggie, still groggy from yesterday's anesthesia, repeatedly blinked trying to bring the face with the pleasant voice, into focus. He noticed her smile.

"What's wrong with my eye?"

"Your eye was destroyed by a piece of shrapnel. You will be fitted for a glass eye. Your remaining eye suffered no damage."

Reggie scowled.

"Got any more good news?"

"You are lucky to be alive, Mr. Windsor."

"Well, my leg is killing me. Got anything for the pain?"

A blank stare on the woman's face sent Reggie into a panic. He yanked the sheet which covered his left side. A clean white sheet, where there should have been flesh and bone, was all that he could see. The stump, extending from his extreme upper thigh less than twelve inches, lay wrapped in bandages. A bloody ball of gauze marked the tip of his amputated limb. Several pins held the red snowball in place.

Reggie's breath quickened. The unbandaged eye bulged and his lips quivered. A loud savage scream filled the hospital ward. He lunged for the nurse. She squealed and jumped back. Two orderlies, one of them as large as Reggie, came running. Some of the patients in nearby beds stared at the screaming amputee. Others looked away. Reggie twisted and turned under the grip of four strong hands. He spit at the orderlies. They restrained him with strips of stained white cloth.

"You butchering bastards. I'm gonna kill you with my bare hands."

The empty irony of a one-eyed, one-legged cripple, threatening to attack anyone, exploded in Reggie's head like the artillery shell in his trench. He stopped moving and grew quiet. His eye glazed over. Reggie's face slowly transformed into a stone-like mask of deep sadness. The tears in his eye rolled down his cheek. The orderlies removed the restraints and stood nearby. Reggie sat motionless, staring into space. The nurse pulled him forward and held the broken man in her arms. Reggie's chest heaved.

The giant man from Newfoundland cried like a child.

Elizabeth left her luxuriously appointed room and entered the hotel dining room.

She wore her nurse's uniform, without the apron or head dress. Billy, in full uniform, rushed to her side.

"I trust your room was acceptable."

"The room was quite nice, but I'm afraid your dinner companion is inappropriately dressed for such beautiful surroundings."

"Most people will never get past those beautiful eyes."

Elizabeth's face, reddened. She looked to the floor and struggled unsuccessfully for the appropriate words.

"Right this way," said the maître d'.

Despite the ravages of war, the hotel restaurant served a full course dinner, complete with beef, a variety of vegetables, bread with real butter, and various pastries and fruit for dessert. Their plates now empty and their appetites satiated, Billy gulped the balance of his wine.

"Walk with me. Please."

"Yes of course. I like being with you, Billy. I don't have to worry that I might say something that irritated you or embarrassed me."

"Thank you. I am very pleased to know that."

Several moments passed, the sound of horse-drawn carriages floating in the cool night air. They found a park bench and enjoyed the street lights of London, in silence. Billy suddenly turned to Elizabeth, reaching for her hand.

"Did you love him?"

Elizabeth yanked her hand from his. Her eyes blinked in disbelief. She stalled for a moment but instantly knew, to whom Billy referred and why.

"Did I love who?"

"Luke Hobbs."

Elizabeth wet her lips. She took a deep breath, opened her mouth, thought better of it, and faked a cough instead.

"It's a bit chilly, this evening."

Billy gnawed on his lower lip.

"Your silence speaks volumes."

It was an unfair question, thought Elizabeth. She chose her words carefully.

"I didn't know I loved him until the day he died."

Billy fidgeted, a pained expression on his face.

"I don't understand."

"Luke Hobbs could be an arrogant ass at times. It drove me mad. And then, one day, I realized that the two of us were very much alike. I too can be self-absorbed and often think of myself as the smartest person in the room."

"Is that why you fell in love with him? Birds of a feather?"

"At first, I was just curious. I became less critical. He wrote often. I rarely replied. It didn't seem to matter. He changed."

"How?"

"He was less concerned about himself. More concerned about his men. Like you, he witnessed so much death, that he began to appreciate life. Especially the important things in life. Suddenly, I became a part of his life that he did not want to lose."

"And you? Was the feeling mutual?"

"Billy. You are making me very uncomfortable."

"I apologize."

"No. Don't apologize. You deserve an answer. Honestly, I was too busy and too absorbed with my own life to give Luke much thought. I didn't respond to his overtures. I didn't realize what was happening."

"What happened?"

"He became one of my patients. I could see the change in his eyes. I could hear the difference in the way he spoke. And that's when it hit me. That's when I realized I could lose him and I didn't want to lose him."

Elizabeth used a coat sleeve to wipe her teary eyes. Sniffles prompted Billy to offer a handkerchief. She continued.

"But it was too late for me to do anything about it. He was dying. We both knew it. And honestly, I am still struggling with the whole thing."

"And Billy Windsor is the consolation prize. I win by default."

Elizabeth jumped to her feet, took a few steps in the opposite direction, and then spun in place.

"That's not true. How can you say that?"

Billy, still sitting on the bench, folded his arms, took a deep breath, and slowly exhaled.

"This war has changed all of us, Elizabeth."

"Perhaps. But you are *not* a consolation prize."

Billy rose and slowly approached the angry woman.

"Oh, but I think I am, Elizabeth. You see, when I first met you, I fell hopelessly in love. I was willing to do anything, to say anything, and frankly, to be anything, just to have you at my side. And it didn't matter to me if you loved me or not. I just wanted to be with you. It was obvious to me, however, that Luke Hobbs came first. Even then."

Elizabeth didn't move.

"And then, we made love."

Billy looked at the sky, the full moon reflecting in his glistening eyes.

"But it wasn't really love, was it Elizabeth? Curiosity perhaps? Lust maybe. Or genuine affection. I really don't know. But it wasn't love. I know that now."

Elizabeth snapped at the man.

"I thought you wanted this visit as much as I did."

"I did. I wanted to see your eyes and hear your voice. I had to know for sure. Did our first night together mean something to you or not."

"I'm sorry if I hurt you, Billy. I am truly sorry."

"You were my first, Elizabeth, and I suspect I was yours."

Elizabeth whispered.

"Yes."

"And that's why we have separate rooms this evening. The boy who was obsessed with you, the boy who readily succumbed to your considerable charms, is no longer a boy. I love you, Elizabeth. I always have. But I cannot and will not go any further in this relationship until I know for sure that you truly love me."

Billy rose to his feet.

"I will not compete with a memory."

When Billy and Elizabeth returned to the hotel, a desk clerk motioned to them.

"Captain Windsor, you have an urgent telegram."

Billy turned his back to Elizabeth and read the cable. His head drooped. He slowly turned to face her, biting his lip.

"I'm sorry, Elizabeth."

"What is it?"

"I must go. First thing tomorrow morning."

"Where are you going?"

"I am not at liberty to say."

"Is it dangerous?"

Billy twitched. *Any trip behind enemy lines is dangerous*, he thought.

"No. Not at all."

"I don't believe you."

Billy leaned forward and tenderly kissed her cheek.

"The rooms are paid for. Please stay for a few days and take in the sights."

"I came to see you, not the London Bridge."

"I have to go."

"Can we at least have breakfast together, in the morning?"

Billy looked away. Elizabeth could not hide her growing anger and frustration. She raised her voice.

"So. You choose to end our conversation this way? Using an RFC telegram to take your leave? Are you afraid of me, Billy? Maybe it's you who is unsure of your feelings, toward me."

"I am simply following orders, Elizabeth. Please try to understand."

Elizabeth stormed off.

Chapter Fourteen

SPIES AND LIES

Billy's new orders were to meet his mystery passenger, at 0800.

After a night of fitful sleep, he shoved a few personal items into his haversack, and reread the telegram before leaving the room.

MEET YOUR PASSENGER AT 0800 HOURS TOMORROW. ALL PREVIOUS INSTRUCTIONS REMAIN IN EFFECT.

Billy arrived at the north center gate of Buckingham Palace 20 minutes before the scheduled meeting.

He lurked in a nearby clump of bushes, hoping to see the mystery man before they met. A man's loud and sudden cough spun Billy in the opposite direction. A tall man, wearing a black bowler and sporting a suit and tie, flashed a toothy grin. He wore a jet-black mustache which highlighted two rows of yellow-stained teeth when he grinned. He carried a small satchel in one hand and an umbrella in the other.

"I need a lift to Shoreham,"

"I have a boat."

The passenger stepped forward; his hand extended.

"You can call me Nigel, Captain Windsor."

Billy's eyebrows arched. He smiled.

"I'm impressed. You know my name."

"Your sweetheart calls you Captain Windsor. Is that not your real name?"

"You spied on us?

Nigel's eyes rose skyward.

"A beautiful nurse dressed in white, a captain in the RFC, with a crisp clean uniform in the middle of a war, a medal for valor pinned on his chest, and two rooms at the Saint James in London. You wished to go unnoticed?"

Billy took a deep breath, anxious to confront his cocky passenger, but Nigel cut him off.

"Shall we?"

"Shall we what?"

"Take our leave?"

"Where are we going?"

"You will know soon enough."

On his trip to London, Billy took the train from Shoreham to the St. James block when he first arrived. He assumed he would make the same trip now, but in reverse.

"The train station is behind us, Nigel.

"So it is, Captain Windsor. So it is."

Nigel, walking quickly and with confidence, took a sudden turn into an alleyway. Billy noticed a parked vehicle blocking the alley's exit. The driver stepped out, lit his cigarette, and took a single, long drag. Nigel stopped and opened his umbrella. Billy looked up. The sun was shining.

The vehicle, a French made Unic, was still common in the streets of London, despite the war. Often used as a taxi, the motor car was neither fast nor comfortable. *It would be a long ride to Shoreham*, thought Billy.

When Nigel approached the driver, he tipped his hat.

"My residence is just outside the city. Are you willing to make the trip?"

"It's a pleasant day for a long drive."

Nigel flashed his dirty, yellow teeth once again. He and Billy climbed into the rear seat. Billy admired the shiny, maroon color of the car and its spotless interior. Although Nigel gave no instructions, the cab driver quickly found the main road to Shoreham. The muddy, rut-filled dirt road would not deposit its passengers at the landing field for several hours. Billy assumed the driver carried extra cans of petrol. He turned to Nigel, hoping to strike up a conversation.

"Have you lived in London for long?"

Nigel exhaled loudly. He closed his eyes, pulling the brim of his Bowler low over his face. Billy gave him a scornful look.

"Have a nice nap, Nigel."

The RFC pilot stared out the window as trees, farms, and pastures floated by. In minutes, he too drifted off to sleep.

"Captain. We have arrived."

Nigel exited the cab, tendering no more than a 'good day' to the driver.

Billy blinked the sleep from his eyes and quick-stepped to his BE2c. The biplane lay on a grassy patch very near the runway.

"Are you going to tell me where we're going?" asked Billy, as he inspected the propeller.

"Cambrai."

Billy's head twisted in Nigel's direction.

"That's 20 miles behind enemy lines."

"You are correct, Captain. And we must proceed with haste. You do not want to make the return trip after the sun has set."

Reggie stopped eating.

He lost weight, refused to leave his bed, and often soiled himself. The nurses, several orderlies, and fellow patients urged him otherwise but to no avail. A surgeon, accompanied by a double amputee, accomplished no more than a terse response.

"Send me back to the tunnels. They can't kill me twice."

Reggie's hunger strike prompted urgent telegrams to Reggie's father and his younger brother. Clarence destroyed the cable for fear that Reggie would start drinking again. Billy, otherwise occupied, would not learn of the telegram until much later. Reggie, soon to be discharged, would not survive the journey home, said the doctors. He needed to eat.

When they carried Reggie onto the *SS Corinthian*, he was floating in and out of consciousness. The *Corinthian* regularly shipped cargo between England and St. John's, New Brunswick. Another boat and a train would deliver him to St. John's, Newfoundland. If he survived.

The *Corinthian* did carry the occasional passenger. Reggie would be accompanied by a previously wounded soldier who recently received his medical discharge. The Newfoundland soldier, 16 years old when he enlisted, looked more like a kid. "Boy soldiers" as they were called, were easily able to circumvent the age requirement if they appeared healthy and enthusiastic. This boy-soldier lost an arm at the Battle of the Somme. He worked as a part-time orderly after recuperating from his wounds. The kid visited Reggie at dinner time.

"Are you going to eat that?" he asked.

Reggie, temporarily conscious and still angry at the world, refused to share his food.

"Yes. Now leave me alone."

"No. You're not going to eat it. And I'm hungry."

"Get your own food."

"I ate my lunch already and I'm still hungry."

The amputee reached for Reggie's tray.

Although physically weak, Reggie's hot temper remained. The man's eyes flashed and his nostrils flared.

"Touch that food, kid, and I'll snap your scrawny little neck."

"You've been lying on your arse for more than a week now. You couldn't hurt me if you wanted to."

The orderly grabbed a spoon and shoved a scoop of mashed potatoes with gravy into his mouth. Reggie reached and flipped the entire tray onto the man's chest. Much of the food fell onto the floor. The food bandit stepped back and grinned, a rivulet of gravy running down his chin.

"See you at breakfast."

Reggie lunged for the orderly but the kid ran off.

"You're a dead man. You hear me? You're a dead man."

The young orderly showed up the next morning. Reggie greeted him with a devilish grin.

"You're too late, ya bum. The food is all gone."

"The name is Mickey, you big lug," said the orderly, scanning the room in search of the food.

"You threw it out, didn't you?"

"I'm not saying a thing," said Reggie.

The boy soldier searched under the bed and then on top of the bed. His hands slipped under the bed covers. Reggie, still capable of a vice-like grip, grabbed the kid's wrist and pulled him close. They struggled. Reggie's face suddenly twisted. His face turned a light shade of green. He released his grip. The kid jumped back. Drops of sweat appeared on Reggie's forehead. His chest heaved. A gusher of vomit flew across the length of Reggie's bed, landing on his remaining leg and spattering the cabin floor. The orderly recognized that morning's menu.

"You bloody idiot. Look at the mess you made."

Reggie gagged from the remains of vomit in his mouth. The orderly fumed as he yanked on the bedcovers and began the clean-up. Unbeknownst to Reggie, Mickey's orders were to feed and care for Reggie Windsor until they reached St. John's, Newfoundland. He worked in silence as Reggie watched.

"What are you, some sort of a nurse?"

"I work as an orderly's assistant."

Reggie, although still queasy, begrudgingly thanked the boy.

"Thanks, kid."

"You're welcome."

"What's your name again?"

"Mickey. Mickey Wells. And if you do this at lunch, I am not going to clean it up. Understand?

"Understood."

Wells turned to leave. Reggie's head jerked up.

"Wells?"

"Yes."

"Sorry."

Wells grinned.

"That's alright. I got you to eat, didn't I?"

Reggie laughed for the first time in weeks.

At lunchtime, Mickey came into the room balancing a single food tray. He sat in the chair, the tray on his lap. Reggie glared.

"What the bloody hell are you doing?"

The boy spoke with his mouth full of fresh carrots.

"Having my lunch. The grub on this ship isn't half bad."

Reggie continued to glare.

"Where's my lunch?" asked Reggie.

"You're looking at it, Windsor. Want some?"

Reggie, too proud to beg, glared at the boy.

Mickey threw a slice of unbuttered bread. Reggie shoved all of it into his mouth.

"Don't overdo it, Windsor. I'm not cleaning up your mess again."

Reggie finished chewing, studying the bowl of soup on Mickey's food tray.

"You can have the soup, but that's all you get until dinner time."

Reggie rolled his eyes.

"All you orderlies are a pain in the arse."

Reginald Windsor arrived at Clarence's office. On time.

Clarence, although pleased, commented on the owner's appearance.

"Looks like you got into a fight with your razor."

Reginald frowned, deliberately exhibiting his violently shaking hand instead.

"Look at this."

"Withdrawal symptoms. It will get better, Mr. Windsor."

Reginald wiped the sweat from his forehead using a sleeve from his jacket.

"I'm freezing in here, Clarence. Can we get some more heat in this room?"

"It's not cold in here, Mr. Windsor. It's you. That too will get better."

"What do we do now?"

"We have contracts to review, pricing decisions to make, and a proposal from the war cabinet to consider. Are you up to it?"

"Do I have a choice?"

Clarence and Reginald worked for three hours straight, took a short break for lunch, and worked several hours more.

"I'll bring you home now, Mr. Windsor."

"Sounds good. I'm exhausted."

"We start tomorrow morning at eight."

"Can you pick me up, Clarence?"

"Yes, sir."

Reginald fell asleep in the back seat of the car. When they reached the Windsor home, Clarence spoke softly.

"Mr. Windsor, we're here. Time to get some rest."

"Clarence? I don't feel so good."

Windsor's face shown blood red. He clutched at his chest and groaned in pain. His eyes rolled to the back of his head.

"Mr. Windsor?"

Clarence slammed his foot to the floor and rushed to the hospital.

Billy's flight from the Shoreham Landing Field in England to Cambrai in France, would include a fuel stop at Saint Omer, on the west coast of France.

Billy, preparing for their departure, installed Nigel in the forward observer's seat.

"I'm not sure the stop at St. Omer is a good idea. Too many eyes, if you know what I mean."

Billy checked the man's harness and snarled.

"You spy, I fly. Don't tell me how to do my job."

Nigel stared in silence at his pilot. Billy contemplated the circumstances of his trip behind enemy lines. His modified BE2c included several machine guns and could reach altitudes approaching 10,000 feet. It would be no match for the newly minted German Fokker. The German monoplane could reach speeds of more than 100 mph. Billy's plane rarely exceeded 70 mph. As a result, Billy planned to fly at high altitudes until very near the German lines. Landing in German territory would be a different matter entirely.

"Tell me about the landing zone."

"After we leave St. Omer, not before."

It was Billy's turn to glare at his passenger. The engine's roar drowned the sound of Billy's angry voice.

"You sir, are an arrogant ass."

Their flight over the English Channel proved unremarkable except for the occasional view of cargo ships heading out to sea. At St. Omer, Billy jumped from the plane and struck up a conversation with the fuel attendant. As the uniformed private pumped petrol into the plane, he posed an innocent question.

"Where are you headed, Captain?"

Nigel went apoplectic.

"That is none of your concern, private. Now get on with the task at hand or I shall report you to the commander."

The attendant took umbrage.

"I down't see you wearin' no uniform, guv'nor. And I iz havin' me a private conversation."

Billy rested a hand on the young man's shoulder.

"Easy, friend. The ole man's in a hurry and a bit agitated."

The private shot a dirty look at Billy's passenger and finished the refueling. When the attendant was out of earshot, Billy mounted the plane and shoved his face toward Nigel's long, pointy nose.

"Tell me everything you know about the landing zone. Now."

"Sorry, ole boy. There are too many ears in this place. What do you say we get into the clouds first."

"This machine isn't moving an inch until you start talking. Now you can do it here or you can do it in Trenchard's office. He's the man that made me a captain and he doesn't take too kindly to civilians telling his pilots what to do."

"I think you're blowing smoke, Captain."

"And I think you're about to blow your mission."

Billy jumped to the ground and marched off. Nigel hesitated and then yelled.

"Wait."

Billy walked faster.

"Captain Windsor. Wait. Please. I have a map. You'll be quite pleased. I'm sure of it."

Billy turned on one heel, his arms folded and a snarl on his face. He stood on the apron like an Egyptian sphinx.

"Captain. Please. I'm begging you."

Billy stepped forward.

"I'm listening."

After a lengthy explanation from his passenger, Billy grilled the man about the precise location of the landing field. Did it contain foxholes or bomb craters? How close was the landing strip to enemy positions? Are there ditches, water, or anything else that would interfere with his ability to land or take off? Were there woods or hills nearby to hide his landing and take-off? The detailed responses encouraged Billy.

"If it's as good as you say it is, we should have no problems."

"I promise you, Captain, you'll be back in St. Omer having tea with the commander before you know it."

Billy, flying his machine at 9,500 feet, recognized the landmarks that surrounded Arras.

After crossing over the Allied Armies trenches, he flew much lower and relied on his compass. The 25-mile trip into enemy territory, with only a few landmarks to guide him, made his stomach churn. The landing field, and it was not much more than a field, lay almost directly south of Cambrai but west of the L'Escau canal. Two nearby wooded areas, Cheneaux and Vaucelles, would block the view of Billy's plane when it landed and took off.

"Our boys in the area tell us you will have plenty of field in which to land this contraption. I will take my leave as soon as you come to a halt and I can escape this bloody harness."

Nigel's remarks made Billy sneer. *Can't be much of a spy if a simple harness slows him down,* thought Billy. As he searched the horizon for the sparkling, sun-soaked waters of the canal, Billy noticed a dark spot in the bright blue sky ahead. A second look revealed two flying machines, descending fast and heading in his direction. The monoplanes, perhaps shocked to discover a British flying machine so deep in German airspace, approached from Billy's right. Neither of them pulled the trigger on their machine guns, opting first to confirm the identity of the unknown interloper. Billy easily recognized the black crosses painted on white backgrounds. The German planes banked sharply and now approached the British BE2c from the rear.

"We've got company, Nigel. Hang on."

Nigel and Billy twisted in their seats. The Fokkers, now directly behind them, were rapidly closing in. Billy put the machine into a deep dive, hoping to land the aircraft the first chance he got. With 2,000 feet of elevation to go, he could hear the explosive pops as German bullets pierced the highly flammable canvas material stretched tight over the frame of his biplane. Nigel screamed.

"We're on bloody fire, Windsor."

Billy reached down and stroked his sidearm, verifying its comforting presence. For a pilot, burning alive was not an option.

At 1,000 feet, Billy could see a recently plowed field. Whether it was pockmarked with artillery craters, or crisscrossed with trenches, did not matter. The second Fokker closed in for the kill. A torrent of bullets reduced the fabric on one wing to shreds. A bullet zipped past Billy's ear and smashed into the control panel.

"Brace yourself, Nigel. We're going down."

Billy kept the nose up as long as he could. When the two wheels hit the soft dirt, the plane jerked to a violent stop, its nose planted in the field like a farmer's corn. Billy could feel the heat of flames from the wing, now fully engulfed. The fuselage would be next, he thought, as he wrestled with his harness. He hung directly over Nigel, wondering why the man sat motionless. The force of gravity made it impossible to release the harness. Billy shoved a hand into his trousers and retrieved a pocket knife. With one slice of the blade, he fell onto his passenger. For once, Nigel had nothing to say.

"Get moving Nigel, it's a few hundred yards to those woods."

The Fokkers approached, once again. Billy swung his legs over the side, and lunged for the harness that held Nigel in the forward seat. The man's eyes, wide open and fixed on the propeller, explained why Nigel did not react. A rivulet of blood, trickling from the Englishman's mouth, prompted Billy to pull open the man's tweed jacket. Nigel's crisp, white shirt, now covered by a bib of crimson red, made the man's release, pointless.

"Oh Nigel. What did you go and do that for?"

The increasingly loud noise of an oncoming plane reminded Billy it was time to run. He reached for his haversack, grabbed Nigel's satchel, and sprinted to a nearby wooded area.

The first Fokker sprayed Billy's BE2c with both of its 7.92-millimeter machine guns. The British biplane flew apart, several pieces of airborne debris narrowly missing Billy. The second Fokker, not to be outdone, banked left, and zoomed in on the escaped pilot. Billy zigged and zagged, hoping to dodge the inevitable. A sudden deep burning pain in his left leg sent him crashing into the dirt. The Fokker flew low over Billy's writhing body. Billy rose to his feet, screaming in pain. Pure adrenalin pushed him closer to safety. Pieces of bark flew off trees. The ground in front of him erupted into a series of tiny explosions. He didn't stop, stumbling deep into the woods until exhaustion and the loss of blood forced him into the shadow of a large rock. He fell face down, his chest heaving, his pant leg soaked red with blood.

Billy Windsor stopped moving.

Chapter Fifteen

HOME

Reggie and Mickey began to share all of their meals. In time, the boy was forced to deliver two trays.

"Your appetite seems to have returned, Reggie."

"Yeah. I suppose it has."

"Why did you stop eating in the first place."

"Because I wanted to stop living."

"Just because you lost a leg and an eye?"

"Isn't that enough?"

"You're asking the wrong man"

"You're just a bloody kid. What do you know?"

"I know that a lot of my dead friends would love to change places with you. And their sweethearts and kids and parents feel the same way, I'm sure."

Reggie looked away.

"I made a mess of things, Mickey. And when I finally got straightened around, this happened," said Reggie, pointing to his stump.

"My father used to say it's never too late to learn something new."

"Did he? Did he learn something new?"

"When I enlisted, he got angry. He went to the recruitment center and enlisted himself. Said he wanted to keep an eye on me. I told him he was crazy. He was 42 years old, for God's sake. That's when he said 'it's never too late to learn something new.'"

"Where is he now?"

Mickey hesitated, swallowing hard to mask his emotions.

"Our patrol got raked with machine gun fire. He pushed me into a crater. They got him instead. We buried him on the banks of the Somme."

Reggie cursed the Huns under his breath. He waited for his anger to dissipate.

"Is there family back home?"

"No, sir. Mom died years ago. All the next of kin are dead or moved away. I'm not even sure the old homestead is still standing. It wasn't much more than a shack, anyway."

Mickey pasted on a brave smile. Reggie had an idea.

"Well, you've got a job, if you want it."

"Doing what?"

"My father owns the Windsor Land and Lumber Company."

"I don't know anything about the lumber business."

"Aw c'mon, Mickey. Haven't you heard? It's never too late to learn something new."

The man and the boy giggled like school kids.

When Reggie and Mickey said their goodbyes, they agreed to meet up, the following week.

"Oh, I almost forgot," said Wells.

"Forgot what?"

Mickey handed Reggie a folded piece of paper.

"What's this?"

"Your sergeant's report of the incident in the trenches."

The sergeant described how Reggie had saved his life. It also contained the sergeant's recommendation that Reggie's sentence be immediately commuted and that a medal of valor be awarded.

"The commander said no to the medal, but you are now a free man."

Reggie smiled.

"And all it cost me was an eye and a leg."

No one knew that Reggie was coming home. After the goodbyes, which included a warm embrace, Reggie hailed a taxi, directing the driver to his father's office.

The giant soldier appeared in the office doorway, looking gaunt and without color. One leg of his trousers was folded and pinned to the back of his pants. A black patch covered his right eye.

Clarence looked up and screamed his stunned surprise.

"Reggie! You are alive and well. Thank the Lord!"

Reggie shrugged.

"Alive yes, but if this is well, I hope things don't get any worse."

Clarence scrambled from behind Mr. Windsor's large desk and pumped Reggie's hand.

"It is so good to see you, Reggie. So good."

"Where's father?"

Clarence froze. Reggie, tired of leaning on his crutches, took a seat.

"Spit it out, Clarence. I'm a big boy."

"Your father is in hospital. He appears to have suffered a massive heart attack. We have a team of doctors doing everything possible."

"When did this happen?"

"Last week."

Reggie shook his head in disbelief.

"I thought the ole man would live forever."

"I'm sorry," said Clarence.

Reggie closed his eyes and exhaled loudly.

"I need a drink."

Clarence blinked. His face burned red.

"I apologize, Reggie. We don't have any alcohol in the office . . ."

Reggie cut him off.

"I need one, Clarence. I didn't say I wanted one."

"You stopped drinking?"

"Yes. I made a promise. I'll tell you about it sometime."

"Your father stopped drinking, too."

"I don't believe you, Clarence."

"He had to. The booze was killing him. It might still kill him."

"Father would drink, but I've never seen him fall-down drunk."

"That changed when his two boys went off to war."

Reggie stared out the window.

"A lot of things changed when we went to war."

"Have you heard from Billy?"

"No. You?"

"My daughter wrote several weeks ago. She hoped to see him in London. I haven't heard from her since."

"Clarence. I'm missing an eye and a leg, in case you haven't noticed. I was fitted for a fake eye back in France. Should be here soon. But I need you to find me one of those fake legs."

"I'll get right on it."

"Excuse me, Mr. Parsons. A telegram from London."

The woman's voice belonged to one of several assistants, employed by Clarence. She handed the cable to Clarence. The man's face went white.

Reggie scowled at Clarence.

"What's wrong, Clarence?"

The telegram fluttered in the older man's trembling hands. He handed the cable to Reggie.

> REGRET TO INFORM YOU. CAPTAIN WILLIAM WINDSOR MISSING IN ACTION. BELIEVED TO BE POW.
>
> ADJUTANT GENERAL

Reggie fumbled with the cable, throwing it on the desk as if it were toxic. One of the crutches dropped to the floor. Clarence jumped up and scrambled to retrieve it. Reggie, using one crutch, rose from his chair.

"Clarence, would you bring me to the hospital?"

"Right away, Reggie."

Elizabeth remained in London for two more nights.

She wandered the streets of London, her emotions careening from white-hot anger to overwhelming sadness and deep regret.

Her head and heart, a tangled web of passion and grief, made it impossible for the woman to think straight. She knew only that Billy was gone and her long overdue holiday would soon be over.

When she returned to the Saint James, she requested a pot of tea be brought to the room. A memory flashed in the young woman's mind as she sat on an easy chair. She bolted across the room, reached for her purse, and started searching. The folded piece of white paper, for which she desperately searched, was missing. She emptied the bag of its contents, pushing each unwanted item to one side. When she turned the empty purse inside out, she rediscovered a hidden pocket. Elizabeth smiled when her fingers found paper and yanked the document from its hiding place.

She recalled signing the government form, months ago. Elizabeth skimmed the first page.

Terms of Service: Members considered suitable after one month probation and who wish to remain are required to sign the declaration to serve six months including the one-month probation.

She checked the dated signature page. Elizabeth sat on the edge of the bed and took several deep breaths. She reread the date of her signature and did the mental calculation. Twice. Her latest contract would expire in less than a month.

The VAD volunteer spent most of that evening wrestling with the decision to continue her work as a nurse or go home. For her, the war would be over when she returned to Newfoundland. She could leave her awful memories where they belonged—in the trenches of France. Luke was buried out there somewhere. And it seemed inevitable that both Reggie and Billy would join him. Elizabeth, tired of the death and destruction, suddenly wanted no more. She did her best to heal the wounded and comfort the dying. But she was exhausted. Elizabeth needed to tend to her own wounds. Wounds of the heart, to be certain, but no less painful.

She would notify her superiors and cable her father as soon as she reached Etaples.

When Elizabeth reached the hospital, she barely had time to enter the building, when matron shouted her name.

The woman wore an urgent look on her face. She handed Elizabeth a cable.

"From your father. It's urgent."

Elizabeth read the telegram. She lunged for the matron's shoulders, leaning on the woman to prevent a fall. Her face changed to a deathly gray. She took a deep breath to calm her nerves.

"What is it?" asked the matron.

"Billy is missing in action. They think he is in a German prison camp."

Matron, her eyes wide with surprise, spoke softly.

"How can that be, Elizabeth? You were just with him. In fact, you're here several days earlier than I expected."

Elizabeth explained Billy's telegram and his sudden departure at the hotel.

"I knew it was a dangerous mission. He said no, but I suspected otherwise."

"Elizabeth. All we can do is pray."

Elizabeth, her jaw set like stone, snarled her anger.

"I disagree, Matron. There *is* something I can do. And this telegram has made it easier."

"What do you mean?"

"I want to go home."

Clarence stayed in the waiting room, allowing Reggie a measure of privacy with his seriously ill father.

Reggie stood in the doorway, mesmerized by his father's gray face. *The old man wore the look of death,* he thought. A look he had seen many times before, in the trenches and tunnels of Gallipoli and France. Reggie swallowed hard and moved to the bedside. His crutches squeaked in protest prompting the senior Windsor to open his eyes. His lips moved and Reggie leaned forward to better hear the weak and fragile voice.

"Reggie."

"I'm right here, Father."

The old man took a deep breath. It triggered an extended coughing spell. Reggie looked to the door.

"Nurse."

A middle-aged woman rushed in and poured water into a glass. She held her patient's head while he sipped the fluid. Much of it dribbled down the old man's chin. He stopped coughing. The nurse disappeared. Reggie, unsure of himself in such circumstances, tried to make light of the situation.

"Don't be offended, Father, but you look awful."

Mr. Windsor focused on Reggie's face.

"What happened to your eye?"

"Lost it . . . got a glass eye on order. They say you won't notice the difference."

The patient's eyes darted in every direction. Reginald spotted his son's crutches. He whispered.

"And your leg?"

Reggie faked a grin.

"Clarence says he's going to find me a new one."

The old man's head twisted. He frowned.

"Billy?"

Reggie ignored the pang of jealousy that a mention of his younger brother, often triggered.

"He's missing, Father. They think the Bosch took him prisoner."

The patient squeezed his eyes shut. For the first time in his life, Reggie saw tears on his father's face. *Not surprising*, thought Reggie. His father cried for Billy but said nothing about the half-blind amputee. His long-standing jealousy made yet another appearance. Reggie forced himself to focus on his father, instead. The boy struggled to say something, anything, to comfort the old man. But his mind, a huge ball of anxiety, worry, and hurt feelings would not cooperate. He stood in silence near his father's deathbed, overwhelmed by the gravity of the moment. *The old man was dying. His little brother could be dead. The company was at risk. What now?*

Clarence appeared at the doorway.

"He's been like that for several days now."

Reggie reached for his father's hand and squeezed. The old man did not seem to notice. Reggie hobbled to the door.

"Let's talk," he said to Clarence.

Reggie did not stop until they reached the waiting room.

"I've seen that look before, Clarence. Men who were wounded. Thought they lucked out, getting a blighty that would get them home. They got home alright. In a box."

"You can't lose hope, Reggie."

"I don't think my ole man is gonna make it."

"I don't want to admit it, Reggie. But I am forced to agree."

"Now what?"

"I'm running the company the best way I know how, Reggie. But it's not my company to run and I don't feel right about it."

"Well, I sure as blazes can't do the job."

"I can teach you."

Reggie flinched.

"Are you serious?"

"Yes, I'm serious. You're a smart, young man, Reggie. All you really need is someone like me to show you the ropes."

"You forgot something. The son who got all the brains is in a German prison camp somewhere. I'm the dumb one. Remember?"

"Reggie. I don't believe that for a moment. Come on. Let's get back to the office."

After her giving her notice, Elizabeth worked as a VAD nurse for several more weeks.

Despite the daily chaos of hospital work, she remained preoccupied with Billy Windsor. *Was he alive? Was he a prisoner? Where did his plane go down? Were there witnesses? And precisely what did they see?* In a desperate search for answers, she called Commander Trenchard's office at Saint Omer.

"Good afternoon. I'm calling with respect to my fiancé, Captain William Windsor. He was reported missing in action and possibly taken prisoner by the Germans."

Elizabeth lied about her relationship with Billy as a ruse to get information. While the lieutenant who answered the phone went in search of the commander, she wondered if her deception was also wishful thinking.

"Miss Parsons, the commander cannot come to the phone at this time. He instructed me to inform you that we have learned nothing more about the captain's whereabouts, since his plane was shot down."

"How do you know that he was shot down. How do you know that he survived."

"I am not authorized to reveal such matters, Miss Parsons. I am sorry."

Elizabeth's voice cracked.

"Can you tell me anything at all?"

The lieutenant lowered his voice.

"There was an eyewitness. One of ours."

"Do you know if he was hurt or wounded?"

"I'm sorry ma'am, I must go now."

The officer hung up. Elizabeth slammed the phone into its cradle just as Matron returned to her office.

"If you destroy my phone, Elizabeth, I will have to terminate your services here at Etaples, effective immediately."

Elizabeth turned, the smile on matron's face triggering a wave of guilt. Elizabeth's eyes glassed over with tears.

"I'm going to miss you, Matron. Very much."

"The feeling is mutual, Elizabeth. This place will not be quite the same without you."

Elizabeth squirmed in place but remained silent. Matron guessed her thoughts.

"Any word on Billy?"

"No, Matron, and I leave in two days."

"Don't give up, Elizabeth. Never give up."

Elizabeth could not have known at the time but she would follow Reggie's footsteps on her journey back to Newfoundland.

The *SS Corinthian* traveled as part of a convoy with an escort of battleships. The journey, although uneventful, seemed to last forever. In fact, her entire trip required two weeks. Like Reggie, Elizabeth's arrival in St. John's would be a total surprise to her father.

"You were sitting behind that same mountain of papers when I left, almost two years ago," she said.

Clarence looked up from a journal filled with numbers, refusing to believe what he saw.

"Elizabeth Parsons, you are the most beautiful sight I have ever seen."

Father and daughter rushed into each other's arms, her weeping, and her father trying hard not to show his true emotions.

"I am in shock, Elizabeth. I just assumed we would not see you until the war was over."

"I got tired, Father. My contract with the VAD was expiring and I chose not to renew it."

"A volunteer for almost two years. You have certainly done your share, Elizabeth."

Elizabeth's eyes drifted to Mr. Windsor's nameplate hand-carved in mahogany lying prominently on the huge desk.

"Have you heard from Billy or the RFC?" she asked.

"No, my dear. We've heard nothing. Did you know that Reggie has also come home?"

Elizabeth took a sharp breath. She repeatedly blinked her surprise.

"Reggie? Here? In Saint John's?"

"Yes. In fact, I'm expecting him to arrive momentarily. I'm teaching him the business."

"Where is Mr. Windsor?"

"I thought you knew. He suffered a massive heart attack. Been in hospital for weeks. Put me in charge."

Elizabeth moved quickly to the exit, stopping just long enough to deliver a quick peck to her father's cheek.

"I don't want to be here when that man arrives. I'll see you at home, Father. I will make you a nice supper."

"Please stay. We can have tea."

Elizabeth's eyes flashed.

"Tea? Tea with Reggie Windsor? Are you mad?"

"Elizabeth. The war has changed everyone. Reggie is a new man. You would hardly recognize him."

Elizabeth slowly shook her head.

"Supper will be ready at 6 o'clock."

As she exited the building, a tall, thin man on crutches and wearing an eyepatch appeared on the other side of the door. Despite the loss of a leg, the man held the door open and waited for her to pass. As she walked by, he reached out and touched her arm.

"Elizabeth? Is that you?"

She instantly recognized Reggie's voice, flinched, and then resumed walking. He followed her out the door, struggling to keep up.

"Elizabeth, please. Please stop. I can't walk that fast."

Elizabeth stopped walking but refused to face her tormentor.

"Elizabeth, you don't have to look at me and you certainly don't have to talk to me. I just wanted to apologize for my behavior of long ago. Most men go to jail for that sort of thing. I am truly sorry."

Elizabeth turned and faced the brute. She barely recognized him. Reggie wore no moustache. Streaks of premature gray could be seen in his black hair. The dark circles under both eyes very nearly matched the black color of his eyepatch. He appeared to have lost a great deal of weight. She noticed the crutches and his missing leg. His exertions left the man breathless. She stood and stared. Speechless. Reggie squirmed.

"An unexploded artillery shell. I got lucky."

Elizabeth felt no sympathy. If anything, she secretly enjoyed his suffering. The man's silly grin reminded her of that leering gaze on the night of his attack. Anger and frustration rose in her chest. But not fear. He kept talking.

"I understand if you have nothing to say. I certainly can't blame you for that."

Elizabeth thought the remark patronizing and gratuitous. He bowed slightly, preparing to leave. She stepped forward.

"Wait," she said.

He faced her. The fingers of her right hand curled into a fist.

"Yes, Elizabeth?"

"I have something for you."

His limited peripheral vision blinded him to the woman's wild swing. Her closed fist hit Reggie square on the jaw. He fell back, stumbled, and landed on his back side. The crutches flew to the ground. He lay there, stunned by the sharp blow. Two pedestrians stopped and helped him to his feet. They retrieved his crutches. Several more gathered and watched. An older lady stepped forward and wagged a finger in Elizabeth's face.

"Young lady, you should be ashamed of yourself. This man is a war veteran. Lost his leg and an eye for King and Country. Shame on you."

The onlookers grumbled their disapproval. A man's voice, his face hidden, could be heard above the rest.

"A spoiled rotten little girl with no respect for her elders. What in blazes is this world coming to?"

Elizabeth pushed her way through a sea of scowling faces. One spectator shoved her forward.

"Good riddance! A curse be on you, little girl."

Elizabeth marched and then ran to the trolley station.

Nothing changed.

Elizabeth stood in the doorway, soaking in the sights, sounds, and smells of her childhood home. The faint odor of yesterday's fish dinner, the loud ticking of the mantle clock in the parlor, and the faded color of worn upholstery on furniture almost as old as she was, greeted the girl. Her father, opposed to change of any kind, did not move so much as a candlestick during her absence.

After unpacking her modest belongings, Elizabeth curled up in her favorite chair, with Alice, the black cat, hoping to relish those first few moments at home. She often dreamed of this day while serving in the hospitals of London and France. Even in the midst of chaos, with patients screaming in pain and doctors demanding her attention, Elizabeth could always recall the hours spent at home in St. Johns. Writing in her journal, sitting near the fire in an overstuffed chair while reading a book on midwifery, or lying on the couch, with Alice the cat purring in her ear.

The ugly encounter with Reggie Windsor shattered that dream and left the girl thinking she should never have returned home. The fear she experienced two years ago mutated into a profound rage. She trembled with fury and blamed Reggie for her deep-seated distrust of all men. The usual punishments, shame and prison time, would not be enough. She wanted him dead. And, if possible, she would do it herself.

A knock on the door sprang Elizabeth from the chair. She approached the exit with caution, opening the door slowly.

"Your father told me you were back."

Mrs. Newcastle's smiling face triggered tears of relief and joy. Elizabeth choked her gratitude as the two embraced.

"Mrs. Newcastle. You are truly a visiting angel."

Elizabeth made a pot of tea and the two midwives picked up where they left off, long ago. They chatted, nonstop, about midwifery, Elizabeth's work as a VAD nurse, her experiences in the OR, and Luke's tragic death. The reference to Luke pushed Elizabeth into a rabbit hole of memories, good and bad. She changed the subject to Billy Windsor but it did not change the overwhelming hurt and regret in her heart.

"Elizabeth, you seem quite troubled. Are you not happy to be home?"

"Yes, of course. I wanted desperately to be home. But my heart seems stuck in the trenches of France and the skies over Germany."

Mrs. Newcastle examined the back of her arthritic hands, as if the pain would go away with nothing more than a long stare.

"I sometimes think that war is very much like a wound that has healed. The bleeding may have stopped but the scar remains. The physical pain and suffering may have ended, but the mental anguish continues. Sometimes for years."

Elizabeth shrugged.

"Is there anyone in this godforsaken world who has not been changed by this miserable war?" asked Elizabeth.

"No one, in my opinion," said Mrs. Newcastle. "But there are some people who have changed for the better."

"I'd like to meet that person."

"You have. You punched him in the face after he held the door for you."

Elizabeth sprang to her feet, spilling her tea on the braided rug at her feet. She stormed out of the parlor, the rattle of her cup on its saucer, loudly announcing the girl's anger. She shoved the dishes into the kitchen sink and glared out the window. Mrs. Newcastle followed. She spoke softly to the girl's back.

"Elizabeth. I did not intend to upset you. Please forgive me."

The angry girl turned and pushed a finger to within an inch of her mentor's face.

"That animal tried to rape me. Do you understand that, Mrs. Newcastle? He tried to rape me and he very nearly succeeded. Don't you *dare* tell me that he is a changed man."

"You may not want to hear this, but I am going to say it anyway. In the three weeks he has been home, Reggie Windsor has made amends with a number of women. He has stopped drinking. He has contributed a significant amount of money to a number of charitable causes, including a special ward for amputees at Wandsworth Hospital. I'm also told he is learning how to run the family business with your father as his mentor. And in the fall, he will begin classes at the university."

"I don't trust him, Mrs. Newcastle. And I never will."

Mrs. Newcastle reached for her wrap.

"I've learned in my old age to trust not what a person may say, but what a person does."

"Mrs. Newcastle, I don't believe for one minute that a cold, calculating, cruel monster like Reggie Windsor has changed his ways simply because he lost a leg."

"Oh, child. You have a right to be angry. You can be angry about Reggie, you can be angry about Luke, and you can be angry about this horrible war that has caused so much death and destruction. But you cannot be angry forever, Elizabeth Parsons. Your anger will not heal your wounds. Your suffering will continue until and unless you move on. Put it all behind you, my friend. Let it go, and live your life as the Good Lord intended."

Elizabeth stood in place, refusing to face Mrs. Newcastle.

The older woman gently squeezed the girl's arm and let herself out.

Chapter Sixteen

FREEDOM

Billy could hear the long, cooing sound of pigeons and the occasional flapping of their wings somewhere above his head.

His weary eyes slowly opened. The patchwork of rough sawn rafters overhead, along with the faint aroma of cow manure, made it obvious. Billy's new home was a barn. The throbbing in his left thigh prompted him to look down. Although relieved to see his leg still intact and nestled in the hay-filled mattress, Billy scowled when he saw the amputated pant leg of his flying uniform. His wounded limb, wrapped in a dirty bandage just above the knee, appeared swollen.

He could also hear snoring. His head twisted. His eyes darted everywhere. There were at least a dozen other beds in the cavernous chamber, some of them in stalls, others in the barn's large open area. All of them wore bandages on their limbs, torso, or head. When he heard the approaching sound of German voices, his eyes squeezed shut. The noise of boots on the hardscrabble floor, stopped at his bedside.

"Captain Windsor. I trust you slept well?"

The man's perfectly spoken English did not contain a hint of the German tongue. The surprise forced Billy's eyes wide open. A middle-aged man, dressed in the gray-green uniform of a German army officer, bowed low.

"Allow me to introduce myself. I am Colonel Konrad Jager of the Imperial German Army.

"How do you know my name?"

"Your friend, Nigel."

"He's dead."

"His luggage spoke volumes."

"I wouldn't know."

The German officer leaned forward and whispered.

"In Germany, we hang spies."

Billy played stupid.

"Am I not in France?"

"It will soon be a part of Germany."

"May I suggest you save your rope until then?"

The colonel flashed a broad smile. He reached for Billy's leg and gently squeezed the bandaged area. Billy winced.

"Are you a spy, Captain Windsor?"

"Oh, sure. We spies regularly wear the uniform of a captain in the Royal Flying Corps."

The colonel leaned hard on the wound. Billy screamed in agony. He jerked to a sitting position and yanked on the man's hand. The colonel released Billy's leg and swung hard with the back of his arm. The sharp blow forced Billy's head back onto the straw. Blood spurted from the prisoner's nose. Billy's eyes, glassy from the excruciating pain, flashed in anger.

"I am not a spy, colonel. My orders were to fly Nigel to Cambrai. And that's all I know."

"Thank you, Captain Windsor. That wasn't so difficult now, was it?"

"I'll let you know after my nose stops bleeding."

The colonel pulled a handkerchief from his trouser pocket and offered it to Billy.

"I do apologize for the misunderstanding, Captain Windsor. We are at war, you know."

Billy held the handkerchief to his nose.

"Thank you, Colonel. But you will forgive me if I am unable to have it cleaned and returned to you."

The German officer smirked.

"I quite understand."

Billy grew curious.

"Your English is impeccable, Colonel."

"Three years at Eton. A fine school. Even if it is British."

"I will give your compliments to the headmaster."

"That would be nice, Captain Windsor. But you do not sound very British."

"Newfoundland. We are part of the British Commonwealth."

"Of course. Well, the Commonwealth needs all the help it can get, I suppose."

"I disagree, Colonel. I think the Commonwealth has all the help it requires."

The colonel retrieved a pocket watch from his coat, frowning when he saw the precise time of day.

"A genuine delight to meet you, Captain Windsor. On Friday you will be transported to our new officers' camp in Freiburg, Germany. Enjoy your stay."

The colonel turned on one heel, and marched away.

Although Billy's leg throbbed, the hunger pains in his stomach were of greater concern. He swung his good leg off the side of the bed for leverage, struggling to a sitting position. A young soldier came running down the center of the makeshift hospital. His uniform, ill-fitting and splattered with blood, suggested the man served as a medical orderly.

"I'd like something to eat."

The soldier stared at Billy, a blank look on his face. Billy brought an imaginary fork to his lips and opened his mouth. The orderly continued to stare as if he did not understand. Billy understood. He reached into an inside pocket of his flying jacket, retrieved a half pack of Kenilworth cigarettes, and flashed them at the German. The boy grinned and stuck his hand out. Billy shook his head.

"First, you bring me some food."

"Ja. Food."

The boy scurried to the exit. He returned in minutes, with a cloth and leather bag. Billy recognized Nigel's blood covered satchel. His hunger pangs were worse than the guilt pangs. Billy rifled through the bag with a vengeance. He discovered a half loaf of bread, some dry beef, a potato, and an onion. *Whatever Nigel carried with him into Germany would stay in Germany,* Billy thought. He surrendered the smokes to the young orderly and ate half the food, uncertain if he would be fed again, anytime soon.

After the meal, Billy removed his bandages and examined the wound in his left thigh. The bullet had gone clean through and there was no sign of gangrene or infection. Just a few crude stitches. He dressed the wound with the same bloody bandages and decided to explore the barn-turned-hospital. A handful of the bedridden soldiers appeared to be German officers. They eyed Billy suspiciously as he hopped to a large door, hoping to learn more about his surroundings. Billy calculated that after retrieving his unconscious body, the Bosch brought him to the barn. He heard no gunfire or exploding artillery shells and concluded the barn lay well behind enemy lines.

On the next day, he ate the rest of his food rations. On the third day, the orderly with access to food stood at Billy's bedside. He motioned to Billy and pointed to the door.

"Du gehst jetzt."

Billy knew enough German to understand the boy's invitation. ("You go now.")

They journeyed to Freiburg in a lorry. The trip consumed most of the day. Billy was given a slice of moldy brown bread in the morning and again in the afternoon. His two guards, sitting in the rear of the open-air truck, left him one canteen of smelly water. Billy took mental notes of the signage, the approximate speed of the lorry, and their general direction. He did not intend to spend the rest of the war as a POW in a German prison. Assuming he could escape, knowledge of the geography around the city of Freiburg would be critical.

When he arrived in Freiburg, Billy's thigh no longer throbbed. He was desperately hungry and thirsty, however. The commandant of the prison camp, a major in the German army, saw no need to introduce himself, much less offer his newest prisoner a bite to eat. The short, stocky man greeted Billy upon arrival. He spoke English with a heavy accent.

"This is an officers' camp. I trust you will conduct yourself like an officer and a gentleman, at all times. You are not allowed off the campus but will be given free access to the yard. You are otherwise confined to your barracks or the dining hall. Any attempt to escape will lead to your immediate execution. Are there any questions?"

"When do I get to eat?"

"Prisoners are fed in the morning at seven and again in the evening at six. You are dismissed."

Billy estimated that the prison, a half dozen separate buildings configured around a large yard, was located in the middle of the city. It looked more like a small university. He counted more than 200 inmates lying, standing, and sitting, shoulder to shoulder, as they jostled for space. He quickly discovered two other captains, one a native of London and the other an Aussie from Sydney. The three of them were the highest-ranking British Army officers on the campus. He waited until he and his fellow captains were alone.

"Have there been any attempts to escape?"

"No. And we shan't recommend it," said the Brit.

"We are very near the Black Forest and no more than 90 miles from Zürich, perhaps 40 miles from the Swiss border," said Billy.

"How do you know this?"

"I rode here in an open truck from somewhere near Cambrai. There are signs and I calculated mileage based on our approximate speed."

The Aussie was not impressed.

"Well, aren't you the clever one?"

Billy turned to the British captain. The man shook his head 'no,' while tapping his chest.

"Don't count on me, laddie. I swallowed a chest full of Bosch gas. My lungs are shot. I would just slow you down."

The Aussie chimed in.

"It's not so bad here. The food is edible and the guards are fair. I say we're better off here than in the trenches."

Billy studied the Aussie's unkempt appearance and his soiled uniform. Despite Billy's anger and disgust, diplomacy trumped honesty.

"Well, I certainly understand your reasoning, gentleman. Thank you for your time."

Reginald Windsor, still in the hospital, showed no improvement.

His older son absorbed the details of his father's business at a record pace. Clarence, clearly ecstatic with his new role as mentor and instructor, patiently encouraged Reggie without shaming him.

"You should have been a teacher, Clarence. I am understanding most of what you have told me."

"I am pleased to hear that, Reggie. And you must never be afraid to ask me questions."

Reggie's face grew solemn. He stared into the distance as if mesmerized by a beautiful sunset.

"I do have one question."

"And what is that?"

"How do I make amends with your daughter?"

Clarence tossed his pencil on the pile of papers which covered the boardroom table. He sat back in his chair, took a deep breath, and exhaled loudly.

"Honestly, Reggie, next to my late wife, my daughter Elizabeth is the most hardheaded woman I have ever known."

Reggie's head drooped. After a moment, he spoke to Clarence through watery eyes.

"Clarence. I know that Elizabeth and I will never be friends. I understand that. But I must make amends. What I did was terribly wrong and I can't forgive myself. At least not until she forgives me."

"You have changed, my friend. You are a different person since losing your leg and coming home."

Reggie gnawed on a thumbnail.

"I thought I was going to die, Clarence. My leg was hanging on by a flap of skin. I was bleeding like a stuck pig and I couldn't see from my left eye. I prayed, Clarence. For the first time since I was in grade school, I prayed. And I made a promise to God. Take my leg if you must, but if you spare me, I'll give up more than my leg. I will give up the booze, the bullying, and the broads."

Clarence leaned forward.

"What happened?"

"I don't know. I passed out. I woke up in a hospital. My leg was gone and there was a patch over my eye. I didn't want to live, Clarence. Not with a leg missing. And I'm afraid I wasn't a very good patient."

"But you hung on."

"Just barely. I refused to eat. They put me on a ship to home, figuring the trip would kill me. I wanted to jump overboard but I was too weak to get out of my bed."

"What changed your mind?"

"Not what, who. I woke up on the ship and this skinny kid was eating my food. We got into an argument. I treated him like shit. But he would not leave me alone. I thought he hung around for the food. He didn't care about the food. He cared about me. Wanted me to live. That boy saved my life, Clarence.

I promised him a job at Windsor Land and Lumber Company. Hope that meets with your approval."

"My approval is not required, Reggie. You're the boss."

"When I said good bye to Mickey, he gave me this."

Reggie reached into a pocket and showed Clarence the Sergeant's recommendation.

"Reggie. This is most impressive."

"The Commander said no to the medal but the letter is proof, to me anyway, that I earned my keep."

Clarence pursed his lips.

"I'll talk to Elizabeth. You have earned and deserve a second chance. But I can't promise you anything."

"Thanks, Clarence. Now I have another question.

"Where in blazes is my fake leg?"

Elizabeth, feeling more like a caged lioness, worked hard to keep occupied.

The transition from VAD nurse to an unemployed homemaker did not go as expected. The girl cleaned, baked, did some sewing, read books, weeded the flower beds, washed bed linens, and prepared her father's garden for the cold winter months ahead. She thought about approaching Mrs. Newcastle, or even the hospital, for work as a midwife or nurse. The hospital would most likely refuse her services, absent any formal medical training. And, despite Mrs. Newcastle's intentions, Elizabeth continued to harbor a deep frustration and considerable anger with the senior midwife.

The nerve of that woman. Telling me to move on from that monster's vicious attack. Elizabeth sat in the overstuffed chair, dinner cooking in the oven and every imaginable chore, completed. Still, she fumed and fidgeted, unwilling to "let it go."

Surprisingly, she thought of Reggie's dying father. Despite her simmering animosity for the man, the nurse in her wondered if she could help him, perhaps even make a difference in his final days. Elizabeth immediately abandoned the idea when she considered that Reggie could be at hospital when she called on Mr. Windsor. When the front door suddenly opened, she panicked.

"It's only me, Elizabeth. I'm home early."

Elizabeth started breathing again, the vision of Reggie on that fateful evening disappearing as fast as it flashed in her mind. Instead, she expressed irritation that her dinner would not be ready for at least an hour.

"Dinner is not ready yet, Father.

"Good. We have time to talk."

"About what?"

"Reggie."

"Mrs. Newcastle has already lectured me on the need to, as she says, *let it go*. That was your idea, I suppose. Must I now sit through another sermon, this one from my father?"

Clarence closed his eyes, as if searching for the perfect words. Elizabeth bit her nails.

"Well?"

Her father leaned forward.

"Elizabeth. Have you ever made a mistake?"

"Of course."

"Did any of those mistakes require the Lord's forgiveness?"

"You're not my confessor, Father."

"No. No indeed. But I am your father. And I have the right and the duty to remind you what it says in the Bible about forgiveness. Luke, chapter 6, verse 37."

Do not judge and you will not be judged. Do not condemn and you will not be condemned. Forgive and you will be forgiven.

"Thank you, Father, but I do not need the instruction. You and Mother forced me to read the Bible, daily. You do remember, don't you?"

"Is there nothing in your past, Elizabeth, for which you must ask God's forgiveness?"

"No. There is not."

"You mean there is nothing you can recall."

Clarence handed Elizabeth an opened envelope. It contained a letter from Elizabeth, sent to her father, long ago. The missive was sent shortly after the encounter with Private Sutherland. Elizabeth pulled the letter from its envelope, frowning as she did so.

"I'll save you the trouble of reading it, Elizabeth. It's the letter you wrote to me shortly after you administered a fatal dose of morphine to Private Sutherland. He was the young man whose entire head was bandaged because he was missing most of his face. The sentence in your letter that I can still recall is, *I pray the Lord will forgive me for what I have done*."

Elizabeth threw the letter to the floor and stormed into the kitchen. Clarence followed. Elizabeth turned her back to him. She yelled at the window.

"You and your stupid Bible. Who in blazes do you think you are? God?"

She spun around, pushed past him, and yelled over her shoulder.

"You are no saint, Mr. Parsons. You have no idea what I've been through."

Clarence followed her into the parlor. He spun the girl around and pulled her close. She pushed back. He wouldn't release his grip. She yelled.

"No. I do not want a hug from you. Don't touch me. I hate you."

She hit him on the chest with a fist. When he didn't budge, she used both hands, Clarence did not back away. She screamed and continued to pummel the man.

"Did you hear me, Father? I hate you. I hate Reggie. I hate the war and I hate this miserable world."

She looked up. Her father's sorrowful eyes, blinking back the tears. She stopped hitting him. He pulled her head to his chest. Elizabeth began to sob.

"It's alright, Elizabeth. Perhaps, a good cry is just what you need."

The tears turned into a torrent.

"I'm sorry, Daddy. I'm so sorry."

Father and daughter ate in silence.

When she poured the tea and sat down, he reached for her hand.

"Elizabeth. It is *your* mental health and well-being that concerns me most. Not Reggie's. Do you understand?"

"I do not wish to be in the same room with that man."

"I have a meeting with Reggie tomorrow morning at 8 o'clock to review the sales journals. Please come with me."

Elizabeth took a long sip of tea.

"I want to move on, Father. But I will not meet with him.

"You must try, my dear. You must try."

"If I meet with him, will you be satisfied? Will you leave me alone?"

"Yes, I promise."

Elizabeth considered her options. She was not prepared to reconcile with Reggie. Not even close. A meeting, however brief, would end her father's constant nagging.

"Fine. I'll do it."

"Hi, Clarence, what do you have for me today?"

Reggie's jaw dropped. He jumped to his feet, using the boardroom table to keep his balance. Elizabeth, just two steps behind her father, walked into the room with an air of confidence. Reggie, staring in disbelief, gulped large amounts of air.

"I'll leave you two alone," said Clarence, shutting the door behind him.

When Clarence left the boardroom, Elizabeth took a seat at the end of the long rectangular table, opposite Reggie and near the door. Reggie sat down and fidgeted with his pencil. Elizabeth spoke first.

"Good morning, Reggie."

The pencil snapped in Reggie's hands. He grabbed the two pieces, shoving them into his jacket pocket. He took a deep breath.

"Good morning, Elizabeth."

She leaned into the table, her voice strong and confident.

"Is it possible that you are more nervous than I am, Reggie?"

"Yes, ma'am. I mean Elizabeth. Yes. I am very nervous. I didn't think you wanted to see me."

"I didn't."

Elizabeth studied the large picture window.

"A very nice view."

"Thank you. And thank you for seeing me."

Elizabeth shrugged.

"It wasn't *my* idea."

Reggie understood her meaning.

"I am very indebted to your father."

"My father usually gets his way. And if you don't cooperate, he'll pester you until you surrender. I'm only here because I surrendered."

"He's arranged for me to receive an artificial leg."

"How sweet."

"You have experience working with amputees?"

Elizabeth shot a dirty look across the length of the table. Reggie's face turned pink.

"Yes, of course you do. I'm sorry. I wasn't thinking."

"My father says you are a different man since returning from the war."

It was Reggie's turn to gaze out the window. He turned to Elizabeth; his eyes shining.

"I . . . I almost. Well. Truthfully, I was close to giving up, Elizabeth."

"You mean you wanted to kill yourself?"

Reggie studied her eyes.

"I am ashamed to tell you. Yes. I thought seriously of killing myself."

"Why?"

"I've made a lot of mistakes in my short life, Elizabeth. Here at home and overseas. I didn't know how to fix that. And I was suddenly missing an eye and a leg. It was too much. I wanted to give up."

"What happened?"

"A kid named Mickey. Someday, I'll tell you all about it."

"That's so sad, Reggie."

Reggie's head jerked up.

"Do you mean that, Elizabeth?"

"Yes. You see, I was hoping you would be killed by the Germans. But suicide would have been even better."

Reggie took a sharp breath. *She is still very angry*, he thought. He struggled to rise. Elizabeth stiffened. Reggie, without his crutches, hopped a few steps to the window. He gazed at the pedestrians four floors below. He turned, leaned against the windowsill, and murmured.

"My heartfelt apology wouldn't mean a thing to you, would it?"

"No, sir. Not a thing."

"Then why are you here?"

"To get the old man off my back. I think he's taken a liking to you. God knows why."

"Your father treats me like I'm a normal person."

"He's got a big heart, Reggie. But I don't. And you are not a normal person."

Reggie stood a bit taller.

"You may be right about me, Elizabeth, but you are dead wrong about yourself. You have suffered greatly for two whole years. You have seen and done things that would drive most people insane. You *do* have a big heart. And it's made of the purest gold. Don't sell yourself short."

Elizabeth jumped to her feet and pointed an accusing finger at him.

"What do you know about big hearts or for that matter, self-sacrifice? When have you ever given something to somebody and not wanted something in return? You have spent your whole life getting everything you ever wanted from your rich daddy. And when he couldn't buy it for you, you would just go out and take it. But you didn't take me, Reggie Windsor. You failed. You failed miserably. In fact, your whole life has been a miserable failure. You are not worthy of the air you breath."

Reggie leaned hard against the window behind him, his legs less than steady. Tears burned in his eye. His face went white. He hung his head and covered his ears with both hands, as if blocking the sound of her voice would erase the memories. When he looked up, his face twisted in sorrow, he sobbed the apology she did not want.

"I'm sorry Elizabeth. I am truly sorry. Please forgive me. I'm begging you."

Elizabeth marched to the end of the table, retrieved his crutches, and threw them on the floor at his feet. She hissed her response through clenched teeth.

"I hope you rot in hell, Reggie Windsor."

After Elizabeth left the building, Clarence returned to the board room.

"Well. How did it go?"

Reggie, ignoring the crutches at his feet, reached for the table and hobbled back to the chair. He cleared his throat and did his best to flash a quick smile.

"Clarence, your daughter could not have been nicer to me. She is a young lady of whom you can be very proud. I consider it a privilege to know her and sincerely hope that we will one day be good friends."

Reggie pretended to review the stack of papers in front of him. He refused to look up, scared that his face would expose his lies. Clarence stood at the door, oblivious to Reggie's suffering.

"Reggie. I am truly amazed. I thought for sure you would get nothing but venom from that girl. I cannot tell you how happy I am that she has moved on."

"Me too, Clarence. Now tell me about these land deals."

Clarence got home at the usual time.

"Reggie told me about your conversation with him."

Elizabeth stiffened. Clarence, his back to the girl, stood an umbrella in the corner. He did not see the stunned look on his daughter's face. She spoke haltingly.

"What did he say to you?"

Clarence turned around, his smile as wide and bright as Elizabeth had ever seen.

"He said you were the perfect lady and that I should be very proud of you."

Clarence pulled her into a long and warm embrace. He talked into her ear.

"Now you can move on, Elizabeth. And you will be all the happier for it."

She withdrew to the kitchen. Her mind raced. *Reggie did not misconstrue her message. Of that, she could be certain. Her comments about suicide were designed to hurt and humiliate the man. Obviously, it didn't work. The monster turned into a nice guy. Perhaps he was pretending. He was more cunning than she thought.*

Elizabeth had to know for sure. But how?

"I propose a working lunch today. In the boardroom," said Clarence."

"That would be fine with me," said Reggie, still rattled from his meeting with Elizabeth the day before.

"I've ordered sandwiches to be brought in. There is something I want to show you."

"You seem very excited, Clarence. What is it?"

Clarence pulled a handful of papers from the large manila envelope in his hands.

"It's from J. E. Hanger. They make artificial limbs."

Clarence showed Reggie a series of colored sketches. They depicted a variety of artificial limbs for AK (above the knee) amputees.

"This one is called the *Dural.* It's made of aluminum. Weighs as little as 4 pounds. Ball-bearing knee joints and it comes in a flesh color. Brand new on the market. Considered 20 to 40 percent stronger than the competition and much lighter."

"How much?"

"$1500. They are manufactured in Pittsburgh, Pennsylvania."

"The ole man will have a fit."

"You need a leg, Reggie. Why not get the best?"

"I've got to go to Pennsylvania?"

"No, sir. I spoke to their sales office. We will send them a series of measurements. But if the artificial limb fits poorly or causes discomfort, we will then send them a plaster mold of your, your, uh, the . . ."

Clarence let his voice disappear into the awkward silence that now filled the room.

"Stump. It's my stump, Clarence. No need to be embarrassed."

"Yes. Yes, of course."

At home that evening, Clarence rattled on about Reggie's new leg.

Elizabeth's curiosity triggered an idea.

"I can do the plaster mold. And I know the measurements they will need."

Clarence looked up at his daughter, a stunned look on his face.

"I know you've moved on, Elizabeth. But, are you sure about this? It's rather soon, don't you think?"

Elizabeth answered. Almost too quickly.

"Yes. Have him come here after dinner, tomorrow evening."

"Thank you, Elizabeth. And I am sure Reggie will thank you, too."

Reggie, greeted at the door by Clarence, followed him into the parlor, sweating profusely and looking nervous.

"Reggie, if I didn't know better, I'd say you were nervous or afraid. I am sure Elizabeth will be gentle."

Reggie removed his suit coat, revealing large patches of wet material under each arm. Beads of perspiration could be seen on his forehead. He used a shirt sleeve to wipe the moisture from his face and brow. When Elizabeth swept into the room, a nurse's satchel in her hand, Reggie stood motionless.

"Father, could you run upstairs and bring my box of sewing needles and thread? Please?"

When Clarence left the room, Elizabeth immediately approached Reggie. He flinched.

"Why didn't you tell my father what really happened in the boardroom?"

Reggie exhaled loudly. He closed his eyes for a moment and slowly shook his head.

"Because I'm tired."

"Tired? I don't understand."

"I'm tired of the fighting, Elizabeth. In France, we used guns and artillery. Here at home, we use our eyes and our tongues. But one way or the other, I am sick and tired of fighting. I truly want and need your forgiveness. But apparently what I did is unforgivable. I have no choice but to move on. There will be no more fighting between us. It takes two to fight, Elizabeth. And if you want to keep on fighting, you'll have to do it by yourself."

Elizabeth's eyebrows arched. Her eyes bulged. Reggie's speech left her speechless. She came prepared to humiliate him. She wanted to crush his soul, to make him beg for mercy. And what does the miserable bastard go and do? He goes soft on her, refusing to beg or even to fight. She thought of Alice, the cat. Alice would catch a mouse, release it, and capture it again. But when the mouse no longer tried to escape, Alice would lose interest. She just walked away. Elizabeth didn't want to admit it, but she was feeling a lot like Alice the cat.

"I have your sewing kit," said Clarence as he walked in.

The woman slipped into nurse mode. She forced her emotions to one side and proceeded with the task at hand. She motioned to Reggie, pointing to a high-back chair.

"I need you to stand here, Reggie. No crutches. And you must be standing straight as an arrow. We want the measurements to be accurate."

Reggie did as he was told. A very awkward silence ensued as Elizabeth released the pin from Reggie's folded pant leg and rolled it up, until the stump was entirely exposed. Reggie, his face now red, looked straight ahead. Elizabeth reached into the satchel for her tailor's tape, asking Clarence for pencil and paper. She measured the circumference of the stump at various points along the entire length of the severed limb. She measured the distance from the very end of the stump to the hardwood floor. She also recorded the width and length of his stockinged foot. When finished, Elizabeth let the pant leg drop, refolded the material, and re-pinned the cloth to the back of Reggie's trousers.

"Shall I do a plaster mold of the stump?"

"No," said Reggie, a firm tone in his voice.

Clarence explained that J. E. Hanger would not require a mold unless the artificial limb proved ill-fitting or seriously uncomfortable. Elizabeth rose to her feet and faced Reggie. She spoke in a business-like manner.

"The artificial leg will be clumsy and painful at first. You will need to practice every day. After a while, its use will come naturally to you. You must prepare the stump, in advance, by rubbing methylated spirits on it. The liquid will shrink the skin and make it less sensitive. I will get you a bottle of the spirits. Your bandages should be wrapped as tightly as possible, from now on. When you get the artificial leg, you will also require a special sock to cover the tip of your stump. The sock will reduce the pain and discomfort when the stump is inserted into the leather portion of the artificial limb. I suppose I can knit several of them, as they tend to get dirty and must regularly be replaced. Until you grow some callouses down there, it will be uncomfortable. Do you have any questions?"

Reggie blinked and held his breath.

"No, ma'am. And thank you."

A young civilian worker, who took an instant liking to the British pilot, confirmed Billy's suspicions.

In its first life, the officers' prison at Freiburg served as a university campus. When the war commenced, enrollment declined to almost nothing, The City of Freiburg, with a population of 85,000, also suffered. Food shortages, massive unemployment, and bombing raids by the French, became commonplace. The conversion of the university to a prison was viewed as a potential boost to the city's failing economy. It did not go as planned.

Billy's new-found civilian friend, Otto, was 18 years of age and missing a hand. The boy seemed to enjoy the opportunity to practice his broken English. He gave Billy a quick history lesson.

"The university was founded in the mid-1400s. Before the war started, there were 3500 students here. I was one of them."

The kitchen worker described the old Freiburg as a city of pensioners and a popular destination for tourists.

"The Black Forest is just west of the city. Visitors would come here for the spas. The hotels were quite nice, back then."

Otto also described the economy, before the war.

"We had jobs for everyone. Construction, manufacturing, textiles, publishing, and my personal favorite—breweries. We had more than 20 breweries before the war started."

"And now?" asked Billy.

"And now, there is nothing left. Everyone is hungry and there is no work. The bombing raids are getting worse. And the rumor mill says that the British will soon join the French, conducting bombing raids of their own. We will be terrorized on a regular basis. Everyone wants to leave but no one has the money."

Billy reached in his pocket for some British money, the bulk of his funds, wrapped in cloth and sewn to the inside of his jacket. He carefully scanned the horizon and handed Otto a three-pence piece.

"I appreciate the instruction," said Billy.

The young boy looked for anyone close enough to hear the conversation. He spoke in a whisper.

"You're looking to leave too, aren't you Captain?"

Billy slowly nodded.

"You will need a bicycle."

Billy sneered.

"Is that what I get for my 3 pence?"

"You'll get a bicycle. And for three pence more I will give you an escape plan that works."

"Keep talking."

"No. Not now. Tomorrow, after breakfast."

The Rathaus, Freiburg's town hall, stood just north of the University, but on the opposite side of the street. Otto instructed Billy to meet him behind the inmates' mess hall, facing the Rathaus building. The post-breakfast meeting went better than Billy anticipated.

"Where is the money?" asked Otto.

Otto arrived, pushing a bicycle with his remaining hand. Billy flashed a silver coin in the boy's face.

"First, you talk."

"Go west on the street behind me. It will bring you to the rail station. Follow the tracks until you are well out of the city. There is a freight train that leaves almost daily, just before dusk. That's your ride all the way to the Swiss border. After that, you're on your own."

"A Brit on a bike. I'm sure that will attract no suspicion."

Billy put the coin back in his pocket.

"You won't pick the evening of your escape. The French will."

Billy leaned in.

"Explain yourself."

"The French planes bomb the city at least twice a week. Usually on Wednesdays and Saturdays, about thirty minutes before sunset. They can't see much and their aim is terrible."

Billy shook his head in agreement. In France, the pilots simply tossed bombs over the side. The Brits did it too. That's why the pilots preferred populated areas. Hitting a target would be more likely.

"So, I get to ride my bike in between the French bombs."

"When the first bomb hits, the city goes into a panic. The camp guards, the police, even the handful of soldiers that are still here, will run for cover. There is a shelter under the

Rathaus. They will go there. You will be able to follow the tracks and you will be alone. This, I guarantee."

"You seem very sure of yourself," said Billy, as he flipped the coin into Otto's waiting hand.

"One makes very little money as a one-handed dishwasher. I do much better as a travel consultant."

The boy chuckled; Billy laughed.

After burying his newly purchased two-wheeler in a nearby pile of garbage, Billy returned to the barracks. He made a mental note of the twists and turns required to keep him in the shadows and away from the prying eyes of camp guards and suspicious residents. The kitchen worker also warned him that bicycles were an item in great demand, on the black market. Billy assumed that his "purchase" was itself stolen, but chose not to ask questions.

After a two-day wait, Wednesday evening arrived, but no bombs. Billy settled in and mentally prepared to wait several more days. On Thursday evening, he jumped out of his cot. A loud explosion startled everyone in the barracks. The prisoners flocked to the windows and the guards, originally posted outside the barracks door, left the building. Billy slowly wandered to the exit and watched the uniformed soldiers as they beat a path across the street toward the Rathaus.

When another explosion occurred, even closer than the first, Billy took his leave. He followed the guards from a safe distance, grinning at the irony. After crossing the street, the guards disappeared. Billy retrieved his bicycle in the heap of garbage and walked it along the railroad track. He mounted his two-wheel escape vehicle just moments later and rode until he heard the squeal of steel wheels on iron rails and the hissing noise of steam engines.

Billy stashed the bike in a nearby clump of bushes and started walking in the direction of the Swiss border. He utilized the windowless sides of buildings, and a mixture of sheds, trees, and bushes to avoid being seen. On occasion, an open area left the escapee fully exposed. He simply crouched low and made a run for it. In a half hour, he could no longer see lights or buildings, on either side of the track. He sat down, his back to a large tree, his view of the track back to Freiburg, perfect. Now he would wait.

Billy estimated, from the moon's movement, that the freight train described by Otto should have left the railyard several hours ago. Although tempted to walk to the Swiss border, Billy decided that a 30- mile hike would be too risky and exhausting. As if in response to the debate in his head, the sound of an approaching train, with its loud whistle, filled the air.

Otto's information, although not entirely accurate, proved correct. When the slow-moving freight train came into view, the crescent moon afforded just enough light for Billy to hop on to one of its empty cars. Billy did not have to worry about luggage. His haversack would be discovered by the lackadaisical guards or his fellow inmates, when they pulled off the blanket which covered Billy's "double." Unfortunately, he now carried no food, no extra clothes, no water, and, of course, no weapon.

Although trains in both England and Germany could regularly reach speeds of 80 mph, Billy assumed that a long and fully loaded freight train would travel much slower. He calculated a ride of less than sixty minutes to the borderline. He would exit the train well before then.

German guards would be stationed at all border crossings.

Clarence took the call from the General Hospital in St. John's.

Reginald Windsor was failing. Fast. Reggie summoned a driver and left the office immediately. Clarence would follow but only after a quick call to his daughter.

"I will meet you there, Father. Perhaps I can help in some way."

As the trolley car rumbled its way through the streets of St. John's, Elizabeth questioned her decision to visit the old man. After young Reggie attacked her, Reginald Windsor offered her money and then threatened to fight back if the Windsor family was publicly attacked. His response did nothing to ameliorate Elizabeth's stress and humiliation. *Why would she visit the man? Why should she offer to help him?*

In truth, Elizabeth could not resist, much less ignore, the nursing instincts deeply rooted in her heart. If someone became ill or suffered an injury, Elizabeth Parsons could not be stopped. She would do everything she could to help the patient, even when circumstances allowed for nothing more than holding the person's hand until the patient breathed their last. Her visit might also send a message to young Reggie. She too, had grown tired of the fighting.

"How is he?"

Elizabeth's appearance in the doorway to Mr. Windsor's hospital room shocked young Reggie.

"Elizabeth. Thank you for coming to my father's bedside. He is unconscious and unable to respond. But I know he would be flattered and genuinely touched that you cared enough to visit him in hospital."

Elizabeth assumed her usual post, on a chair nearest the patient's head. But only after she straightened the sheets, fluffed the man's pillows, and wet his lips with a moist towel. She spoke to the doctor on the way in and conveyed the news to Reggie.

"He does not have much longer, I'm afraid. The doctor says his organs are showing signs of failure. He is extremely weak and his breathing is very shallow. His heart will give out. Sooner than later, I'm afraid."

Reggie, despite the crutches, leaned over the frail form that once dominated any room occupied by Reginald Windsor, Founder and CEO of the Windsor Land and Lumber Company.

"Do you think he can hear me?"

"It is a distinct possibility, Reggie. I have witnessed such a thing in dying men, on several occasions."

"I'd like to speak with him."

"I'll give you some privacy."

Elizabeth tiptoed from the room and stood in the hallway.

"Father, I'm hoping you can hear me. I've been thinking about something. I never got around to telling you that I loved you. And now, it's probably too late. Looking back, you were pretty good to me. Probably too good. I grew up thinking that I could have anything I wanted. But life doesn't really work that way, does it?"

"I've made a lot of stupid mistakes over the years, Father. But I wanted you to know that I have turned over a new leaf. I'm staying away from the booze. I'm not bullying people anymore and I'm leaving the women alone. I'm also learning the business. Hell, I'm even going to take some courses at university this year. I will be thinking of you every day, Father, and hoping that I finally do something you can be proud of. I'm never gonna be as smart and as brave as Billy. But I hope you will be proud of me, anyway."

Reggie choked up and his voice cracked.

"Goodbye, Father."

Reggie hobbled out of the room. He took no notice of Elizabeth. She stood off to the side wiping the tears from her eyes.

"How long have you been here?"

Elizabeth did not have to respond. Clarence knew the answer to his question.

"Sorry, I'm late. I got held up at the office."

"How is he?"

He stopped breathing on several occasions. But then, he recovers."

"Is that normal?"

"It happens often."

"You look very sad, Elizabeth. I am a bit surprised. Mr. Windsor was hardly your best friend."

"He's dying, Father and I feel obligated to help in any way I can. But he's not the reason I'm sad. That's Reggie's fault."

"Was he disrespectful?"

"No, not at all."

"Well. What happened?"

"He said goodbye to his father. I waited outside but I could hear everything he said."

"And?"

"Reggie has changed."

Despite his doctor's pronouncement, Reginald lingered for days more.

The death vigil cast a gloomy shadow in the office of the Windsor Land and Lumber company. Mourning the founder's loss was not yet appropriate, but tackling the day's assignments with good humor and a spirit of joy seemed in poor taste. And then Elizabeth arrived. She carried a long box, flashing a big smile to Clarence. Reggie too.

"Good morning, Elizabeth," said Clarence.

Reggie bowed his head.

"Good morning, Elizabeth. Clarence, I'll be in the board room, if you need me."

"Reggie, this is for you," said Elizabeth, holding the long package aloft.

"What is it?"

"Your new leg has arrived."

Reggie, forgetting the awkwardness of the moment, reached for the package.

"I've been waiting weeks for this. How did you know that it arrived?"

"Well, I might have asked the nice folks in the mail room to notify me," said Elizabeth, a sheepish grin on her face.

"Why did you do that?"

Elizabeth put on an air of authority.

"These things can be tricky. You will need some help."

"Thank you."

"If you do well, my father may promote you from 'tenderfoot' to 'sure-footed' business executive."

Reggie laughed. Elizabeth smirked. Clarence shook his head and grinned.

"If I didn't know better, I'd say that the two of you have signed a truce."

After a silent moment of clumsy looks, Clarence intervened.

"Well. Are you going to try that thing on or not?"

Elizabeth got busy removing the contraption from its box. She loosened the laces which pulled the coned-shape leather opening tight around the amputee's stump. Reggie pulled his pants leg up high, tucking the excess material into the waist of his trousers.

"Take a seat," said Elizabeth.

"Have you been using the methylated spirits I gave you?"

"Yes, ma'am."

She produced a sock-like covering for Reggie's stump, handmade from thick yarn.

"Put this on," she said, as she prepared to slide the man-made limb onto Reggie's thigh.

Elizabeth pulled on the crisscrossed leather laces until they tightened the cone-shaped leather harness around Reggie's stump. The amputee stared in silence at the artificial limb. He sat motionless. Elizabeth sensed a problem.

"Reggie, are you afraid?"

Reggie leaned forward, eying the foot made of wood.

"Yes. I'm afraid I left my other shoe at home."

Clarence howled. Elizabeth chuckled. Reggie yelled.

"Who needs shoes."

He suddenly sprang to his feet and promptly fell forward into Elizabeth's arms. She braced herself and steadied her tormentor-turned-patient.

"Easy, Windsor. Easy. You've got to get used to this thing before you start running around with it."

Reggie took a few tentative steps, the wooden foot sliding out of control on the boardroom's hard wood floor. Clarence held up a hand.

"Wait a minute. I know where I can get a pair of shoes."

He left and returned in a few minutes, holding a pair of black shoes aloft. They were a bit scuffed but otherwise suitable.

"These are your father's. He left them in the store room for when we toured standing timber lots."

Reggie grinned.

"And we both have big feet."

With the shoes on, Reggie walked with ease and confidence. He circled the boardroom table several times. When he unexpectedly exited the room, Clarence and Elizabeth scrambled to keep up. At the end of the hallway, Reggie quickly pivoted to turn. Such a maneuver required more experience with a prosthesis than Reggie possessed. He collided with the wall and fell to the floor, sprawled on his back. Elizabeth's instincts kicked in. She rushed to his side.

"Are you hurt? Are you in pain? Don't move, until I've checked you over."

Other than his mangled pride, Reggie suffered no injuries.

"I'm fine, Elizabeth. I just need a hand getting up, that's all."

She instructed Reggie in the proper way to get up off the floor and insisted that he perform the maneuver several times. She also made him practice the removal and attachment of the prosthesis.

"I think you're ready to go solo. But please go slow."

When Eizabeth announced her intended departure, Reggie instinctively reached for her hand and squeezed.

"Thank you, Elizabeth. Thank you for everything."

Elizabeth didn't flinch this time. She squeezed back.

"You're welcome, Reggie. In my opinion, you are well on your way to a complete recovery."

She started to leave but turned suddenly.

"In more ways than one, Reggie Windsor. In more ways than one."

Billy, poised and ready to jump from the empty box car, strained to see what lay ahead of the moving train.

As the freight train came around the bend, he could see lights ahead. The border. Although the ground beneath him was mostly dark, he noticed the outline of trees. *A good place to hide*, he thought. Billy took a deep breath and plunged into the cold night air.

He landed on even ground but his left foot slammed into a rock, protruding from the forest floor. Billy heard the snap of a bone as it broke. An excruciating pain, much like a bolt of lightning, raced through his body. Not wanting to remain trackside, Billy hopped on one foot in to the deep woods. Each step brought a searing pain. He wanted to scream. His eyes filled with tears that stung. He took shelter in a stand of thick trees. Their low-hanging branches made it almost impossible for him to be seen. Unfortunately, his own view would be completely blocked.

As he sat in the inky darkness of his hideout, Billy tenderly caressed the already swollen leg. He could feel a large bump where there should have been a smooth flat surface. He could feel the jagged edge of broken bone just beneath the skin's surface. The entire area throbbed. The biology he learned at the Anglican school of St. Thomas, in St. John's, Newfoundland, failed him. He did not know if he broke his fibula or his tibia. It didn't matter. He needed a crutch or he would never leave the forest.

Billy knew, instinctively, to keep his boot on. He also used a sleeve, torn from his shirt, to tightly wrap the swollen area, just above his ankle. After a few loud groans, the bandage was secured. His head swiveled, in search of something he could use as a crutch. Several dead branches, lying on the ground, were his best chance. Using his weight and his good leg, Billy first broke and then hand-trimmed the limb into a crude walking stick. A fork in the dead limb would serve as a grip. He practiced with his rough-hewn cane and managed to walk, albeit slowly. Exhausted and unable to see, Billy decided to get some rest. He laid his back against a large tree and closed his eyes.

The escaped prisoner woke hours later, the rising sun casting long shadows in the woods. A slight breeze carried the sound of approaching voices. Billy scrambled to his feet and hobbled behind the largest of the trees, which enclosed his hideout. The voices grew louder but remained on the track. They walked a short way and then left. If they were searching for an escaped prisoner, they exerted very little effort. Billy recalled the words of the prison commandant. *"If you attempt to escape, you will be executed immediately."*

Billy dragged himself deeper into the woods, sat with his back to a large rock, and considered his options. He possessed neither food nor water. The nights were getting colder. One of his legs, shorn of a pants leg, lay almost entirely exposed to the elements. His survival, alone in the woods and without a weapon, would be unlikely. He had no choice but to follow the tracks. When he got close to the line, he would turn either east or west, in search of an unguarded crossing point. He waited until after sunset, grateful that the waxing moon and a cloudless evening would make his journey less difficult.

As the last rays of sunshine disappeared into the western skyline, Billy examined his broken leg. The swelling grew worse. The pain, although bearable, had not lessened. He thought of the Aussie and the Brit, back in Freiburg, enjoying the comforts of the University-turned-prison camp. He could feel the anger rising in his chest, that two of his kind would so willingly aid and abet the enemy. The adrenalin pumping through his body pushed him forward.

He would make it to the borderline or die trying.

"Elizabeth says we're having moose stew this evening. Why don't you join us?"

The invitation by Clarence did more than startle Reggie. It paralyzed him. He sat at his end of the board room table in his usual chair, surrounded by charts, maps, and government reports. Reggie was always hungry. He bit his lower lip and blinked repeatedly.

"I. Well. I'm not sure."

Clarence interrupted him.

"One of Mrs. Newcastle's patients gave her a dozen jars of moose stew. She brought two of the jars to Elizabeth last night.

My daughter said it was some sort of peace offering from Mrs. Newcastle. I didn't ask questions. I haven't had moose meat since my wife was alive."

Reggie apologized for his mixed feelings.

"I am truly sorry, Clarence. I would like to go. Really, I would. But it may be too soon. I certainly don't want to upset Elizabeth."

Clarence sat back in Mr. Windsor's huge leather chair, hands in front of him, clasped together with his fingers forming a steeple.

"Reggie. Please. It was her idea."

Reggie's face shown like a full moon. He jumped to his feet, stuck his chest out, and looked to the ceiling.

"Thank you, Lord. Thank you. Thank you. Thank you."

"I hope you like moose stew, we have two jars of it."

Reggie nodded as Elizabeth took his coat.

"Yes, ma'am. Our cook used to make it all the time, but I let him go when I got back from France. One person does not need a cook."

Clarence headed to the dining room.

"I'm hungry. Feed me, please," he said with a smile.

The dinner hour flew by, as far as Reggie was concerned. The trio talked about the business, Reggie's new leg, Elizabeth's previous work as a VAD nurse, what she would like to do going forward, Billy's whereabouts, and Mr. Windsor. When the dishes were cleared, Elizabeth washed and Reggie dried. Clarence read a newspaper, puffed on his pipe for a while, and then announced his intentions to retire for the evening.

"Don't forget, Reggie. We leave at 7 o'clock tomorrow morning for a tour of that timber lot near Clarenceville."

"I'll be waiting for you," said Reggie, sitting on a chair and watching, as Elizabeth planted a quick kiss on her father's cheek. She turned to Reggie.

"Would you like some tea?" she asked.

Reggie shook his head.

"No, thank you. I really should be going home."

"Please. Stay just a bit longer. I have something I wish to discuss."

"After that stew, how could I refuse?"

Elizabeth's hands, trembled. She cleared her throat.

"I want to know why."

Reggie squirmed in his chair.

"Why what?"

"Why did you attack me that night?"

Reggie's chin dropped. His chest heaved. He folded his arms, not because he was angry. Because his hands were shaking and he didn't want her to notice. For minutes, the only sound in the room was the man's heavy breathing. Elizabeth waited for a response. Reggie took a deep breath.

"I don't know."

"I don't believe you."

Reggie rose from his chair and walked to the door.

"I wanted to be seen with you, Elizabeth."

"Nonsense. You always had a pretty girl on your arm."

He turned, anger in his voice.

"I wanted to be seen with the smartest girl in town."

"Me?"

Reggie raised his voice.

"Yes, *you*. I was always the dumb brother in the Windsor family. I had lots of friends, mostly because I had lots of money. But I could hear them when they thought my back was turned. I was the dumb one. I thought, if you were my girlfriend, things would be different."

Reggie reached for the door.

"I have to go,"

"Please, Reggie. This is important to me."

His voice softened.

"I must have asked you out a dozen times. But you always said no. I guess you reached the same conclusion."

"I made you angry when I said no."

Reggie whispered in a monotone, as if in a trance.

"Yes. And I wanted to punish you for turning me down. No girl had ever done that to me. I just wanted to scare you. But things got out of hand."

Elizabeth approached him, but kept her distance.

"Reggie, I have a confession to make."

"You? A confession?"

"Yes."

"You were right."

"About what?"

"I said no because I thought the same thing. I thought you were the dumb one. And I did not want to be seen with you."

Reggie squeezed his eyes, shut.

"Goodnight, Elizabeth."

"But I was wrong, Reggie."

Reggie stopped and turned, his mouth agape.

"What did you say?"

"You *are* smart, Reggie Windsor. Very smart. But I am most impressed with your strength and courage. Not the strength that comes from muscles or the courage that's required to fight Germans. I mean the strength and courage one needs when you've hit bottom. When you have no reason to live. The strength to go on. The courage to persevere. And the will to live."

Reggie took a deep breath.

"Do you really mean that, Elizabeth?"

"If I could give you a medal, my friend, I would do it."

Chapter Seventeen

WARS CHANGE PEOPLE

Billy followed the railroad tracks for at least a mile.

Seeing lights in the distance, he decided to go west. The thick brush and dense forest made his progress nearly impossible. Although reluctant to reverse course and already exhausted, Billy turned in the opposite direction. After listening and looking he crossed the tracks. Within several yards, he came to a road. He wrestled with the decision to follow the road or plunge into the thick underbrush once again. The road would be an easier trek but he might be seen. The thick underbrush would be very difficult but he would be hidden from view.

As if the Lord himself wanted a voice in the matter, a flash of lightning lit up the evening sky. The ground shook with thunder and the skies dumped sheets of rain onto the escapee. The thunder continued as Billy slowly made his way across the muddy road. He needed to find a large tree under which he might take cover. The road, now pockmarked with deep puddles and inches of mud, posed a severe challenge to the cane-wielding pilot. The sudden oncoming lights of a motor vehicle sent Billy into a panic. He stabbed at puddles to gauge their depth, slowly moving across the road.

The headlights grew closer. He quickened his pace. The cane got stuck in the mud. He pulled it free but lost his balance. The lights blinded him. He fell face forward. His cane flew into a nearby pool of muddy water. The escapee instinctively turned away, covering his head with both arms. The car braked to a noisy stop. Billy lay in the mud, inches from a tire and out of breath. He thought he heard male voices, cursing loudly.

Two doors opened. He could hear footsteps sloshing in the water. Two sets of boots came into view. The boots spoke.

"Hey ole chap. I'm assuming you're a bit lost."

Billy's eyes open wide. In the glare of headlights, he squeezed them shut.

"Are you with the British Army?"

"No sir. Red Cross. Got a dead one in the back."

Billy sat up, his rear end in a small puddle.

"Where are you going?"

"Our base is in Zürich. Got a small hospital there. Looks like you could use some help."

"Broke my leg."

"Well, let's get you on board."

Billy got a good look at the field ambulance. The lorry, covered with a white canopy and decorated with a large red cross on either side, was open in the front and the back. The driver and his mate enjoyed a windshield but no roof. Both were soaked to the skin. Billy stopped when they got to the rear of the vehicle.

"Just a minute, boys."

"What's the problem, Captain?"

"You may not want to cross the line with me in your ambulance."

"Why not?"

"I am an escaped POW. The prison in Freiburg."

"You didn't crash your flying machine?"

"I did. But the Bosch rescued me. So to speak."

"That does pose a challenge," said the driver.

His buddy reached for the driver and squeezed the man's arm.

"No worries, mate. I think this man has the fever."

Billy and the driver spoke in unison.

"What fever?"

"Typhus fever. And you are covered with lice. That's how it spreads, you know. Especially after dark, they say."

Billy shook his head.

"Even if that's a genuine affliction, I don't see how that's going to help me."

"It's real. Trust me. And you, good sir, have not yet been deloused. We will have to wrap you in rubber sheets from head to toe. I don't believe the guards will be anxious to unwrap our little present."

Billy smiled his understanding despite the throbbing pain in his leg.

"Thanks fellas. That might work. Thanks a lot."

The two ambulance drivers chatted with their new passenger as they carefully wrapped Billy in three separate rubber sheets. They tied yards of bandages around the "body," making it difficult to inspect the "patient."

"We should be at the line in about 15 minutes. When you hear voices, that means we're at the border."

Billy, though anxious, savored the ride and every moment he did not have to stand. When German voices filled the night air, he laid deathly still. He could hear the driver.

"One of them is dead. Died before we could pick him up at Hueberg. The other one has lice-borne typhus. He has not been deloused. We wrapped him up in rubber sheets."

The German guards look at each other, uncertain as to what they should do. The ambulance driver, added a little fluff to his bluff.

"If you're going looking for lice, please take him out of the vehicle. We don't want those things infesting our ambulance."

The older guard decided to peek in the back, shining his torch on the shrouded dead man and then on the lice laden passenger.

"How can he breathe all wrapped up like that?"

"Ask him yourself. But we gave him something to stop the itching. I think he's out cold."

The older guard shook his head and motioned the ambulance forward.

"Get them out of here. Now."

Billy, hearing the entire conversation, did not experience any difficulty breathing.

It was his laughter that proved almost impossible to stifle.

"Mr. Parsons. A telegram arrived for Mr. Windsor."

The secretary smiled as she handled the cable to Clarence. He questioned her with his eyes.

"It's good news, Mr. Parsons."

Clarence read the message, jumped to his feet, and screamed.

"Reggie! Come here! Quick!"

The irregular sound of Reggie's footsteps could be heard in the hallway.

"I was on my way to see you. What's going on?"

"Read this," said Clarence, the grin on his face lighting the room.

CAPTAIN WILLIAM WINDSOR LOCATED IN ZURICH, SWITZERLAND. SLIGHTLY INJURED.

Reggie showed no reaction. He slowly reached for the chair in front of the desk and sat down. He ran fingers through his hair and scanned the room as if looking for answers.

"Aren't you pleased, Reggie?"

Reggie, washing his hands with imaginary water, seemed to take offense.

"Yes. Of course. Why wouldn't I be pleased?"

Clarence announced his intention to call Elizabeth.

"Yes. You should do that. I'm sure she will be quite pleased."

Reggie excused himself.

"I've got to finish reviewing that report. Excuse me."

Reggie could not concentrate on his work and left for the hospital instead. He didn't know why, only that he must see his father, immediately. The scene in Reginald Windsor's room could best be described as chaotic. Nurses marched in and out. A doctor at Windsor's bedside barked a series of orders. Reggie caught a glimpse of his father's ashen face, eyes fixed and dilated. At one point, the doctor, using his fist as a hammer, pounded on the patient's chest. Mr. Windsor's limp body showed no signs of life. When Reggie appeared in the doorway, everyone stood motionless, a white-coated wall of blank stares. An elderly doctor stepped forward.

"I am very sorry, Mr. Windsor. We did everything we could. It wasn't enough. Your father is gone."

Reggie blinked repeatedly but there were no tears. Only silence. A nurse used a hand to brush the eyelids closed, and pulled a sheet over Mr. Windsor's gray face. Reggie stepped to one side, no longer blocking the doorway.

"I would like a moment alone with my father. Please."

Several of the white uniforms acknowledged Reggie with quick bows of their heads or a few words of condolence. Reggie responded to each sympathetic gesture with a soft thank-you. When he stood at the bedside, he reached for the shroud and exposed his father's stone-like face. For the first time, he noticed a few strands of gray hair in his father's unruly mane of jet black hair. The man's mustache, trimmed to perfection, appeared unchanged by death. Reggie used the fingers of one hand to caress his father's cheek.

The body, already cool to the touch, triggered painfully vivid memories of Reggie's time in France. *One man's death mask was very much like all the others*, Reggie thought. Unmoving, Sphinx-like. And eerily haunting. It did not seem to matter if the victim was one's friend, foe, or father. In death, they all looked the same. *God's way of reminding us that we would all come to the same end,* thought Reggie.

Reggie leaned over, kissed his father's forehead, and left.

Hundreds of people, politicians, business leaders, and laborers, attended Reginald Windsor's viewing and funeral service.

Reggie received more questions about the absence of his little brother, than he did expressions of sympathy. He left the funeral home frustrated and unsettled. A telegram from Billy announced that he would be arriving in St. Johns, the following week. He would be nursing no more than a broken leg.

After the service, Reginald refused to return to the Windsor mansion. The memories of his father invaded every nook and cranny of the large house. He drove to the office, instead, sitting in his father's oversized chair behind his father's oversized desk. For the better part of an hour, he fantasized about a life where he served as the company's Chief Executive Officer. He would then be known as Mister Windsor. He would take calls from parliamentary ministers, business executives, union managers, and newspaper editors. And, in Reggie's fantasy world, everyone would love and respect him. They would forget the misdeeds of his youth and would acknowledge him as a war veteran, an educated businessman, and as a kind and generous soul. He would be described in the newspapers, as "beloved."

The sound of a door, as it opened and shut, interrupted the grieving son's dream of fame and fortune. Elizabeth's face appeared at his door. Reggie could not disguise the pink blush that covered his face, embarrassed that she might be capable of reading his innermost thoughts. He used his sense of humor to camouflage his thoughts.

"We're closed, ma'am. You'll have to buy your lumber somewhere else."

"I'm not looking for lumber. I'm looking for you."

Reggie tried to smile. The result was a twisted grimace.

"Have a seat."

"Actually, it was my father who was looking for you. Neither of us imagined that you would be here. Working."

"I'm not really working. Daydreaming, mostly."

"Is something wrong?"

"I can't imagine life without his booming voice ringing in my ear."

"I can't imagine life without my own father telling me what to do or force-feeding me his opinions," she replied.

Elizabeth fidgeted in her chair. Reggie sensed her anxiety.

"Why are you here, Eilzabeth?"

"I am unsure if this is a good time to discuss this."

"Discuss what?"

"As Executor, my father was reading your father's *Last Will and Testament.*"

"And?"

"He left the house and some money to you. He left the company to Billy."

Reggie's eyes rolled to the ceiling.

"The homecoming hero will be most pleased."

"And you? How do you feel about that?"

"Does it matter how I feel? It never mattered before."

"I think you and Billy would make a great team, don't you?"

Reggie wore a pained expression.

"You *would* say that."

Elizabeth's eyebrows furrowed.

"Why are you saying that?"

"I saw your reaction when you learned he was coming home. And I know that the two of you are more than friends. He told me, in a letter."

"What exactly did Billy tell you?"

Reggie shook his head.

"It doesn't matter."

"Billy and I have been friends for a very long time."

Reggie loosened his collar, tugged on his tie, and rolled up his sleeves. His voice trembled.

"Yes, I know. Good friends. Really good friends."

Elizabeth got up to leave, her face red. She stood in the doorway, her legs apart and a closed fist on each hip.

"We were young and stupid. And going off to war. It meant nothing. You, more than anyone, should understand that."

"Well, I don't."

"Well then, maybe I was right."

"Right about what?"

"You *are* the dumb one."

Clarence met Billy at the docks.

Although wearing a cast and using crutches, Billy insisted his leg was healing nicely. Clarence delivered the bad news about Billy's father.

"We didn't know where you were or even if you were alive. I am sorry you weren't here for the funeral."

Billy watched as their driver negotiated the streets of St. John's, surrounded by trolleys, pedestrians, and horse-drawn carriages.

"Funerals are for the guilty, Clarence. Makes them feel less guilty."

"I'm not sure what you mean."

"I mean that I have no regrets. I worked hard for my father. And I was loyal. I have nothing to feel guilty about."

Clarence moved on to a more pleasant topic.

"Elizabeth has put together a nice dinner to welcome you home. Reggie will be joining us."

Elizabeth greeted Billy at the door with a big hug.

Reggie, forced to attend despite the chill between him and his host, greeted his brother with a handshake.

"Glad you made it home, little brother."

Billy waved a crutch.

"A broken leg, but otherwise I'm good."

"Better broken, than missing."

Billy gave Elizabeth a quizzical look. She explained.

"Reggie lost a leg and, as you can see, and he's still waiting for his glass eye."

Billy stared at Reggie's legs.

"I would not have known. You hide it well."

"Yeah. I suppose from 10,000 feet, we trench rats all look the same."

Billy winced.

"You haven't changed a bit, Reggie."

Clarence stepped between the two brothers.

"Dinner is ready, gentlemen. How about we all sit down? Elizabeth has made a feast."

Reggie sat at the head of the table, Billy, at the opposite end. Clarence and Elizabeth took seats on either side. Elizabeth offered small talk.

"I'm betting it's been a while since you enjoyed a decent meal, Billy."

"Yes. German POWs don't get much to eat. But I'm told that the guards and their families don't do much better."

Reggie scanned the dining room.

"Where can a man get a drink around here?"

"Reggie, I thought you decided to abstain from the consumption of alcohol?" asked Clarence.

"Reggie? Give up the spirits? Surely you jest!" said Billy.

Reggie rose to his feet.

"As a matter of fact, I have. But you're home now, Billy, and soon you will be my new boss. I think that's a good reason to start drinking again."

Elizabeth flashed Reggie a dirty look and got up to clear the plates.

Billy reached into a pocket and retrieved a cigarette.

"Who says I'm going to be the new boss?"

Reggie pointed to Clarence. Clarence swallowed hard and cleared his throat.

"I have reviewed your father's *Last Will and Testament*. He has bequeathed 100% of the Windsor Land and Lumber Company to you, Billy. But I think the two of you would make a great team."

Billy took a long drag on his cigarette, leaving the table's center piece engulfed in smoke.

"I won't be staying."

Elizabeth dropped the plate she was holding. It landed on the table and broke into several pieces. Reggie leaned forward.

"What do you mean you won't be staying?"

"Just what I said. The war is not over yet. Not by a long shot. The Americans will soon join us. I intend to keep flying."

Reggie sat back in his chair, the tension draining from his face. Elizabeth, clearly stunned by Billy's announcement, stammered a question.

"What about the company?"

Billy pointed to Reggie.

"My older brother can handle it. He'll need Clarence to help out, of course."

"What about your share of the estate?" asked Reggie.

Billy pointed again, this time to Clarence.

"Add it all up, Clarence, and then divide by two. But I wouldn't sign the bank draft until the war is over." Billy smirked. "If you know what I mean."

Elizabeth cleaned up the shards of china and placed a freshly baked apple pie next to Reggie's place setting.

Billy winked at Reggie.

"Hope you can handle it, big brother."

"The pie or the company?" asked Reggie.

"Both."

Reggie sprang out of his chair and extended a hand in Billy's direction.

"Clarence has been working with me, Billy. I intend to do you proud. I promise."

Billy chuckled.

"Father must be spinning in his grave."

Clarence offered an observation.

"This war has changed everything and everybody."

Billy turned to Elizabeth.

"Have you changed, Elizabeth?

Elizabeth did not hesitate.

"At one point, I thought I might be falling in love with a dashing and daring pilot."

Billy and Reggie spoke in unison.

"And now?"

"I've made a decision," she said.

"Tell me," said Billy.

"I want to be a doctor."

"Don't be silly," said Billy. "There is no such thing as a woman doctor."

Elizabeth fired back.

"Maria Louisa Angwin, a native of Newfoundland, licensed in Nova Scotia, and practiced in Halifax."

Reggie laughed out loud.

"That's the second time you've been shot down, Billy."

Billy grinned and nodded.

"I think Elizabeth could teach the Germans a thing or two."

Clarence joined in.

"And how do you propose to do this, young lady?"

Elizabeth looked at Reggie when she responded to her father.

"Well, if Reggie has no objection, I would like to work for him, part-time. And I too, want to attend university. He will be working on his degree in business and I will be working on my degree in nursing."

Reggie's face lit up.

"Are you serious, Elizabeth? Do you really mean that?"

"Yes, Reggie. With all my heart."

Billy lit another cigarette.

"Well, I almost fell in love with a VAD nurse. But I too, changed my mind. I have fallen in love with another woman."

Reggie grinned.

"What's her name, Billy?"

"Is it somebody we know?" asked Clarence.

Elizabeth stopped eating.

"What does she look like? Is she pretty? How did you meet her?"

"I don't know. I have yet to meet her myself."

Clarence scratched his head.

"I don't understand."

"She is called a Sopwith Camel. The RFC's newest fighter plane."

The room erupted in laughter. When the discussion turned to the mechanical details of Billy's new flying machine, Reggie and Elizabeth decided to leave Billy and Clarence alone.

"We would like to be excused."

Billy and Clarence nodded their approval and continued their chat. Reggie and Elizabeth walked down the street, silently enjoying the afterglow of a convivial dinner. Elizabeth reached for Reggie's hand. Reggie came to a sudden halt.

"I owe you an apology."

"For what?" asked Elizabeth.

"What happened between you and Billy was none of my business. I was acting like a jealous monster. I am truly sorry."

"Actually, it was kind of nice knowing that I was the cause of someone's jealousy. But honestly, Reggie, we were two inexperienced kids, filled with lust and wondering if we would survive the war. Seems like years ago, now. But it ended the night it started."

"I understand that, now."

"I could have told you but we were hardly a couple, back then."

Reggie's eyes bulged.

"Wait a minute. Are we a couple?"

"That's up to you, Mr. Windsor."

Reggie leaned forward and looked into her eyes. Elizabeth wrapped her arms around his waist.

"Are you sure?" he asked. "I'm the dumb one."

"Not anymore," she said.

"How's that?"

"You are with the smartest girl in town."

Reggie softly pressed his lips against hers.

"Elizabeth?"

"What?"

"I'm feeling smarter already!"